CUCKOO

Camilla Lackberg is a worldwide bestseller renowned for her brilliant contemporary psychological thrillers. Her novels have sold over 39 million copies in 60 countries with translations into 43 languages.

www.camillalackberg.com

Also by Camilla Lackberg

Patrik Hedstrom and Erica Falck
The Ice Princess
The Preacher
The Stonecutter
The Stranger (previously titled *The Gallows Bird*)
The Hidden Child
The Drowning
The Lost Boy
Buried Angels
The Ice Child
The Girl in the Woods

The Faye Novels
The Gilded Cage
Silver Tears

Short stories
The Scent of Almonds & Other Stories

WRITTEN WITH HENRIK FEXEUS
Mina Dabiri and Vincent Walder
Trapped
Cult

THE CUCKOO

CAMILLA LACKBERG

Translated from the Swedish by Ian Giles

HEMLOCK
PRESS

Hemlock Press,
An imprint of HarperCollins*Publishers*
1 London Bridge Street,
London SE1 9GF
www.harpercollins.co.uk

HarperCollins*Publishers*
Macken House, 39/40 Mayor Street Upper,
Dublin 1, D01 C9W8, Ireland

This paperback edition 2025
1

First published in the United Kingdom by HarperCollins*Publishers* Ltd 2024
Published by agreement with Nordin Agency, Sweden
Copyright © Camilla Lackberg, 2024
Translation copyright © Ian Giles

Originally published in 2022 by
Bokförlaget Forum, Sweden, as *Gökungen*

Camilla Lackberg asserts the moral right to be
identified as the author of this work.

A catalogue copy of this book is available from the British Library.

ISBN: 978-0-00-828388-9 (PB b-format)
ISBN: 978-0-00-828389-6 (PB a-format)

Typeset in Meridien by
Palimpsest Book Production Limited, Falkirk, Stirlingshire

Printed and bound in the UK using 100% Renewable
Electricity at CPI Group (UK) Ltd

FSC
www.fsc.org

MIX
Paper | Supporting
responsible forestry
FSC™ C007454

For Simon

1

SATURDAY

He gazed at the photographs. He knew that Vivian was upset because he had decided they weren't going to the party, but he simply couldn't bring himself to go. Time had finally caught up with him and forced him to face the truth. Perhaps he should have done so long ago.

What had happened had been like a millstone around his neck all these years. He had been afraid of the questions, of the answers, and of everything in between. The choices he had made had shaped him as a human being, and what he now saw in the mirror was not particularly attractive. Choosing to live life with your eyes shut never was. In the end, he'd forced himself to tear the blindfold off and act based on what he saw.

Slowly and carefully, one by one, he got out the framed photographs. He propped them up against the wall and counted a total of sixteen pictures. They were all there.

He took a few steps back and gazed at them. Then he turned towards the simpler frames he had: his place-holders. He wrote the names of every single photograph on scraps of paper in large, uneven letters, before taping them to the respective frames. He didn't need the actual photographs to be able to picture them as he moved them around on the white walls of the gallery. Each photo for the upcoming exhibition was etched into his retinas, and he could quite easily summon them from memory and see them clearly.

He knew that it would take many hours – probably well into the early hours – to hang the exhibition, and that he would pay the price for it in the morning. He was no longer a young man. But he also knew that at the opening in two days' time he would feel lighter and freer than he had in many years.

The consequences of what he had chosen to do would be dramatic, but that wasn't something that he could take into consideration. He had been far too considerate for far too many years. They had all been living in the dark shadow of their lies. Admittedly, they ran the risk of being crushed, but he still meant to reveal his truths. And theirs.

He had never felt as free as he did now, carefully fixing the piece of paper with the word *Guilt* to one of the frames.

Not even death frightened him any longer.

Erica Falck stretched. The warmth of the bed meant it was tempting to linger, but she had promised to meet up with Louise Bauer for a power walk in an hour. Quite why she had done so she wasn't sure. But Louise was probably stressed about the festivities and needing to blow off some steam.

'Do we really have to go tonight?' Patrik groaned beside her, covering his face with the pillow.

Erica yanked it away and used it to gently pummel him.

'It's going to be wonderful! Good food, some decent wine, your wife all dressed up . . . for once!'

Patrik closed his eyes with a grimace.

'A golden wedding anniversary, Erica. Just how festive

2

can that be? A bunch of stuck-up guests and endlessly long speeches. You must know what kinds of people will be going.' He groaned again.

'We're going anyway, so you might as well bite the bullet and bring a positive attitude,' said Erica.

Sensing she had crossed the bounds of enthusiasm, she leaned towards Patrik's side of the bed and gently stroked his ribcage. His heart was beating so powerfully – it was hard to believe that he had ever had heart problems, even if the worry was still there.

'Louise expects us to come. Anyway, I love seeing you in a suit. You're wildly handsome in them – especially that dark blue one.'

'Oh, give over!'

Patrik kissed her on the mouth, gently at first before it turned into a deeper kiss. He pulled her very close to him, and Erica felt her body turn soft and warm throughout, like always.

'The kids might come in any second,' she mumbled, her mouth against his.

Patrik responded by pulling the duvet over their heads. It quickly got hot under the covers – nothing else existed inside their bubble except the two of them. Their bodies. Their lips. Their breathing.

Then a heavy thump confirmed what Erica had feared.

'Hide and seek!'

Noel shrieked with joy as he bounced up and down on the bed. As if he'd been fired from a cannon, Anton arrived shortly thereafter, landing right on Patrik's family jewels.

'Ouch! Fu—' He stopped himself after a glance from Erica. 'Fiddlesticks!'

Noel and Anton were choking with laughter. Erica sighed, smiling. She and Patrik had carved out a few seconds alone, just the two of them, and that would have to do. She bent over the boys and tickled them, making them howl like wolves.

'I tried to get them to watch TV, but they sneaked up here as I was getting out the yoghurt.'

Maja was standing in the doorway in her nightie – the one with a unicorn on it – her hands held out in resignation.

'Sweetheart, you don't have to look after them in the mornings. They can get up by themselves,' Patrik said, waving at her to come in.

Maja hesitated at first. Always so responsible. Then her face cracked into a smile and she hurled herself onto the bed too, joining in the game. Erica caught Patrik's eye over the kids' heads. Their family was perfect – just perfect.

'Do you think they'll call in advance, or do we have to wait until Thursday? We know they sometimes provide advance warning.'

Henning Bauer drummed his fingers on the tabletop. It was the first weekend in October. Beyond the window, autumn had taken over and white-crested grey waves were breaking against the smooth rocks lining the shore of the small island. *Their* small island.

He looked at Elisabeth, who was sitting opposite him with her teacup.

'We've heard that I'm into the final five. Although obviously that doesn't mean I'll win. There are no guarantees. But if it's true, then I have a one in five chance.'

His fingers continued to drum against the table.

His wife sipped her tea calmly. Henning admired her calm. That had always been their reciprocal dynamic when it came to his writing. He got worked up, she calmed him down. He worried, she reassured him.

Henning continued drumming his fingers, waiting for her reply. He needed her confidence. He needed her to tell him that it would all work out.

After a few sips of tea, Elisabeth carefully set down the cup on the saucer. They had been drinking from those very cups their entire marriage – one of the countless wedding presents from their extravagant wedding, though he couldn't for the life of him recall who had given it to them.

Outside, one wave larger than the others threw a cascade of water against the picture window running the full length of the house. The salt from the sea always left its traces on the glass, and their housekeeper Nancy had her work cut out trying to keep up with the polishing. The archipelago was relentless in its capriciousness, as if it were constantly trying to displace civilization and reconquer lost territory.

'Don't worry, darling. Either they'll call today or tomorrow, or they'll wait until Thursday. Or they won't call. But *if* they call, which of course I believe they will, you *must* pretend to be surprised. You can't give away that we know you were on the shortlist.'

Henning nodded, his gaze fixed on the window.

'Of course not, darling. Of course not.'

He tapped out a diffuse rhythm as he regarded the pattern left by the water on the window. One in five. He ought to be satisfied with that, but knowing what was in reach – what a single telephone call could give him – left him almost struggling to breathe.

'Come on, have a bite to eat,' Elisabeth said, nudging a basket of freshly baked bread towards him. 'We have a long day ahead of us – not to mention a long evening – and I don't want to find you nodding off at the table at ten o'clock.'

Henning reached for a still-warm French roll. He knew better than to disobey his wife. He spread a thick layer of butter across it, which immediately melted into the bread.

'Tonight we're going to dance,' he said, his mouth full of bread as he winked at Elisabeth, who smiled slightly.

'Tonight we're going to dance.'

'Good grief – just how early did you catch the boat? And in this weather?'

Erica held up a hand in front of her face to shield herself from the wind as she struggled to keep up with Louise Bauer. As ever, it was a challenge. No matter how fast she walked, Louise walked faster. It wasn't made any better by the fact that she could feel the spatter from the waves breaking on the shore only a few metres behind them. The wooden houses provided them with some shelter, but Erica thought even they were almost crouching in the wind.

'Oh it's nothing – I always wake up at six anyway,' said Louise. 'And today's going to be a long one – I'm responsible for everything to do with the party, so it felt like I had to start with a power walk.'

Erica rolled her eyes. At the same time, she understood that Louise needed to clear her head. Being assistant to Henning Bauer – her father-in-law and one of Sweden's most celebrated authors – was probably not the easiest job.

'I don't think I've ever felt like I *had* to take a power walk,' she muttered. 'In fact, on reflection, I don't think I've ever felt any form of physical activity was a necessity.'

Louise laughed. 'You're so funny, you really are. Of course you like to get moving. It energizes you for the whole day!'

Erica struggled to speak as they climbed up the incline of Galärbacken at far too brisk a pace. She tugged her blue Helly Hansen coat more tightly around her torso. Louise was naturally wearing perfectly fitting sports gear that was both windproof and water repellent.

'I love the feeling afterwards, if that's what you're getting at. But before lunchtime? Nope. Nyet. Nein. Even though I know I need it.'

Erica paused for a moment to catch her breath. Louise slowed down and looked at her.

'To be perfectly honest, I've been feeling pretty lousy lately,' Erica continued, 'and I think it's to do with the wrong diet and being too sedentary. Not to mention my advancing years. Let's not forget about the march of time. I've already started to feel the menopause creeping up on me. Haven't you felt the same?'

Louise began to move again.

'I'm a few years older than you, but . . .' Louise paused, picking up pace as they passed the pharmacy. 'But I had a hysterectomy when I was a young woman. Cancer. So now something that's been the source of great sorrow in my life is slowly transforming into a blessing.'

'I'm so sorry, I didn't know.'

Erica grimaced. Typical of her to put her foot in it.

'It doesn't matter. It's not a secret – it just rarely comes up in conversation. "Hi, my name's Louise and I don't have a womb."'

Erica laughed loudly. This was what she loved about Louise. Her forthrightness and sarcastic sense of humour.

They had met through the children. Maja had become immediate best friends with Louise's stepson William, who was around a year her senior, while they were both playing in the playground at Ingrid Bergman torg. And since their kids had been playing together, Erica and Louise had got talking. That had been last summer, and now they took the opportunity to meet up whenever Louise came back to Fjällbacka with her family.

But Erica had to admit to herself that she appreciated their wine nights more than Louise's objectionable habit of power walking at all times of day.

'So, how are you feeling about tonight?'

Erica waved to Dan – her sister's husband – who was pulling out of the car park at Konsum. He waved back.

She could almost sense that he was laughing at her for being out on a power walk.

'What can I say? Utter torment. My parents are due in an hour or so, same as usual. But they're getting to borrow a house by Badis, so they're happy. And then there's the party. Henning says one thing about what they want, and Elisabeth says another. And we all know that it'll be Elisabeth who gets her way, but it's always me who has the honour of being the messenger.'

'It should be lots of fun tonight,' said Erica.

Louise turned and smiled at her.

'You're only saying that to be polite. "Lots of fun" isn't how I'd describe a golden wedding anniversary. But the food will be good – I've tasted the menu personally, and the wine will be flowing. I've also made sure that you and Patrik have got good seats. Patrik will have the tremendous pleasure of having me at his table, while you'll have my infinitely charming husband as your dining companion.'

'Splendid,' Erica said, clutching her side. A stitch was beginning to make its presence felt.

They had begun to make their way round the hill on their way back towards civilization, and had just passed a steep slope to their right; Erica had called it the Seven Jumps when she'd been little, and it allowed you to get a sledge up to what felt like lethal speeds. She tried to figure out how much of their circuit was left, and concluded the answer was far too much.

In front of her, Louise's dark ponytail bobbed rhythmically as she seemingly effortlessly maintained a brisk pace. Erica bent down and picked up a stone that she clenched tightly in her fist, hoping it would distract her from her increasingly painful stitch. She simply had to face facts: working out wasn't her thing.

* * *

'Have you talked to her?'

Tilde opened her beautiful blue eyes wide and held up a very décolleté dress in front of her.

Rickard Bauer spotted the letters D&G on the label, and guessed it had set him back thirty or maybe forty thousand kronor. But that wasn't something that troubled Tilde. Or rather, it wasn't something that had troubled her until now – now that there was suddenly not a seemingly infinite line of credit on her Amex to be blown in Stockholm, Paris, Milan and Dubai.

'I'm going to,' he said, unable to conceal his irritation. Her voice had begun to annoy him more and more. Had it always been so whiny? And that childish?

'I don't want to talk to her until after the party. You know what my mother's like – she worries – and I don't want to ruin tonight for her.'

'Yes, Rickard, but will you promise me you'll talk to Elisabeth tomorrow then? Definitely?'

Tilde pursed her lips and thrust out her chest. She had showered and was naked, apart from a white towel wrapped around her hair. Rickard could feel his own reaction. It fascinated him how his brain could be bugged by her, while his cock reacted to her mere presence.

'I promise, darling,' he said, pushing her down onto the bed they had only recently left.

She let out a shrill giggle.

'Come to me, baby,' she said in a childish voice. 'Come, just come.'

Rickard buried his face between her big breasts, shutting out the world.

Elisabeth Bauer held up the red earrings. They had been her grandmother's. They would go perfectly with the dress she had chosen for the dinner. The black one she was going to wear during the dancing was suspended from a hanger next to it. It was cleaner cut and easier to move in than the rather extravagant one she would only be sitting down in. YSL and Oscar de la Renta. Bought in Paris in the spring, when she and Henning had spent a couple of weeks in the flat there. If you were shopping for a special occasion – like a golden wedding anniversary – well, there was nowhere but Paris to do it.

Elisabeth carefully placed the earrings in their dark blue velvet box. She jumped as yet another cascade of water struck the bedroom window. They lived in a single-storey house on the island of Skjälerö, and spray from the breakers reached all the windows. It was their most fastidiously turned out residence. The Stockholm apartment, the Paris flat, and the house in Tuscany were all far more luxuriously decorated. But this was the place on Earth she loved the most. She had spent every summer here since her birth. Some might have mistakenly thought the name Skjälerö had something to do with souls, but they would have been wrong. It came from the word for mussels in the old local dialect: 'skjäler'. All over the island there were drifts of beautiful, blue mussel shells. The gulls dropped the mussels from a great height, letting them shatter on the pink granite so that they could get at the fleshy interior. But the shards of shell were left behind, giving the barren island little flashes of blue.

Her grandfather had bought the island, and now it was hers. This little place outside Fjällbacka had always had an almost magical effect on her. As soon as they got out here, it was as if all her troubles were blown away. No one could reach them here. They were impregnable. Unreachable.

For many years, they hadn't even had a telephone on the island – only a communication radio, although that had been several decades ago. Now they had all the modern conveniences. Phone, electricity, Wi-Fi and far too many channels on the TV for the grandchildren. Louise and Peter were too lax when it came to their kids' viewing habits. Hour after hour, they were left to watch bright, colourful characters fighting and making terrible scenes. All instead of reading a good book. She was going to bring it up with them sometime. But offering good advice about the children was always such a sensitive topic. Come to that, it was probably extra sensitive in light of what had happened to Cecily.

Elisabeth shook off the unpleasant thought and carefully slipped each dress into its own garment carrier. She knew she could ask Nancy to do it, but she loved handling the expensive fabrics with their exquisite quality. There was no one who made dresses like Oscar.

'Henning?' She shouted in the direction of his study, expecting nothing more than a hum in response.

As expected, a 'Hmm' emanated from behind the closed door.

'I thought we'd go with the dinner jacket from Savile Row. The one we had made up for you the other year. Will that do?'

'Hmm' emanated from the study once again, and Elisabeth smiled.

The jacket had already been packed along with the other items bound for the mainland. But something she had learned in her many years of marriage was that it was important to make her husband feel involved and consulted. Even if the decision had already been made. That was a tip for her to share with Louise – with the best of intentions.

2

STOCKHOLM 1980

P'tite loved to watch Lola getting ready for the evening.
It was like magic. They had the same routine every night.
P'tite would lie on the big velvet cushion, her chin resting
on her hands, while Lola sat in front of the cluttered
dressing table and made herself beautiful.

'What are you going to wear tonight?' P'tite asked,
looking towards the wardrobe with twinkling eyes.

She loved everything in Lola's wardrobe.

'What do you think about the pink blouse with the
lace on the back? With the hot pink slim-fit trousers? A
simple chignon on top, and my diamond earrings?'

Lola turned to face P'tite, who nodded eagerly.

'Yes, I love the pink blouse! It's my favourite!'

'I know that, sweetheart.'

Lola turned back to face the mirror and began to carefully apply make-up. It was usually the same each night.
For a party, she might go with more, and P'tite loved
those nights. But tonight it was work, which meant some
cream foundation first, then powder, kohl, mascara, a
little bronze on her eyebrows using a brush, and finally
one of the many lipsticks stored in mugs on the dressing
table. Tonight, she opted for a hot pink.

Lola carefully painted inside her lip lines, smacking her lips audibly before blotting her lipstick on a tissue and then applying a little more. Then she chose a wig. Lola's own hair was long, shiny and copper-coloured, but she often wore one of her wigs when working. After looking at the five mounted on Styrofoam heads, she selected a brown shoulder-length one. She placed it on top of her own hair, which had been carefully gathered under a hairnet, adjusted the wig and made a chignon at her neck with a practised hand.

Next she went over to the wardrobe, taking care as she put on the pink blouse and pink trousers to ensure she didn't catch them with her long painted nails. Last of all, she picked up a beautifully ornate bottle of perfume from the dressing table and dabbed a little behind her ears and on her wrists. Then she stood in front of P'tite.

'Et voilà! What do you say? Do I look good enough to go into battle?'

'You look good enough to go into battle,' P'tite said, laughing loudly.

When she grew up, she wanted to be as beautiful as Lola.

Lola grabbed a pretty little pink handbag and made for the hallway.

'You will be all right, won't you, sweetie? There's food in the fridge. You can warm it up in the oven – but don't forget to turn it off again. And I want you in bed by ten – don't wait up for me. I'll lock the door behind me, so don't unlock it and don't let anyone in. Okay, sweetheart?'

Lola was already halfway out of the door and had inserted the key in the lock.

'Love you!' she called out to P'tite.

'Love you, Daddy!'

Then the door slammed shut again, leaving only the scent of perfume in the hall.

3

'I just think it's very weird. Why aren't we going?'

'Because I said so.'

Rolf Stenklo gave his wife Vivian an annoyed look. For him, the matter had been concluded long ago.

Vivian looked at him from the doorway of the bright space that he was going to fill with all his dreams – all the things that made his heart both ache and sing.

'But Rolf, it's our best friends' golden wedding anniversary. I don't understand you. Everyone we know will be there, and plenty of people that it would honestly be good for us – for *you* – to meet.'

Vivian's voice rose to a falsetto, as it always did when she was agitated. They had been married for twenty years, and that voice always made him feel like it had been at least nineteen years too many.

'I just don't want to. Is that such a problem? Big parties don't do it for me – that can't come as a surprise to you.'

Rolf fired a nail into the wall using the nail gun and swore when it went in too far. The nail gun was a little too powerful.

'Fuck's sake.'

He grabbed a hammer and used it to prise the nail out slightly.

'You could get someone else to do that,' said Vivian.

Rolf could see that she was peering curiously at the framed photographs leaning against the wall by the entrance. For once, he hadn't let her get involved in planning the exhibition. He'd said it was too personal, and oddly enough she had accepted that.

'You mean like Henning and Elisabeth? They can't even wipe their own arses without help,' he muttered.

'What the hell's wrong with you today? I know you like Henning and Elisabeth. But first you refuse to go to the celebration of their big anniversary, and now you seem to be getting worked up about them completely unreasonably. You know what? You're really not being nice!'

Vivian folded her arms across her chest. Rolf turned towards her, tired.

'Being nice is apparently the most important thing in the universe to you. Don't make a fuss. Don't rock the boat. Don't ever mention what hurts – or the things that actually matter.'

'You're being completely impossible.'

Vivian swept out of the door, finally leaving him alone. He looked around the room at the empty walls that he was going to fill with the most beautiful work he had ever done.

He picked up the nail gun and fired off another nail. Then he grabbed one of the cheap frames with the names of the photographs, hung it on the nail and took a step back. As always, he felt a blow to his heart when he saw the name he had written on the sheet. Out of guilt. Out of love. Out of longing for a bygone era that would never return. But soon the brightest of stars would shine again.

'How are we getting on?'

Louise Bauer paced restlessly around the large room known as Mademoiselle, which was to the right of the foyer at Stora Hotellet. The wooden floor creaked softly beneath her feet. The clouds had still been low, the waves still lashing the jetties, when Louise had hurried into the venue.

Barbro, the hotel supervisor, was following her nervously.

'Everything is going according to plan,' she said. 'The food preparation is in full swing, we have everything ready to be laid on the tables, the tables will be set up just after lunch, the staff are well prepared and we've got plenty of drinks to serve. And we've managed to source everything you requested in that respect.'

'Good,' Louise said, stopping. 'The kids. Will they be getting special meals? Max and William won't want to eat the same menu as us grown-ups.'

Barbro nodded.

'There are burgers for the kids. And ice cream with chocolate sauce for dessert.'

'Brilliant. Yes, I must say you really do seem to have it all under control. Do you have the place cards? Have you checked them off against the guest list to ensure you've got them all? You can't mess up the seating plan – it's taken months to finalize it.'

Louise saw that beads of sweat had formed on Barbro's brow.

'Naturally we've checked, but I'll ask the maître d' to check one more time,' the supervisor said.

'Good.'

She could hear how curt she sounded. But Louise had no patience for other people's failures and shortcomings, or their lax carelessness.

She looked around. Right now, the room was cool but, just in case it became too hot due to the many guests, she had ordered fans that could be set up. The walls were painted pale green with exotic features in the interior decor, which matched the rest of the hotel's theme.

16

Louise pictured the crowds of people turned out in their best dancing the night away to the sound of the jazz band that would be playing on a small stage currently being built at one end of the room.

It was going to be a magnificent event. It was going to be perfect. Like everything she did. Nothing was ever left to chance.

Henning Bauer pushed his teacup away from him and stared at the blank document on the computer screen. The cursor was flashing mockingly at him. His nemesis. Emptiness.

Outside the closed door, he could hear noise and movement. Elisabeth was excited about the evening ahead – that much he knew. As was he. It was going to be a great night. The guest list was impressive – just the way he wanted it – and he already knew the speeches were going to be superb.

If only he could cough up a few words before then. Every day he sat there for hours, sipping his tea and staring at the flashing cursor on the display. He knew the words ought to be there – within reach. He had lived with words his whole life – they ought not to be unfamiliar to him – but they eluded him.

Henning picked up the teacup and went over to stand by the window. He contemplated the wild landscape beyond. In the summer, it looked like an advert for seaside life. Blue skies, pink granite rocks glittering in the sunshine, yachts sailing past in all weathers. Now, in October, the sea was lashing the rocks as if it wanted to drag the island into the depths. He preferred it like this, when nature was showing its true power.

Henning cradled the teacup, cursing his fate.

He ought to be able to write here. It was the perfect environment. Behind the large desk by the picture window,

17

he was able to regard himself as a Bergmanian figure – a recluse in the midst of a never-ending flow of creativity. But nothing came. Absolutely nothing.

A timid knock on the door made him start.

'Yes?' he called out, more harshly than he had intended.

'Sorry, Dad, the boys just wanted Grandad's help with something.'

Henning's face softened. He didn't really want to be disturbed in his study, but the grandchildren were always welcome.

'Come in, come in.'

The door opened, and there was Peter with the boys at his side.

Henning waved at them to come in. His heart filled with warmth as he saw Max and William's small faces light up when they saw his smile. He hadn't been much of a presence when Peter and Rickard were growing up, but that had been in keeping with the times. It was different with Max and William. He was able to give them the love he'd never given his own sons.

'We need help choosing ties, Grandad.'

Max, the oldest, precocious and serious, held up three options. William, the little brother who was always up to some mischief and whose hair was constantly standing on end, also proffered three ties.

William had recently lost three teeth, so he lisped audibly as he repeated his big brother's statement:

'Yes, Grandad. We need help choosing ties.'

'Of course. Of course I'll help. It's an honour. A real distinction. And by the way, William . . .'

William looked quizzically at Henning.

'Tomorrow, why don't we put out the lobsterpots?' Henning asked, ruffling the boy's hair. 'That's what we'll do.'

Peter beamed at him over his boys' heads. He was a great son – and a son to be proud of. As well as having

chosen Mammon and being the head of a fund management firm, he was all his father could have wished for.
Henning's gaze rested on him. Sometimes it was obvious
that Peter was still mourning Cecily, but today he was
beaming at his father.

'Right, let's see,' Henning said, returning to the ties.
'Firstly, I need to know what else you're going to wear.
What's the tie going with? It's meant to be the dot on
the i in your ensemble.'

At that very moment, the mobile lying on the desk
began to ring and Henning jumped. He usually put it on
silent when he came into the study, but he must have
forgotten today. Annoyed, Henning went over to the desk
to turn off the mobile as it blared away next to the
computer, but he stopped with his hand in mid-air when
he saw who was calling. They didn't know each other,
but Henning had had his number saved on his phone for
years. Just in case.

His hand trembling, he tapped the green button and
then the speakerphone symbol. He put his finger to his
lips to get Peter and the boys to realize they needed to
be quiet. Then he said:

'Hello? Henning Bauer speaking.'

'This is Sten Sahlén, Permanent Secretary of the
Swedish Academy.'

'Oh, hello . . .'

His heart was pounding so hard in his ribcage that
Henning thought he might pass out. His hand began
shaking and Henning put the phone down on the desk
to ensure he didn't accidentally hang up on Sten Sahlén.

The whistling of the storm outside amplified the rushing
sound in his ears. This was the moment his whole life
had been working towards. When Sten Sahlén began
talking again, Henning caught Peter's eye and he saw that
his son knew how significant this was. The moment when

Henning Bauer was forever written into the history books – not only in Sweden, but around the world.

'Henning, it's my distinct pleasure to inform you that the Swedish Academy has decided to award you this year's Nobel Prize in Literature. You'll receive more information about all the formalities in due course, and I hardly need add that this news must remain within a strictly limited group until it's announced publicly.' A short laugh. 'Most people still think we wait to notify the recipient in the moments before I step through the famous door at the Stock Exchange.'

Silence. All Henning could hear was the wind, the crashing of the waves and the sound of his own heart. Peter was standing still, his hands on Max and William's shoulders.

Henning took a deep breath and straightened his back.

'I'm grateful for the honour,' he said. 'Please tell all the members that I am very, very honoured.'

When he had ended the call, he looked at the cursor that was still flashing on the blank document. Then he closed the lid of the laptop.

'Is Auntie's favourite awake?' Erica called carefully through the front door, which was ajar.

'She's awake! Come in!' Anna bellowed from her office in the house on Falkeliden.

Erica took off her coat and added her trainers to the huge heap of shoes in the hallway.

'How are you getting on?'

Erica couldn't help laughing when she found Anna at a table covered in drawings, fabric samples, fittings and colour charts. Not to mention the many toys.

'I've got an interior design commission due in two days' time, but someone has just started walking and if she was all over the place when she was crawling, she's managing to top that now . . .'

'Hence the ocean of toys in here?'

Erica got down on all fours and tried to find her niece amidst the many toys scattered across the floor of Anna's office. She found her behind a huge teddy bear, and a big smile appeared on Fliss's face when she caught sight of her. Erica was a big favourite of Felicia's – or Fliss as she was fondly known by all in the family. Born a month premature but the picture of health, she had turned out to be the world's happiest – and most active – baby. The horror of that time when Anna had begun to bleed had almost been forgotten.

'It's like working in the middle of a tornado,' Anna sighed, getting up and surveying the mess on her desk with a look of resignation.

'I can take her for a while so you can get some work done in peace and quiet,' Erica said, cooing at Fliss, who was now amusing herself by tugging as hard as she could at Erica's nose.

'Oh, would you? That would be the best.' Anna groaned. 'The client is the demanding kind and I've got my hands full trying to ward off all the proposals for curtains adorned with lighthouses and cushions with shells on them.'

'Isn't the customer always right?' Erica said, pinching Fliss's nose gently, which made her laugh loudly.

'Nope – in fact, it just so happens that the customer is actually very, very rarely right.'

Anna scratched at her blond hair, which now reached down to below her shoulders, hiding all trace of the scars she'd acquired on her head from the accident. Erica thought her little sister was glowing, even though she was complaining. Anna seemed to have been haunted by misfortune for so many years but she was now happily married to Dan, Erica's childhood sweetheart, and they had a happy blended family as well as their own little darling that all the siblings fought to fuss over.

'Have you been out for a workout?' Anna said suspiciously, only now noticing Erica's leggings.

'Louise dragged me out for a power walk,' Erica sighed.

'Of course she did. Of course she needed to go for a power walk,' Anna said. Erica stuck out her tongue at her, which Fliss found hilarious and immediately began to imitate.

'What exactly is it you have against Louise?' Erica said, putting Fliss down on the floor.

'Oh, I guess I don't have anything in particular against her. And I know you like each other. I just think that Bauer family have broom handles shoved up their arses. Did you see Henning on the box? My God! I'll only say two words: cliché bingo.'

'No, I missed that,' Erica said, going to fetch a bag of corn puffs from the kitchen to bribe Fliss with.

She'd had plenty of practice with Noel and Anton, who had always been two prairie fires who could barely be allowed in furnished rooms. Now they had finally started to calm down a little, but there was a long way to go until she could take the child locks off the cupboards.

'Perhaps I'm oversensitive. Might be a hang-up from Stockholm days with Lucas. All those dinners with people who seemed to think they were better than everyone else, and who always had a way of talking down to you so you felt . . . stupid.'

'Louise isn't like that – you know that,' said Erica, fending off Fliss's attempt to insert a well-chewed puff into her own mouth.

'I guess not. But they are a bit stuck-up. Admit it.'

'Well, I've hardly done more than say hello to Elisabeth and Henning, or the sons for that matter. But the boys are sweet. Max and William. Maja and William are basically inseparable. He winds her up and she calms him down.'

'Typical girl's role to calm down wild lads,' Anna muttered, rooting through the samples on her desk.

'When did you become a feminist?' Erica said, cocking her head to one side and regarding her sister.

'You don't need to be a feminist to realize that the world is unfair. I can see what it's like at school for Emma right now. The disruptive boys get all the attention, while the calm girls like her get barely any time or attention at all.'

'I know, you're right,' Erica said, opening her arms as Fliss came steaming towards her at top speed for a hug. 'Oh heavens, you're a beauty.'

'How's the writing going, by the way?'

Anna reached towards a hidden biscuit tin high up in the cupboard. Oat snaps, of course. They'd been a constant presence in their childhood home.

'Ugh, don't mention that miserable subject,' Erica said, accepting a biscuit. 'I've got writer's block. No new ideas whatsoever. No case I find interests me. I've even ploughed through every volume of the *Nordic Crime Chronicle* hoping to find inspiration, but I haven't turned up a thing. My publisher is on to me demanding that I at least come up with a synopsis soon, but I can't write about something I don't have.'

Erica shook herself to dispel the feeling of discomfort. 'Do you mind if we change the subject? It's making me anxious.'

'Of course,' Anna said, grinning. 'So what do you think about tonight's dinner?'

She placed a piece of fabric on top of a colour sample, muttered glumly, picked up a different fitting and held it against a new colour before shaking her head in dissatisfaction.

'Come on, let's have a coffee. I need to rest my brain for a bit. So, the dinner?'

Erica picked up Fliss, put her on her hip and followed Anna into the kitchen.

'It's going to be . . . interesting. Patrik is suitably amused. But we're only going because Louise invited us. It's still a bit awkward – we hardly know Elisabeth and Henning.'

'But you're an author – that must count for a lot in their world?' said Anna, her back turned as she shovelled ground coffee into the filter of a battered coffee maker.

'I don't know whether people like Elisabeth and Henning consider me to be an author. I'm too easy to read and normal people like what I do.'

'No, of course. Good sales figures must be a proper author's worst nightmare.' Anna grinned as she poured water into the machine.

'I expect so,' said Erica. 'But all joking aside, it should be okay. Louise has promised me good food and good wine.'

'Well then. Ah, here comes Dan. He's been down to secure the boat. When you're done with the marauder, you can pass her on to Dan. She can be his daughter for a couple of hours.'

Erica sniffed Fliss's head. She was sitting on her aunt's knee playing with her keys – always a safe bet.

'Sweetheart, when Mum is mean you're always welcome to come to Auntie Erica's. She's the stable one, don't you know. The safe one.'

'Go on then, give me a kiss,' said Anna, setting down a cup of coffee in front of her big sister but at a safe distance from the baby.

She leaned forward and kissed Erica on the cheek.

'Love you.'

Erica gulped. Anna had always been stingy with her affection.

'Love you,' she whispered back.

Vivian Stenklo hesitated. She usually left most things up to Rolf – she wasn't all that fond of making decisions. But this was something she neither understood nor liked.

Why was she supposed to stay at home just because he didn't want to go? It was absurd. Downright ridiculous. For twenty years, Vivian had let Rolf be in charge; she had adapted to his schedule, his exhibitions, his travels, his habits. She had known when they'd met that was how he was used to having things. His first wife, Ester, who had died the year before Vivian had met Rolf, had taken care of everything in his surroundings. That was also what life had been like for Vivian before Rolf – her ex-husband had been an artist and their life had been dominated by his whims. It was a life that was very familiar, and felt – in some strange way – safe.

She could usually see a logic in Rolf's whims, but this was just weird. Besides, these were new times. The habits of their own generation were as extinct as the dinosaurs. She didn't have to adapt to a man. She could make up her own mind.

Vivian picked up her phone from the coffee table. The small house they rented in Sälvik was pretty but draughty. Each gust of wind could be felt through the walls. She tugged her cardigan closer to her body.

'Louise? It's Vivian. Sorry to bother you, I'm sure you've got a lot on today, but I know Rolf has declined on behalf of the two of us for this evening. Yes, it's a real shame. But I was going to ask you – if it wasn't putting you out too much – if I could come to the party on my own? That's okay with you? Oh, thank you, Louise, that's so kind of you. Yes, no. Well, we felt a bit off, but I'm back on my feet again and Rolf can manage on his own for an evening. Thanks again.'

Once Vivian had hung up, it felt as if the brief conversation had been a huge victory. A first step towards independence. There was so much that was about to change. Rolf was already different. He'd lost his *joie de vivre* – the thing that had made the sacrifices in life with

25

him worthwhile. Over the last few months he'd been replaced by a gloomy, listless man. Rolf was getting old, and this wasn't the existence she wanted.

Vivian went to the wardrobe to see whether she'd brought any party clothes with her. At a pinch, she would have to make a quick outing to Uddevalla.

The boat rocked heavily as Louise Bauer tied up the *Elisabeth II* at the jetty. The old wooden boat was in good nick, having been well cared for over the years, but it was still creaking significantly in the heavy seas. It didn't scare her. She was a practised sailor and had seen worse weather at sea than this. She was, however, soaked through after making her way from Fjällbacka to Skjälerö. When they went to the party, they were due to take a water-taxi since they would otherwise arrive in a real state.

Once Louise had jumped ashore, she deftly moored the boat with a big clove hitch and then strode up towards the house. Her parents, Lussan and Pierre, had complained that Louise hadn't welcomed them when they'd arrived in Fjällbacka, but how was she supposed to have time for that? There were all the minor last-minute changes to the party, all the things she had to think about. The call from Vivian had annoyed her, but she hadn't let her voice give that away. RSVPing *yes* this late on risked turning her entire, meticulous seating plan on its head, but she had quickly decided to resolve it as simply as possible by putting Vivian at the end of one of the tables, next to Erica and Peter. But it was still rude. And it was a little weird that Rolf couldn't make it. Not for one moment did she buy the excuse that he was under the weather – he'd refused the invitation immediately after receiving it, and without a crystal ball there was no way he could have known that he would be ill then. After all, Rolf was one of Elisabeth and Henning's oldest friends.

The rocks were slimy, and she slipped, but managed to regain her balance. The lights were on in both her and Peter's house, and in the main house where Elisabeth and Henning lived. Rickard and Tilde's house was dark. They were probably having a lie-in as usual. Sometimes they slept until early afternoon, which she knew drove Henning mad.

She began to walk towards her and Peter's house, but changed her mind and diverted towards the main house instead. As usual, she went inside without knocking – they all did that on the island. She called out: 'Hello?'

'Louise! Louise! Come here! We're in the study!'

Elisabeth's voice was full of excitement, and Louise hurried to take off her wet outerwear and shoes. Elisabeth was always quiet and collected. They used to joke that she was like that drawing of a duck – outwardly calm but beneath the surface paddling feverishly with its feet. So her tone indicated something big had happened.

When Louise reached them, Elisabeth and Henning were each sitting in an armchair with a bottle of champagne and two glasses on the table between them. Henning stood up quickly, his face fiery red in marked contrast to his silver-white hair. He fetched another champagne glass and passed it to her, his hand trembling.

'Have you started early?' Louise said, taking the proffered glass which was now filled with champagne. She noted the bottle. An Henri Giraud, worth almost thirty thousand kronor.

'Take a seat. We have big news.'

Elisabeth's eyes were shiny as she pointed to the only remaining chair – Henning's desk chair.

'You have to tell me what's happened! I'm bursting with curiosity.'

Louise gently sipped the champagne. It tasted good, although not so good as to merit its price tag.

Elisabeth looked at Henning triumphantly. Then she looked at Louise. She nodded imperceptibly to Henning, who took a deep breath.

'I've had the call.'

'Call?' said Louise, although she knew full well what he meant. Her grip on the champagne glass tightened.

'Yes, *the* call,' Henning said jubilantly. 'I'm this year's recipient of the Nobel Prize in Literature.'

The room fell silent. Then the silence was broken by the sound of Louise's glass cracking.

'When do you think we can go home?' Patrik hissed to Erica as they stood outside Stora Hotellet.

For a while, the storm had seemed to be waning, but now the waves were lashing the shore again. Erica could almost taste the salt in the air. She shushed Patrik and hurried him along to make sure they got indoors before her hair was blown all over the place. He continued to mumble to himself as they took off their coats, but in the end she managed to get him to let go of the tie he was tugging at. If only he knew how incredibly handsome he looked tonight, she thought to herself.

'I gather Louise has given you a pleasant dining partner,' she said, 'and look how inviting it looks. It's going to be a great night.'

There was apparently something the matter with his jacket too, because Patrik was fidgeting gloomily and he cast only a brief glance at the laid-out long tables in the illuminated room.

'Did you tell Anna and Dan to call if the kids become too much?'

The hope in his voice was much too obvious.

'They won't call. And we get a child-free evening and a child-free lie-in – don't forget about that. I can't remember the last time we had that.'

'True,' Patrik said, discreetly squeezing Erica's rear end. 'And I know exactly how we're going to make use of that time . . .'

'Sleep?' Erica said, winking at Patrik. How she loved this man!

She kissed him on the cheek and pointed to the large seating chart on the wall by the door. 'Look. You've got the best spot at the party. You're sitting with Louise.'

Patrik looked relieved and Erica pointed to her name. 'I'm on the table next to yours. In between Louise's husband Peter and Ole Hovland.'

'I've met Peter, but who is Ole Hovland?' Patrik said, looking towards Erica's seat where a man in a dark suit with dark, slicked-back hair was sitting.

'He's married to Susanne Hovland, who's a member of the Swedish Academy. They're close friends of Elisabeth and Henning. They run a . . . well, how to describe it . . . a cultural club in Stockholm – together with Rolf Stenklo. You know, the one who's so well known for his nature photography. It's called Blanche. It's where all the culture vultures go. In other words, I've never been invited. It'll be very entertaining having him on the table. It may be that he needs his smelling salts when he realizes what a cultural philistine he has at his side.'

'Are you bothered by that?' Patrik said, supporting Erica so that she didn't stumble as she descended a flight of steps in her heels.

'Not one bit,' said Erica, squeezing Patrik's arm. 'I mostly find it entertaining.'

'Well then. Have fun,' he said, heading for his table.

Louise tapped her glass and asked everyone to take their places.

'Hi Erica!'

Peter pulled out her chair and welcomed her with a

broad smile. Erica was once again reminded of how much she liked Louise's husband.

Ole turned guardedly towards her when she sat down, and only after scrutinizing her unabashedly from head to toe did he take her hand, kiss it and then say:

'Enchanté.' He had a strong Norwegian accent.

Erica stifled a laugh. This was most certainly going to be a very interesting evening.

Elisabeth Bauer looked around the room. This was where they'd held their wedding reception fifty years earlier. That had also been a stormy night, and there had been an equally beautiful arrangement with white tablecloths, flickering candles, pale pink roses and beautifully dressed guests.

She glanced at Henning, who had Lussan – Louise's mother – on his other side. He was so incredibly happy. He was talking loudly, gesticulating, his laughter booming between the walls, and Lussan was allowing herself to be charmed by him as always. In that moment, Elisabeth realized it had all been worth it. Even the hard bits, the ulcerous bits, even the bits that had sometimes pushed her down so deep she'd thought she would never resurface.

She sought out Henning's hand under the table. He took it. He caressed the back of her now liver-spotted hand with his thumb. How young they had been on that night fifty years ago! So naive. So unprepared for what life had in store for them.

But now they were here, in a room full of family, friends and colleagues. The rich flora that came together to form their lives. Many of the faces around her were aged. These were people she had got to know when they had been young, and now they weren't even middle-aged any longer. Henning would be turning eighty soon, while she would be turning seventy. But tonight, life felt rich.

It felt worth every wrinkle of anxiety, every curvature of the spine.

She squeezed Henning's hand and then let go of it. Someone tapped a glass. Oscar Bäring. A close friend, but also one of the authors whom she had published for decades. Over the years, he had won many prestigious literary prizes. Basically the lot – except the one that her husband would soon be awarded. As Oscar cleared his throat to begin his speech, which would doubtless be lengthy, she once again felt fireworks of happiness in her breast. And not just happiness. Triumph. Because that was in truth what tonight was: a triumph.

The guests continued to chatter and Oscar cleared his throat even more loudly with a hint of irritation. Once it was finally silent, he raised his chin, picked up his notes and began to speak:

'Henning! As Thomas Mann said, "Books are the life-blood of the soul." No one personifies that better than you. For almost forty years, you have enriched our souls and filled our veins with your texts. Your tribute to woman has flown to all corners of the world, been read, discussed, studied and praised in countless languages . . .'

Elisabeth took a big sip of her wine. She loved Oscar. But a whole speech by him without wine would be impossible to endure.

They were approaching the main course, and Patrik Hedström was tugging ever more frantically at his tie and shirt collar. His dining companion, Louise, hadn't spent long at the table, but the woman on his other side had turned to him since her own dining partner was mostly interested in the wine.

'For goodness' sake, take off the tie,' she said with a smile.

Her name was Patricia Smedh, and apparently she wrote novels that not only sold well but were also heralded by the critics. 'Although nothing like your wife's sales,' she had confided in him.

'I don't intend to take anything off in this company,' Patrik said, although he did loosen the tie slightly before taking a sip of the full-bodied wine. He didn't dare contemplate which glass of the evening this was.

'Elisabeth wouldn't mind,' Patricia said, smiling even more widely, the fine lines around her eyes getting deeper. 'Although Henning has probably always been a little more . . . prim.'

'Isn't Elisabeth Henning's publisher? Have I got that right?'

Patrik dug deep to recall what Erica had told him earlier that day. He loved his wife, he admired her profession, but when she began talking about things that related to books and the publishing world, he usually zoned out, if he was honest.

'Yes, Elisabeth is a legendary publisher. Her family founded Bauer's a few years after Albert Bonnier started his place. She's been Henning's publisher since the very beginning, and he took her last name when they married.'

Patricia took a small sip of wine. She had barely touched the wine during the two courses they had hitherto eaten. She seemed to be mostly sticking to water.

'Isn't it hard? Working together like that?' Patrik asked, curiously.

'It's clearly worked for them,' said Patricia with a shrug.

Suddenly a hand caressed his neck. Erica was apparently heading back to her table after a visit to the ladies. From her breath and her somewhat swaying centre of gravity, he guessed she'd also drunk her fair share of the wine. It was lucky they had a lie-in in the morning.

'Have you been taking good care of my husband?' Erica said, tousling his hair.

'He's a dear,' said Patricia. 'So nice to see you in your

own neck of the woods for a change, rather than at a book fair somewhere. How are you getting on with Ole over there?'

Erica rolled her eyes.

'He intends to teach me to write and achieve my ultimate potential instead of casting pearls before swine.'

Patricia let out a low laugh.

'All while taking the chance to put his hand on my thigh,' Erica added.

'What the hell?' Patrik was on the brink of getting up.

Erica put her hands on his shoulders and kissed his cheek.

'I can handle it, sweetheart. It's frankly almost entertaining.'

They smiled at each other and he cast his gaze over the room.

'By the way, who are the two people sitting next to Henning and Elisabeth? The woman who looks like she's sitting on a pitchfork and the chap who looks like he's straight out of *Farmers Weekly*?'

'Your powers of observation are not altogether off the mark – despite their prejudiced nature,' Erica said in a low voice. 'Those are Louise's parents – Lussan and Pierre. He's the heir to one of the largest estates in Skåne, with all that entails, and he and Lussan have been married since they were young.'

'Did you get that from some women's weekly at the hairdresser's?' Patrik asked, smirking.

Erica snorted. 'No, it was actually Louise who told me. You know, we do talk while we're on our walks. But I should be getting back to my tactile companion. I can see that their youngest is about to give a speech.'

Patrik's gaze lingered on Erica as she left. He had the best-looking wife here tonight – no doubt about it. And tomorrow they could stay in bed as long as they liked . . .

A tinkling glass proved Erica right. Another speech.

Patrik had lost count around speech number twelve. Most of them were long, too.

'Hello, everyone!'

A man in his forties had stood up. Patrik vaguely remembered that Erica had said he was called Rickard. Patrik's first impression was that he was an entitled arsehole. Slicked-back hair, Rolex on his wrist, haughty expression. And what was more, he'd clearly had one too many. He swayed as he raised his wine glass and tried to focus his eyes on his celebrating parents.

He held up two envelopes.

'I have two different speeches here. Dad – you get to choose one . . .'

Rickard laughed out loud at his own joke and then cast the envelopes aside.

'No, it's not that bad. And I know this night is for both of you, Mum and Dad. But I thought I'd start with you, Dad. You haven't been a very good father . . .'

Patrik's sip of wine caught in his throat and he watched the man with the slicked-back hair in horror. How was this going to pan out?

Henning clenched his fists under the table. Rickard. Always Rickard. Ever since he'd been a kid, it had been as if he was determined to ruin everything that came his way. Not like Peter, who always did everything right.

Henning glanced at his eldest son. Peter looked as angry as he felt. Over on the children's table, Max and William were sitting there in the blue and grey striped ties that they had chosen together earlier that day. They were listening to their uncle, wide-eyed.

Elisabeth placed a hand on Henning's thigh. He'd never understood her weakness for Rickard. Their son was her only blind spot – she forgave all and gave him constant second chances.

'He's had too much to drink,' she pointed out in a whisper, and Henning leaned in towards her.

'He's making a fool of himself,' he said in the same low voice. 'He's making fools of us all.'

From the corner of his eye, he saw Lussan's horrified gaze, and he felt ashamed. He knew how careful Louise's parents were when it came to etiquette, and in the circles they mixed in, behaviour such as this was simply unacceptable.

'You'll probably get an apology tomorrow.'

Elisabeth squeezed his thigh even more tightly. Henning gritted his teeth. More than anything, he wanted to stand up, grab his youngest by the collar and drag him outside. But everyone's eyes were on them. And he now had a responsibility greater than himself. He wasn't just Henning Bauer, author. Not just Henning Bauer, husband and father. Soon he would be Henning Bauer, Nobel Laureate in Literature. He couldn't afford a scene. So while his son stripped him of credit and honour, swaying on unsteady feet, his eyes shiny with booze, Henning merely smiled stiffly. And once the speech finally reached its end after far too long, he was the first to applaud.

'Good God,' Erica exclaimed, turning to Ole.

Dessert had been eaten and the room was beginning to empty. Many of the guests were staying at the hotel and had gone to change ahead of the imminent dance, to powder their noses, or simply to catch their breath after Rickard's speech. The mood was one of unrest, and Peter had excused himself to speak to his parents.

'Even in the best of families . . .' Ole drawled, waving at one of the young waitresses before pointing to his whisky glass.

Vivian Stenklo leaned closer. She hadn't said much

during dinner, but it was clear that the younger Bauer son's speech had shaken her.

'Rickard has always been the black sheep,' she said. 'Always at Elisabeth's skirts asking for cash. Living life well beyond his own means, jumping between jobs that Elisabeth sorts out for him, or starting some business that she invests in before it goes down the tubes. If Rolf had been here, he would have given him a talking to.'

'Yes, what a pity that Rolf couldn't make it,' Erica said. When Vivian lowered her gaze, she added tactfully:

'He must have a lot to prepare ahead of his exhibition. I saw that he's going to be in the gallery over the road – I'm looking forward to it. His photographs really are in a class of their own. What's the theme this time? Borneo? Antarctica?'

'I don't actually know,' Vivian said. 'He says it's a retrospective. Speaking of Rolf's past, there's actually a mystery that it might be worth your while to take a closer look at. A murder mystery . . .'

She smiled conspiratorially as she stood up.

'Right, I need to go and freshen up. I've forked out for a room here tonight so that I don't wake Rolf up by getting in late. Stop by the gallery next week and I'm sure Rolf will tell you more.'

'Absolutely. Thanks,' said Erica.

What was it Vivian had said? A murder mystery?

Her thoughts were interrupted by Ole, who didn't seem to have bothered to listen to what Vivian had said.

'Do you know?' he said, leaning even closer to Erica.

He had been constantly getting too close to her throughout dinner. Now he reached indolently for the refilled whisky glass and knocked back a gulp before continuing.

'Do you know that Henning is going to win the Nobel Prize in Literature?'

Ole peered at her with moist lips. His hands once again sought out her leg, and once again she pushed them away.

'And how do you know that?'

Erica didn't take his drunken ramblings very seriously. The identity of who was going to win the Nobel Prize in Literature was a secret strictly guarded by the eighteen members of the Academy – everyone knew that. Admittedly, there had been rumours of leaks, but she had attached no importance to them. Cultural Sweden loved nothing more than a gossip.

Ole didn't reply at first, instead taking another gulp of whisky. His glass would soon be empty. He half-turned and pointed to his wife sitting at the far end of the room on another table. Susanne Hovland was a strikingly beautiful woman. Raven-black hair, high cheekbones and a perfect fair complexion highlighted by the bold purple dress she was wearing.

'Susanne tells me everything. We have no secrets from each other. She loves me.' He waved an arm in her direction, almost knocking over every glass in his vicinity. 'He got the call today,' Ole chortled.

He drained his glass and gesticulated towards a waitress, trying to get her attention. When he lowered his hand, it landed once again on Erica's thigh and immediately began to make its way up. This time she'd had enough. She stood up, picked up her small evening bag and thanked him for a pleasant evening. A crestfallen Ole watched her leave.

As Erica headed for the ladies, she glanced towards Henning, who was deep in conversation with Peter. Could it be true? She snorted and shook her head. Of course not. The Academy didn't leak.

His whole body ached, but Rolf was finally satisfied. He'd lost count of how many times he'd rehung the photographs – or rather, the placeholders that symbolized the photographs – but there were probably hundreds of them. It was nothing out of the ordinary. It was his usual process. But it had never been as important as this time. He had to get it right.

He stood with his back to the door, trying to assume the role of a visitor seeing the photographs for the first time. He walked slowly through the gallery, stopping by each note, the way the visitors would. In his mind's eye, he saw each photograph before him. His goal was for all the pictures to give the observer the same feeling he'd had when taking the photo – that was why the order was so important. Only amateurs chucked their pictures onto the wall in any old order. The feeling had to be just right.

Hubbub and music from the hotel trickled into the gallery. Rolf could picture it. Elisabeth and Henning in their glad rags, both delighted to be at the centre of the party. Ole – probably well on the way to being hammered and getting handsy – and Susanne, probably keeping a watchful eye on her husband. Vivian, who was hopefully having fun while very probably beaming the occasional angry thought in his direction.

He was conscious that their relationship would require tender love and attention once he was done with the exhibition. It had never been his intention to make Vivian sad or upset. It had simply turned out that way. He loved her. Not like he'd loved Ester, because she had been in his blood, while he and Vivian were more like two celestial bodies in the same orbit around a common sun, his art being the sun. But he knew that she would be there when he needed her. And he would need her.

A knock on the door made him jump. He had just positioned the photograph he'd titled *Guilt* beneath his placeholder. It was the most important photo in the entire exhibition and its position was critical.

Reluctantly, he went to open the door. He didn't like

being disturbed when he was mid-process, but the knocks were insistent.

'Oh, hello there,' he said after opening the door. 'What are you doing here?'

Then he stepped aside to let his visitor in.

'Can I dance with you later?'

William tugged at Erica's skirt and looked up at her hopefully.

Erica's heart melted.

'Of course! It would be an honour! Why don't we make the first dance ours?'

'I've promised that one to Louise,' William said, his face falling before he perked up. 'But how about the second dance? The second is almost as good as the first.'

Erica crouched down to look William in the eye.

'Don't tell anyone, but I happen to think the second dance is better. During the first dance you're never quite sure what to do and it's all a bit awkward and wobbly. The second dance is completely different. So that's ours!'

'Great!' William said cheerfully, and ran off.

Erica stood up and met Peter's amused gaze.

'I think my son has a bit of a crush on you.'

'He's lovely,' Erica said, grinning. 'He and Maja play so well together. You should see them. They're on the same wavelength.'

'Hmm, well, from what I've heard she has a calming effect on him. He can be something of a tornado at home.'

'Oh really?' Erica said, laughing. 'I haven't seen that side of him – maybe you're right. Maja really does have a calming effect on everyone around her.'

'A fine quality to have,' Peter said, leaning against a pillar in the centre of the room. Erica agreed but couldn't help thinking about what Anna had said – about girls being expected to keep boys in check.

There was feverish activity under way around them, transforming the venue into a dance floor. The clusters of guests had thinned out and the room had cooled down. Erica took a deep breath and smoothed her dress.

'Cecily was like that,' Peter continued, looking tenderly towards William, who was now talking to the band with big gestures. 'She kept her composure in every situation and had a stabilizing energy that everyone around her could feel. Harmonizing, I think that's the word I'm looking for. Cecily spread harmony.'

'Do the boys miss her a lot?'

As always, it tugged at her heartstrings when Erica thought about the fact that William and Max had lost their mum.

'Yes. And I try to let them do that. We talk about her a lot – look at photos of her and watch videos with her in them. She's always with us. And Louise has been incredible in her attitude towards it all.'

'It can't always be easy?' Erica said cautiously.

'Living with a ghost? No, probably not,' said Peter. He fingered the wine glass he was clutching. 'But Louise is sensible enough to recognize that they're two distinct things. The fact that the boys and I miss Cecily has nothing to do with our love of Louise.'

'Do you stay in touch with Cecily's parents? The boys' maternal grandparents?'

'Sadly, they died before the boys were even born. And to be perfectly honest, Lussan and Pierre aren't much of a substitute.'

He grinned, and he and Erica exchanged meaningful glances.

'I know what you mean. Not exactly the warmest people I've ever met.'

'Sitting on the floor and playing with the grandkids isn't in their nature. Their focus is different, and I think

Louise had a tricky childhood on that monstrosity of an estate down in Skåne.'

'She still seems to have come out of it on her own two feet,' Erica said, raising her glass towards Louise who had just entered the room with a stressed look on her face.

'People are all over the hotel. I've no idea how we're going to get them back in here when the dancing begins,' she said when she reached them. 'Rickard is sulking in his room and Ole is shitfaced and fell asleep on the stairs. I had to shake him back to life. Jesus Christ. Darling, next time your parents ask me to arrange something like this, shoot me.'

'Pfft, I know you love it really,' said Peter, kissing her on the cheek. 'Bringing order to chaos. The party is a smash hit. Forget Rickard. Mum's spoiled him all these years, and now she only has herself to blame.'

'You're right,' said Louise, composing herself. 'Now I'm going to enjoy the rest of the night. I've already got the first dance on my card bagged by the most handsome man at the party.'

'I heard about that,' said Erica. 'I had to settle for the second dance.'

'You snooze, you lose,' Louise said, smiling broadly.

She went over to talk to the band, who looked ready to start, and put an arm around William.

'When God closes a door, he opens a window,' Peter quipped, following his wife with his gaze. 'Louise is my window. And the boys'. It might be cheesy to say so, but it's true in my case. And I'm not even religious.'

Erica didn't reply, merely squeezed his arm instead. She knew it wasn't just Peter who had been lucky. Louise could count herself as lucky too.

She went off to find Patrik. The first dance would be his whether he liked it or not.

4

SUNDAY

Soon. Soon she, Fanny Klintberg, would be able to leave this fucking place behind. She was saving every single penny this shitty job gave her so that she could leave. Eighteen years in Fjällbacka was more than enough. Endless winters in a place with only a thousand inhabitants, where everyone knew everyone else, and no one was allowed to stand out. Then there were the stuck-up summer visitors to the seaside, coming here and thinking they owned the place and could act however they pleased.

Fanny retrieved the cleaning gear from the boot of the old Fiat she'd been given by her parents as an eighteenth birthday present. It wasn't exactly a flash set of wheels, but she loved the little red car since it had at least made her a little freer.

After checking that she had everything, she closed the boot, sighed deeply and dug in her pocket for the bunch of keys for the places she cleaned. Once she got to Bali, she wouldn't ever clean again. Well, except perhaps for her bungalow. She was going to work in a bar – that was the plan. She'd already started boning up on drinks online. And she'd seen that ancient movie *Cocktail* that her mum loved so much because she had – for some unfathomable

42

reason – a crush on that dodgy guy from the cult who played the lead.

She opened the door and used the bucket filled with cleaning equipment as a doorstop while she lifted in the vacuum cleaner. This was a relatively easy job. The gallery space was usually empty and didn't have loads of knick-knacks that needed picking up, wiping down, or working around. She heaved in the vacuum cleaner and picked up the bucket of mops and detergent, the door slamming shut behind her. Then she turned around, and screamed shrilly.

'You up for it?'

Patrik Hedström's voice was husky. It felt as if his mouth was filled with carpet.

'No.'

Erica's voice from her side of the bed left no room for doubt about the sincerity of her answer.

'Jesus Christ, is this why we don't hit the town anymore?'

'That and three young kids,' Erica groaned, turning to face him.

A whiff of her breath made him grimace. Then he grimaced even more as he realized that his own was probably just as bad.

'I don't know what I was thinking, drinking that much,' Patrik said, unable to raise his head from the pillow.

'In my case, I blame Ole. He was definitely trying to drink me under the table. How did we even get home? Did we walk?'

Patrik racked his memory and found nothing about the journey home. But at home they most certainly were, tucked up in their own bed.

'When do we have to pick up the kids?' he said, clearing his throat. His voice had an interesting, smoky character.

'We said eleven. But I think I'm going to have to ask Anna and Dan for a few more hours of respite.'

Erica pulled the duvet even further up towards her chin. She licked her lips and fumbled for the bottle of water she always had on the bedside table. She drained half of it before passing it to Patrik, who received it gratefully.

'I'm too old for this,' he sighed, trying to work out whether there was any part of his head that wasn't aching.

'You have to admit that it was a pretty fun night, at any rate,' Erica said. 'Perhaps not quite good enough to merit *this*, but still.'

'Agreed. Although that was mostly thanks to my dining companions and that speech by the son that wouldn't have been out of place in a Lars Norén play.'

'Did you just name-drop Norén in casual conversation? I didn't realize I'd been cohabiting with a covert intellectual all these years . . .'

Erica smiled at him. Her curly blond hair framed her face, and he noted that even when he felt rougher than a badger's bum, his wife was still incredibly attractive.

'I've always been ragingly intellectual,' he said, managing to prop himself up on his elbows and lift his upper body slightly. 'It's only commercial authors like you who don't understand my greatness.'

A pillow came straight towards his face, making the whole world rock. Once he'd collected himself, he sought revenge by tickling Erica. Slowly his sunken spirits began to revive, and just as soon as he popped a paracetamol and an ibuprofen, he'd be more or less human again.

When his phone began buzzing on the bedside table, he considered ignoring it.

'It might be Anna and Dan,' said Erica, heaving herself up on one elbow so that the duvet slid off one of her breasts.

After giving her a long look, Patrik reluctantly reached out for his phone.

'It's work, not Dan and Anna.'

He cleared his throat a couple of times before answering.

'Patrik speaking. What the hell? Okay, where? I'll be there right away. Is forensics en route? Good. I'll wait for them there.'

It was as if the hangover was gone. Patrik kicked the duvet away and got out of bed.

'What's happened?' Erica said, sitting up slowly.

Patrik pulled on a pair of jeans and a T-shirt which were at the top of the heap of clothes beside the bed, then he searched for his socks.

'Someone's been found dead at the gallery on Galärbacken.'

'Someone? Is it Rolf? Or Vivian?'

Erica also began to get dressed. She chucked a pair of black socks over to him.

'I don't know any more than that right now. The cleaner found a dead body this morning. That was Annika on the blower. I'm heading straight over there. Will you deal with the kids?'

'Yes, I'll deal with them,' Erica said, tugging a sweatshirt over her head. 'Keep me posted!' she called to Patrik, but it was too late.

The door had already slammed shut behind him.

5

STOCKHOLM 1980

Lola could hear P'tite getting up quietly so as not to wake her. She had worked late – later than usual – and her eyelids were heavy and impossible to open. But the sound of P'tite's tiny feet tripping across the wooden floor to the kitchen made her smile with her eyes closed.

Lola often wondered whether P'tite knew that she was her whole world. P'tite was the light streaming through the white curtains at the window. She was the sound of gravel underfoot after a long winter.

Lola stretched in bed. It had been a rowdy night at Alexa's. Several drunk, angry men had come in and started yelling. Fortunately, that didn't happen very often. The club was a wonderful place. She loved working there and being part of the community. Being loved. It was that simple. It made all the rest worth it. The men from the night before didn't know any better. They were ignorant. Narrow-minded. Small.

There was a clatter of saucepans and frying pans in the kitchen. Lola smelled the scent of coffee and reluctantly began to come fully to life, even though she knew she could sleep as long as she wanted. P'tite was fine on her own. But she missed her. Time spent with her daughter was always more worthwhile than sleep.

She turned on the radio. 'Don't Do Me Like That' with Tom Petty and the Heartbreakers blared out at full volume and Lòla hurried to turn it down before the neighbour began hammering on the wall.

When she opened the curtains, Stockholm was sparkling in its full summer beauty beyond the rooftops. She had been lucky to bag this flat on a sublet. One of her colleagues at Alexa's was going to Los Angeles for a few years and had asked if she wanted to rent her one-bed flat in Vasastan. Late nineteenth-century tenement. Top floor. Morning sun. She'd said yes on the spot. It was perfect for her and P'tite. Much better than the poky hole they'd been in before in Bandhagen.

A crisp white dressing gown was hanging on a hanger at the foot of the bed. White was her favourite colour. It always had been – ever since she'd been little. Perhaps it was because she'd had a white pony as a kid. Or perhaps because she thought it contrasted so beautifully with her copper hair. It was dyed, but what difference did that make?

'What luxe breakfast will I be enjoying today, sweetheart?'

By the kitchen table, Lola almost tripped over P'tite's pink rucksack with a Barbie face on the pocket. P'tite took it everywhere she went, and Lola was strictly prohibited from looking inside. She feigned a dramatic sigh and set the bag down by the wall before taking a seat at the battered pine kitchen table and lighting a cigarette. P'tite put a coffee cup down in front of her and then grandly presented the menu, which had generated a considerable amount of washing up on the side.

'Scrambled eggs. Skogaholm bread with cheese. No butter. And bacon. Fried so crispy you'll get cancer just from looking at it.'

'Darling, where did you get that from? Bacon never gave anyone cancer. It's those awful nuclear power plants that cause cancer.'

Lola exhaled a few perfect smoke rings at P'tite. She loved poking holes through them – she had done since she was a baby.

'I'm ready. Let's dine.'

P'tite giggled. She liked the word dine.

'Start with the scrambled eggs, Daddy.'

'Yes, boss. I'll start with the scrambled eggs.'

She took a bite.

'Lovely! Heavenly!'

When P'tite turned back to the hob, Lola carefully removed the eggshell from her mouth.

6

Vivian wiggled her toes contentedly as she lay in bed. She felt proud. She had stood up for herself, demanded her place in her marriage to Rolf. It was a small yet important victory.

Otherwise, everything revolved around Rolf. His exhibitions. His travels. His friends. His club, Blanche. She was nothing more than a cog in the machine ensuring that his wheels kept turning. But last night had been the beginning of something new. She'd had fun at the party without being Rolf's shadow.

Vivian looked around the room. Like all the rooms at Stora Hotellet, the decor was inspired by one of the major port cities of the world and its good-time girls. One floor of cities, one of girls. Her room was Tokyo. On the wall outside each room were fictitious letters from one Captain Klassen writing home to his sister from the city evoked by the room in question. She had been disappointed when she'd realized that the letters were made up. But the rooms were nice.

The hotel had actually been fully booked long before the party, but Vivian had been fortunate. Just as she'd asked in reception on the off chance, someone had called to cancel. She hadn't been surprised. The position of the moon right now meant that luck and fortune were coming her way. Rolf thought that was nonsense, but Vivian knew better.

There had been powerful flows of energy at the dinner the night before. Many emotional currents, and much going on beneath the surface that she hadn't quite been able to interpret. Admittedly, her intuition was always gravely impaired when consuming alcohol.

Vivian hoped that Elisabeth and Henning had enjoyed themselves. She liked them. She knew they had spent a lot of time with Rolf and Ester during the years of their marriage, but they had always welcomed her with open arms. They probably had one of the suites.

Some time she would like to book one of the suites with Rolf, but he didn't enjoy staying in hotels. He always said he'd stayed in enough hotels around the world for work.

Yesterday's dress was neatly hung up on the wardrobe door – she'd slept in a threadbare long T-shirt. It was probably at least ten years old, but no matter how much she tried she could never find anything more comfortable to sleep in.

Vivian crawled out of bed and opened the curtains. The sky was imperceptible – almost everything beyond the window was a murky haze. The window faced Galärbacken, and the gallery was just out of sight, even when she looked as far to the right as she could. But she was able to sense through the haze that something was going on outside the exhibition venue. At this time of year, the hill running down to Ingrid Bergmans torg ought to be more or less deserted, other than the odd pedestrian, but right now there were cars and people pouring down the hill. She couldn't see where they were going, but something made her feel a gnawing sense of unease in the pit of her stomach. She hadn't heard from

Rolf that morning, which was unusual even when they'd had a row. For almost twenty years, he had sent her a *Good morning my love* message at seven o'clock if they had slept separately. But today there was no such text on her mobile.

That should have occurred to her earlier, but her brain was as thick as cold treacle before she had her first cup of coffee. Now the anxiety hit her with full force.

She quickly grabbed a pair of trousers and a top from her bag and got dressed. The plait she'd had in overnight was tangled and messy, but that didn't matter. Something told her that she needed to get down to the gallery.

Vivian jogged down the stairs, pulling on her cardigan over her top, and hurried past reception. One of the girls there tried to stop her, but she carried on outside. Then she stopped. The door to the gallery was wide open. Outside in the tiny car park beneath a steep rock face there were police cars and an ambulance. Vivian ran across the street without looking and almost got hit by a car that honked angrily at her. She carried on towards the gallery without taking any notice but was stopped by an older man with a stern expression.

'You can't go in there.'

'My husband? Rolf?' she said, her voice trembling while her legs threatened to give way.

'Is your husband the gallery owner?' the older, white-haired man asked.

'No, he's a photographer. He's due to have an exhibition here.'

'Best you wait here with me.'

Vivian pulled the cardigan even tighter around herself. But nothing could shield her from the icy cold spreading through her.

* * *

'How long until forensics get here?' said Patrik, stepping carefully inside.

He wanted to get abreast of the situation quickly, while not destroying any traces or evidence.

'They'll be here any minute now,' Gösta said from the doorway, pointing towards a woman with grey-blond hair wearing a grey cardigan and pale blue trousers, who was staring at them intently. A curious local was holding her by the arm. 'That's probably the wife. If it's the photographer due to have the exhibition that we're dealing with here.'

'It is,' Patrik said, nodding. 'I've seen his photo. It's Rolf Stenklo.'

'Should I get someone to take care of her?' said Gösta, turning back to the woman, whose teeth seemed to be chattering with the cold in the mist shrouding Galärbacken.

'Is Martin on his way?'

'Five minutes.'

'Ask him when he gets here. He's best with people.'

'Shall I call in Paula and Mellberg?' Gösta asked – Patrik knew it was mostly for appearance's sake.

'No, too many chefs . . . We don't need more people at the scene of the crime. I asked Annika to get them down to the station. They'll wait for us there.'

Gösta pointed up the hill through the haze.

'Here come forensics.'

'Good,' said Patrik, backing up to the doorway.

He pulled out his phone and slowly filmed the surroundings and as much of the room as he could capture without stepping into the crime scene. The simple frames with the scraps of paper on the walls. The body of Rolf Stenklo on the floor; the thin trickle of blood from his head.

'Torbjörn and his team always do a stand-up job,' he said.

'Well, that's the thing, Patrik,' Gösta said hesitantly. 'It's not Torbjörn who—'

'Hello! This seems to be the place!'

A perky female voice resounded towards them as the woman whose voice it was waved eagerly at them.

'My name's Farideh Mirza. I've taken over from Torbjörn Ruud.'

'Taken over from Torbjörn?' Patrik said quizzically. Then a bell began to faintly ring – he'd seen a memo somewhere.

'He took early retirement,' Gösta said, placing a reassuring hand on Patrik's shoulder.

Patrik gritted his teeth.

'What's the status of our crime scene? How untouched can we assume it is?'

Farideh looked at them sternly and Patrik found himself standing up straighter. She had a commanding presence.

'It was the cleaner who found him first thing this morning. We've taken her statement and, according to her, she came straight in, and then legged it straight out again without touching the body. The on-call doctor has been and confirmed the death.'

'Good. And what about you guys?'

She eyed Patrik and Gösta from head to toe. Behind her, two of her team approached in full protective gear and awaited her go-ahead to enter.

'I popped inside,' said Patrik. 'Gösta waited here, by the front door.'

'Brilliant. That's a good place for us to start.'

She stepped inside. Then she turned to Patrik.

'Next time, it'd be best if you didn't go inside at all.'

'Okay,' he said submissively, feeling like a rebuked schoolboy.

'Battleaxe,' Gösta said admiringly.

'Hmm,' Patrik said. He missed Torbjörn. Why couldn't things just stay the way they were?

In the distance, he could see the medical examiner approaching.

* * *

53

There was a loud fizz when the Samarin tablet hit the water. Or perhaps loud was an exaggeration, but to Erica's aching head it sounded like a huge waterfall. A paracetamol and an ibuprofen had preceded the Samarin, but they still hadn't kicked in. Good God. She really wasn't up to much these days. There might have been copious wine the night before, but a few years ago that wouldn't have caused her anything more than a gently throbbing forehead. Now she had an entire symphony orchestra inside her skull. With a voluble percussion section.

Erica replaced the box of Samarin in the cupboard above the cooker hood and managed to topple another packet out of it at the same time. She turned it over sullenly. It had been given to her by Kristina, her mother-in-law, after she had complained a little too much and a little too often that her body was beginning to give her grief. It hadn't crept up on her slowly – it had shown up more or less overnight, or at least over a few days, which was apparently not unusual.

The menopause.

That word alone made Erica shudder with discomfort. That was at least the diagnosis that Google offered her, and Kristina seemed to agree, given that she had given her a natural remedy that would alleviate her discomfort for that particular condition.

Erica couldn't quite put her finger on why the thought precipitated such an acute sense of discomfort. Surely she and Patrik weren't that old? Or were they? Was it all downhill from here? Her periods had become irregular, she was constantly hot and sweaty, and she no longer recognized her own body. She didn't really know what was different – it simply was. Men didn't have those concerns. They sailed through those years without any hormonal changes – all they had to grapple with was a receding hairline and a swelling gut. On the other hand, she thought Patrik had started to become increasingly fixed in his habits and more reluctant to change. Surely that was a clear sign he was turning into an old man . . .

She brusquely replaced the pack of tablets that promised harmony and happiness and shut the cupboard door. The headache had lost its sharpest edges and she poured herself a big glass of water and downed it even though she wasn't thirsty. She needed to restore her fluids. Especially given that she planned to have a big cup of dehydrating coffee and head out onto the terrace.

She intended to max out her hours without the kids as much as she could. She knew everyone said you had to enjoy the early years, because once they were over you missed them, but she couldn't quite bring herself to agree. She loved her kids to death, but goodness gracious she longed for these chaotic early years to be over.

The glazed terrace was chilly, so she turned on the heater and wrapped a thick blanket around herself before flopping into one of the wicker chairs. Only now did she manage to think about what might have happened at the gallery. Patrik had sent a brief text in which he had written: Rolf murdered. Don't know when I'll be home.

It was actually against all police regulations to tell her anything about a crime scene. But they had long ago erased that rule – Patrik regarded Erica as a resource to bounce ideas off during his cases.

Erica jumped when the doorbell rang. She cast off the blanket and went to open the door. A rosy-cheeked Louise was standing on the threshold.

'I didn't ask whether you wanted to meet up today – I thought the two of you might want a lie-in! But you must be up by now! Any chance of a coffee?'

'Come in,' Erica said, stepping to one side. 'How early were *you* up?'

Louise took off her weatherproof fitness jacket.

'Very early. I couldn't tip back bucketloads of wine last night like the rest of you since I was in charge. So I've already been out walking for an hour. It feels great! And with a little luck, my parents will have had breakfast when I get back! I thought I'd do 10k today!'

Erica could but grunt in response. Bile rose up in her throat at the mere thought of going out to exercise.

'You look a bit green about the gills. Are you hungover? Where's Patrik got to?'

Louise glanced around the living room and towards the kitchen. Erica realized that her friend must have left the hotel before the body had been discovered. Could she tell her anything? Though as soon as Louise got back to the hotel, she'd find out anyway.

Playing for time, Erica filled her own cup and passed another to Louise, who took her coffee black. Obviously. Erica couldn't fathom how anyone could drink coffee without full-fat milk in it.

'Come on, let's sit on the terrace.'

'There's not much to see out there today,' Louise said, peering through the beautiful windows.

Ordinarily, there was a sea view from the terrace, but today almost everything was shrouded in grey mist that seemed to be growing thicker.

'No; this weather doesn't cheer anyone up.'

Erica sipped her coffee, wondering how to break the news to Louise. She didn't know how well Louise knew Rolf Stenklo, but she knew that he was close to Elisabeth and Henning, and that they were all very involved in their club, Blanche. Given how closely Henning and Louise seemed to work together, surely she had come across Rolf too.

'You didn't say where Patrik was . . .' Louise said, providing Erica with the perfect opening to embark on the subject.

'He's at work. He got an urgent summons not long ago. There's . . . something's happened at the gallery.'

'The gallery? Where Rolf's having his exhibition?' Louise said, horrified. 'Has there been a burglary? Oh no – not Rolf's photographs. He was so looking forward to exhibiting them here in Fjällbacka. He must be crushed.'

'Rolf's dead.'

That sounded more brutal than Erica had intended, but there probably was no gentle way to deliver that kind of news.

Louise recoiled, spilling her coffee, and stared back at Erica. Erica passed her a napkin to wipe the coffee up with. She took it hesitantly but didn't start mopping up. Her eyes were wide.

'Dead? From what? Heart attack? I know Vivian was worried about his weight. It can strike when you're least expecting . . .'

'He was murdered.'

Louise continued to stare at Erica. Slowly, she set the coffee cup down on the table and began to dab at her leg where the coffee stain was now beginning to spread across her pale leggings.

'I have to get back to the hotel,' she said, getting up abruptly.

Without saying another word, Louise walked through the living room, retrieved her jacket from the hook in the hall and disappeared.

'Martin!'

Gösta was calling to him from the steps leading into the gallery. Martin Molin hurried over and looked up at the older policeman, who was leaning against the banister.

'The victim's wife. Can you . . . ?'

Gösta pointed to a woman with a long, pale plait and

big cardigan who was standing stock still and shivering as her gaze followed everything that was happening.

'Sure,' Martin said, going over to her. He tried to put his police officer's hat on. He'd abandoned Mette, Tuva and wee Jon at the kitchen table when Gösta had called.

Sometimes the change was just too abrupt.

'Martin Molin, Tanumshede Police. I gather you're married to Rolf Stenklo?'

Vivian Stenklo nodded.

'I heard someone say he'd been found dead in there,' she said, despair in her voice. 'But surely that can't be?'

She looked hopefully at Martin, who shook his head. Gösta had called him en route. It had already been confirmed that it was the exhibitor himself who was the deceased. Patrik had identified him.

'Unfortunately, we've confirmed that it's your husband who has been found dead.'

Vivian trembled and looked like she was about to collapse.

Martin gently took her by the arm.

'Why don't we get back into the warm?'

Gently gripping Vivian Stenklo's arm, Martin made for the entrance of the hotel. When they entered the foyer, the two women behind the reception desk fell silent, and avoided looking at Vivian. News had spread quickly. Soon it would be all over Fjällbacka.

'Can we get some coffee?' he asked the receptionists.

'There's some already made in there – please help yourselves,' was the reply.

He held Vivian with great care as they descended the steps to the dining room. The final remnants of breakfast were just being tidied away. Martin parked Vivian on a chair by one of the tables at the window facing the harbour and poured them each a cup of coffee.

'Milk?'

She nodded mutely.

'Here, drink a little. It'll warm you up.'

Martin contemplated the woman before him. He'd lost a spouse too – albeit to illness, but he could still largely understand the pain she was feeling at this moment.

Vivian did as she was told while staring into the mist covering Ingrid Bergmans torg. More and more curious onlookers were gathering. In a small community, an incident like this assumed far greater proportions than it ever did in the city, where police cars and ambulances were merely part of the daily backdrop.

'When was the last time you saw Rolf?' Martin asked, taking a sip of coffee.

He grimaced. It had spent far too long on the hotplate at the bar and tasted acrid – not unlike the coffee down at the station.

'Yesterday afternoon. We . . . we had a row.'

'What was the row about?'

Vivian shook her head, making the bedraggled plait move.

'It was stupid. Insignificant. And stupid. Sorry, I already said stupid.'

She brushed a strand of hair out of her face with a trembling hand.

'It doesn't matter. What was the stupid thing you had a row about? Sorry if my questions seem intrusive and personal. I'm afraid it's my job to ask questions – even uncomfortable ones – so that we can quickly find out as much as possible. Right now, we don't know what's relevant and what isn't.'

'I understand,' Vivian said, looking down into her coffee as if she didn't understand what it was. 'We were arguing about a party. Our good friends Elisabeth and Henning Bauer were celebrating their golden wedding anniversary yesterday – in this very room, as it happens. And for some unfathomable reason, Rolf didn't want to go. And as usual, he assumed that I wouldn't want to go either. But I put my foot down. I called Louise – that's Elisabeth and Henning's daughter-in-law, and Henning's secretary; she was organizing the party – and I asked if I could join at the last minute. And she sorted it all out. Louise sorts everything out. As a sort of protest, I stayed at the hotel overnight. I suppose I thought deep down that Rolf might be sitting there at home on his own, thinking over his . . . his mistake.'

Vivian clapped her hands to her face. Martin sat still, watching her trembling body. After a minute or so, Vivian raised her head. She didn't look at Martin – instead she once again looked out at the mist.

Martin gently cleared his throat.

'So the last time you saw him or spoke to him was yesterday afternoon?'

Vivian nodded, her gaze still on the window.

'No, I was sulking. But I did think it was strange this morning. He always sends me a text in the morning if we're not sleeping in the same place. Whether we've quarrelled or not. And this morning I didn't get one . . .'

Her gaze seemed to move towards the square, and Martin followed it. The previous day's storm had abated, but he actually preferred it when there were white horses out on the waves and the water was lashing the quayside to this heavy torpor that had settled on the place.

Sensing that Vivian needed a moment to herself, he allowed his mind to wander to the recently announced plans to reinforce the square. Fjällbacka was one of several communities on the Bohuslän coast built on clay, which were now threatened by future landslides. It probably had something to do with climate change and rising sea levels, although he didn't feel up to ruminating on those issues. He had his hands quite full with the leaks in his own home. There was no room to take in the thought that the world was slowly being engulfed by the oceans as the ice sheets melted.

'So you don't know how long Rolf was at the gallery? When was the exhibition due to open?'

'Tomorrow. Monday. He'd been preparing this one in situ for a week. And before that for six months at home in Stockholm. He'd picked his theme, picked his photos. Developed them. For his exhibitions, Rolf worked exclusively with platinum prints.'

'Platinum prints?' Martin asked.

It was a concept he'd never heard of, but then he knew nothing about photography. He took as many photos as he could of his daughter Tuva, his partner Mette and her little boy Jon using the portrait feature on his iPhone – he thought the results were good enough.

In the most recent photo, Tuva had her hand on Mette's belly. Martin swallowed as he thought about them.

'I'm not an expert, but over my years with Rolf I've overheard this and that,' said Vivian. 'It's a way of printing images where you use the precious metals platinum and palladium. It's expensive, but Rolf said it gave the best and most unique quality to the pictures.'

'So the pictures in the gallery were valuable?'

Martin frowned and leaned forward. This was important information. It increased the possibility that this might be a burglary gone wrong.

'Yes, although not just because of the printing method. Rolf is one of our most internationally successful photographers. His originals sell for hundreds of thousands of kronor at auctions and galleries the world over.'

'Impressive. Forgive my ignorance.'

'No problem. Naturally, not everyone knows.'

For the first time during their conversation, Vivian smiled. It softened her tense face, and Martin saw what a beautiful woman she was. Beautiful in a brittle, fragile kind of way.

'I suppose it's likely a lot of people were aware that there were valuable pieces in the gallery?'

'Yes, it was common knowledge that Rolf was going to have an exhibition. There are posters all over the place – up and down the coast too. But he didn't start arranging the photographs until I was there yesterday. At first, he works with sheets of paper on which he writes the names of the photographs so that he can move them around and feel his way forward. It takes several attempts before you get the perfect composition and experience for the gallery visitors. He didn't need the originals there for that. The images were in his head – just as clearly as if they were there in front of him.'

'He was a . . . nature photographer, right?' Martin said hesitantly.

'Yes. Nature and indigenous peoples. His most famous photos were taken during the year he spent living with the Penan tribe in Borneo.'

'And this exhibition? What was its theme?'

Martin reluctantly found himself intrigued. He'd always been drawn to people who had a passion for their work, as one surely must have to spend a year living with people from the Stone Age in Southeast Asia.

Vivian shook her head.

'The strange thing is that I don't know much about it. He always used to show me the pictures, but not this time. All I know is that it was about the past. If I remember correctly, he'd hung fifteen of his sheets of paper on the walls.'

'Did Rolf have any enemies? Sorry, the word enemy sounds so dramatic. But is there anyone you're aware of who might have wanted to harm him?'

Vivian shook her head emphatically. 'No, everyone liked Rolf. He had no enemies.'

'Okay, but if you think of anything that might be

important to the investigation, please get in touch. Here's my number.'

Martin passed Vivian his card and she tucked it into the pocket of her knitted cardigan.

'When will I get him back?'

When she said those words, the realization seemed to strike her with full force. Her face contorted and wrinkled.

Martin spontaneously placed his hand on hers.

'As soon as possible,' he said. 'And I think that's enough for now. If I can just have your phone number and then we're done here. Is there anyone who can be with you right now?'

Vivian nodded. She gave him her number and stood up.

'I have to pack,' she said, making for reception without saying goodbye.

Martin continued to look in the direction she'd gone for a long time. Sometimes other people's grief was more than he could bear. His own had begun to settle and soften at the edges. He had Tuva, who reminded him of all the things he had loved about Pia. He'd inherited his dream home and then a few months ago Mette and he had found out they were expecting their first child together. But encounters like this were always a reminder of how suddenly death could snatch everything away.

'What do we have?' Patrik said, following Farideh Mirza impatiently as she made briskly for her car while removing her gloves.

Once she reached the vehicle, she began to remove her coveralls which she inserted neatly into a bag.

'Someone shot Rolf Stenklo in the back of the head with a nail gun,' she said at last, after leaving Patrik shifting from foot to foot while she finished her own tasks.

'We've swabbed it and also secured some fibres from the grip.'

'And how long will it take to analyse that?' said Patrik. However, he knew the answer already.

'Impossible to say. They're having a tough time at NFC right now.'

'Other evidence?'

'Not much. There are obviously plenty of fingerprints in the place but, given it's somewhere lots of people pass through, finding anything that might have been left by our killer is pretty much like finding a needle in a haystack. We'll do our best, though.'

Patrik irritably surveyed the gaggle of onlookers pressed up against the police cordon. Vultures. He spotted a familiar face coming down from the square. Louise. Erica's friend. She was stopped at the cordon, but a nod from him indicated she was to be admitted and after a quick wave to him she ran inside the hotel.

'Can you say roughly when Rolf Stenklo died?' he asked Farideh, who shrugged.

'We'll get final confirmation on the time of death later, but according to the medical examiner's preliminary assessment, somewhere around midnight – give or take two hours either side.'

'The medical examiner can't be more precise than that?' he said, glancing towards the window into the function room.

In other words, it was very likely that Rolf had been murdered while Patrik had been only a few metres away.

'No, not right now.'

'Okay, I'll take that.'

Patrik nodded curtly. He had nothing against Farideh Mirza personally, but he was familiar with Torbjörn's way of doing things after so many years working together and knew how to talk to him about a crime scene. This was just . . . new.

'I hope we'll work well together. Torbjörn sends his best from Torrevieja,' said Farideh, as if she had heard his very thoughts. 'My colleagues will need another couple of hours before we're done here.'

'Please let me know if you find anything else,' Patrik said, waving to Gösta and Martin.

They came over to him and Patrik pointed towards the windows of the hotel.

'Rolf was most likely murdered while a party was taking place right next door. I myself was at it. We'll need to interview all the guests. All it needs is for one person to have nipped out for a smoke or to have glanced through the window and seen something and we might have more to go on. Martin, you spoke with his wife – did she have anything to give us?'

Martin cleared his throat.

'The photographs that Rolf was going to exhibit – the ones he was in the process of hanging on the walls – were very valuable. So we might be dealing with a break-in gone wrong. Fifteen photographs – each one worth a couple of hundred thousand kronor. That's a lot of cash.'

'Not easy to sell, but we might be looking at stupid burglars. Wouldn't be the first time . . . Or perhaps they can be sold on the black market, where buyers don't ask too many questions. Good work, Martin. That gives us something to work on. I'm going to talk to Louise Bauer who was running the party and ask her for a list of guests and their phone numbers. There were around eighty guests. We need to contact them all right away by phone if we're going to have any chance to get through the whole list in a reasonable time.'

'Gösta and I will head to the station. Will you come as soon as you've got the list?' said Martin, beginning to make his way up Galärbacken to his car, which he'd left in the car park by the church.

Patrik responded with nothing more than a thumbs up. He was already en route to the hotel.

'Elisabeth? Henning? Are you awake?'

Louise was standing outside Henning and Elisabeth's hotel room, breathing erratically. She forced herself to take long, deep breaths. She knocked again. Then she heard footsteps on the other side and Henning opened the door.

'What's up?' he said, knotting the hotel robe tighter around his waist.

His hair was wet, and Louise guessed that he had come straight from the shower. Standing behind him was Elisabeth, also clad in a robe. Her hair was wet too. She had – in other words – actually interrupted them in the middle of a bath in the turquoise spa tub that she knew was sunk into the upstairs floor.

'What is it?' said Elisabeth.

Both she and Henning were regarding her with questioning eyes. Louise took a few deep breaths to stabilize her voice and then she said:

'Rolf's dead. Murdered.'

Elisabeth gasped. All colour drained from Henning's face. They beckoned for her to enter the room and closed the door behind her. There was only a small sofa to sit on, which was under the stairs, and she collapsed onto it while Henning and Elisabeth remained standing.

A small puddle had begun to form around Henning, but he didn't seem to have noticed.

'I just heard about it, but it's all going on outside. The police are there.'

'Outside? You mean the gallery?' said Elisabeth, going over to the window and trying to look to the right as best she could.

'He's been murdered in the gallery?' Henning echoed.

'Yes, I think so,' said Louise.

She looked at her hands. They were red from her chilly walk. She was surprised they weren't shaking. They ought to be shaking, because inside she was shaking.

'I'm going upstairs to get dressed,' said Henning, making for the stairs.

Elisabeth lingered for a few moments. She met Louise's gaze. For a second, it looked as if she wanted to say something. Then she tugged the gown tighter around her torso and followed Henning upstairs.

'Louise!'

Patrik raised his voice when he caught sight of Louise Bauer at the top of the stairs, heading away.

'Oh, hello, Patrik,' she said, hurrying towards him. 'I heard. About Rolf. Erica . . . Erica told me.'

She hesitated, probably unsure whether it had been okay for Erica to tell her. He smiled to reassure her.

'I need to have a chat with you,' he said.

He pointed enquiringly towards the dining room.

'Impressive that they've already managed to clean it up,' he said lightly, once they'd taken seats at a table by the wall. 'Thanks for a great party, by the way.'

'Thanks for coming.' Louise's voice was cordial but absent. 'What did you need to talk to me about?'

Straight to the point. Concise. But he could tell she was shocked.

'The guest list. We think Rolf was murdered while the party was going on, so we need to get in touch with all the guests to check whether anyone saw anything.'

'Of course. Give me an email address and I'll send it over as soon as I'm in front of my computer in my room.'

'We'll need phone numbers too.'

'All guests are listed with their phone number, email, home address and local address. You'll have everything you need.'

'Thanks. That's very helpful.'

Patrik glanced towards the coffee pot on the bar and noted with disappointment that it was empty. The raw weather meant he was shivering right down to his bone marrow, and damn it, he thought he'd started to feel a slight ache in his joints when the weather was bad. Was it his age? Though he was inclined to think it might be his imagination. That was what Erica thought. 'Hypochondriac,' was the word she used.

'Do you . . . know anything?'

Louise looked at Patrik hopefully. He shook his head.

'I can't comment on an ongoing investigation. But . . . we're at a very early stage. So no.'

'Rolf was a good man,' Louise said slowly. 'He and his late wife Ester were Elisabeth and Henning's closest friends. I never met Ester – she died of cancer many years ago – but I really like Vivian. How . . . how's she doing? Have you spoken to her?'

Louise ran her hands over the table, brushing away a few breadcrumbs left over from breakfast.

'We've spoken to her. And of course, she's shocked.'

'Of course,' Louise said, before falling silent.

Some German tourists noisily entered the room but turned around as soon as they saw the bare tables. He heard the word 'Polizei' and guessed they were talking about what they had seen outside.

They both jumped when Louise's phone rang.

'Sorry. Is it all right if I take this?' she said, pulling the mobile from the pocket of her windbreaker.

'Of course. Go for it,' said Patrik.

'Louise Bauer? Yes . . . Yes, no. We've no comment to make. No. We've only just heard the news, and the Bauer family won't be offering any comment at this time. Yes. No. No. No. Yes, of course I understand. But right now, our only comment is "no comment".'

She ended the call and shook her head angrily.

'The press?' Patrik asked rhetorically.

'Yes, *Göteborgs-Posten*. I don't understand how they've found out so quickly. But I suppose people call their tip line hoping to make a quick buck.'

'A quick buck, or sometimes the satisfaction of seeing something in the paper that they know they tipped them off about,' Patrik said levelly. 'Odd behaviour, if you ask me.'

He was no longer outraged by the public's conduct around crimes. Empathy no longer seemed to be in vogue. If it ever had been. He hoped that Farideh and her team were working quickly. Before long, the media would flock to the police cordon and while they wouldn't dare to cross it, you never knew what they might get up to. It was always disruptive, regardless.

'I'd also like to talk to Henning and Elisabeth. Preferably now,' Patrik said amicably, while still managing to make it sound more like an order than a request. They had been close to Rolf and together with Vivian they might be able to provide important information.

Louise nodded.

'They're still in the hotel packing. I'll call them.'

'Thanks,' said Patrik, standing up.

As they made their way out of the room, a member of staff arrived with a freshly brewed pot of coffee. Typical.

'The press are calling like crazy.' The police station secretary Annika's face was pink with stress. She pointed to the persistently ringing telephone in reception.

'Tell them we aren't able to comment right now, but we'll call a press conference when the time is right,'

Martin said automatically, glancing at Gösta for his colleague's approval. 'Where's Mellberg?'

'On the way in. He and Rita were apparently at the swimming baths in Strömstad with the grandkids when we called. But he's coming. Paula's here – she's in her office.'

'Thanks.'

Martin walked ahead of Gösta into the station. As far as he was concerned, Mellberg would have been welcome to stay in the pool in Strömstad. The reason for his reinstatement as chief following the debacle that had taken place in Tanumshede a year or so earlier was a mystery. Presumably the brass in Gothenburg had been worried that they might end up with him otherwise; that was the only plausible explanation.

'Hi Paula.'

Martin stopped in the doorway to Paula Morales' office while Gösta continued on to his own room. Paula still had the smallest office as the most recent hire, but she didn't seem bothered by it. She had her things ordered with military precision, unlike Martin, whose own office always looked like it had just been burgled and the thieves had been searching for something they hadn't found.

'Hi. How's Mette?'

He grimaced. Mette had rushed into the bathroom the moment he'd switched on the coffee maker that morning.

'So-so. She's sick as a parrot all day long. And most of the night too. If she doesn't start keeping her fluids down soon, they're going to have to put her on a drip.'

'Jesus Christ.' Paula grimaced sympathetically before frowning. 'Why do they say "sick as a parrot", by the way? Are parrots known for vomiting a lot?'

Martin mused. Then he shook his head.

'I don't know. Just do.'

'In the absence of any other orders, I've started reading

up on Rolf Stenklo,' said Paula. 'Do you have anything else for me to do? When's Patrik coming?'

'He should be on his way soon. We're going to get a guest list with potential witnesses that we'll need to go through. And the press are already on our backs. Annika's swamped with calls on the phone in reception.'

'Yes, I heard. They made quick work of that.'

'By the way, Torbjörn's retired.'

'You mean forensics Torbjörn? Gosh – how's Patrik taking it?' Paula said with a smile.

Patrik's growing aversion to all that was not as usual was a running joke between her and Martin.

'Not well is my guess. It's a woman now. Relatively young. Farideh something-or-other.'

'Relatively young? What's relatively young?' Paula laughed.

Martin blushed.

'Well, maybe thirty-five. Forty?'

'So, I'm "relatively young"?'

'Well, yes, young . . .' His blush deepened – as it always had a tendency to do. 'And I suppose in that case I'm "relatively young" too.'

Paula's grin broadened.

'Martin, you're always going to be young.'

He understood what she meant. His boyish appearance with his strawberry blond hair and freckles meant he was reminiscent of the boy in the Kalles Kaviar logo and made him look much younger than he was. Sometimes it was to his advantage, while sometimes he thought it robbed him of a little gravitas.

His mobile buzzed as a text message arrived from Patrik. He read the text and turned to Paula.

'Patrik will be here as soon as he's spoken to yesterday's honourees. They were the victim's closest friends. But he's got the guest list and has sent it on to us.'

Paula nodded and pulled up the email on her computer.

'Yep, here it is.'

'Great. Would you divvy up the names between you, me and Gösta? We can take it from there.'

Martin took a deep breath as he entered his own office. Time to call a bunch of hungover witnesses.

Rickard Bauer woke up with the unpleasant feeling that there was something he couldn't remember – something disagreeable. It wasn't an unfamiliar feeling to him, but today it was particularly palpable.

He groped for Tilde on the left-hand side of the double bed. For some unfathomable reason, hangovers always left him furiously horny – promptly busting a nut would deal with that issue. It didn't even demand anything of her – she just had to lie there. Any rapid movements would only cause his head to split even more than it already was.

But her side of the bed was empty.

'Tilde?'

No reply, but he heard the splashing of water from the bathroom. She must be taking a bath. He sank back into the pillows again.

Memories of the day before resurfaced before slipping away again – just beyond reach. Catching them was like trying to grasp fog in your bare hands. He heard Tilde get out of the bath. Good. Soon he'd have help with his increasingly pressing needs.

'Oh, you're awake.'

Hopes of a hangover shag evaporated as soon as Rickard heard Tilde's tone.

'Yes . . . ?' he said slowly, hoping for more information.

It would probably have been better to hover in uncertainty, but that state rarely lasted indefinitely. He supposed he might as well grab the bull by the horns.

'You sound upset?'

Tilde sighed pointedly and began to dry her hair with a towel. She was otherwise naked. Rickard's horniness was struggling against the torment of his hangover. The signals that something wasn't as it should be still hadn't reached his cock, which was standing to attention under the covers.

'Well, what the fuck were you expecting? You embarrassed yourself yesterday! And me, and your parents! Do you have any idea how embarrassing it was? Your parents celebrate their golden anniversary, and you stand up and slag off your dad! You went over every single fucking time you think he wronged you throughout your whole damn life. For twenty fucking minutes! And you do that while we're in the shit and need your mum's help! Do you think we're going to get any help from your mum after this? Huh? And who was it who paddled us up shit creek in the first place? That'd be you, sunshine!'

His cock went limp in response to Tilde's bollocking. Rickard sat up in bed feeling frustrated, his back against the headboard.

'I've had plenty of help on the way – you're hardly bringing in the dough yourself!' he snapped. 'And how much do you think you've blown on shopping in the last year? And all the fucking trips. Dubai, Paris, Marbella, Ibiza. You just love to swan around playing the glamorous housewife! Then it's all *us us us*. But when there's the slightest headwind, it's all my fault! Do you think that's fair?'

Tilde said nothing. Rickard irritably swung his legs over the side of the bed and slipped his feet into the hotel slippers. His cock had definitely got the memo now and had shrivelled away between his legs.

'Okay, so yesterday was bad timing, but the old man deserved it. I stand by every word I said. Whatever it was

I said. Anyway, Mum isn't our only option, though we're running out of alternatives. I'll get back onto them – I know how to weasel my way in with Mum. Don't you worry. I've pulled off worse shit than this and she's still forgiven me.'

He pulled on a pair of jeans and a T-shirt.

'I'm her favourite.'

'Yes, for some unfathomable reason,' Tilde muttered, but she was beginning to look slightly less pissed off.

'It's impossible not to love me,' he said, flashing his most charming smile.

Tilde snorted, but he caught a glimpse of a smile.

Rickard pulled her towards him and felt his dick perk up again. He unbuttoned his jeans and pushed Tilde's head down.

Erica was still sitting on the terrace although Louise had rushed off. The fog refused to release its grip on the world beyond the window, but the painkillers were beginning to take effect.

The more the headache faded, the more Erica thought about what Vivian had said the night before. Something about the fact that there was a murder mystery in Rolf's past. Could there be something in that? Feeling resolute, she went into the hallway and pulled on her Helly Hansen coat and a hat. The hangover meant she felt colder than usual, and after consideration she slipped a pair of gloves into her pocket.

Erica knew which house in Sälvik Vivian and Rolf had been renting during the festivities. Nothing went unnoticed in this community. She set off at a brisk pace but had to slow down after just a few hundred metres because she was panting and her lungs felt fit to burst. The walks with Louise still hadn't had any significant effect on her.

Soon enough, she caught sight of the small yellow cottage. The house actually had a stunning view of the bay, but today it was obscured in the grey mire.

Erica hesitated the closer she got, and she stopped outside the door, her hand raised to knock on it. She had no idea how Vivian had taken the news of Rolf's death, let alone whether she was at home. But then it was as if her hand made the decision for her and knocked hard on the wood.

Erica took a step back and waited. At first there was complete silence. Was there no one at home? But then she heard slow footsteps getting closer. The door opened and Vivian was standing there.

'Come in,' she said, as if Erica were expected, before stepping to one side.

The ceiling was so low that Erica almost had to crouch despite being no more than 1.68m in her socks.

'I haven't got any coffee, but I do have tea.' Her voice was toneless.

Erica followed Vivian into a tiny kitchen with decor that couldn't have been updated since the fifties.

'Rooibos?'

'That's fine.'

Erica was about to sit down at the kitchen table – a rickety round table with a threadbare waxen cloth on top – but Vivian stopped her.

'Sit down on the terrace. We need all the light we can get at this dark time of year. I'll bring the tea in a second.'

Erica sat down in one of the wicker armchairs on the terrace. They too were well worn and she guessed that the house was only rented out to summer visitors and no longer inhabited by anyone who cared about it. Likely as not, the place would soon be sold – probably to some Germans or Norwegians who would rip out the old interior and embark on a luxury renovation. Maybe Anna would get the assignment. She was the only interior designer in the area.

The floorboards creaked gently as Vivian padded across them with a pot of piping hot tea. She set it down on the table along with a small porcelain bowl filled with sugar cubes.

'Help yourself to sugar if you want. Do you take milk?'

'Sugar's fine.'

Erica waited until Vivian had sat down, then she asked softly:

'How are you doing?'

Vivian shook her head.

'I've spoken to the police, but apart from that I can't talk about it. I can't talk about Rolf's death any more today. But I can talk about his life – I guess that's what your visit is about?'

Erica nodded.

'You said something at dinner yesterday. About a murder mystery that was somehow connected to Rolf's background?'

'I have to admit I was hoping to spark your curiosity. I suppose I thought if you got interested in the case it might drum up some extra publicity for Rolf's exhibition.'

'I was very curious. But are you sure it's okay for you to talk about this right now?'

Erica gulped. Here she was intruding on the time of a grieving woman in a state of shock. Her timing wasn't always the best, as Patrik often pointed out.

Vivian extended a hand covered in liver spots. She patted Erica's hand a few times.

'I'm not really sure what Rolf's exhibition was supposed to include. I just said as much to that sweet young policeman. But over the last year back home in Stockholm, I would find Rolf standing in front of a photo of Lola he took years ago.'

'Who was Lola?'

Erica sipped her tea – apart from rooibos she could make out the taste of ginger. It was good. She added another sugar cube and stirred.

'Lola was one of Rolf's friends when he was young. I don't have many details. Rolf was taciturn about that period in his life. But he did once say that Lola and her daughter lived in Vasastan and that they were murdered. They were killed in a fire and the killer was never found.'

'How terrible.'

Vivian fidgeted with her cup without drinking anything from it.

'It must have been. I think it affected them all in different ways.'

'Them?'

Vivian winced.

'Rolf and his friends. Henning and Elisabeth. Ole and Susanne. Sometimes I wonder whether it was actually because of Lola that they started Blanche.'

She shook her head. 'Excuse an old woman her rambling,' she said quietly.

'What was Lola's last name?' Erica asked. 'And what kind of era are we talking? Eighties?'

Vivian nodded.

'Yes – the early eighties. And other than Lola, I don't have anything more by way of a name. I think Rolf said the daughter had a pet name like Mini or Little'un or something like that. But I can show you the picture. Did I mention that it's hanging on our bedroom wall at home?'

Vivian realized she had said 'our', and stopped. She seemed to slump over. She screwed her eyes shut for a few seconds and then stretched.

'I've got a copy of that interior decor magazine with the feature on our flat. One of the few things I managed to get Rolf to agree to. He knew how much time and love

77

I put into that flat, so he agreed even though he hates everything like that. It's on my bedside table.'

Vivian went back into the cottage and Erica surveyed the hazy sea, letting her thoughts wander. There was something alluring in what Vivian had told her – something that roused the writer in her. She looked up again when the wood began to creak. Vivian re-emerged onto the terrace clutching a magazine.

'You can see the photo here.'

Erica took the magazine from her. In one of the photos in the feature depicting Vivian and Rolf's bedroom she could see the black-and-white photo on the wall. It was a small photograph, but Erica could clearly see a beautiful woman with long, flowing hair and perfect make-up. She was wearing a gossamer blouse that was unbuttoned to reveal a glimpse of an embroidered bra and cleavage.

Erica examined the picture more closely. Something about Lola had made her react. She spotted that the bra was padded.

'Was Lola a man?' she asked.

Vivian shrugged and sat down.

'Lola was beautiful,' she said. 'At any rate, judging by this photo – which is the only one I've seen. Rolf used to call it *Innocence*.'

'So the name Lola and the fact that she lived in Vasastan is all the information you have? And that she and her daughter were murdered?'

'Yes, I'm afraid so. While Rolf never talked about it, I realized that her death affected him deeply. We lived together for almost twenty years. You learn to read each other. Lola was important to him.'

'Why do you think he called the photo *Innocence*?'

Erica contemplated the picture intently. The urge to write was back. There was a story to be discovered here. That was how all her books got started: human fate and

Erica's desire to find out what had happened and tell it all in a way that plunged the depths. A woman and her daughter had been murdered – and their murderer had never been held accountable. It was an injustice that Erica wanted to remedy.

'I don't know,' said Vivian, taking a few sips from her tea. 'As I said, Rolf didn't tell me much about that time.'

'Didn't you wonder why?'

Vivian smiled wryly.

'Rolf was capricious. He was an artist. A creator. I learned to live with his whims. I stopped asking questions long ago. But I've always wondered about Lola.'

'You've really got me interested in her. I'll see what I can turn up about Lola and the circumstances around her death,' said Erica. 'Can I call you or pop round if there's anything else? How long will you be staying here?'

The woman in the armchair suddenly looked tiny. Erica wanted to give her a hug, but she wasn't sure how Vivian would take the gesture.

'I . . . I don't know. We took this place for a month. But I won't stay that long. Although I have to find out when I can take him home . . .' Her voice drifted off.

'Is there anyone who can be with you?'

Vivian nodded slowly.

'Henning called and said I can stay with him and Elisabeth on the island for a few days. I think I'll pack up here and accept their offer. At least until I know more.'

'That sounds sensible,' said Erica, relieved that Vivian had somewhere to go.

She stood up.

'Thanks. I'm going to find out more about Lola.'

'Keep me posted,' Vivian said, her voice heavy with emotion. 'I can't know for sure, but I believe this is what Rolf would have wanted.'

Erica walked homewards, deep in thought. Halfway

up the hill she turned around. Vivian was still standing on the terrace of the small yellow cottage, her gaze fixed on the great greyness.

'I've just called the taxi-boat – they'll pick us up in fifteen minutes' time, down by the tourist information point,' said Elisabeth.

'Good,' said Henning as he placed his party shoes from the day before into the top of his bag. He was only half-listening to his wife.

'The clothes underneath will get dirty if you put those shoes in without any protection,' she said.

Henning looked at her.

'Does that matter in the slightest right now?'

'No, not at all,' she sighed.

'I've invited Vivian to the island for a few days. Ole and Susanne too.'

'Why on earth would you do that?' said Elisabeth, turning towards him.

He took a few deep breaths to avoid getting worked up, then propped open the door into the corridor with his bag and gathered the rest of their luggage.

'Inviting Vivian felt like the right thing – the compassionate thing – to do. And we need to talk to Ole and Susanne. About Blanche. And we may as well do so in peace and quiet on the island.'

'Peace and quiet? It'll be a circus. Couldn't you have asked me first? And where were you thinking we'd put them?'

Elisabeth swept past him and out the door.

'Can't they take Rickard and Tilde's house, and they can stay ashore?' Henning muttered.

There always had to be a fuss.

'Out of the question. Rickard was drunk and didn't know what he was saying. He's probably full of remorse today and you'll get an apology.'

'I'll believe that when I see it . . .'

Henning closed the door behind them and locked it. They laboriously conveyed the luggage down the stairs. Louise was waiting for them in reception with Pierre and Lussan, and hurried over when she spotted them.

'Here, let me help you with those.'

She took Elisabeth's bag and carried it down the stairs before returning and taking Henning's.

'I've been trying to call you. There's a policeman who wants to talk to you. He just went in there.' She nodded towards the large room opposite the reception desk.

'The boat will be here in five minutes,' Elisabeth said with a sigh.

Henning leaned forward to kiss Lussan's cheek and shake hands with Pierre. He had always liked Louise's parents. Good people. Fine ancestry stretching back many generations. You couldn't buy that kind of thing. It was one of the reasons he had always liked Louise.

'We heard. How dreadful,' Pierre said, shaking his head.

He was a head shorter than Henning, but as straight-backed as if he had a poker stuck down the back of his blazer.

'Awful,' Henning agreed, putting an arm around Elisabeth. 'Are you heading back to Skåne?'

'No, we'll stay on for a while in the house we've borrowed from our good friends Giggs and Joy,' said Lussan. 'They live near the old spa hotel – Badis. It's absolutely wonderful. And they were generous enough to lend it to us when they heard we were coming here to celebrate with you. Anyway, they're in their place in Marbella right now.'

'Splendid,' said Henning. 'Then you must come out to the island for dinner. Get in touch with Louise and she'll arrange the details. But I gather we have a policeman waiting for us.'

Henning turned towards the large dining room.

'The whole thing is just so awful,' said Lussan. Her immaculate dark hair in its pageboy cut was so firmly sprayed that it barely moved as she shook her head.

'Louise, would you ask them to hold the boat?'

Louise nodded, and Henning gently gripped his wife's arm and led her into the big room. There they saw a serious, dark-haired man sitting alone at one of the tables, and Henning assumed he was the one who had been looking for them.

'Patrik Hedström – Tanum Police,' he said by way of introduction as they approached.

Henning glanced discreetly at the time as they sat down. Hopefully this wouldn't take too long. He wanted to get to the island.

7

STOCKHOLM 1980

Today P'tite had been allowed to choose what they would do. Admittedly, she was usually allowed to. Daddy was kind like that. P'tite always chose the same thing. The playground in Vasaparken. It was closest to home and she had been playing there ever since she was little.

The park was full of mummies and children. None of the mummies were as beautifully dressed as Daddy. Their clothes were boring. Grey. Or brown. None of them had clothes as beautiful as her Daddy did. Or hair as nice.

Daddy knew most of the mothers at the park – it wasn't just P'tite and Daddy who had been regulars there for a long time. In the beginning, some of the other kids had stared at Daddy. When P'tite thought someone was staring too much, she would simply walk over, put her face close to theirs and say: 'Have you finished gawping or what?' That made them stop. Occasionally, someone would start crying and run to their mother – when that happened Daddy told her off.

'It's not their fault,' she always used to say. 'Someone said something at home, so they're curious. We treat everyone with kindness.'

P'tite listened. She wanted to do everything as Daddy

told her. She just couldn't understand how she was supposed to get someone to stop staring by being kind.

'Hasn't she grown!'

P'tite eavesdropped as the mother Daddy usually talked to most pointed in her direction.

'I can barely keep track,' Daddy replied. 'Where does the time go? It feels like only yesterday I brought her home – tiny as a baby bird.'

It was a description she'd heard many times. Mummy had died in hospital, and she had almost died in Mummy's tummy, but instead she'd come out alive, but tiny as a baby bird. Daddy said she'd fitted into the palm of her hand. P'tite didn't really believe her. Surely no baby could be so small that it fitted into the palm of a hand. Even if Daddy had big hands . . .

She went over to the swings. This was her favourite spot in the park. There was no one who dared to swing as high as she did. Now she was swinging high, high towards the clear blue sky, and when she was at the highest point, she always thought that she was closest to Mummy in heaven. Not that she really missed her. Daddy was both her mother and her father. She couldn't really contemplate a world in which there was anyone other than her and Daddy.

Daddy always said such kind things about Mummy. And she always said that P'tite was so very much like her. So of course, she was curious . . . And when the swing was so far above the ground that her toes seemed to be grazing the clouds, it sometimes felt as if she could almost see her.

'P'tite! Don't go so high!'

P'tite ignored Daddy's worried voice. She was free. Nothing could hurt her, nothing bad could happen to her as she flew through the air. Out of the corner of her eye, she could see Daddy looking at her anxiously. P'tite swung her legs, increasing her speed even more. And when she reached the top, she let go. She fell through the air, feeling the wind in her long hair.

She fell and fell and fell. She was a bird flying free out of the sky. Then she landed hard on both her feet in the sand. She grinned towards her father. Daddy shook her head and hugged P'tite's rucksack, which she had promised to look after while P'tite was on the swings. Then she leaned towards the mother next to her on the bench and remarked:

'That kid! I swear she's going to give me a heart attack one of these days.'

Then she met P'tite's gaze, and everything was right in the world.

8

'We're going to have to use aggressive treatment on your cancer, Rita.'

Bertil Mellberg stared at the doctor in front of him. Firstly, this doctor was still practically wet behind the ears. Was he even thirty? Were you really allowed to treat people when it was impossible that you had any experience whatsoever? And how could he deliver news like this without even a tremor in his voice? Breast cancer. Triple negative. It sounded like a death sentence.

Rita brushed something off the doctor's much-too-large desk.

'What does "aggressive treatment" entail?' she asked the whippersnapper.

Bertil couldn't understand how she could be so calm. Everything had just come tumbling down around them. They'd been doing so well – but then Rita had developed that cough that never went away, and begun feeling tired. When she'd found the lump in her breast, Bertil had been on the brink of fainting.

'Radiotherapy. And chemotherapy. Before *and* after the operation. You'll probably be aware of the side effects. Nausea. Hair loss. Et cetera. It's not pleasant. But it's the only thing that will give us a chance of killing off the cancerous tumours.'

'When do we begin?'

Rita was clasping her handbag tightly. Bertil looked at her in dismay.

'Surely we can't just take this man's word for it. He looks like he just graduated. We ought to go to Gothenburg – to a bigger hospital. To see someone more experienced . . .'

'I've been in this line of work for fifteen years,' said the doctor in a voice that gave no hint he had taken any offence. 'Of course, you're most welcome to seek a second opinion, but I can assure you that you'll get the same answer, and it'll cost you time that I'm afraid you don't currently have. It's my strong recommendation that you begin treatment immediately.'

Bertil looked down at his hands. There was a roaring in his ears. He didn't want to hear what the doctor was saying. This wasn't possible – it couldn't be. Not his Rita. They'd barely had any time together.

Rita placed her hand over his. He recognized the absurdity of her comforting him. It ought to be the other way around. But the abyss was so deep and so dark that he was incapable of averting his gaze from it.

'Let's get started right away,' said Rita.

The doctor nodded. He cleared his throat behind a clenched fist.

'A lot of people choose to shave their own hair off before it falls out. But it's very much a personal choice.'

'We'll see,' Rita replied brusquely. 'For now, I just want to make a plan and get started.'

'Then we'll do that.'

The silence hung heavy in the room. Bertil couldn't breathe. He had lied to his colleagues and said that he and Rita were taking Paula's kids on some stupid outing to the swimming baths in Strömstad. Now he desperately wished it was the truth.

Bertil took a juddering breath and held Rita's hand. Her hand was warm in his. He never wanted to let it go.

Erica smiled with satisfaction and set her phone to silent. Anna had agreed to keep the kids for a few more hours so that Erica could work on her new writing project.

She settled down at the computer and cracked her fingers, then started googling. Much of her success with biographies of female authors and depictions of murder cases boiled down to her ability to dig up the most inaccessible details. But Lola was going to be a challenge. Erica had very little to go on. Stockholm in the early eighties, a fire in a flat and someone who had been born a man but lived as a woman and was known as Lola, murdered together with their child. That wasn't much information at all. Her inner cynic told her that it was most likely that the case hadn't been written about very much. It wasn't easy being transgender now, so she could imagine what it must have been like in the eighties, with all the prejudice and hate crime.

The keywords that Erica tried didn't turn up many hits, and she found nothing that seemed particularly relevant in the context. She deleted the word 'murder' and searched more generally on the themes of Stockholm and the trans community in the eighties. Once again, she was surprised at how few hits there were. Was there really nothing more from that time? Offhand, she had thought there would be pictures, stories, narratives – people giving that era and life a face. But the results were scant to say the least.

She continued to google and soon enough found photographs by Christer Strömholm. Like many others, she loved his pictures from the Quartier Pigalle in Paris taken in the fifties and sixties where he had lived among the trans community and got to know his subjects. Those photos were among the most beautiful she knew of. Rolf's photo of Lola had something of an air of Strömholm, but there was also something distinct and unique to it. Erica couldn't forget it.

At the same time, contemplating Christer Strömholm's oeuvre made her examine her own interest in the case. There was an unfortunate history of examining the trans community from the outside looking in – as a spectacle, or as a shop window onto something exotic and titillating. And she in no way wanted to be part of the exploitation of already vulnerable people. She was confident enough in her own self-awareness to know that she wasn't drawn to Lola's story because she was a trans woman, but she was aware she might face that criticism.

Erica stood up and paced back and forth across her small study. The sea view from upstairs always took her breath away, and the mist that had formed an almost impenetrable filter on the world had finally begun to lift.

Writing was a lonely job. Over the years, Erica had spent many hours alone with her creative anxiety, but looking out to sea and the islands always brought her calm and a sense of being part of something bigger. Absurdly, she seemed to need that calm even more now that she was successful. The more books she sold, the more dogged the world became in its onslaught on her. Requests for interviews, podcast appearances, PR trips abroad. Invitations to book fairs and signings. There was so much that drew focus away from what she really wanted to do: write and spend time with her family.

She returned to the computer, wondering how to find the information she was looking for. Who was the mysterious Lola? Who had murdered her and her child? How well did she and Rolf know each other when she was murdered?

With renewed energy, she googled new keywords.

* * *

The yellow break room had looked the same for far too long. There was neither the budget nor the inclination to make any changes. Annika sometimes muttered that they ought to 'freshen the place up a bit', but this never elicited any show of support. Her colleagues liked the place as it was. Maybe the coffee could be somewhat improved upon . . .

'How long has the pot been on?' said Paula Morales, sceptically examining the coffee pot.

'Do you really want to know?' Martin asked.

'Probably not.'

Paula boldly poured herself a cup and sat down at the table opposite Martin. A plate of green marzipan-clad punsch rolls was at its centre, and Paula reached for one before nudging the plate towards Martin.

He shook his head.

'I'm starting to put on sympathy pregnancy weight.'

'Comes with the territory,' said Paula, laughing.

She was pleased to see him happy again. For a while, she had been afraid the sorrow in his eyes would never go away. But time healed most wounds, at least to the extent that life could carry on without drowning in bad memories.

Paula took a sip. The coffee tasted metallic and burnt, but she didn't even grimace. Just like the faded yellow decor, it was part and parcel of the place. It was home.

'I heard Mellberg was in Strömstad for a splash about with the kids. That must be a sight for sore eyes. Mellberg in his trunks.'

Martin reached for a punsch roll and devoured it in two bites. So much for abstinence.

Paula looked down at the table. She hated lying to Martin, but Bertil had insisted they weren't to say a word about Rita's doctor's appointment, and she had been disposed to agree. She didn't want sympathetic glances from her colleagues. Especially not from Martin, who had been through the same journey with a loved one. Besides, perhaps there would be good news today. If so, they need never mention to anyone how close they had come.

She glanced at her mobile phone. Still no call from her mother or Bertil. But then again, doctor's appointments were always running late.

'How's that list coming along?' said Martin, sweeping together a few crumbs on the table.

After throwing the crumbs into the sink, he took a piece of kitchen roll from the dispenser and gave her a sheet. He'd become so tidy, Paula thought to herself. It must be Mette's influence.

'Getting there,' she said. 'But I haven't turned up anything that stands out as yet. It was a party, people were drunk, everyone's memories are pretty vague, and I'm struggling to get any exact times out of people. But as I said, no one saw anything out of the ordinary, nothing you'd notice.'

'Same here,' said Martin once he'd sat back down.

He reached for another punsch roll. He did seem to have got a little chubbier around the cheeks lately, but Paula thought it suited him.

'I think the simplest explanation is the likeliest one,' he said eventually. 'A break-in. Rolf was there. There was a scuffle. He died, and in a panic the intruder legged it without taking anything with them.'

'The part that bothers me is that it seems a bit far-fetched for us to have art thieves in Fjällbacka,' said Paula, helping herself to another pastry as well. 'We know all the usual suspects around here when it comes to breaking and entering, and photographic art doesn't seem like something that would be their cup of tea.'

She picked up a crumb that had fallen onto the piece of kitchen roll.

'I've been thinking that too,' Martin agreed. 'But we don't know what the word on the street is. There's been a bit of coverage in the local press on Rolf's exhibition and his successes. And don't forget the raid on the Munch Museum in Oslo. The perpetrators weren't exactly art connoisseurs.'

Paula whistled. 'Oops! I didn't realize we had a specialist on art theft in our midst.'

Martin blushed, making his many freckles less visible. 'We streamed an episode about it on Viaplay.'

'Ah.' Paula grinned. She regarded the plate of punsch rolls. There was one left. She pushed the plate towards him.

'You take it. You've got a pregnant partner to catch up with.'

'Thanks,' said Martin ironically.

Nonetheless, he helped himself to the roll.

Paula got up after quickly checking her mobile. Still no call from her mother. There was a dull ache of worry in the pit of her stomach, but all she could do for now was focus on her work. And she had a list to be getting on with.

'First of all, I'm sorry for your loss,' said Patrik in a low voice.

Henning and Elisabeth Bauer nodded mutely. They looked tired and worn out. That was no surprise after the evening's party, but nowhere in their fatigue was there any hint of satisfaction after a successful event. Their gazes were vacant.

'Was it a burglary?'

Elisabeth's tone of voice was stern. She radiated gravitas and an authority that made Patrik sit up a little straighter.

'We don't know yet. And even if we did know, we wouldn't be able to disclose that at this stage.'

'I see.'

'The police must be allowed to do their jobs,' said Henning, putting a hand on top of his wife's. He turned to look at Patrik.

'We want to assist you in any way we can. We've been good friends with Rolf for many, many years.'

'How come he wasn't at the party?'

Patrik frowned. If they had been as close as Henning claimed, then surely he should have been at the festivities?

'Rolf was a bit of a loner. And it got worse with age. As things do for all of us.'

Henning extended his hands while seeking the support of his wife with his gaze.

'Rolf became increasingly reclusive the older he got,' Elisabeth agreed. 'More than anything, he wanted to be behind his camera – preferably in some godforsaken corner of the earth. He regarded those of us living in the real world with ever greater contempt.'

'That's a little harsh,' said Henning, looking from Patrik to Elisabeth.

His wife glared at him.

'It's true, and you know it. He was surly and distant, especially in recent months. Quite honestly, we weren't all that surprised when he turned down our invitation to the party.'

Patrik jotted away in his notepad as they talked.

'But his wife was there.'

'Yes. From what I've heard from Louise, Vivian accepted at the last minute. Probably against Rolf's will.' Elisabeth snorted. 'But I consider that a salubrious sign. Rolf could be very dominating, and poor old Vivian has been bending to his will for almost twenty years.'

'Were they unhappy?' Patrik asked.

'Not to the extent she would have cause to kill him – if that's what you're wondering.'

'They had their relationship problems, just like everyone.' Henning Bauer once again toned down and softened his wife's words. Patrik wondered whether that was peculiar to this conversation or whether it was the pattern followed throughout their relationship.

'But nothing serious?'

'No, nothing serious,' said Henning.

'How did you first get to know Rolf? You said you went back a long way.'

Henning looked at Elisabeth once again. She had turned her head and seemed to be studying the hotel guests at other tables. The mist had kept people indoors.

'We've known Rolf since the seventies,' Henning said at last. 'There was a small and motley collection of us brought together by our love for cultural forms of expression.'

'Cultural forms of expression?' said Patrik.

'Literature, photography, art, music. Everything that separates us from the apes,' Henning said, laughing, and Patrik guessed it was a joke he'd told many times.

'So you've known each other since then?'

'Yes, we've mixed both personally and professionally,' said Elisabeth, whose gaze was now directed at Patrik again. 'Rolf is the godfather of our youngest son, Rickard. And we've also run a club together for many years – Blanche.'

'Yes, someone mentioned that yesterday. Could you tell me a bit more about what kind of club it is?'

Henning leaned forward.

'You could say that Blanche is our way of giving something back. Paying it forward. Blanche's backers are successful in our own cultural fields, and we know how small the eye of the needle is for those who want to succeed. This club is simply our way of offering a forum where fresh talent can grow and thrive.'

'Talent in what?' Patrik asked.

'All the forms of expression that I just mentioned. Literature, photography, art and music. We have regular receptions featuring everything from art exhibitions and poetry recitals to musical performances. We've had dancing too.'

'We provide a venue where talent can encounter the cultural establishment, where they can grow through each other and create new cultural worlds,' Elisabeth supplemented.

Patrik scratched his head. He was none the wiser. It was all pretty woolly, as far as he was concerned.

'Who are the people behind Blanche?'

Henning looked even more eager now.

'That would be me, and Elisabeth and Rolf, as well as Susanne and Ole Hovland. Do you know who Susanne and Ole are?'

Patrik nodded. Henning's tone indicated that he didn't expect Patrik to say yes.

'I heard them mentioned yesterday. Susanne's a member of the Swedish Academy, and Ole is her husband.'

'Yes, that's right. Ole actively presides over Blanche – he's its host.'

'And how have things been between those of you involved in Blanche?'

Elisabeth snorted again and Henning placed a hand on her arm.

'Our partnership has always worked perfectly,' she said. 'I don't understand what these questions have to do with Rolf's murder. That was obviously connected to the break-in. What has Blanche got to do with it?'

Patrik parried her query with his hands.

'Our first step is always to obtain as much knowledge of the victim as we can.'

'Let them do their jobs, Elisabeth,' said Henning, caressing her hand soothingly.

She withdrew her arm, not looking at her husband or Patrik.

'Did Rolf have any enemies? Problems with anyone?'

Henning shook his head fiercely.

'No, no. Good God, Rolf didn't have any enemies. Who even has enemies? It sounds very dramatic. Sure, he could be a little abrupt – especially in recent years – and he was in an extremely competitive industry. But enemies? No, nothing like that.'

Elisabeth looked at her watch. It was a beautiful, elegant, silver-coloured timepiece. Patrik guessed it was worth a fortune.

'I'll let you get going in just a moment,' he said. 'But my last question is about yesterday evening. Did you see or hear anything you thought was strange, that stood out, or that you think might have anything to do with Rolf's murder?'

'So it happened during the party?' said Elisabeth.

'As I said before, I can't make any comment on the investigation. But is there anything you feel you want to mention from last night's party?'

Henning and Elisabeth looked at each other. Then both of them shook their heads.

'No, there's nothing that springs to mind,' said Henning.

'Well then, I'll let you be on your way, but I'm sure we'll be in touch.'

Henning Bauer stood up. 'I'll make sure Louise passes on our contact details to you.'

As they swept out of the room, Patrik's gaze lingered on their backs. Something told him they hadn't been wholly truthful. He just wasn't sure about what. Not yet.

'Does everyone have their bags?'

Louise surveyed the small gathering on the quayside. They'd had to book a big water-taxi to head out to Skjälerö since Henning had decided to invite Vivian, Ole and Susanne along on the spur of the moment.

'How are you feeling?' she asked Vivian, who was standing next to her, bag in hand.

Vivian was staring out to sea where the fog was lifting but the waves were now white-crested. It was going to be a bumpy ride out to the island.

'I don't know how to answer that . . .' Vivian said flatly. 'It doesn't seem real. I can't feel anything about something that doesn't seem real.'

Louise patted her arm but said nothing more.

'Susanne, Ole, do you have your luggage?'

Susanne nodded while Ole winked at her. With a sigh, Louise went to talk to the captain charged with ferrying them to their destination.

'We need to get under way soon – the wind has really picked up,' he said, pointing towards the sea.

'We'll be off as soon as Henning and Elisabeth are here,' she said, peering up towards Galärbacken and the entrance to the hotel.

'Was it really such a good idea for Dad to invite people over right now?' Peter hissed from the corner of his mouth as he kept an eye on Max and William, who were standing slightly too close to the edge of the quayside, albeit wearing sturdy life vests.

'No, it's an utterly dreadful idea,' Louise agreed. 'But what do you suggest we do about it? Are you going to tell him that?'

She threw out her arms helplessly. Peter's gaze shifted from the boys and he placed his hand against her cheek.

Louise stiffened in surprise at his touch. It was unusual for Peter to engage in public displays of affection. Well, it was unusual for her too, for that matter. That wasn't the kind of relationship they had. Private matters were kept private.

'No, I don't want to – and you know that. There's no point trying to talk Dad round when he's set on something. Maybe it's his way of grieving for Rolf. Surrounding himself with people who knew him. Maybe Dad's right and we're wrong.'

'Elisabeth didn't exactly look thrilled either.'

'Does she ever?'

Peter smiled before taking a few brisk steps towards the quayside where the boys were pushing and shoving each other dangerously close to the water.

'What are you two up to?'

He took a firm grip on the collar of each boy's life vest and pulled them apart.

'He started it! He called me a baby because I've been given a baby life vest.'

William, on the brink of tears, pointed at the orange life vest with the huge collar that he was wearing. Max stuck out his tongue. He was wearing a considerably slicker-looking life vest in a shade of dark blue. It was a smaller edition of the ones the grown-ups were wearing.

'That's not a baby life vest. And stop teasing him, Max.'

'Here they come!' Louise shouted, pointing towards the hill. 'I'll go and help them with their bags. Get on board and we'll cast off soon.'

'Yes, Captain!' Ole hooted cheerily as he performed a salute.

No one laughed.

Once everyone was aboard and the boat had departed from the harbour in Fjällbacka, Louise allowed her shoulders to slump for the first time since Erica had told her that Rolf's body had been found. The motion of the sea soothed her. Water was her element. Always had been. Slowly, she made her way towards the bow, holding the rail. The boat was being tossed back and forth on the waves, but she rode the movements with practised accomplishment.

Once at the very front, she let the cold wind scour her face and she savoured the water splashing up in huge cascades. There was a salty taste in her mouth, but the feeling of freedom helped her to breathe. She wanted to keep that feeling in her body for as long as she could. Dark clouds were gathering on the horizon. There was a storm on the way – and none of them would be able to avoid it.

'Bertil!'

Gösta Flygare called after the station chief Bertil Mellberg, but the Detective Chief Inspector made his way straight along the corridor to his office and shut the door behind him.

Gösta sighed. Mellberg was apparently not in the best of moods today. Given that he wasn't the easiest to deal with even on his good days, that was not great news.

He knocked on the door frame of Martin Molin's office.

'Mellberg is on the warpath,' he notified Martin, who was sitting behind his desk.

'Jolly good,' said Martin, angling his neck and making it audibly crack.

'They say that's meant to be bad for you.'

'Old habits die hard. How are you getting on with the list?'

Gösta leaned against the doorway. Apart from Bertil, everyone at the station kept their doors open – it was both more agreeable and easier to work with.

'Getting there,' he said dryly. 'I've churned through around a dozen guests. But everyone says the same thing. No one saw anything unusual at the party or saw anything around the gallery. But judging by how hungover everyone sounds, the real question is how reliable any of them are. Seems to have been a pretty boozy do.'

'We'll have to ask Patrik about that. He was there.'

'Yes, he did look a bit green about the gills as well,' Gösta chuckled. 'What about yourself? How are you doing?'

Martin waved his hand towards a list on which he had ticked off name after name.

'Same here. No one saw or heard anything.'

'Neighbours? Who lives on the hill, full-timers or second-home-owners?'

'Full-time residents, to my knowledge. So, we should definitely do door-to-door enquiries.'

'The staff? At the hotel?'

'I've asked Paula to compile a list of staff too.' Martin sighed and rolled his shoulders to disperse more tension. 'I think we should have a chat with the local miscreants as well. Just in case there's some genius who got big ideas.'

'We don't have anyone we know to be violent. It's a pretty big step from burglary to murder.'

'True. But you and I both know that situations that start one way can spiral into something else entirely. And given that the weapon used seems to have been on the premises, my impression is that this wasn't planned – quite the opposite, in fact. A murder in the heat of the moment.'

Gösta looked at his young colleague. He really had filled out his uniform in recent years.

'I dare say you're right about that,' he said. 'But let's run it by Patrik first, eh? So that he's in the picture about who we're talking to and in which order.'

'He should be here soon,' Martin said, picking up his phone to carry on calling the numbers on the list. 'He'll probably want a briefing when he arrives.'

'No doubt. Well, I suppose we'll have to see what kind of mood Bertil's in then,' said Gösta, glancing towards the closed door at the far end of the corridor.

Their work would have been much easier if Patrik had been allowed to continue in charge. But you couldn't have everything.

'What are you doing here?' said Erica in surprise when Patrik stepped through the front door.

She had made a pot of coffee and was about to return to her computer to continue her research.

'Just a flying visit. I thought I'd grab a paracetamol, an ibuprofen, and a packed lunch, and then be on my way to the station.'

'You've got time for a coffee,' said Erica, pouring him a cup and another for herself.

'Okay, five minutes then,' said Patrik, pinching the bridge of his nose hard and screwing his eyes shut.

Erica got the painkillers out from the cupboard above the cooker hood and passed them to him with a glass of water.

'No kids home yet?' he said, looking around.

'I don't have to pick them up until three,' said Erica, sitting down opposite him at the kitchen table.

She gave her husband a searching gaze.

'How are you getting on?'

'We've barely got started,' he said, averting his gaze down into his coffee cup.

'Not well, in other words,' she said, reading between the lines. 'I went over to see Vivian. She was surprisingly composed, although I think she's still in shock.'

Patrik looked at her questioningly. 'Vivian? Why did you visit her?'

'She said something last night . . . about a murder in Rolf's past.'

'A murder? What do you mean?'

Patrik's eyes narrowed. Erica's tendency to stick her nose into all manner of places it didn't belong – especially Patrik's investigations – was a regular topic of disagreement.

'Way back, a good friend of Rolf's and a child were murdered in Stockholm. Vivian thought it was in the early eighties, but she wasn't sure. Right now, I'm on the lookout for a new book idea and this is a case I've never heard of. The unsolved murder of a trans woman and her daughter. There might be something in it.'

'Trans woman?'

'Yes, the murder victim was called Lola. I've started looking for more information but so far, I've only hit dead ends. Rolf once photographed her. Vivian had a copy of an interiors magazine with a feature about them. You could see the photo hanging on the wall in a picture of their bedroom.'

Patrik smiled at her. Was he impressed by her idea or had the painkillers already begun to take effect?

'You're a bit of a culture vulture,' he said. 'Tell me what you know about that club Blanche you mentioned yesterday?'

'Culture vulture? I don't think so! Wasn't it painfully obvious yesterday at dinner that people from the echelon of culture don't consider me one of them? But Vivian and I actually talked about Blanche while I was there. She said something mysterious about this Lola influencing them into starting the club.'

Erica frowned, reflecting. Wasn't it all a bit fateful if that was the case?

'At any rate: Blanche is a club in Stockholm that's as overbearingly snobby as you'd expect it to be. The whole thing is predictably chic and underground – they permit a selection of blessed chosen ones to perform for an audience at poetry nights, string instrument soirées, art installations . . .'

'Sounds more like a punishment,' Patrik groaned.

'I'm not exactly devastated that I've never been invited. But I assume you're asking since Rolf helped found it?'

Patrik nodded and grimaced. So, the headache hadn't let up after all, she thought to herself.

'Yes, I asked Henning and Elisabeth a few questions about it. As I understand it, they're still actively involved in running it together with Rolf, Ole and Susanne.'

'Yes, it's largely thanks to Susanne that Blanche has assumed such a desirable status. Everyone wants to be close to a member of the Swedish Academy.'

'Why?' said Patrik. 'Sorry if that's a stupid question.'

'As we tell the kids: "there's no such thing as a stupid question." But it's hard to explain. In the cultural world – especially in the Stockholm cultural world – the Swedish Academy is practically royal in status. And Susanne Hovland is most definitely the uncrowned queen of the Academy. Her star quality, together with Henning's, Elisabeth's and Rolf's networks of contacts within the cultural elite, means that Blanche has been a favourite watering hole for years for those who want to be admitted into a world that is otherwise very hard to access.'

Erica took a sip of her coffee and looked at her husband. She always felt a tingle when he looked at her that intensely.

'What about Ole then? Where does he fit in? Henning mentioned something about him looking after Blanche?'

'Ole has gained access to that world thanks to Susanne. He's a wannabe film director, and rumour has it he spends most of his time chasing girls who are much too young. And I've heard he doesn't have anything against older ladies either.'

'How does his wife put up with it?'

'That's what everyone else wonders too. But they've been together for years and years and have no children – who knows what their arrangements are? Because if she doesn't know that Ole sleeps with anything that has a pulse and a vagina, then she's deaf and blind.'

Patrik snorted.

Erica looked at him. Should she tell him what she'd found out? Yes, he needed to know.

'Ole said something while he was pissed yesterday that I can't quite let go of. It might have been the drink talking, but . . .'

'What?'

Patrik leaned forward with interest. Outside the window, the wind had begun to splatter rain against the glass and Erica shivered and pulled her cardigan tighter around her.

'He said Henning's going to be given the Nobel Prize in Literature.'

Patrik roared with laughter.

'Oh, right. I thought it had something to do with Rolf's murder. But fine – nice for him if it's true.'

'That's not information you're allowed to leak in advance. It's one of the best-kept secrets in Sweden. And the world.'

'Okay, maybe it's a big deal in your circles. But in my little world where I've got a murder to investigate, who gets the Nobel Literature Prize isn't really of much interest.'

'Of course, that's true. But I still thought it was interesting that he claimed to know. It's a secret worth both money and power.'

Patrik shook his head and stood up. He walked around the table and kissed her tenderly on the cheek.

'As I said, in my world that's worthless information. Take care, darling. I'll be back when I'm back.'

'Of course. I'll get the kids.'

Erica waved goodbye to Patrik and went back upstairs to her study. She hadn't given up hope of finding out more about Lola.

* * *

'Why do we have to move?' Tilde snapped.

Rickard shook his head at her as she threw her belongings pell-mell into a large Louis Vuitton weekend bag.

'Dear God – they're only borrowing our place for a night or two,' he said. 'You don't have to pack everything. Leave it hanging there and come over if you need to fetch anything.'

'I don't want people going through my stuff.'

'I think Vivian's got other things on her mind than your clothes.'

'She doesn't seem very upset.'

Tilde held up a slinky dress from Valentino and then stuffed it into the bag.

'People take it differently. Vivian's always been . . . a little standoffish . . . and she's a bit kooky too. Not religious, but there's probably some sort of soul guide or something that she's being supported by.'

Rickard smirked at the words 'soul guide'. They had always been intriguing – those spiritual people. The ones who claimed to be above all material things and didn't care about money. The ones that hadn't understood that money was what determined how you were judged and defined as a person. Not even his parents understood that. They thought it was their intellectual capital that gave them their exalted position in society. But their intellectual capital meant diddly squat. Without money and a household name, they would have been starving artists – the kind of people despised by those with power. Talent, intellect, gifts – none of it gave true status in the way that money did.

That was something he had understood early on. If he had money, then he didn't have to make an effort. He didn't have to work, he didn't have to be talented, he didn't even have to be nice. Money opened all doors. People who sought advice from crystals would never understand that.

'Did you like Rolf?'

Rickard looked at Tilde in surprise. It was a surprisingly multifaceted question, given it had come from her.

'Liked? I don't know . . . Do you ever like your parents' friends? He was always there in the background. Before I found out more about him, all I knew was that he was my godfather and that it meant I got slightly nicer presents from him at Christmas and on my birthdays than Peter did. Granted, that was something I appreciated.'

Tilde sighed. She did, however, seem to be satisfied for the time being.

'It's going to be a real squeeze if we stay with Peter's family. And the kids are shits.'

'No, Max and William are lovely. Come on, Tilde. Stop whining. It is what it is, and given that I need to ask Mum for help perhaps now is a good time to be accommodating?'

Tilde pulled the zip on the bag and pouted.

'Okay, you're right. I'll do my best. But you need to talk to your mother soon. Especially since the other plan has hit the buffers. I don't want to have to cancel Nice. Everyone's going.'

'We won't have to cancel Nice. Mum always helps me in the end. She just needs to . . . get a few things off her chest. Needs to feel like a responsible mother. And I'll pretend to be remorseful and promise never to ask for money again. That's how we play the game. Right, baby? In two weeks, you and I will be in Nice.'

He picked up her bag and left the bedroom. It would all work out. One way or another, it would sort itself out. It always did.

'I still don't think this was a good idea.'

Elisabeth stirred the fire with a poker. Nancy had lit the fire as soon as she'd seen them tying up, and now it was taking.

106

'Not at all – it's a splendid idea,' said Henning, pouring a glass of red wine for her and another for himself.

He couldn't quite understand why Elisabeth was so unsure about it.

'I've told everyone we'll eat in an hour,' he said. 'Nancy already knows – I asked Louise to make all the arrangements.'

Elisabeth sat down on the sofa cupping the glass of wine in her hand.

'I just can't believe he's gone,' she said.

'It's hard to take in. I'd been looking forward to telling him about the prize. He would have been delighted.'

'He would.'

They sat in silence for a moment. Henning had a warm feeling in his breast as soon as he thought about the prize. To think that the Nobel Prize would soon be his – one of the most honourable awards a man could receive!

'Do you think this will . . .' Elisabeth hesitated before continuing. 'Do you think this will mess it up?'

'Mess what up? You mean the tabloids sniffing around? There's nothing to be messed up. Gossip and lies – it is what it is. We're above that kind of thing.'

'I don't know . . .'

His wife took another sip of the wine. It was a 2009 Châteauneuf-du-Pape. He had chosen it with care. It had been Rolf's favourite. 'Good legs on this,' was what he'd usually said when drinking it.

'Everyone is settled in.'

Louise's voice right behind him made Henning jump. He turned around.

'Has everyone got a bed?'

'Yes. We've put Rickard and Tilde in the boys' room in our house. The boys can sleep in our room. And Vivian and Susanne and Ole are sharing Rickard's house.'

'Brilliant. Did you ask Nancy to make her saddle of venison?'

'Of course. With crushed potatoes and port wine sauce. And seafood tonight. Fresh oysters.'

'Wonderful. From Åsa at Kalvö Oysters?' said Henning, smacking his lips.

'Not today. Today they're from Lotta Klemming,' said Elisabeth.

'It's great that there are so many incredible female business owners along this coast,' Henning said cheerfully. Then he realized the occasion called for a more sombre tone. 'Well, the circumstances are unfortunate, but there's no reason why we can't try to make the best of the situation. And we'll need to make some decisions together – about Blanche.'

Louise nodded.

'Let me know if there's anything I can do to help.'

'You're always a help,' said Elisabeth, raising her glass towards her daughter-in-law.

'Take a seat. Have a glass of wine,' said Henning, patting the space next to him on the sofa.

Louise appeared to hesitate, but then she shook her head.

'I've got a few things to prepare. But you enjoy yourselves. Lunch will be ready in an hour and the guests are comfortable. Should I tell them they can join you earlier if they'd like?'

'Of course,' said Henning, ignoring a tired look from his wife.

He raised his glass to her again, and saw the flames of the fire reflected in the well-polished crystal as they took on the blood-red hue of the wine.

'To Rolf.'

Elisabeth also raised her glass. 'To Rolf.'

* * *

'Would you ask everyone to gather in the conference room?'

Annika nodded and Patrik hastily tapped the counter at reception by way of thanks as he dashed past.

He wasn't stressed but felt acutely nauseous as his hangover had brought on a bout of travel sickness on the way from Fjällbacka to Tanumshede.

He ran into the toilet and barely had time to raise the lid before he threw up. He remained on the floor for another thirty seconds before he slowly got up. He felt much better after vomiting. He gargled with water, splashed a little more of that cold water over his face, examined his reflection in the mirror and managed to convince himself that his bloodshot eyes weren't all that noticeable.

He made his way towards the conference room on legs that weren't *too* unsteady to find the majority of them there waiting for him: Gösta, Martin and Paula, and also Annika, the police station's secretary. He couldn't wish for a better team. Only one person was missing from the room.

'Annika, would you find Mellberg?' he said.

Paula cleared her throat. She was unusually pale – perhaps she'd been on the town the night before too.

'He'll be along later. He had . . . an important errand to run.'

'Important errand,' Patrik muttered.

He had a pretty good idea what that entailed: Mellberg was in urgent need of a nap. But he didn't insist. Things were usually more straightforward when Bertil wasn't there.

'Okay, I thought we'd start by summing up the situation as it currently stands.' Patrik picked up a marker and began to write on the large whiteboard. 'Rolf Stenklo, a photographer due to exhibit at the gallery on Galärbacken, was found murdered, by the cleaner, Fanny Klintberg.

The call came in at 08:05 and the cleaner says only a few minutes elapsed between her finding him and calling it in to the police. We know the results of the autopsy will take time, but according to the new head of forensics, the medical examiner gave an approximate time of death for Rolf of around midnight. But we need to bear in mind that this is only a preliminary assessment and that there may be a margin of error.'

'I heard the weapon was a nail gun. Is that true?' said Annika.

Patrik nodded and wrote 'nail gun' on the board.

'That's right. A nail gun that was most likely already on the premises. So that probably means it was an impulsive crime rather a planned one.'

'One shot?' Gösta put up his hand.

Patrik nodded again.

'Yes, only one shot. The nail must have really hit home.'

Martin pointed to the board.

'There was no sign of a break-in, but the door was unlocked when the cleaner arrived.'

Patrik wrote down what he had said.

'What else do we have? Have the guests given us anything?'

'Not yet,' said Paula. 'Martin, Gösta and I haven't been able to glean anything worthwhile from them.'

'I suggest we have a chat with all the local miscreants,' Martin said to Patrik. 'Gösta and I talked about it, but we wanted to run it by you first. We're happy to check out that angle.'

'Sounds good. Make a list, putting them in order of priority. I trust your judgement – we know who our frequent flyers are and how they act and how far they'll take things. Do you think it's a break-in gone wrong?'

Gösta clasped his hands on his belly.

'Don't you?'

Patrik was silent for a moment before replying.

'That's the most likely version of events. The photographs were worth a lot of money. It's highly likely that one of our local muppets found that out, not realizing how hard it would be to sell them. However, we don't believe there are any photographs missing.'

'According to his wife, only Rolf knew which photographs were going to be part of the exhibition,' said Martin.

Patrik thought out loud: 'We could ask her to take a look at them, but we can't make the mistake of only pursuing one line of enquiry. There are plenty of examples of investigations where the solution seemed to be obvious at first glance and then turned out to be more complex than that.'

Paula nudged the plate of buns towards Martin. He glared at her, but then took one.

'So have we got any alternative motives?' she said.

Martin shook his head. 'Rolf and his wife Vivian had a quarrel the night before the party, but it doesn't seem to have been anything beyond a common or garden marital squabble. Rolf also seems to have been more abrupt in recent months, from what I've understood, but I haven't seen any indications of threats against him. There's nothing to suggest that anyone disliked him enough to kill him.'

Patrik wrote 'motive' in large letters on the board, added a question mark afterwards and then circled the word.

'So we have no signs of a personal motive,' he summarized.

Annika waved to catch his attention.

'What should we do about the media? They're calling the front desk. What do you want me to say?'

'Tell everyone we'll hold a press conference tomorrow. Not that we'll have anything to report at it, but at least we have a bone to throw them for the time being.'

'Should I tell them eleven o'clock?'

'That'll be perfect. Check with Mellberg before you notify the press. I'm sure he'll want to take it.'

'Most likely,' Annika said dryly.

Paula coughed. 'I can't say any more right now, but I would ask you to show . . . show Bertil some consideration over the coming days.'

Everyone looked at her in astonishment. Gösta was the first to speak.

'Consideration? We've done nothing but show him consideration for years. What is it you're not telling us?'

'Nothing.' Paula stared down into her lap without meeting their gazes. 'Just . . . give him some space.'

'Okay.'

Patrik looked at Annika quizzically and she shrugged. Normally she knew everything going on at the station, but this time even she seemed to be in the dark.

Paula's face was tense. Patrik looked at her kindly. Something had happened, but Paula was apparently not ready to tell them. They would find out in time.

Annika put a comforting hand on Paula's – her colleague looked like she might burst into tears at any moment.

'We could do with finding out more about our murder victim,' said Patrik.

Paula blinked a few times. 'I've already made a start on that.'

'Good. What else do we have?'

'Not much until we hear back from NFC and forensics,' said Gösta.

'I've got a video of the crime scene on my phone. Let's watch it together.'

Patrik pulled up the recording on his mobile and passed the device to Annika. She was the only one who could achieve the feat of connecting it to the temperamental screen in the conference room.

'Here's the gallery – there's only one room and it's easy to take it all in,' said Patrik. 'As you know, Rolf's exhibition was due to open in twenty-four hours' time, on Monday morning.'

'What's that hanging on the walls?' Gösta asked, leaning forward to get a better view.

'According to Vivian, Rolf spent a lot of time on the positioning of the photographs,' said Martin. 'And to avoid constantly moving the photographs around – since they were pretty heavy and unwieldy, not to mention valuable – he used cheap frames with notes inserted showing the names of the pictures.'

'Which means that every frame represents one of the photos that was due to be exhibited,' Patrik clarified.

'Exactly,' said Martin.

'There are the pieces.' Patrik pointed to a neat row of framed photographs at the back of the venue.

'There's not much blood, is there?' said Paula.

'No, the nail was still in his head, and there wasn't much spatter.'

Patrik shivered and looked at the others in the room. 'Does everyone know what they need to do?'

Everyone nodded, gathered their things and went about their duties. Outside, the wind had intensified and was verging on gale force in strength. Patrik remained in the room, alone. There was something gnawing at him. Something he'd seen or heard that didn't add up. But it was just out of reach. And now his headache had returned with a vengeance.

He stuffed the phone back into his pocket and headed for reception, where he knew Annika ran a small pharmacy out of her desk drawer.

9

STOCKHOLM 1980

Lola was always worried about leaving P'tite at home on her own on the evenings that she was working. But she had no choice – there was no one else. It was just her and P'tite.

'You're ten minutes late.'

Jack, her boss, glowered at her in irritation. She snorted and swept past him. Jack's bark was worse than his bite.

'Show up on time, Lola!' he called after her.

She turned around and blew him a kiss.

'Love you too!'

'Busy night,' said Maggie when Lola arrived behind the bar.

Maggie was right. The place was teeming with people. Alexa's was the club everyone wanted to be at, and everyone was welcome. The clientele were as mixed a bag as the staff, and one of the attractions of a night at Alexa's was that you never knew who you'd bump into. Royalty, foreign rock stars, notorious robbers, famous politicians. They all came to Alexa's.

Lola stowed her handbag under the bar and began to help Maggie taking orders.

Maggie was a drag queen with a penchant for particularly glittery dresses. Tonight he was shimmering in a turquoise creation. He was mixing drinks at breakneck speed and glanced only quickly at Lola.

'Love the blouse!'

'Oh, this old rag.'

Lola tugged at the silky fabric of the top and fluttered her eyelashes. She appreciated the compliment. She'd found the blouse in a charity shop in Södermalm for a price that was as close to a steal as she was going to get. It wasn't easy dressing like a queen on a maid's budget, but thanks to good contacts in several charity shops, she pulled it off. She looked incredible, and she knew it.

'Lola, give me a Tequila Sunrise and a smile.'

Kent – one of Alexa's regulars – leaned over the bar and gazed at her with infatuation.

'A smile will cost you extra,' she said with feigned sternness as she began to mix the drink he had ordered.

She could pretty much mix drinks in her sleep now, and the customers usually ordered the same night after night. Once the red and orange cocktail was ready, she produced a shot glass, poured in coffee and Galliano and topped it off with whipped cream before pushing it towards Kent along with his order.

'Have a Hot Shot on the house,' she said, also flashing him the requested smile.

Kent was one of the nice ones. There were others she did her best to keep at as much of a distance as she could.

'When can I take you out to dinner?'

Kent was still hanging around the bar and hadn't taken his eyes off her. She shook her head. There wasn't really anything wrong with Kent. He was pleasant and always well turned out. Tonight he was wearing a grey blazer with the arms rolled up to reveal the shiny lining, smart jeans and brown loafers with tassels. But he was in his seventies and definitely too old for her, which she had told him on countless occasions. But hope was the last thing to abandon Kent.

'Just an itty bitty dinner can't do any harm, can it?' he said, tilting his head to one side pleadingly.

Lola greeted another patron who ordered a beer and she turned around to get it out of the fridge.

'You're old enough to be my dad, Kent,' she said. 'Find someone your own age. I don't want someone who needs help cranking up their todger.'

Kent laughed loudly and resoundingly. He only became more enamoured when she insulted him.

'Now why don't you toddle along to a table so that you can admire me from afar. I've got customers to see to.'

Reluctantly, Kent took his drink and made for a table. He had already downed the Hot Shot and Lola retrieved the empty glass and set it down behind her.

'I need a ciggie soon,' Maggie hissed as he coolly opened a beer.

'You nip off for a crafty one – I've got this,' Lola said, gesturing to the queue for the bar.

She meant it. She was practised and had the situation under control.

'Thanks, darling.'

Maggie sneaked off, leaving the scent of Dior Poison in his wake.

'Lola!'

A familiar voice cut across the sound of Boney M's 'Rivers of Babylon'. Rolf Stenklo had arrived at the bar and was smiling at her with that Hollywood smile he had.

'Is the whole gang here?' she said, and Rolf nodded.

'We're sitting over there! We're heading out for a bite to eat, but we can pick you up afterwards. How long are you working tonight?'

'I get off at one. We can go back to mine after!'

116

'OK! We're only having one now, but we'll pick you up later!'

'I'll make sure two bottles of wine and some glasses are sent over to the table.'

'You're a sweetie, Lola.'

Lola followed Rolf's bouncing shock of blond hair as he made his way towards the round table in the corner with his characteristically quick gait. She smiled, raised her hand and waved. The gang all waved back eagerly and she felt a warm glow inside. She was already longing for closing time. In truth, that wasn't exactly what she'd thought when she'd left home. She wasn't alone. She lined up six shot glasses. She was going to give them Hot Shots with their wine.

10

'Hello! Are there any hungover mums here?'

Anna's cheerful cry was audible from the hall, and Erica turned off the computer and jogged down the stairs. She was met by a hooting chorus of children, and she hugged them each in turn before they ran into the living room to play.

'Come on, let's have a cup of coffee,' she said to Anna. 'I'm afraid I haven't got anything nice to go with it. I've put on a couple of kilos so I'm trying not to keep that kind of stuff in the house.'

'You're beautiful, Erica – and your constant dieting is . . . completely unnecessary.'

'Easy for you to say, having inherited Dad's genes. Did you know that Mum used to force Dad to eat cream for breakfast because she was so afraid that people would think he wasn't being fed at home?'

'No, I've never heard that,' Anna laughed, before beginning to peruse the cupboards in a familiar way. 'Why don't you sit down? You need to take it easy. I'll make the coffee.'

Then she turned towards Erica with a serious expression.

'Have you heard any more about the murder of the photographer?'

'Rolf Stenklo? No; Patrik popped back briefly before he went down to the station and I haven't heard anything since then. But I went over to have a chat with Rolf's wife, Vivian. They've rented a house here in the bay.'

'Why did you do that?' said Anna in surprise. Then she shook her head. 'You just can't help yourself . . .'

'I didn't actually go there to talk about Rolf's murder. Vivian was sitting at the end of my table at the party and mentioned an unsolved murder in Stockholm in the eighties.'

'And you thought it would be a good idea to go and talk to her about it on the very morning her husband was found murdered?'

When Anna put it like that, Erica reluctantly admitted it might seem a little inappropriate. Her greatest strengths as a writer – her insatiable curiosity and occasional pushiness – were not necessarily always her greatest strengths as a person. But she hadn't got the impression that Vivian had taken offence.

'What murder case was that?'

'A trans woman. Lola. And her daughter. I've been trying to find more information for hours, but I can't find anything online.'

'What was the connection to Rolf?'

'They were friends, according to Vivian. But this must have happened when he was married to his late wife – Vivian never met Lola.'

Anna looked at Erica thoughtfully.

'Are you sure you're not getting yourself into something that you don't really understand?'

'What do you mean?'

Erica looked at her sister in surprise. Anna was usually her biggest supporter, no matter what.

'Yes, but you know Marianne . . .'

A penny dropped for Erica. She most certainly knew Marianne, who was one of Anna's friends in Stockholm.

Ten years ago she had sent shockwaves through conservative Sweden when, as the CEO of one of Sweden's biggest banks, she had announced that effective immediately she was no longer Kjell Sundholm, CEO, but was instead Marianne Sundholm, CEO.

'Marianne taught me a lot that I hadn't thought about,' Anna said, seemingly searching for the right words. 'There's so much prejudice. So much history that is downright shameful. And that includes a tendency for the trans community to be regarded as entertainment. As a phenomenon. As a spectacle. Not to mention something that people outside that world have profited from. When you talk about Lola, you specify that she was a trans woman. Why don't you just say "woman"?'

Erica sat quietly without answering at first. She realized that Anna had a devastating point. And she'd followed the same train of thought too. Erica was confident in her motives. Nonetheless, it would be all too easy to misstep because she didn't know any better.

'I'll put my cards on the table. My ignorance is enormous. But I promise that I'm going to approach this story with the utmost respect. And I'll acquire the knowledge I lack before I publish even a single word in print. Okay?'

'Okay,' said Anna, taking her hand with a smile.

Erica sighed.

'The first problem, however, is how to make any progress whatsoever. I can't find anything online.'

'Well, go to Stockholm then.'

Erica raised her eyebrows. Then she pointed at the kids playing in the living room.

'With a husband in the middle of a murder inquiry and a bunch of kids, I don't exactly see how I'm going to manage a trip to Stockholm at the moment.'

'Pfft, you know how often Kristina says she wants to see more of the kids. Ask her for help. Surely you need to drop in to visit your publisher? You seem to do that at regular intervals. Take a couple of days. I can help Kristina too, if necessary. We'll figure it out.'

'Are you sure?'

Erica still wasn't entirely convinced that it was a good idea. Admittedly, she loved her mother-in-law, but it might be a tactical error to end up owing her a debt of gratitude. The price tag was usually revealed sooner or later – often in the form of some family celebration they were forced to attend. But in this case it might actually be worth it.

Anna poured coffee for them both.

'Call Kristina and ask her to take the kids for a couple of days, and then head off to Stockholm.'

Erica nodded. 'You know, I think I will. I can ask around about Blanche as well.'

'Blanche?'

'Yes, it's a cultural club that Rolf was one of the backers of. I've heard some rumours about Blanche and I'd like to find out if there's anything to them.'

'Do you think there's a connection to the murder?' Anna asked.

Erica leaned back and glanced towards the living room.

'Maybe, maybe not. But it won't hurt to ask around. And I don't believe in coincidences . . .'

'Do you have a way in?'

'I think my publisher can help out on that front. Stockholm's cultural sphere isn't that big.'

'And how are you going to find out more about Lola?'

'I've already emailed Frank – my police contact in Stockholm – saying that I need help finding a police file from 1980. I also thought I'd see whether I could find out more from anyone who knew Lola at the time. Someone from the trans community, for instance.'

'Sounds to me like you had already decided to take a trip to Stockholm.' Anna grinned.

Erica blushed. Yes, she supposed she had.

Maja came into the kitchen pinching her nose shut with two fingers.

'Fliss smells really badly of poo,' she said in a nasal voice, and Anna glanced meaningfully at Erica.

'Well, she is Auntie's favourite . . .'

Erica sighed and stood up. Changing a shit-filled nappy while hungover – exactly what she needed.

'It feels like we only just ate,' said Susanne, stretching on the sofa.

Beyond the picture windows the wind was blowing wildly and roiling waves surged against the shoreline. Henning had warned everyone that the rocks were slippery and that they had to exercise care when moving from house to house.

'We don't have to eat yet if you don't want to,' said Louise.

William had fallen asleep on her lap and her legs were beginning to go numb from his weight. He and Peter had been out setting lobster pots and the boy had spent the whole afternoon talking about it. Now Peter was playing chess with his eldest, who appeared to be winning, judging by his expression.

'No, no, we'll eat now.'

Elisabeth stood up and poked Henning, who was snoring gently in the armchair by the fire.

'Henning. Dinner.'

'Er, what? Didn't we just eat? What time is it?'

'It's past eight. It'll be late for the boys if we don't eat now.'

'Yes, yes, I just have to get up. This armchair is a dream, but it's hell to get out of it.'

He groaned as he readied himself and then got to his feet.

'Right then, ladies and gentlemen. Let's take our seats at the table.'

'But Grandad! I'm winning!'

Max looked at Henning, disappointment writ across his face.

'You can carry on after dinner. Leave the chessboard there and remember whose go it was,' said Louise, gently nudging William.

It was a shame to wake him, but she'd asked Nancy to make spaghetti and mincemeat sauce for the boys instead of oysters, and since that was William's favourite dish it would make it easier to get him to the table.

'Gosh, what a feast!' Ole clapped his hands together exuberantly as they entered the dining room. He'd been drinking whisky all afternoon and his face had assumed a fiery hue that was particularly conspicuous against his beige polo-neck.

Louise drew out a chair and sat down next to Peter. The table really was set for a party. There were lobsters, langoustines, crab, shrimp and oysters. To go with that there were fresh baguettes, lemon, aioli, Västerbotten cheese and a delicious vendace roe sauce from the fishmonger in Fjällbacka.

'Would someone let Vivian know?' Elisabeth, taking a seat at one end of the dining table, looked at the others commandingly.

'I'm here,' Vivian said from the doorway.

She had pillow marks on her face, but she had changed into a pale blue dress and braided her hair neatly to one side.

'Come and sit here.'

Louise patted the chair next to hers. Vivian sat down and Louise stroked her arm lightly.

'Are you sure you're up to this? We can ask Nancy to send food to your room if you'd prefer?' she said softly.

Vivian shook her head.

'No, I need energies around me.'

'Okay.'

The atmosphere was subdued during dinner and no one wanted to prolong it unnecessarily. Conversation was strained, so the thing that was most audible was the noisy consumption of shellfish.

Louise managed to eat half a lobster and some shrimp, but that was as much as she could manage. There were too many thoughts spinning around in her head. Peter had no trouble eating – he could always eat, regardless of the circumstances – and the 10 kilometres he ran every day meant he could do so without any trace of it being visible on his person.

Louise looked around the table. Henning and Elisabeth were seated at either end. The patriarch. The matriarch. Like royal couples of old. Susanne and Ole. The odd couple. Beauty and the Beast. The love between them was hard to comprehend, but it was apparent and palpable. Vivian. Brittle and fragile in her grief. Lost without Rolf, who had been the anchor of their relationship. Rickard and Tilde. Selfish, egotistical. Unable to love anyone but themselves. Leeches living on the blood of their hosts. She wondered how people saw her and Peter. He and Cecily had been a beautiful couple. Did they make comparisons with her and Peter? Probably.

Louise was completely unlike Cecily. Cecily had been small, dainty and blonde. Louise was tall and dark. The boys had Peter's dark colouring, so they looked more like her kids than Cecily's. As if it had always been intended that they would be hers. Louise forced herself to think about something else. She couldn't go there.

Henning tapped the table a few times from his prominent position.

'We've got some matters to discuss in relation to Blanche, so I'm afraid we must ask for privacy. I apologize,

124

Vivian, although I dare say you may find it a relief to be spared our dreary affairs.'

'I'd like to go to bed,' Vivian said, wiping her hands clean.

Louise noticed that she hadn't touched the food on her plate.

'Good, good. Louise, would you join us in case we need to take notes?'

'Of course,' she said, opening a wet wipe sachet and wiping her hands thoroughly. 'Peter, would you put the boys to bed? Don't forget that they're sleeping in our room.'

'Of course. I'll probably turn in early too, so tiptoe when you come in.'

He kissed her on the cheek. She called the boys over and they ran to her. Max glanced longingly towards the sofas.

'I was going to finish playing.'

'Tomorrow, sweetie,' she said, taking his face between her hands. 'Tomorrow.'

She kissed him on the cheek and reached out to William. 'Be a good boy.'

'I am a good boy.'

'Yes, you are. You're a very good boy. Now go and give Grandad a goodnight hug and then it's off to bed with you.'

Both the boys did as she told them and gave Henning a hug. Louise watched them intensely. There was a lot of Henning in the boys. Sometimes she saw only him in them. Tonight was one such occasion.

As they left with Peter, they blew kisses to both her and their grandfather.

Henning cleared his throat.

'Well then. We've got some business to attend to.'

* * *

125

'Good God, we barely fit into the beds!'

Tilde waved her arms about in frustration and Rickard could only agree with her as they looked around the boys' room. He'd drunk too much wine at dinner – in fact, for the majority of the evening – and Tilde's agitated movements were making him dizzy.

William entered wearing PAW Patrol pyjamas, a toothbrush in his mouth.

'Are you going . . . to schleep here . . . ?' he said, looking at them wide-eyed.

Rickard clutched a chair and tried not to show his nephew how drunk he was.

'Yep. Tonight Tilde and I are going to sleep in your room.'

'Unfortunately,' Tilde muttered, yanking the duvet matching William's pyjamas off the bed.

Rickard grimaced at William, which made him start laughing, making toothpaste spray everywhere.

'Finish brushing your teeth then come in to say goodnight. All right, champ?'

He ruffled William's hair and the boy giggled and ran off.

'Don't tell me you've changed your mind and want one of those,' Tilde said, settling herself under the PAW Patrol duvet. 'Because it ain't happening.'

'Don't worry,' said Rickard as he unbuttoned his shirt. 'I've never seen you as mother material.'

'Good. Then we agree.'

Tilde sat up again with the duvet pulled up over her chest.

'What was it they needed to talk about? It sounded serious.'

'How serious can it be?' Rickard managed to step out of his trousers without falling over and hung them over a miniature desk chair. 'The mime artist has broken a leg?

The Czech poet has sold more than two thousand copies and lost all credibility?'

Tilde giggled but quickly turned serious again.

'But what if it's something about money? What if it's something that means your mother can't help us? Why didn't you talk to her this evening?'

'I'm *going* to talk to Mum, but maybe you've noticed that a few things have happened in the last twenty-four hours!'

'What are you going to talk to Mum about? Money? Again?' Peter was standing in the doorway with William and Max next to him. 'Boys, go and get into our bed. There's something I need to discuss with Uncle Rickard.'

'Okay. Good night!'

William waved enthusiastically and he and Max disappeared in the direction of Peter and Louise's bedroom.

Once his sons were not in the vicinity, Peter's neutral expression vanished. His gaze darkened.

'You shouldn't ask Mum for another penny. And you should be grateful that I haven't told Dad how much you've got out of her in the last few years, Rickard. I know exactly how much you've swindled out of Mum with your lies and your empty promises – down to the last penny.'

Peter took a step into the room and Rickard backed away involuntarily. He almost fell over and cursed himself for having that final drink. He'd never seen Peter angry before. Peter was always the calm one, the stable one. The one whose surface never rippled in the slightest.

'I haven't swindled . . .' Rickard began, but stopped when his brother stepped up so close to him that he could feel his breath.

Peter jabbed his index finger into his chest and Rickard squirmed.

'What the hell?'

'I'm only going to say this once: stop asking Mum for money. I have an overview of Mum and Dad's finances. I *will* see if you get money again. The tap is off. I guess you'll just have to . . . Oh, I don't know. Get jobs?'

Peter stared hard at his little brother. Then he turned on his heel and left the room.

Rickard pulled off his socks in frustration. Tilde's eyes were wide and terrified. Her lower lip was trembling.

'Rickard . . .'

'Not a word. I'll explode if you do. Not a word.'

He made his way around Tilde's bed to the other bed against the far wall. He angrily pulled back the Spiderman duvet, crawled under it and pulled it over his head. He could hear Peter reading a story to the boys in the room next door.

'You're home early . . .'

Erica looked at Patrik in surprise as he came into the kitchen. She was clearing up after dinner. The kids were in front of the TV in their pyjamas.

'We're not going to make any further progress today, so I wanted to get home before the kids went to bed.'

His head was splitting, but the worst of it settled down when he rested his gaze on Erica.

'We've just eaten – we could have waited and eaten together,' she said. 'But there's leftovers if you'd like some.'

'Don't worry. I ate at the station.'

'Would you like to put them to bed?'

'Gladly,' said Patrik, making for the living room.

His arrival was met with jubilation, which was quickly replaced with downturned expressions when he announced it was time for bed.

When he came downstairs twenty minutes later, Erica had lit candles in the living room and made a pot of tea.

'Come and sit down. You look completely done in.'

Patrik flopped onto the sofa.

'It never gets easier.'

Erica leaned in against him, stroking his bicep.

'That's what makes you such a good policeman, Patrik. You never allow yourself to be unmoved by people dying.'

'I guess so,' he said tiredly. 'But that doesn't make it easier.'

'Have you got anywhere?'

'I wouldn't say so. We don't really know any more than we did this morning. And we've been inundated with phone calls from the media. We're having a press conference in the morning, but I don't have anything to give them.'

'Hasn't Mellberg bagsied it?'

'That's what's so weird. He spent the whole afternoon shut up in his office and then he went home without anyone noticing. And Paula looks utterly devastated. I wonder if something has happened, but I don't want to intrude. And I've got an investigation to focus on.'

Erica caressed his cheek and he took her hand.

'Have some tea,' she said. 'It's chamomile so you'll sleep better.'

'Thanks, sweetheart.'

He took a sip then turned to her. Her blond curls shone in the candlelight.

'How was your day?'

Erica suddenly looked self-conscious. 'I've decided to go to Stockholm for a couple of days.'

'Stockholm?'

'I've spoken to Kristina – she'll take the kids, so there's no need for you to worry about that. I'd like to find out more about Lola. And . . . I can also ask around about Blanche.'

'Erica . . .'

'I know you don't like me snooping around. But what

129

harm can it do? Your investigation into Rolf's murder is here – I'm not barging in on that – and you must admit that what Vivian hinted to me about secrets might be of importance to you.'

'Yes, but . . .'

'I'll be careful. I'll be diplomatic. I'll be discreet. I'll be all the things you think I can't be . . .'

She grinned at him.

'Now you're pulling the wool over my eyes,' he said. 'Smiling like that. It's doping. Bribery.'

'Wait until you see the rest of my repertoire.'

She put her arms around him and hugged him before suddenly letting go.

'If you're not too tired?'

Patrik pulled her close. 'I'm never too tired.'

'Liar.'

He kissed her. Tonight – more than ever – he needed to be close to his wife.

Peter didn't know why, but tonight – for the first time since Cecily's death – he'd got out the storybook she always read to the boys. *The Wind in the Willows*. The book was old and worn out. It had been Cecily's when she had been a child.

It had usually been Cecily who read to the kids. He had always worked late. There had been few nights when he'd got home before the boys had gone to bed. At the weekends, she had been the one at the park with the boys or at the swimming baths or on fun outings to child-friendly museums.

All that had changed when she died. His priorities had changed the very moment an untraceable car had struck her body. All those hours of overtime, all the bonuses, all that pursuit of success had in a second become meaningless. All that mattered was the boys.

Telling them what had happened to their mother had been the hardest thing he'd ever done. Two-year-old William had been far too little, but Max had been five and he'd understood the gravity of what Peter had said. The howl that had emanated from him had sounded like it had come from a wounded animal. It was a primal cry of sadness.

After talking to the psychologist at the hospital, Peter had been advised to bring the kids in to say goodbye. Cecily was lying in a hospital bed, hooked up to tubes and with no prospect of ever waking up again. The staff had been so nice. They had prepared her ahead of the boys' arrival. They had covered as many of the tubes as they could, wiped away the blood and brushed her hair. She'd looked peaceful.

They'd curled up next to her on the hospital bed, pressing themselves against her like two small puppies seeking out warmth and reassurance. After an hour, Peter had lifted them down and carried them out of the room – then he'd given the doctor permission to switch off Cecily's life support.

He hadn't thought they'd survive those first few months, let alone ever feel happiness again. Louise had changed all that. At first, she'd been his best friend. Then she'd been a safe harbour for the boys. Then love had blossomed. Both he and the boys loved her. She wasn't Cecily. She wasn't their mother. But she was Louise.

'Don't make a habit out of sleeping here,' he said with a sly smile.

'We promise,' Max said gravely.

Peter tickled his side. He'd been serious since the day he'd been born – and it had only been reinforced by Cecily's death.

'Are you going to snore?'

'Daaad! I don't snore,' said Max. 'I'm a child.'

'That's true, Dad. We don't snore because we're kids,' William added.

'So what are you saying? Who snores so loudly it raises the roof every night?'

'You, Dad! It's you!'

'What? No? Me?'

'Yes, it is!'

Both boys laughed out loud.

Peter closed the book and put it on the floor by the bed. He tucked the extra duvet more tightly around the boys and turned off the bedside lamp.

'I love you.'

'We love you, Dad.'

Peter smiled in the dark. He wasn't religious, but part of him was certain that at moments like these Cecily was still with them.

'If someone had told me a couple of years ago that I'd be grateful for Bertil's existence I would have thought they were unhinged.'

Paula stifled a sob. Rita had gathered them all in the kitchen and told them in a steady monotone what the doctor had said. The silence that had followed had echoed around the small room. Bertil had looked so terribly small.

She and Johanna hadn't talked about it since. The kids had come rushing in. They'd been romping about and making a racket and simply being lively in the way that only children could be, so it hadn't been possible to be serious. But now as they were lying next to each other in the double bed, each with their book, desperately trying not to think about Rita's cancer diagnosis, it was no longer avoidable.

Johanna put down her book and removed her reading glasses. She turned to Paula and caressed her cheek.

'It'll be okay. You heard what Rita said – they're going to start treatment right away. They wouldn't do that if there was no hope.'

'I know. But . . .' Paula wiped away the tears that stubbornly insisted on running down her cheeks.

She hated crying. She hated being weak, being afraid.

'Sweetie . . .'

'Ugh, don't look at me like that. It's not me you should be feeling sorry for – it's Mum who is in a difficult place. I'm just . . . I'm so afraid.'

'Of course you're afraid – that's what happens when someone you love is sick,' Johanna said, stroking some of the tears away. 'I could tell that Bertil is bloody terrified too.'

Paula took a deep breath. She needed to regain control. Her mother needed her. 'Yes, I don't suppose I've ever thought how much Mum means to Bertil.'

'Please! She's his everything. Her and our kids.'

Johanna smiled at her.

'You're right. I know you're right,' said Paula. 'But what happens now? Will he be able to cope? Bertil isn't exactly famous for staying steady when the wind picks up.'

'Sometimes people can surprise us.'

'You think? I find people do that very rarely. And I'm worried that this is more than Bertil can handle.'

'I think you're wrong. But *if* that turns out to be the case, then we'll be there for Rita. Rita won't be alone, no matter what happens.'

'I know. But . . .'

Johanna caressed her cheek again.

'No buts. You'll drive yourself insane if you worry about crossing bridges you haven't even reached yet. Bertil may surprise you.'

Paula sighed and turned off her reading light.

'Can we sleep now? I can't bear to talk any more.'

Johanna switched off her lamp and pulled the covers up to her chin. Then she whispered: 'Love you.'

Paula didn't answer, but she sought out Johanna's hand under the duvet, and didn't let go until she was overcome by sleep.

'Are we really going to do this now? Rolf's body is barely cold!' Elisabeth slowly swirled her wine glass.

'I don't think we have any choice,' said Susanne, standing up to refill her own glass.

She had kicked off her high heels and was barefoot. Her long, silky kaftan from Rodebjer undulated on her slender body as she moved across the room.

'We can start with something more pleasant,' said Henning.

He could hear the joy in his own voice. The more it sunk in, the more that joy and expectation grew.

'Yes, how did you feel when our good friend Sten called?' slurred Ole, who had now lain down with his head in Susanne's lap.

Henning pursed his lips. Of course Susanne and Ole had talked about this at home.

'It's really well-deserved,' said Susanne, raising her glass in a toast. 'We were unanimous.'

Ole sat up, reached out for his whisky glass and did likewise. Henning looked at his wife, who also raised her glass towards him.

'It's going to be magnificent for Blanche,' said Ole, lying back down in Susanne's lap. She slowly stroked his hair.

'This is one of the reasons why we need to have this conversation now. We're going to be placed under the microscope. What with the investigation into Rolf's death and with my . . . announcement. There are certain things that need dealing with.'

'Gossip. Bullshit. Jealousy,' Ole slurred.

'We all know there are lots of people who want to take us down – want to take down Blanche,' Henning said. 'They want to destroy what we've built. Poisonous tongues.'

'Bastards, the lot of them.'

Ole spat out the words and Susanne caressed his cheek. 'Calm down, darling.'

'We're not going to give them the opportunity to get at us.' Henning leaned forward to give his words emphasis. 'How long have we known each other? Forty-five years? Longer? We can never allow ourselves to be divided.'

He turned to Louise.

'Isn't it incredible? We've known each other almost fifty years.'

'Amazing,' said Louise. Henning thought she looked tired.

She cleared her throat.

'What do I say if the police ask me about . . . certain matters?'

Susanne looked at her sternly. She'd always had the ability to transform her gaze to ice.

'It's not a problem, Susanne,' said Louise. 'I'm on your side. I just want it nice and clear what you want me to do.'

'Bloody bury it. That's what we want you to do, Louise.'

Ole laughed and poured more whisky into his glass.

'That's not what we mean,' Elisabeth said in a conciliatory tone. 'We simply feel it's unnecessary to draw focus away from the investigation by bringing up things that are irrelevant and will only waste police time and resources. And it would be tragic if false accusations were to draw focus from what Henning has achieved.'

'I quite understand,' said Louise. 'Naturally I won't share irrelevant information with the police.'

'Irrelevant! That was the word! Irrelevant!' Ole slurred.

He reached for the whisky bottle again, but Susanne took it from him.

'No more for you now.'

'Oh darling, I love it when you're so stern.'

Ole pressed his face between her breasts and shook his head. Susanne laughed and pushed him away.

'Save that for the bedroom.'

'I think we should raise a toast to Rolf,' Elisabeth said suddenly. 'We've barely talked about him. Why don't we talk about him?'

Henning immediately raised his glass. 'To Rolf.'

'To Rolf,' the others said in chorus.

For a few seconds, all that was audible was the sound of them drinking. Then Elisabeth laughed.

'Rolf really could not stand whisky.'

'Bloody hell, I'd forgotten that!' said Ole. 'Half a glass and he'd be snoring away in the corner.'

He looked questioningly at Susanne, who now nodded. With a smile, he poured himself another glass.

'Poor Ester. All those times she had to drag him home. And he was a big guy.'

'Where did you used to hang out?' Louise asked.

She'd settled down on her side on the sofa and was looking at them intently. Outside, the storm was raging – the strongest gusts of wind made the entire house rattle.

'Our first watering hole was a place called Alexa's,' said Henning. 'A Stockholm version of Studio 54. Everyone was there in the late seventies and early eighties. It was a crazy time. Before the mobile phone. No risk of being filmed.'

He winked at Louise.

'It was amazing,' Ole slurred. 'Gays, dykes, trannies and drag queens rubbing shoulders with finance yuppies and plumbers from Bagarmossen. Everyone was welcome.'

'Yes, those were the days,' said Henning.

He looked down into his wine glass. He found the deep red colour soothing. But it also evoked memories. Memories of a bygone era. He felt Elisabeth's gaze resting on him, but right now he didn't want to look her in the eye. There was something about this evening that felt unreal to him. The convergence of timelines. Old, unresolved memories emerging that wanted to rise to the surface.

In the end, he raised his head and looked at Louise.

'You're like a daughter, you know that, right? You're more than a daughter-in-law.'

Henning's words surprised even himself. He must have been drunker than he realized, but he meant what he said.

Louise didn't reply, but she continued to look at him.

'I think we should raise a toast to Lola,' said Ole.

The room fell deadly silent.

Henning hesitated. Then he saw that Elisabeth had raised her glass and he did the same.

'To Lola.'

'Who was Lola?' Louise asked.

Henning looked around the room. He met the others' gazes. Eyes he had seen age. Eyes he had seen lose their naivety – their innocence.

'Lola was Lola.'

He said no more. There was no more to say.

'I'm going to put some music on.' Elisabeth got up and went over to the record player beside the bookcase. It had been a seventieth birthday present to Henning after he'd long complained about difficulties connecting to the advanced speaker system that Peter had had installed.

Nat King Cole's voice flowed across the living room with the characteristic crackle of vinyl. They spent an hour talking about unimportant things. Irrelevant things. Not about Rolf. Not about Lola. Not about any of the secrets that they collectively needed to keep.

When Henning stood up, he could feel how unsteady he was on his feet – and he wasn't alone. Ole had to support himself against Susanne.

'Louise has nodded off,' Henning whispered, pointing to his daughter-in-law.

She was snoring gently on her side on the sofa. Elisabeth spread a blanket over her.

'Shouldn't we wake her?' said Henning.

Elisabeth shook her head.

'Let her sleep. Peter has the boys in their bed. She'll sleep better here.'

'Well then. To bed, my beauty.'

He offered his arm to Elisabeth and she took it, just as she had done so many times before. Outside, the wind was whipping up ever-bigger waves.

'Can't you sleep?'

Rita was only visible as a dark silhouette in the doorway. Bertil was sitting in the sheepskin-covered armchair in the living room. He had turned it to face the window so that he could look out into the dark.

Ernst was lying with his head at Bertil's feet. The big dog had sensed Bertil's state of mind and had padded over to him. Ernst would stay at home with Rita from now on. She needed him more.

'Quite a storm. A lot of trees are going to come down tonight,' he said.

Rita stood behind him. She put her hands on his shoulders.

'We've been through storms before. And we'll face more of them in future.'

'Not like this one.'

Neither of them was talking about the weather any longer.

She kissed him on the top of his head.

'Can you handle it?'

Her words left Bertil short of breath.

'You shouldn't be asking me that,' he said, putting his hand over hers. 'It's me who should be asking you.'

'Yet it's you sitting here in the middle of the night while I was actually sleeping pretty well . . .'

'Sorry if I woke you.'

'You didn't. I needed the loo. But come back to bed.'

'I'll be there soon.'

'You need to sleep. You've got a murder inquiry to oversee.'

'How am I supposed to care about that now?'

Rita gently punched his shoulder.

'Now you're talking nonsense. Do you think you're any use to me in this state? Bertil Rufus Mellberg, look at me.'

Rita moved around the armchair and stood in front of him with her arms crossed. Ernst let out a heavy sigh and went over to the rug, where he lay down.

'Time for you to go to bed. Now. You need some decent sleep for a couple of hours. Then you'll take a shower, get dressed, go to work and do your job. And when I talk, you'll listen. When I don't want to talk, you'll leave me alone. When I need a hug, you'll give me a hug. Simple as that. To hell with the storm – come to bed. The storm will do whatever the storm does, regardless of whether you're watching it.'

'Yes, yes. I'm coming.'

Mellberg sat there for a few more minutes staring at the swaying trees. Then he got up. Rita was right. As ever.

11

MONDAY

Erica loved this time of day, when the kids had been dropped off at kindergarten and Patrik had gone to work. It was just her, a cup of coffee, her computer and the whole working day ahead of her.

The first thing she always did was to check her emails. She replied to anything urgent right away and kept the rest to be done in batches over the day. One of the morning's emails immediately caught her attention. It was from Frank, her police contact in Stockholm. She opened it and noted with disappointment that he was only acknowledging receipt and said he'd do what he could. Erica knew it had been vain to hope for more than this early on, especially since she'd only been able to give him very scant details. But still . . . There was always that hope.

She pulled up the booking with SJ and double-checked the departure time from Dingle. Thank goodness Kristina could pick up the kids that afternoon.

The departure time was fine, she noted. She had plenty of time. She also double-checked the hotel booking to make sure she'd entered the right date. As always, she'd gone with the Haymarket – it was so central.

There was a rattle at the mailbox outside. The post had arrived early today, she thought to herself as she descended the stairs to retrieve it. After concluding there was nothing important – just junk mail and a bill – she pulled her mobile from her pocket and checked the news. Rolf's death was dominating the headlines, but there was also a mention of the police press conference at eleven o'clock. She clicked on some of the headlines and read the tributes offered by friends and colleagues of Rolf Stenklo. Erica realized that she had probably never grasped how big he was in his field – photography had never really been her thing. Blanche was also mentioned in passing – but only that Rolf had been one of the founders.

She sent a text to Louise to thank her for her most recent visit and to ask how Vivian was doing. She hoped that poor woman was being cared for by her friends out on the island.

Erica opened the fridge but then closed it again. Her trousers were rather tighter these days, and she'd read that periodic fasting was the new way of losing weight. WeightWatchers didn't seem to work for her anymore. She'd been doing pretty well with her points in recent weeks, but the pounds kept piling on. Bloody hormones. It was one thing after another for women. Men had no idea just how good they had it.

She pulled out the natural remedy she'd been given by Kristina and gulped down two tablets with some water.

Then she checked her phone – still no reply from Louise. Strange. She was usually quick to reply, but was doubtless busy with work. The media were probably in hot pursuit of Henning. Erica stuffed the mobile back into her pocket and headed for the stairs. She could work for another hour, and then she needed to catch her train.

* * *

Elisabeth set down the manuscript on the small table by the armchair in the living room. There was no doubt about it: it had potential. But the author would have to go over it a few more times.

When Henning came in, Elisabeth put a finger to her lips and pointed to the sofa where Louise was lying.

'Is she still asleep?' he whispered.

'Leave her be. She worked around the clock to organize the party – she's probably exhausted.'

'Is everyone else asleep too? It's almost nine – I've no idea how people can sleep away the day like that.'

Elisabeth peered at him over her reading glasses.

'Not everyone is an early rising pensioner, like we are. But Vivian was up and had some breakfast a while ago, although she's gone back to hers.'

'What do you think?'

'About what?'

'Yesterday's conversation. Do you think everyone understands the gravity?'

Elisabeth took off her reading glasses and put them on top of the manuscript.

'Do they have any choice?'

'Not as I see it. We're all in the same boat. But you can't underestimate people's stupidity. Or vanity.'

'True.' She looked at Henning intently. 'I'm not going to let anyone take what we've worked so hard for away from us.'

Her husband came over to her and put his hand against her cheek. Henning's hand. The hand of the man she had loved for more than fifty years. It was true that love could move mountains. Her love had – in sickness and in health. That was what she had promised him – before God and this parish. She wasn't particularly religious, but she had always believed in love as a divine power. That power was theirs. It always had been. And always would be.

'We can do anything. Can't we?' Henning said softly, caressing her cheek.

She placed her hand on top of his. Her heart swelled at the warmth of his touch.

'Anything, Henning. We can do anything.'

There was the sound of movement from the sofa behind Henning. Louise stretched, yawned and looked around herself in confusion.

'Why am I lying here?' she said in a husky voice.

'You were so sound asleep here yesterday that we couldn't bring ourselves to wake you. Anyway, you've got the boys in your bed.'

Henning settled down in one of the armchairs and unfolded the newspaper from the day before, which they had bought in Fjällbacka.

Louise slowly sat up. She shook herself sleepily.

'Yes, that was probably sensible. What time is it? Is everyone up?'

'It's just gone nine,' said Elisabeth, heading for the kitchen. 'Vivian was up a while ago, but we haven't seen anyone else yet. It seems Peter and the boys are having a lie-in.'

'They don't usually sleep this long,' said Louise, getting up. 'I'll go and kick some life into them.'

'Tell them there's breakfast. I've promised the boys they can have their favourite cereal.'

'That's not cereal – it's sweets in cereal form,' Henning muttered.

'On that we are agreed, but I'll have to let it slide today,' Louise said with a chuckle, neatly folding up the blanket and hanging it over the back of the sofa.

She made for the front door and a few seconds later they were able to follow her progress across the rocks towards the house she and Peter used. The storm had died down and the only trace of it was the driftwood

143

that had floated up to the rocks and was now bobbing in the water.

Elisabeth sat down in the armchair again with her hands clasped around a hot cup of tea. The boys would be so happy when they saw their bowls of sweet cereal. It wasn't often they got to eat it. After all, Henning was right. They might as well eat sugar straight out of the bag for breakfast. But it was a grandmother's privilege to spoil her grandchildren and ignore principle.

The cottage door opened. Louise emerged. Elisabeth squinted out of the window. She couldn't see the boys anywhere. Or Peter. But then again, they probably needed to get dressed first.

Something about Louise's movements made Elisabeth stiffen. Her daughter-in-law appeared to be moving in slow motion. Her arms were no longer wrapped tightly around her body against the cold – they were hanging limply by her sides, moving clumsily as she stumbled forward.

'Henning,' Elisabeth said, standing up. 'Come here.'

'What? What is it?'

Henning put the newspaper to one side and got up laboriously from the armchair. It always took a while for his joints to warm up in the mornings.

'Something's the matter with Louise.'

Elisabeth walked closer to the window and gestured to Henning that he should follow. He stood next to her and they watched the figure outside.

'What? Surely it's not . . .'

Henning abruptly fell silent, and Elisabeth gasped. Louise appeared to have stains on the front of her top. And on her hands.

Louise took another few steps, then stopped and raised her hands towards them. Now they could see the blood covering her. They watched her mouth open. It was as if her gaze was fixed to theirs. Then came the scream. The scream that rose into the grey sky and made the earth quake under their feet.

Patrik had to force himself up from the chair. He trembled at what awaited him; he would never get used to holding press conferences. All those eyes. The waving hands. Journalists interrupting each other with their questions.

He slowly made his way to the kitchen. If he was going to do this then it would take more coffee. Gösta and Annika were by the coffee maker when he entered the small yellow room that became so insanely hot in the summer.

Gösta patted Patrik on the shoulder. He knew how uncomfortable Patrik was ahead of his encounter with the press.

Patrik had no sooner filled his cup than the sound of brisk footsteps made him look up. Mellberg entered the kitchen with such a spring in his step that his hair was bouncing.

'We'll take it in the conference room, right?'

Patrik exchanged a look of surprise with Gösta.

'Do you want to take the press conference?'

'Yes. Why wouldn't I?'

'Well, no. We thought . . .'

Patrik cleared his throat and bit back what he had been about to say. Mellberg truly did move in mysterious ways.

'Well then. Is everyone here?'

Annika nodded.

'They're all here. Do you have all the information you need?'

'Are you saying that I usually don't?' Bertil snorted.

No one replied.

Patrik and Gösta followed hot on Mellberg's heels. It was going to be a squeeze in the conference room, but they didn't have anywhere better. The police station was small and badly designed.

145

He noted with surprise that in addition to the local press, there was a strong turnout from the national media. There were representatives of *Expressen*, TV4, *Aftonbladet* and SVT squashed into the small room. Journalists began firing questions at them immediately, but Patrik held up a placatory hand, which surprisingly transformed the hubbub into silence.

'Detective Chief Inspector Bertil Mellberg – officer in charge of Tanumshede police station.'

Patrik steeled himself and didn't dare look. He stood close by Gösta and whispered from the corner of his mouth:

'Has he even been briefed?'

'Unclear,' Gösta replied glumly. 'We'll soon find out.'

One of the journalists at the back of the room raised their hand. It was a well-known face – Kjell from *Bohusläningen*.

'Could you start by summarizing where the investigation is at right now? For instance, do you have any persons of interest?'

Mellberg solemnly cleared his throat and pompously straightened his back. His hair fell across the side of his face, but he quickly adjusted it with an automatic movement.

'As I'm sure you understand, I can't go into any details about our investigation. What we know so far is this: we can confirm Rolf Stenklo was found dead in the gallery on Galärbacken. He was last seen alive on Saturday evening and the body was discovered yesterday morning. We therefore believe he was killed sometime during the night between Saturday and Sunday.'

'Was he shot?' asked *Expressen*'s reporter. 'We've heard he was.'

Mellberg paused for effect. Patrik held his breath. Mellberg at a press conference was always like watching a car crash in slow motion.

'At this stage, we can't provide any details whatsoever about how he died. That's something that we need to keep to ourselves due to the nature of the investigation. The forensic autopsy and subsequent reporting have not yet been completed, which makes it too early to confirm a cause of death.'

Patrik exhaled. Mellberg was surprisingly and unusually alert – especially given his absence the day before. On the other hand, Patrik wasn't surprised that the rumour mill was already up and running. It seemed to be human nature to immediately begin speculating whenever there was a murder.

Aftonbladet's reporter waved his hand feverishly. Patrik recognized the young man from his byline photo.

'Is there any possible connection between the murder and Rolf's co-ownership of Blanche? There have been some strange rumours about the club of late.'

Mellberg looked at the journalist in confusion. It was obvious he didn't have the foggiest what the man was talking about. Patrik swore silently. He leaned towards Gösta to whisper, but stopped himself when he spotted Annika in the doorway. She took a step into the room, gripped Gösta's arm and pulled him out into the corridor, while waving to Patrik that he should follow. Martin and Paula were already waiting for them – they'd chosen not to listen in to the press conference. Judging by their expressions, something terrible had happened.

'We have to stop the press conference,' said Annika. Her face was flushed.

Patrik felt as if he had been gut-punched – there wasn't much that could knock Annika off-kilter.

'The cars are ready. We have to go right away,' Martin said gravely. Then he took a deep breath. 'Something's happened on Skjälerö.'

Martin told them what they knew and Patrik's mouth went dry with horror.

147

'Get the engines running. I'll interrupt the press conference and be there in a second.'

His legs shaky, he went into the cramped room, whispered into Mellberg's ear and then said in a voice that he was unable to keep steady:

'I'm afraid we have to stop. We've just received an alert that requires our immediate presence.'

A buzz spread around the room. All the journalists craned their necks with intense interest. There would be chaos at the police station, but that couldn't be helped. The whole force needed to go to Skjälerö. There, a nightmare awaited them.

12

STOCKHOLM 1980

Lola loved them. They were a motley crowd. They were loud, rowdy, unruly, intelligent, unreasonable, reasonable, broad-minded and narrow-minded. They'd been hanging out ever since that time Rolf had brought them along to Alexa's. On the very first night, they'd ended up back in her kitchen after closing time and since then it had become their gathering place.

'Do you seriously think Ted Hughes was the cause of Sylvia Plath's suicide? Isn't that rather over-egging his role and significance? Sylvia would never have allowed a man to have such a bearing on an important choice.'

Elisabeth's gaze was ablaze with strong emotion and conviction.

Lola could see that her eyes were shiny from one too many drinks, but that was when Elisabeth was at her best – when she discarded the heavy burden of her family name and became a wild unruly intellectual.

Ole made a dismissive gesture and took another swig from his beer bottle. Lola knew he loved provoking Elisabeth and that it was impossible to tell whether the views he advanced were truly his own or merely ones being used to add fuel to Elisabeth's fire.

'It's an established fact that Ted Hughes caused her suicide. They saw each other a couple of days before her death, and his influence was so significant that on that occasion she asked him to leave the country, because she had such difficulty writing while he was in the same country.'

'We only have his word for that,' Elisabeth replied, tossing back the blond hair that was always hanging loosely across her face. 'Men have always wanted to emphasize their own importance at women's expense.'

'I'd say it was the other way around,' Ole said in a drawl.

Henning raised his eyebrows at them in amusement. This was an eternal and ongoing spectacle and a source of great entertainment to them all. The angrier Elisabeth got, the more interesting it became.

'How many women in history haven't got a free ride from their husbands? Especially in literary circles. Sylvia Plath was no exception. First Richard Sassoon, then Ted Hughes. I find it hard to believe that she hooked up with famous male literary figures by pure chance when she wanted her own success in the same field. And she herself attacks women in *The Colossus*.'

'And men in *Ariel*,' said Elisabeth, who was now red with anger.

'I'm on Elisabeth's side here,' said Ester in her soft voice. 'What's more, Ted Hughes tried to manipulate the narrative about Sylvia's life after her death. If that isn't autocratic, I don't know what is.'

'Exactly! Exactly!' Elisabeth said vehemently.

Henning placed a hand on her shoulder.

'Calm down, darling – we're discussing literature. Not life and death.'

Elisabeth turned her gaze to him and jutted her chin forward angrily.

'Literature *is* life and death. People come and go. We live. We die. But the literature we create lives on.'

'Elisabeth has a point.' Susanne settled down on Ole's lap.

Lola had always thought Susanne was the spitting image of Ali MacGraw in *Love Story*, with those soulful eyes and her long straight dark hair parted in the middle. Her hair wasn't very modern, given that hair was meant to be big right now – fluffy and permed – but beauty like Susanne's was untouched by time and fashion.

Rolf was quietly contemplating Lola and now he nodded to her in encouragement.

'What do you say? You usually give the sharpest critique of all of us. Why so silent?'

Lola smiled at him. He knew her so well. She hesitated, then she said in her soft voice:

'Because I think you're both right. And both wrong. Ted and Sylvia. Man and woman. Thus we quickly reduce them to something far smaller than they were. People. Authors. Tormented souls.

'I believe that creativity and love are the words we should seek our guidance from – not man or woman. It was creativity and love that were the defining features of their relationship as well as their creations. For better or worse. With creativity comes destructiveness. With love comes hate.'

'Words of wisdom as a worthy conclusion to the night,' said Henning, standing up. 'The literature we create will hopefully outlive us. And it's that realization that makes you such a brilliant publisher, Elisabeth. That being said, we have to break the party up now. We have a book launch tomorrow.'

'Bloody hell, that's right! Congratulations!' Rolf exclaimed, raising his glass.

The others followed his example. They solemnly clinked

their glasses against Susanne's. Rolf's photographs were already internationally recognized, Henning had long been regarded as a promising author, and now Susanne was releasing yet another novel.

'What did you end up with as your title?' said Ester curiously. 'I heard you were struggling.'

'In the end we picked *Shadow Side*,' said Elisabeth.

The discussion of Plath versus Hughes was forgotten and her eyes shone with joy.

'I think it's your best to date, Susanne,' she added. 'By several furlongs.'

'So you don't think the others were any good?' said Susanne teasingly, although there was no sting in her question.

'They've been brilliant. But this one . . . it has something extra. You've created your own literary landscape, you've claimed your own territory with your very own language. Few publishers have the privilege to watch from close quarters while that kind of magic takes place.'

'Well, you've done more than watch, Elisabeth. *You* are brilliant.'

'Brilliant, brilliant, brilliant! Let's break up this mutual admiration club,' Henning said, chuckling. 'Because Susanne is right. Tomorrow is launch day. Anyway, Lola probably wants to get shot of us. She's got a young child to deal with.'

'So have we,' Elisabeth protested glumly, pointing to her wine glass which had just been refilled by Ole.

'Yes, but we've got a nanny, my dear. Lola doesn't.'

Amid clatter and laughter, the party broke up and they blew kisses to Lola before departing, leaving her with a chaos of glasses, bottles and cigarette butts in the kitchen. But she didn't mind. She was more than happy to tidy up, and always made sure she did so before going to bed, so that P'tite wouldn't see the mess in the morning.

Once it was all put away, she went into the bedroom.

P'tite had settled down well as usual. She was sleeping peacefully on the left-hand side of the bed with a tatty giraffe in her arms. She'd had it since she was a baby and refused to sleep without it. Lola carefully undressed, hanging up her clothes and putting on her nightie before sitting on the edge of the bed. She opened the drawer of her bedside table as quietly as she could. It squeaked slightly, but P'tite only stirred in her sleep without waking.

The blue notebook was at the back of the drawer behind the red velvet box. She kept the full notebooks in the wardrobe, but she liked to keep the current one close. She took it out, picked up the pen on the bedside table and plumped up a pillow to lean against. A smile still on her lips from the evening, she began to write. The words came easily, as they always did when she was happy. And right now she was – something she had thought would never be possible earlier in her life.

13

There was something about travelling by train that was so completely relaxing. Not that Erica fell asleep. She wasn't one of those people who slept on trains, planes or the like – though Patrik usually nodded off before they had even departed. But she revelled in being conveyed safely towards a destination while she binge-watched episodes of one of her favourite shows – the more light-hearted the better. Right now she was addicted to *The Real Housewives of Beverly Hills*. It was bliss to be able to watch undisturbed without Patrik whining about how pointless it was to watch a bunch of women bitching at each other.

The landscape slid by outside. She saw traces of the storm from the night before beside the line. Trees had been toppled all over the place. She realized she'd been lucky not to hit delays caused by the bad weather. On the other hand, she hadn't got there yet and she was loath to jinx things. Travelling with SJ and *not* encountering a delay was about as likely as winning the lottery jackpot these days.

The nausea had slowly begun to make itself known. This was in spite of the fact that she'd taken care to book a seat in the direction of travel. She got travel sick easily but this time it had come on quicker than usual – and she'd started sweating. Bloody hormones. Maybe she ought to get some tests done while she was in Stockholm. The quicker she got to the bottom of it, the sooner she could look into what she could do herself about it. She'd read in a magazine about patches, and about some gel that could be applied to the inside of the thighs.

She'd bet anything that this was yet another situation in which yoga or meditation would be recommended. These were two things she had tried a few times but most definitely lacked the patience for. After five minutes' meditation, her brain had managed to rattle off the order of succession to the British throne, all of Elizabeth Taylor's husbands, and every pasta shape in the Barilla range. It hadn't exactly been mindfulness.

She'd heard about women who had their wombs removed to avoid all the hassle, but that seemed like overkill. She had a tough enough time getting her hair trimmed. She'd rather have a cream to slather on, pills to pop or a patch to stick on.

A voice on the tannoy announced that they were approaching Gothenburg and that passengers should change there for Stockholm. Erica stowed her iPad in her rucksack. Kyle, Lisa and Denise would have to pause their argument until she had changed trains.

Once she had stepped onto the platform, she pulled out her phone. Still no response from Louise. The silence was now becoming unsettling. But there wasn't much more she could do, other than wait. She pulled up her list of recent calls and tapped on Patrik's name. It kept on ringing, but there was no answer. She checked her watch. The press conference ought to be over by this stage. She sent him a hasty text.

Changing trains in Gothenburg. Call when you can. Love you. Xxx.

The lifeboat was making for the island at top speed. Paramedics were already on the scene. Farideh Mirza and her forensics team would take the next boat – they had to drive in from Uddevalla and hadn't reached Fjällbacka yet.

Gösta gazed across the grey water, his expression not even flickering as spray splashed his face. His stomach was a tight knot of anxiety in anticipation of what they were going to have to encounter. They'd received a report by phone, but the account had been incoherent and messy. The most important part – the worst part – had got through though.

'I feel sick,' said Martin.

Gösta jumped. He hadn't heard his colleague approaching him over the rushing sound of the boat carving its way through the water.

'Me too.'

Neither of them was referring to seasickness.

'I just spoke to the captain. The forensics team have arrived in the harbour and will get there about fifteen minutes after we do.'

'Good. That makes our most important task to preserve the crime scene. And to start taking witness statements.'

'Patrik said the same thing.'

They fell silent and stared out across the water. The day after a storm, the air felt clean and fresh and the sea was calm, as if it were pretending there had never been any high waves at all. The islands they passed were deserted. The hordes of tourists were long gone. There was no one lying on the rocks with their picnics and beer. No boats in the inlets with their anchor chain lowered over the stern. The people on the islands now were the handful of permanent residents. People who were tough enough to withstand an environment that could be beautiful and welcoming, but also brutal and dismissive.

156

The odd fishing boat passed them by, and they raised their hands in response to greetings from them.

'Has lobster season started?' Martin asked.

The question passed through the air between them, banal and flimsy. But Gösta gratefully accepted the chance to briefly talk about trivial everyday matters.

'Yes, it has. Has been for a few weeks,' he said.

'Do you fish?'

'I used to. Had a bunch of my own pots. But in the end, it wasn't worth the hassle. People pinch the lobsters from the pots, don't they? It just winds up being a waste of bait.'

'Bloody hell, that's the worst. No one has any sense of decency these days. Not even when it comes to lobster fishing.'

'I do occasionally head out with my brother to fish mackerel on hand lines.'

They both knew they were keeping up conversation to avoid thinking about what awaited them.

Soon they saw Skjälerö directly ahead of them. The boat quickly approached its destination and Gösta realized that he was grasping the rail so tightly that his knuckles were white.

'So it's time,' he said.

'Yes,' said Martin. 'It's time.'

Patrik was careful where he put his feet on the rocks. He knew how treacherous they could be. Someone yelled at them, and he looked up.

Henning Bauer was coming towards them, and Patrik gasped when he saw him. He was a shadow of the man Patrik had spoken to the day before. His face was deathly pale, and his teeth were chattering, making him stutter when he reached them.

'Louise . . . she found them . . .'

Henning flinched and let out a cry when Patrik touched him. Patrik quickly backed away. Then Henning pulled himself together, realizing who he was dealing with, and allowed Patrik to place a calming hand on his arm. Paramedics were already there, and he had been notified that there were three dead who could not be saved. It was now of the utmost importance that all investigative work be dealt with in an exemplary manner characterized by calm and rationality, even if what he wanted more than anything was to turn on his heel and not see what awaited them.

Through the big picture windows on the main house he could see Elisabeth. She was standing still as a statue, her arms hugging herself for protection.

'The second room on the left, straight off the hall.'

With a hand shaking from a storm of emotions, Henning pointed to the cottage on the left.

'Go back to the others,' said Patrik. 'We'll take over.'

He squeezed Henning's shoulder and gestured to his colleagues that they should follow. Once they were out of earshot of Henning, he reminded the officers with him of what they knew:

'According to the information we've received from the paramedics, we're dealing with three dead. Remember to be cautious in all you do now, as we're probably looking at a crime scene.'

They nodded grimly and hurried towards the house.

There was a doormat by the front door emblazoned with 'Welcome'. The commonplace nature of it seemed grotesque, and Patrik stepped across it without treading on the message. He pulled down the sleeve of his coat and opened the door using the material as a glove. It was important not to leave his own fingerprints behind at this stage; that would only impede the investigation.

He propped open the door and let the others in, but

signalled to Martin, Gösta and Bertil to stay in the hall with him. They stood there for a few seconds, breathing heavily. The paramedics emerged, their faces stiff masks, and hurried past them out of a house that had been transformed into a scene from hell.

Patrik could feel the knot in his stomach tighten. He pictured Maja, Noel and Anton in his mind's eye. Erica's little niece Fliss. Then he forced the images out of his head. He couldn't mix up his personal and private lives. Not now – not like this.

He exchanged glances with the others, and they carefully approached the bedroom the paramedics had just left. They stopped in the doorway. Patrik inhaled sharply and audibly when he caught sight of the bloody beds. Bile rose in his throat and once again his thoughts were drawn to Maja, Noel and Anton. It was impossible to prevent these visions – he would never forget what he was now seeing before him.

Out of the corner of his eye, he saw Martin press his hand to his mouth before clutching Patrik's arm tightly.

'I can't handle this. I've got to get out.'

Patrik nodded and Martin rushed off. Patrik also wanted to leave. He wanted to run until he could go no further – he wanted to cross the water, cross the islands. He wanted to run until he could no longer see what was now before him – but it was too late. The sight would be etched into his mind's eye for all eternity. And as he stood there, frozen to the spot, something crumbled within him.

It was mid-afternoon when Erica reached Stockholm. The nausea had lingered throughout the journey, and she stopped on the platform breathing deeply before setting off. She made the mistake of taking the lift up to the bridge. The smell of urine – poorly concealed with vanilla-scented cleaning solution – made the nausea well up again, and she hurled herself out of the lift as quickly as she could when she reached the upper level.

A row of taxis was standing outside the entrance and Erica took care to get into one from one of the main companies. Once she'd given the name of her hotel, she checked her phone again. Still nothing from either Patrik or Louise. She shook her head but decided to let it go. Instead she called Kristina to check that picking the kids up had gone well. It had been a dream, according to her mother-in-law, and now they were on their way to the supermarket where Kristina was probably going to buy them something unnecessary. Erica had long ago given up that battle, and since the kids didn't have a maternal grandmother, she let Kristina have a slightly longer leash. Both of Erica's parents had died in a car accident before the kids had been born, and Patrik's father was pleasant enough but not much of a presence in the kids' lives, so Kristina had many shoes to fill.

The taxi stopped and Erica realized to her embarrassment that she had forgotten just how close the hotel was. She tipped the driver extra by way of compensation for the over-short journey.

Greta Garbo welcomed her from a large photograph in the foyer, and Erica was struck as always by how well they had succeeded in transforming the old department store into an Art Deco-style hotel showcasing the movie stars of the Golden Age. Patrik preferred more modern hotels with lots of glass and gleaming gold, so she always made sure she picked according to her own taste when travelling solo.

Once she had checked into the room, Erica sat down on the bed and went over what she needed to get done during her sojourn. She had booked a train home in two days' time – not wanting to impose on Kristina's babysitting for any longer – so she would have to be efficient and make the most of her time.

She texted Frank to find out how he was getting on with digging up the old investigation about Lola and got a reply right away. He'd found something, so they agreed to meet for a coffee in the bar of the Haymarket at five. Erica smiled. Now she was cooking with gas. She knew from writing her past books that the preliminary investigative report was the very best place to begin. That would provide her with the basic details she required. Threads to follow. Names to unravel. Facts to get her teeth into. This was the phase she loved most in the process of creating a new book. She loved writing too, but using facts to build a picture of the course of events and the people involved was what fascinated her the most.

Erica walked over to the window. Outside in the square in front of the Concert Hall commerce was in full swing. When she had lived in Stockholm, she had loved going to the flea markets there at the weekend, but during the week it was mostly flowers, fruit and vegetables – as well as an array of knick-knacks.

She went back to the bed. She had another appointment to make. Rolf was the connection to Lola, but he also had connections to Blanche, and Vivian had hinted that there were secrets there.

Erica opened her computer and pulled up Blanche's website. It was pared back, indicating its elite power while offering very little information. 'If you know, you know,' seemed to be the motto. But when she spotted the event scheduled for that evening in the calendar that they nonetheless provided, Erica couldn't help but smile. She wouldn't need to check with her publisher. She had found a way into Blanche.

'So, what's going on? Why was the press conference interrupted so suddenly?'

Paula jumped when a man in his thirties appeared

161

in the doorway to her office. She recognized him as one of the journalists but couldn't place which paper he was with.

'Markus Reberg, *Aftonbladet*.'

Paula placed a magazine over the papers she had been looking at and turned off her monitor just to be on the safe side.

'I've got no comment to make. And I thought you'd all been asked to vacate the building?'

Her sharp tone didn't seem to bother him.

'I was in the loo – must have missed that.'

'Well, now you know too.'

Paula glowered at Markus Reberg as angrily as she could. The tabloids were not favourites of hers, and she was already in a bad mood. As if things weren't bad enough with her mother's terrible cancer diagnosis, Mellberg had ordered her to remain at the station while the rest of the team went to Skjälerö. She had been at Tanumshede police station for several years now – how much longer was she going to be the newbie? Paula had told everyone else to take it easy on Mellberg, but personally she wanted to . . . She didn't know what she wanted – all she knew was that she didn't want it to be like this.

'Well now that I'm here anyway, why don't I ask you some questions?'

'I just told you that I've got nothing to say.'

She was surprised at how annoyed she sounded.

'Does it have anything to do with the murder of Rolf Stenklo?'

Markus Reberg remained stubbornly rooted to the spot and Paula sighed. Getting rid of hacks was like trying to shake off a piece of toilet paper stuck to your shoe.

'I've got nothing to say.'

He ignored her and entered the office, sitting down on the chair in front of her desk. Paula was on the verge of calling Annika – she would grab him by the ear and drag him out of the place if that was what it took. But Annika was a powerful weapon best kept for special occasions.

'I may have information of use to you. It's about Rolf Stenklo and his association with club Blanche,' the journalist said.

'Oh?'

Paula endeavoured not to lean forward, but he definitely had her attention now.

'Our newspaper has been looking into what is going on at Blanche for a long time. We'll be ready to publish soon. We're sitting on a lot of information that might be of importance to your investigation.'

'And I dare say you're envisioning some sort of swap? Or are you proposing to do the right thing out of sheer decency, by sharing relevant information with a murder inquiry?'

Markus Reberg extended his arms. 'You and I both know that's not how the world works.'

'I think you and I probably have very different perspectives on the world,' Paula said curtly.

'That doesn't mean we can't cooperate.'

Paula leaned back in her chair. She couldn't deny that it was tempting. One of the things they had given a high priority in the Rolf Stenklo investigation was finding out more about Blanche. Here was an opportunity to take a shortcut. Part of her quietly noted that sometimes the ends justified the means. Yet she had very little to offer in exchange if she was perfectly honest. Except . . . She was still hesitant. Then she took a deep breath.

'Do you have a summary of the material?'

Markus Reberg gave a thumbs up. She could tell from his face that he knew he had reeled her in.

'We've got a working draft of the full series of articles for the feature. We're just waiting to confirm certain sources.'

'And can I have access to the full draft?'

'If what you give me is good enough then yes, you can have the full draft. But I'll only make that decision once I hear what you can give me.'

Paula looked at the dark screen. They had so little to go on. And it wouldn't be easy for them to find out information about a business in Stockholm. She made up her mind.

'We don't know whether the alert that came in has anything to do with Rolf Stenklo,' she said, 'but I would say the probability that it does is high. The alert was to notify us of a murder on Skjälerö.'

'Skjälerö? Henning Bauer's island?'

Paula nodded. Markus Reberg let it sink in – then he stood up.

'I'll email the draft over right away.'

'Thanks. And this stays between us?'

Paula couldn't look him in the eye.

'Well, journalistic sources are protected by law, so yes.'

Markus Reberg grinned before hurrying away. Paula leaned back in her chair. She felt dirty and she already regretted her decision.

14

STOCKHOLM 1980

P'tite didn't really mind that she didn't have lots of friends. One was enough. Daddy said she'd make more friends when she started school, but she just wanted Sigge.

'I'm counting!' she crowed from the kitchen.

She heard Sigge giggle. P'tite already knew where he would be hiding. He always hid in the same place. In the big trunk where Daddy kept summer clothes in winter and winter clothes in summer. Right now it was empty and the best place in the flat to hide.

'Here I come!'

She hooted loudly so that he would hear her through the thick wood of the trunk. She had sat inside it with the lid closed and knew it muffled all sounds from outside. She crept dramatically around the small flat.

'Where are youuuu, Sigge? Where are youuuu, Sigge?'

He opened the lid a crack and peered at her, but she pretended not to have seen. Hide and seek had many unwritten rules and she and Sigge followed them closely. That was why it was so much fun. She checked behind the curtains, looked under the sofa, opened the door to the pantry. And when she could no longer hold out, she threw herself onto the sofa and kicked the cushion with her heels.

'Nope. No Sigge here! He must have gone home!' she said as loudly as she could, using exactly the same voice as that lady at the park. She and Sigge had been sneaking around in the bushes and had heard her and the children. Daddy said it was a playgroup. P'tite couldn't understand what the point of that was – you could play on your own.

'Squeeeak,' said the box, and P'tite leapt up from the sofa.

'What was that? Was it a mouse? Or have we got rats here?'

'Squeeeak!'

'Oh my, that sounds like a big rat! I wonder where it could be! It almost sounds as if it's stuck in the big . . . TRUNK!'

P'tite threw open the lid of the trunk and saw Sigge's eyes shining with laughter. She helped him out.

'Imagine if I'd thought you were a real rat and got the mousetrap.'

'Did I sound like a real rat?' Sigge asked happily.

'You sounded like a really big and scary rat,' P'tite affirmed, taking him by the hand. 'Do you want to play mums and dads and kids?'

She pulled him towards Daddy's bedroom and opened the wardrobe door. Sigge looked hesitant.

'Hmm. I don't think it's very . . .'

'No, come on!'

P'tite knew that with a little persuasion, Sigge agreed to most things she suggested, and she loved playing mums and dads and kids.

'I'll be the mum and you be the dad,' she said, giving him one of Daddy's necklaces. It was one of her favourites. Daddy said it was from Finland and made of bronze.

'Okay,' Sigge said submissively, hanging it around his neck.

The round disc with patterns on it bounced on his belly, so he tucked it into his trousers.

P'tite looked through Daddy's clothes. What else could Sigge wear? She wasn't really sure whether she was allowed to play with Daddy's stuff, but she was always careful to put everything back where she found it and as yet Daddy hadn't said anything.

Anyway, Daddy was off seeing that man today so she only had herself to blame. Well, not that Daddy had told P'tite that, but she'd heard them on the phone.

'Here, wear this skirt,' said P'tite, pulling out a frilly skirt that rustled when Daddy wore it. She liked the colour too. It was almost the same as her Barbie rucksack.

The skirt didn't rustle on Sigge, so she put a belt on him to hold it up, although it still reached down to his feet.

'You're soooo beautiful, Dad.'

'What about you? What are you going to wear?' said Sigge.

In the beginning, he'd thought it was strange that her dad wore a dress, but now he knew that P'tite's dad looked like a mum and that was that.

'I'm going to wear this,' said P'tite, taking a floral dress off a hanger. 'It was my Mummy's before she died.'

She pulled on the dress. It was much too big, so she tucked a lot of it in under the belt at her waist to avoid tripping.

'My mum's dead too,' said Sigge, adjusting the necklace so that it didn't catch in his belt.

'No,' P'tite said. 'Your mum's not dead. She's a whore.'

She reached for a bright red lipstick and began to painstakingly apply it to Sigge's lips.

'How do you know that?' he said, wriggling so that the lipstick missed its mark.

'I heard your grandmother say so. She said your mum's a whore and beyond all salvation.'

'What does whore mean?' Sigge said thoughtfully.

P'tite carefully wiped the stray lipstick off him with a finger.

'I don't know. But it must be better than being dead. Like my mum.'

'Yeah, I suppose so.'

Sigge sounded hesitant but cheered up again when P'tite spun him around so that he could see himself in the big mirror.

'I don't look like a dad. I look like a clown.'

They exploded with laughter. P'tite took a step back and looked at him.

'You do, actually. You look like a clown. A dad clown!'

They laughed so hard they cried. P'tite put her arms around him and hugged him. The disc of the necklace was hard and cold between them and she moved it out of the way. She didn't need any other friends. She loved Sigge. And she wished that her mum was a whore instead of being dead.

15

'I don't want a sedative!' a woman shouted as Martin, Gösta and Patrik entered through the front door.

Martin tried to shake off the feeling of being an intruder. It was irrational, but grief was lingering in the air like a thick veil and now they were barging in and ripping it to shreds.

Mellberg had chosen to remain outdoors. He'd claimed that someone needed to wait to meet the reinforcements they had requested to come and comb the island, but the truth was probably that they had far too many hours' work ahead of them inside the house.

'But Louise, you'd feel better if you just . . .'

Henning Bauer's voice was insistent and concerned, but Martin saw Louise shake her head firmly as they came into the living room.

'I want to be able to think clearly – we've got to find out what's happened! And I can't trust any of you! We're on an island – the most likely explanation is that it was one of you!'

Her voice rose hysterically towards the ceiling and reverberated around the room.

'Louise! Don't talk like that,' Elisabeth Bauer said sharply.

'Of course it wasn't any of us. Someone must have come from outside in the night by boat.'

Louise didn't reply. She collapsed into an armchair and sobbed.

Elisabeth leaned over her.

'Why don't you have a little lie down?'

The only indication that she had just learned that her son and grandsons had been found dead were the red rims around her eyes and a few twitches at the corners of her mouth.

'We're sorry to intrude on your grief,' said Patrik. 'But we're going to need to talk to each and every one of you.'

'Now?' Henning said, his expression full of dismay. 'You need to talk to us now? Can't it wait? We've just lost . . .'

The older man couldn't bear to continue and merely waved his hand in the air. Gösta shifted anxiously at Martin's side.

The two paramedics looked at the officers questioningly.

'It seems you're not needed anymore,' said Patrik. 'Make sure you provide prints for your shoes so we can rule you out, but then you're free to go.'

They nodded and left. Patrik coughed gently. 'As I said, we need to start taking your witness statements.'

'I'll go first.' Louise wiped her nose and sat up straight in the armchair.

Elisabeth leaned in closer to her again, but received a sharp look in response from her daughter-in-law.

'I was going to suggest that,' said Patrik. 'But I think we should split up. Louise, can we find somewhere to talk in private? Elisabeth, you can talk to Gösta, and Henning, you can talk to Martin here.'

'Of course,' said Henning.

The room fell silent and Martin looked around. Everyone seemed to be in varying states of shock. Ole and Susanne were sitting closely entwined on a sofa, Vivian was staring into the fire from an armchair, and Rickard and Tilde were simply standing in a corner of the room.

Martin felt the nausea coming in waves. He would never be the same again. He wanted to go home and hug Tuva and Mette and her belly – hug them tight and never let them out of his sight again. But he had a job to do. He and his colleagues had many hours of interviews ahead of them, with people who might be in mourning or might be killers.

He couldn't help but agree with Louise. The most logical conclusion was that one of the people in front of him had brutally shot dead a father and his two boys. Two little children.

None of them looked like a murderer. Everyone seemed completely devastated by grief. But if there was one thing that Martin had learned in his years as a police officer, it was that evil was never easy to recognize.

'First Rolf. Then Peter and the boys. It can't be a coincidence.'

Vivian's voice by the fireplace made everyone turn towards her. Elisabeth opened her mouth to say something. Then she closed it again.

Outside there was the sound of a helicopter. Martin peered out of the window and up towards the sky. Damn it. The press had arrived. How on earth had they caught wind of this so fast?

'Tell me in your own words: what happened?'

Patrik spoke calmly and clearly. They were sitting in Henning's study, on the only couch. Louise's eyes were wild and her hands were shaking, as if she was forcing herself to keep it together. The effort involved had to be superhuman.

'I . . . We were up late – there was a lot of wine and I ended up falling asleep on the sofa. Elisabeth and Henning left me sleeping there and tucked me in. It would have been a squash in bed with . . .' Her voice stumbled, but then she regained her thread. '. . . the boys there.'

She stared at Patrik.

'Everyone must have assumed that I was sleeping in our room last night. That means that I must have been meant to die too.'

'We can't draw any conclusions at this stage,' said Patrik.

He tried to ignore the sound of the helicopter outside. He couldn't understand how the media had found out so quickly. Someone must have tipped them off – it was the only explanation. So far there was just one helicopter, but it would probably be followed by more. And by boats. The place was going to turn into a full-blown circus.

He gritted his teeth. Bloody hyenas. Although given the helicopter above, perhaps a better comparison was vultures circling their prey.

'But isn't it likely?' said Louise.

She took a blanket from the armrest and wrapped it around herself. The older woman that Patrik assumed to be the housekeeper had discreetly brought in a tea tray. Neither he nor Louise had touched it.

'I can't speculate on that, Louise. But please do go on. You fell asleep on the sofa?'

'Yes. I woke up pretty late in the morning. Unusual for me – I'm an early riser. Well, you know that . . .'

Patrik forced a smile.

'Yes, I do – Erica is always muttering about it.'

'But like I said, it was late, there had been a lot of wine and there was a lot of tension – first the party and then Rolf's death. I guess I was all in and my body needed to sleep.'

172

'What time was it when you woke up?'

The blanket rose and fell as Louise shrugged.

'Ask Henning and Elisabeth – they were up earlier. I can't fathom how they handle their booze so well. I suppose it must be decades of drinking wine.'

Louise smiled slightly, then reality struck and she sobbed.

'It's . . . it's as if my brain won't take it in.'

Patrik placed a hand on her arm, patting it through the blanket.

'We'll try to get through this as quickly as possible, and then you can rest. Did you go straight to your cottage? As soon as you woke up?'

'Yes, I thought it was strange that Peter and . . . the kids weren't up. Max can sleep, but William wakes up . . .' Her voice faltered. '. . . always woke up early. So I went over to the cottage to wake them.'

'Did you meet anyone on the way? Was there anyone other than Henning and Elisabeth awake?'

Louise brushed her fingers under her eyes.

'No . . . Well . . . I heard someone rattling around in the kitchen. That must have been Nancy. But I didn't see or hear anyone else. Rickard and Tilde were sleeping in the kids' room – I passed it – but their door was shut.'

She lost her thread again, began shivering and tugged the blanket closer.

'Then . . . then I saw them. There was so much blood. William's eyes were wide open. I . . . I ran over and shook them, but . . .'

Her head slumped towards her chest. Her body was racked with sobbing.

Patrik waited for a minute or so before saying as gently as he could:

'Do you remember whether you saw a weapon anywhere?'

'No,' Louise said, shaking her head slowly. 'But I don't know, I didn't look for . . .'

She was breathing with increasing intensity and Patrik put his hand on her arm again.

'Let's move on from that. What happened next?'

'I came back to the main house. Henning and Elisabeth saw me through the window and came out to meet me. Then it was just chaos . . . Everyone heard me screaming and came out . . . Chaos . . . Just chaos . . .'

She wrung her hands in her lap and the blanket slipped down. Patrik had a hard time looking at her bloodied top, but he realized it was also evidence.

'I'm going to have to ask you to give us your clothes. I imagine you'd like to get out of them anyway. And please don't wash your hands or shower until we've had time to secure evidence.'

'Evidence?' Louise said in confusion, looking at her hands.

'Among other things, we'll be testing for gunshot residue on your hands – on everyone's hands.'

'I understand.'

'Is there anyone on the island that you know had any kind of grudge against your husband? Something that might have led them to act like this?'

'Grudge?' She shook her head fiercely. 'No one had a grudge against Peter. Everyone loved him. And why would anyone hurt the boys?'

'You said yourself that you might have been a target. So I'll ask the same question about you. Do you know of anyone with a grudge against you?'

She laughed. It was a short, grief-stricken laugh.

'Me? No. I'm not important enough in this family for that.'

'What was Peter's relationship like with his brother? Rickard was in the house when Peter was shot?'

'Rickard and Peter's relationship was okay. Not good. Not bad. It was really Henning that Rickard was in conflict with.'

174

'Yes, I gathered that on Saturday. What's the conflict about?'

'Money.'

'In what way?' Patrik coaxed.

Louise hesitated. She appeared to be torn between loyalty to the Bauer family and her desire to help. Finally, she seemed to make a decision.

'Rickard is a good-for-nothing. Money slips between his fingers. He's always after a quick buck. He's never been interested in working. And Elisabeth always helps him out of his financial straits. Over and over again. She's been providing for him his whole life. And now I suppose she must be providing for Tilde too . . .'

Her voice was terse.

'Why?' asked Patrik.

'What do you mean, why?'

'Well, why does Elisabeth do it?'

Louise was looking increasingly tired and her face had a greyish pallor. Patrik hated this part of the job, but it had to be done. The greatest gift they could give to loved ones was to find answers.

'She's always had a soft spot for Rickard. He's her youngest – her darling. Peter's always been the diligent one. The good child. He's the one who always does the right thing. Well, I mean . . . did . . .'

She was rocking back and forth.

'We'll be done soon. And was the conflict with Henning because Elisabeth was helping him?'

'Yes, I think finally Henning has had enough. He's been muttering for years, but lately he's sounded like he means it. I think Rickard's speech on Saturday was the straw that broke the camel's back. And Rickard knows that.'

'Okay. Thanks. I think that's enough for now. But we'll need to talk more later. I'll make sure you see one of our forensic team, who will secure your clothing and the other things we need. Then you can rest.'

'I won't be able to rest,' Louise said, looking down at her bloodied hands. 'They're dead. How am I supposed to rest?'

Patrik didn't know what to say. In his mind's eye he pictured the boys in their colourful pyjamas. He clenched his fists tightly. He wouldn't be able to rest until he'd found the perpetrators.

'I should have been allowed to come with you right away,' Paula said sourly as she came ashore. 'You need me.'

She'd become increasingly worked up the closer she'd got to Skjälerö and when she caught sight of Gösta she could no longer contain herself.

'You're here now,' said Gösta.

He greeted the reinforcements from Uddevalla, whose number also included patrol dogs and dogs for detecting firearms. While the island was small, they would need some manpower to cover it properly. Above all, they were looking for the weapon. But they were also looking for traces of the killer.

'Do we think it's one of the people on the island?' said Paula, shading her eyes with her hand.

Ethereal sunlight had begun to stream through the clouds, which were slowly dispersing. Above them, the helicopter emblazoned with the logo of a tabloid continued to circle. Markus Reberg had acted quickly, she thought bitterly. Self-contempt made bile rise into her mouth.

'We don't think anything right now,' said Gösta. 'Right now we need to take everyone's witness statements; you're most welcome to help out on that front. Forensics have arrived and are examining the bedroom and then they'll do the rest of the cottage. And we'll need to carve up the islands into sections and search them all thoroughly. We can't assume it's one of the people here – a person or persons unknown might have come by boat in the night.'

Paula agreed with him. She tried not to look up at the helicopter. The regret was like a big knot in her stomach and she still hadn't received any material in her inbox though the reporter had promised to send it right away. If he'd deceived her and she'd sold them down the river for nothing then she didn't know what she'd do.

Gösta nodded towards the dwellings.

'Go into the main house and have a word with Patrik or Martin and find out who's next in line. We've put them in order of priority. I'll get the search underway.'

'Where's Bertil?'

Paula looked around. Mellberg was nowhere to be seen.

'No idea. He's probably found some nook to take a nap in. I guess he realized the moment he got here that it was too much like hard work for his liking. I'm surprised he hasn't already caught a boat back to the station.'

'Like I said, give him some space,' Paula said, and was met with a surprised look.

She immediately regretted saying anything. But they weren't ready yet – none of the family were. They were circling around each other without talking, without mentioning the unmentionable. But she could see the same panic in Bertil's eyes that was in her own, and she forgave him all his shortcomings because of it. There was no doubt how much he loved her mother.

'Is there something I should know?' said Gösta.

Paula held out her hands.

'I just think we should cut him some slack right now.'

Gösta didn't look impressed by the scant explanation, but he let it be.

Paula walked briskly towards the house in the middle. She'd never heard of Skjälerö before. She wasn't a big boat person – she went out on the water perhaps once a year, and she spent most of that time wanting to be ashore. Water was not her element. She couldn't imagine how people were willing to live like this. Isolated, barren and claustrophobic – with a boat the only way to and from the mainland.

She knew that for many this was the big dream. Houses on the islands out in the archipelago around Fjällbacka went for a fortune. Only recently some artist had bought a place for sixteen million kronor. Insane.

She hadn't really known much about the Bauers either. The literary world was not her forte, and she wouldn't have been able to name the winners of the August Prize or the Nobel Prize even if her life had depended on it. She only read on holiday, and then only easy-reading, thrillers and chick lit. Hardly the kinds of things the Bauers would describe as literature.

The sound of the helicopter faded as she entered through the door without knocking. Martin was standing in the hallway talking to Patrik, and both perked up when they saw her.

'Good that you were able to come so quickly,' said Patrik. 'We need help taking witness statements.'

'Did you see the bloody helicopter?' Martin pointed up towards the ceiling in irritation. 'Who tipped them off so fast? We'll soon be invaded. Nothing is sacred.'

Paula stared at the floor. Then she cleared her throat and looked at Patrik.

'Who would you like me to talk to?'

'We've spoken to Louise, Henning and Elisabeth. Nothing tangible so far. I thought I'd take Rickard next. Could you take Tilde, and Martin you can take Vivian? They're in the living room.'

Paula made for the living room that she'd glimpsed from the hallway. Outside, the helicopter continued to buzz overhead.

* * *

The man in front of Patrik looked like he might throw up at any moment. The other rooms were occupied, so he'd suggested they sit in Henning and Elisabeth's bedroom. It felt a little odd to sit on a bed questioning a witness, but they had to take what was available.

'Do you mind if I open the window?'

Rickard's face was a shade of green. The youngest son in the Bauer family was still a little unsteady on his feet as he stood up to do so. Then he dropped heavily onto the bed.

'As I said, we're trying to find out whether anyone saw or heard anything,' said Patrik.

Rickard ran both his hands through his hair, which was tousled and looked unwashed.

'I can't believe we didn't hear anything. It's the next room along. We should have woken up. But we were knocking the booze back yesterday – I guess we all had a bit too much, and, well . . . I slept like a dead man.'

Rickard grimaced at his own choice of words. He stifled a belch and rubbed his eyes. The effects of last night's drinking were not only visible but could also be smelled in the breath that wafted towards Patrik.

'Might they have used a silencer?' said Rickard, hiccupping.

'We don't know anything right now,' Patrik said, wondering how many times he'd repeated that in the last few hours.

'I can't believe we didn't hear anything,' Rickard said again.

He shook his head but seemed to immediately regret the movement.

'What time did you go to bed? And did you go to bed at the same time? You and Tilde?'

'Yes, we went to bed at the same time. I couldn't get off at first so I thought we'd have some fun, but I couldn't get it up. I don't usually have any problems after I've been on the lash, but I guess I'm not twenty anymore . . .'

He smiled wryly but the smile disappeared when he realized the inappropriateness.

Patrik tried to put his personal emotions to one side, but it was hard to do in this case. He disliked this type of person so intensely, and the speech on Saturday was still resounding in the back of his mind. A spoilt rascal was the most charitable description to hand, and Rickard was by definition too old to be a rascal.

'About what time?' Patrik asked.

Rickard's fringe fell across his face and he tossed it out of the way in a practised move.

'No idea, actually. It's all a bit of a blur . . . But Dad and the others were going to discuss something about Blanche, so we had to leave the house. Mum and Dad had given our place to Vivian, Ole and Susanne, so we had to sleep in the boys' room at Peter and Louise's. Honestly, there wasn't much to do except go to bed. I will say that Tilde wasn't thrilled about it, and I'll need a full session with the chiropractor to sort my back out.'

Patrik gritted his teeth so as not to say anything inappropriate. He had little sympathy for Rickard's back pain.

'What was your relationship with your brother like?' he said instead.

Rickard's expression was blank. Patrik searched for a modicum of emotion in him, but all he saw was a hangover. He tried to persuade himself not to pass judgement. Grief could take many forms, and shock could often delay grief.

'We were very different. Peter was the clever one. The responsible one. I guess I've always been the one regarded as the family fuck-up.'

'What do you think about that?'

'Pretty unfair really. Peter never took any risks. I take risks. Sometimes they pay off, sometimes not. You just

180

have to have a little patience. Mum understands that. But Dad and Peter . . . They think too small. Too narrow-minded.'

'Did that lead to conflicts between you and your brother?'

Outside, the helicopter hovered closer and the down-draught made the window rattle. If it hadn't been fixed on the opener, it would have slammed shut.

'I wouldn't say I had conflicts,' Rickard drawled. 'Peter never really argued. He just looked at you with disappointed puppy eyes. Dad's always been the angry one.'

A part of Patrik wanted to lean forward and shake the nonchalance out of him.

'But I don't know. Peter seemed to grow a pair later on. He talked back more. Probably all Louise's work. She's a tough cookie. I don't think she likes me, but then again you can't charm everyone . . .'

He smiled at Patrik.

'Though I don't know how she stuck all the Cecily chat over the last year. Peter seemed to have got it into his head that he was going to find out who killed her.'

'Killed her?' Patrik said, straightening his back. 'Wasn't it a car accident?'

'Hit-and-run. Some bastard mowed her down while she was out jogging. Driver was probably hammered and did a bunk.'

'And you say that Peter had started trying to find out who it was?'

'Yes. In the early years, he was paralysed with grief. It was Louise who got him back on his feet again. So I think it was only now he felt up to taking it on. I know he called the police every week, and I know he'd also hired someone to find out more.'

'Bloody hell,' said Patrik. 'Do you know whether he'd got anywhere?'

'Not a clue.'

Rickard was looking more and more green about the gills, despite the sea breeze coming in through the open window.

'Do you know if anyone had any quarrel with your brother?'

'Quarrel?' Rickard laughed. 'No. As I've been trying to tell you, Peter lived a life of utmost humility. He avoided conflict, he tried to have no dissenting opinions whatsoever. So no. I don't know anyone who had a quarrel with Peter.'

He gulped and his smile faded.

'I need to throw up. Can we take a break?'

'Sure,' said Patrik.

He watched Rickard rush off to the bathroom. Could he be a killer? He doubted it, but then again you never knew.

Erica got out of the lift and hurried towards the bar. She had lain down to rest, fallen asleep and woken in a panic when she realized there were only five minutes left until the appointed hour. She spotted Frank already there waiting for her. Damn. She knew how scrupulous he was about timekeeping. Well, he was scrupulous about everything – it was one of his great strengths. On many an occasion she'd received the decisive, key details from Frank – the details that lifted a story so that it became more than what everyone had already read in the papers. But she never asked him for things she knew he wasn't allowed to disclose. If that was what she was after, she had to approach other sources.

'Sorry. I fell asleep.'

Frank held up a glass.

'No worries. I'm done for the day, so I ordered a beer. It's on you.'

He was more like a clerk than the police stereotype.

Slim, with a receding hairline and the kind of glasses most commonly associated with bureaucrats in the sixties. He'd been one of her contacts for many years, and she still had no idea what his private life was like. She used to amuse herself trying to guess, but oscillated between him living in his mother's basement and him living a clandestine life with a leather upholstered sex chamber. Admittedly, the two didn't have to be mutually exclusive.

'Have you seen the news?' he said, pointing to his phone.

'No,' said Erica. She hadn't checked her phone before rushing down.

'There's stuff going on in Fjällbacka,' he said dryly, taking a sip of his beer.

'Yes, the murder of Rolf Stenklo,' she said, a little confused.

She looked around for a waiter. She was going to make the most of this break and combine work with enjoying some time on her own. Somewhere behind that bar there was a glass of Cava with her name on it.

'No, no, not Rolf's murder. The massacre on Skjälerö.'

'What? What did you say?' The arm that Erica had raised to summon the server's attention froze mid-movement. 'A massacre on Skjälerö? How many beers have you already had?'

Frank calmly tapped on his mobile, pulling up the *Aftonbladet* website and held it in front of her. The bold headlines yelled at her.

MURDER ON SKJÄLERÖ! UNKNOWN NUMBER OF DEAD!

Erica struggled to digest them. She pulled out her own phone and went to the article. There was a livestream from a helicopter hovering above the small island.

Erica suddenly understood the radio silence emanating from Patrik and Louise. Good God. Louise and the kids. The room began to spin and the screen blurred for a few seconds.

'Just what do you folks get up to in the village? Seems like the Wild West,' Frank said laconically.

He gestured to the waiter and turned to Erica.

'What did you want?'

'Cava?' she said faintly, and the server quickly disappeared.

Erica continued reading. There didn't seem to be much in the way of facts, so most of the article was pure filler. Rolf's murder was mentioned, and there was wild speculation in connection with it.

'It can't be a coincidence for two incidents like that to happen so soon one after the other, with the same people involved,' said Frank, as if reading her mind.

'No . . . no, it's too improbable.'

Erica sent a text to Patrik:

Seen the news. Call when you can.

'Does Rolf's murder have anything to do with what you asked me to pull up?'

Frank grabbed a fistful of peanuts from a bowl next to his beer.

'I've absolutely nothing connecting the two things, but Rolf's widow mentioned Lola's murder as something that had increasingly occupied Rolf's attention. Especially lately. But either way, the story piqued my interest. And I thought I'd ask around about Rolf and Blanche while I was here anyway. I've heard vague rumours about issues. Both murders in the past and problems in the present are things that can lead to someone being killed.'

'I've seen flimsier motives than that,' Frank sighed, taking another sip.

The waiter returned with Erica's Cava and Frank ordered a second beer. He continued:

'Once there was a guy who beat his neighbour to death because his cat had pissed on his flowers. People . . .'

'Do you have the file?' said Erica, trying not to keep glancing at her phone.

She guessed it might be hours before Patrik got in touch, but she still couldn't help looking. Suddenly the sofa she was sitting on felt far too soft and the light cast by the lamp above was too harsh.

'I found the old investigation. The lead officer has passed away, and I still haven't managed to track down anyone else who remembers it, so this is what we've got.'

He handed over a disappointingly thin stack of papers that Erica laid out on the table in front of her. She'd already downed half her Cava.

Frank watched her thumbing through them. She muttered to herself quietly – a habit when reading sources – and occasionally raised her eyebrows.

'Have you ever heard of this case?' she asked as she continued to skim the text.

'Surprisingly, no. I ought to have done. There are some deserving angles and interesting aspects to it. And a lot of question marks. But no. Never heard of it. They must have put a lid on it pretty much straight away.'

'Who did?' said Erica, looking up.

'Hard to tell, but what I can say is that the directive must have come from higher up.'

He quickly drained his beer as the new one arrived. Then he stopped himself and looked intently at Erica with unexpected concern.

'Are you sure you know what you're getting yourself into?'

'Not a clue,' said Erica. 'But someone has to find out what actually happened to Lola and her daughter after all these years. And I guess that'll have to be me.'

'Just be careful,' said Frank.

'I'm always careful.'

Something in his eyes told her that he knew she was lying.

The island was teeming with activity. Police officers were combing every last inch. No more helicopters had shown up, but there were a couple of boats not far offshore filled with photographers armed with huge telescopic lenses.

'Why is there so much attention?' said Farideh Mirza, pointing to the boats.

'You don't know the Bauer family?' said Patrik.

'I can't say that I do.'

'Elisabeth Bauer is the sole heiress of the Bauer family, whose publishing house is the biggest in Sweden, second only to Bonniers. And her husband is Henning Bauer – an internationally acclaimed author, who according to my wife is rumoured to be up for the Nobel Prize in Literature.'

'I suppose that'd do it.'

Farideh looked moderately impressed.

'How are you getting on?' Patrik took a few deep breaths of the fresh air.

He needed a few minutes' break from the grief within the main house and he'd taken the chance to check how things were going with forensics. He and Farideh had met outside Peter's cottage.

'We're almost done in the bedroom. The medical examiner has been and taken samples, and the bodies are being packed up now,' she said flatly, and Patrik swallowed.

The thought of those small boys in the black body bags used for transportation turned his stomach.

'Anything of interest?'

She shook her head. She'd pulled down the hood of her coverall and her dark hair was carefully fastened into an austere ponytail. 'We've gathered and documented as much as we can, and I hope we'll find out more once it's all been analysed by NFC. But there's nothing that stands out right now.'

'Weapon?'

'Not in the bedroom.'

'Guess on the type?'

'I can't say for sure, but judging by the bullet buried in the headboard, I'd say it was a pistol. 7.65 calibre.'

'A common one, then. There's no end of those in Sweden.'

'Yes, not very helpful. But if we find the gun we can match it to the bullet. And we'll find bullets when we do the autopsy – none of the entry wounds had exit wounds.'

Patrik swallowed again.

'We're carrying on in the bedroom next door,' said Farideh. 'There's a small bloodstain on the doorway into that bedroom.'

'Could it be from when the murderer passed by in the hallway?' said Patrik.

'Yes, it could be,' said Farideh.

She pulled the hood back up. Behind them, the door opened. Two members of the forensics team were carrying a black bag. A small bag. Bile began to force its way up Patrik's throat. His eyes filled with tears in response to the corrosive feeling, and he fought against it with all his might, but when the second small black bag followed he could no longer hold it back.

Patrik only made it as far as the outside of the house before he threw up the contents of his stomach. A man on one of the boats offshore photographed him feverishly.

'It must be to do with Rolf,' Vivian said.

She stared at Martin without blinking. They sat down in the dining area at the end of the long table.

'We don't know anything as yet.'

Martin sipped the tea in front of him. It was nice and

187

strong, and he'd added three teaspoons of honey to make it really sweet.

Vivian hadn't touched her tea.

'But anything else is impossible. How can it be a coincidence that Rolf was murdered first and then Peter and the boys were, shortly after?'

'I agree with you and of course we'll be looking into it. But we can't commit to any one theory at the moment.'

'Something was different over the last year. I noticed it so clearly. Rolf was darker. Troubled. And it was something to do with the Bauers. And Blanche.'

'Yes, you mentioned that when we spoke after . . . after what happened to Rolf. But you don't have anything more concrete to go on than that? Nothing that might suggest a possible motive? Did he behave at all differently? Did he say anything?'

Vivian shook her head.

'I don't know. It's hard to put my finger on. It was more that he was quieter. Sometimes he'd disappear and refuse to say where he was going. It wasn't like him. We had a shared calendar and always ran our days past one another. We shared everything. Until, suddenly, we didn't. He'd sometimes withdraw to talk on the phone, which was unusual. We'd never kept any secrets from each other.'

Her voice fell silent. She looked tired and seemed to have aged ten years since Martin had last seen her.

'What were the calls about?'

He turned the mug so that he could see the floral design on it.

'I don't know . . .' The frustration was clearly visible on her face. 'I only heard the odd word. Rolf mentioned Blanche and I know I heard Ole's name mentioned. And Henning's. Then there was his obsession with the exhibition. And the way it had a completely different focus

188

to what he made his name doing. Somehow, I got the impression that he'd started looking back lately.'

Vivian shook her head and finally took a sip of her tea.

'Look at me, rambling. But I didn't recognize him. And the last straw was when he refused to go to Henning and Elisabeth's party. It was so . . .'

Vivian shrugged and Martin leaned forward.

'Well, there was one more thing. He received envelopes in the post. No return address. Just his name and address on the front. I almost opened one. We weren't in the habit of opening each other's post, but I picked it up by mistake and began opening it without seeing who it was addressed to. Rolf flew into a rage and snatched it from me! Which wasn't like him, either.'

'You don't have any idea who sent him the letter you almost opened? Or what it contained?'

Vivian shook her head.

'No, not a clue.'

'Might it have been kept? Is it still in your flat?'

'I don't think so. I didn't see it after that.'

'Okay,' said Martin, lost hope in his voice. 'But if you do think of anything, then please get in touch immediately.'

'I will. May I go home, by the way?'

'We can't stop you.'

'Thanks. I'll stay a few more days in the house in Sälvik, but then I'll head home, and wait for Rolf to follow on there.'

She trembled.

'I understand,' said Martin. 'Before we stop, could you tell me a little about yesterday?'

'There's not much to say. The others were probably up pretty late, but I went to bed early. It had all been so much . . . with everything. It's been a long time since I slept as deeply as I did last night.'

'So you didn't hear anything? Didn't see anything?'

'No, I think it was around half past eight when I woke up, and I popped round to the kitchen in the main house. I was parched and didn't have any water in my room. I had a coffee and a sandwich standing up by the work surface. But I didn't notice anything out of the ordinary then. Everyone was asleep – apart from Henning and Elisabeth, with whom I exchanged a few words. Louise was asleep on the sofa, and I didn't see the others. Well, Nancy was in the kitchen, of course.'

'Okay, thanks.'

Martin closed his notebook.

'Are we done here?'

'Yes. I don't have any more questions for the time being.'

'Then I'll go and check on Elisabeth,' said Vivian, standing up.

There were so many questions buzzing around his head. What was it that had changed Rolf? What had he been brooding over? Something told Martin that some of the answers to their questions would be found there. But how was he going to get hold of them?

'Hello? How are you getting on?'

Anna entered Erica and Patrik's place without knocking. No one replied. The only thing she could hear was a rhythmic, pounding sound.

'Hellooooo?'

She shifted Fliss to her other hip and kicked off her shoes in the hall. The rhythmic sound continued. The kitchen was deserted, as were the living room and terrace. She carried on towards the back where the door into the garden was open, overlooking the water.

'Hi Anna!'

Maja came rushing towards her and hurled herself at her legs. The twins did the same thing when they caught sight of her, and Anna staggered under the weight of three children. She put Fliss down on the grass and looked around.

Kristina came towards her with a big smile.

'Fancy seeing you! Hello! How nice of you to pop in! And little Alicia!'

'Fliss,' said Anna, hugging Kristina.

She liked Erica's mother-in-law, but preferred her in smaller doses.

'What are you doing?' she said, squinting towards the corner of the garden where Kristina's husband Gunnar – known fondly as Bob the Builder to his family – was in the middle of something.

Planks were strewn all over the grass and he was on his knees clutching a large tool.

'You mustn't tell,' said Kristina, flashing her a shrewd smile. 'But we're going to surprise Erica and Patrik with a few minor improvements around the house. They've got so much on their plates with work and young children, so we know it can't be easy to look after a big house, but they're not doing it and there's so much potential here! It's lucky they've got us pensioners! We have all the time in the world to help them sort things out!'

Anna looked at Kristina sceptically. She wasn't at all sure that Erica and Patrik wanted their house 'sorted out', but she knew better than to try and stop Kristina when she was mid-flow. She had to pick and choose her battles, and this was one she was happy to leave to her sister and her brother-in-law.

'So what's this going to be?'

Anna cast her eye towards the lawn where Fliss was being occupied by Maja and the twins, and then she headed towards the building work. Bob the Builder looked up cheerfully and waved, but couldn't talk since he had several nails in his mouth.

'A small extension to the decking,' said Kristina. 'I'm going to put an airer there so they don't have towels all over the place in the summer. And Gunnar's also building some raised beds too. My goodness, this place looks like the Sahara without any flowers. That simply won't do. What must the neighbours say?'

Kristina pointed at the garden in horror – it was indeed rather barren in the floral department.

Anna stifled a laugh and instead said indignantly:

'Yes, good God, what will the neighbours say? You'd better build those raised beds nice and big. I'm sure Erica will be a fan when she gets started. The place will look like Ernst Kirchsteiger moved in once she gets going.'

Truthfully, Erica had never in her life managed to keep a cactus alive for more than a week.

Kristina clapped her hands happily.

'Once you've found joy in seeing it in bloom, there's no going back!'

'That's so true,' Anna said in a deadly earnest tone, while laughing so much inside that she was on the verge of falling over.

She knew she really oughtn't to ask more questions, but she couldn't help herself.

'What else have you got planned? And what does Patrik have to say about it when he's at home?'

Kristina's face turned serious at once.

'Well, Patrik called earlier and said he'll be staying at the station while Erica is away, given the workload in light of what happened. So we've got plenty of time to surprise them both.' Kristina's face lit up again. 'We were lucky enough to find cabinet doors that fit their frames, so we'll have plenty of time to swap the ones they currently have. I'm going to paint them while Gunnar does the carpentry. I was thinking salmon pink, although with a hint of terracotta. Won't that be lovely?

192

And then Gunnar can make an archway from the kitchen into the living room so that they have that wonderful Mediterranean feel. You know, when Gunnar and I were in Positano last summer, we fell head over heels for the style and the architecture, so we've re-done our whole house in the same look. You and Dan must come for dinner one night so you can see. You'd love my lemon curtains. You know, I think I've got some fabric left over . . .'

'Sure,' said Anna, biting her tongue. Terracotta. Roman arches. She really ought to put a stop to it, but it was all too hilarious.

Then she asked curiously:

'What else did Patrik say when he called? I saw the news. What's happened on Skjälerö?'

Kristina shook her head.

'I asked him, but he wouldn't say. It's dreadful – and so soon after that photographer being murdered! You'd think we were living in Stockholm rather than little Fjällbacka!' She shook her head again.

Anna glanced towards the lawn and had to launch herself towards the kids when she discovered that the twins had managed to pick up Fliss between them and were now trying to run away from Maja with her.

'Boys, boys, put her down!'

They only ran faster, laughing loudly, but their legs were short and Anna caught up with them in a couple of steps and gently disentangled her daughter. A daughter who seemed extremely pleased with the situation.

'Aunt Anna, they're hopeless,' Maja said gloomily, and Anna laughed.

She stroked Maja's hair.

'They're little. Not a big girl like you.'

'We *are* big!' the boys howled.

They glared at Anna for a few seconds, but quickly

shifted focus and made for Bob the Builder to watch his hammering with wide eyes.

Anna leaned forward towards Maja.

'How about a coffee break?'

Maja nodded eagerly.

Anna took her hand after putting Fliss on her hip and they went into the kitchen – the one that was soon going to be salmon pink.

Erica spread out the preliminary investigation file on the bed – page after page in the right order. As she'd noted when Frank had given her the papers, there was alarmingly little of it. The murder of a trans woman and her child ought to have been subject to more investigation, and while hate crimes and transgender issues were much more in the public consciousness now, there should have been big headlines even in 1980.

But nonetheless, having these papers was worth their weight in gold. She felt slightly dizzy from the two glasses of Cava she'd drunk, and forced herself to focus. Patrik still hadn't been in touch, but she left her phone on full volume so that she would hear if he called or texted.

First, Erica read through from beginning to end to form an overarching understanding of the case. Then she took out her notepad and pen and began to write down individual points that she would find useful when searching for further information.

First she noted the lead investigator, before adding *deceased* in parentheses based on Frank's tip. The name might still come in handy – there could be colleagues or other people around him who knew something. Then she wrote down Lola's birth name. There was something about seeing the name written down for the first time that deeply touched Erica. The name she had been born with but hadn't been the person she wanted to be. She was

194

Lola, not 'Lars Christer Berggren', which was what the papers said. She silently promised Lola to use that name as little as she could. Even in her thoughts.

Erica noted the personal identity number. She also noted the child's name and personal identity number. 'Julia Berggren.' She'd been six years old when she died.

She examined the enclosed autopsy report. Two different causes of death were listed. Lola had died from two shots to the head. The girl had died from smoke inhalation. There had been no smoke in Lola's lungs, which meant she had been dead when the fire had occurred, while the girl had died from the smoke triggered by the fire.

A few photos of the crime scene were included. It was hard to see anything properly. This was partly because the pictures were of substandard quality and partly because the flat was so smoke-damaged and the bodies so charred that it was hard to make out what was what. But what Erica was able to deduce from the photos and the report was that Lola had been lying on the kitchen floor near the hob, while the girl had been found in a big American-style trunk in the living room.

The firearm had never been found and Erica tried to summon up different scenarios. There was something about the two shots that felt personal. Forming a picture of what had happened at an early stage helped her to visualize which way to proceed in her investigation, even if there was always room to retrace her steps and re-evaluate her assumptions. On occasion she had been wrong. Sometimes things weren't as obvious as you wanted them to be.

She continued to note down details in her notebook. She was more than familiar with the location of the flat. She had lived nearby during her Stockholm years, and knew exactly which building it was in. On the other hand, she had never heard anything about a fire there.

A handful of neighbours had been interviewed as witnesses. None of them had seen or heard anything, but Erica still noted their names. They might have something different to say now that this much time had passed. She'd learned that there were many reasons why witnesses chose to keep things quiet, and the passing of time could sometimes remedy that.

One name made her start. One of the witnesses had been Rolf Stenklo. He had been the last person to see Lola alive, and had therefore been questioned. This had been in connection with a birthday party at Lola's flat. When he'd left the flat, both Lola and her daughter had been alive.

Erica stood up and went over to the window. The market in the square outside was packing up, the traders now calling out 'half price' to passers-by. Wasn't that strange? Rolf had been the last person to see Lola alive. Now, some forty years later, he too was dead after beginning to bring the memory of Lola back to life over the past year.

Erica didn't believe in chance. And she didn't believe in coincidences. Lola and Rolf were linked. Their deaths were linked. She just needed to figure out how.

16

STOCKHOLM 1980

It was almost closing time and Lola's feet ached in her high heels. It had been a quiet night at Alexa's. It was the night before payday, everyone was skint and no one could afford beers or cocktails.

'Where are the others?' she asked Rolf when she saw him sauntering up to the bar.

'What? Am I not good enough?'

He smiled to indicate that he wasn't being serious.

Lola put her hand on his. Her long, hot pink nails shone in the neon light behind the bar.

'You're always good enough. Just asking. You're always together.'

She noted that Rolf always drew looks from the other patrons – men and women alike. He looked like what he was: an adventurer. A free soul. As if he should have been at the helm of the Kon-Tiki or summiting Mount Everest. Blond, with glittering blue eyes and a constant slight tan from his travels, he seemed to have been pulled straight from a Hollywood movie of the forties.

'We were supposed to come here together. But life got in the way. Peter's got an ear infection, so Henning and Elisabeth decided to stay at home. Ole and Susanne have apparently had a row. You can guess about what. Same old song.'

'And Ester?'

Rolf's smile faded. He stared deep into the beer he'd just been handed. It was a while before he answered, but Lola waited. There were no other patrons demanding her attention.

'We had a miscarriage yesterday.'

'My God. I'm sorry I asked.'

Impulsively, Lola put her hand over Rolf's. Without looking at her, he placed his other hand on top of hers, squeezing it warmly. Then he let go and took a deep draught of beer.

'We're starting to get used to it. It's the eighth time . . . But Ester's upset, of course. Well, so am I. But her sister was supposed to be coming round tonight, and she mostly wanted me out of the way . . .'

The words floated away into the muted hubbub of the club.

'Are you going to keep trying?' Lola picked up a cloth and wiped down the bar.

'I don't know. I think Ester wants to. But this whole thing of oscillating between hope and despair . . .' He sighed. 'You're lucky to have P'tite. Even if things turned out the way they did.'

'Yes, I am. But I wish her mother could see her now.'

'Yes, I understand. I think we can still live a good life – Ester and I. Without children. But I don't know whether she sees it that way. She doesn't have a grand passion like I do. In many ways, my photographs are my children, my legacy. But I love Ester. Nothing means more to me than her happiness.'

'Then you'll just have to follow Ester's lead. Let her decide.'

'You know, you're wise.' Rolf took another sip. Then

he set the beer down resolutely. 'You know what, I'm not going to be much fun tonight. I think I'll head home.'

'The bar closes in a moment, so I'm about to leave anyway. See you another time.'

'Kisses,' he said, blowing her a kiss.

Lola cleaned up the last of her station. There wasn't much to sort out when it had been that quiet, so it only took a few minutes. She grabbed her bag from behind the bar, waved to those of her colleagues who were left, then departed via the back way.

The summer night was warm. Lola loved feeling the balmy July air on her face as she strolled home. The sky was never really black at this time of year. The darkest it got was a pale shade of greyish purple, and tonight it also had a streak of pink.

She loved Stockholm. And against all odds, she loved her life. All the grief, all the pain, all the evil of the past had drained away the very moment she'd looked into P'tite's eyes the day she had been born. Everything had become simple. Even the complicated bits.

'Hi.'

A man was standing outside smoking a cigarette. He peered at her from under his fringe. He was shy but with an undertone of something else.

Lola smiled at him. He'd been one of a group of lads who'd been ordering drinks from her all evening and she'd felt his gaze. It wasn't the first time he'd been to Alexa's, but it was the first time he had looked at her so purposefully. She, on the other hand, hadn't liked the way some of his friends were looking at her, but she'd chosen to ignore it. There were so many like them, and it was best to ignore them.

'Hi,' she said, going over to him. 'You got a fag for me too?'

His smile broadened and he proffered a pack of Marlboros.

'Got a light for me too?'

She winked at him and fluttered her eyelashes. She had no intention of taking this any further – she was already in love. And she was much too faithful to do anything. But she liked the attention. And he was sweet, in a boyish way.

Without taking his eyes off her, he lit the cigarette in his own mouth and turned the filter in her direction. She took a few deep drags, then raised an eyebrow and pouted slightly. Men loved it.

'You're beautiful,' he said.

'Thanks.'

She took a step closer. People were emerging from the club, happy, still in the party mood, ready to move on elsewhere or back to someone's place for an afterparty. She was about to go home to P'tite. Just as soon as she had finished smoking the cigarette.

The man raised his hand and caressed her cheek. 'Can I get your number?'

'Maybe.'

He really was insanely cute. She could let him think he was going to get her number for a little longer.

'Ugh! Toby! What the fuck you doing? You getting it on with *that*? Wasn't buying drinks off it all night enough?'

A booming voice behind them made them both jump. The other guys from the same table had emerged from Alexa's. Everything boyish in the young man's face disappeared. All that was left was horror. And something Lola knew well. Shame.

Before she had time to react, his fist cracked something in her jaw. She fell to the ground.

And then they loomed over her. They kicked, punched, spat. Shouted at her with their awful, roaring voices.

Lola turned on her side and tried to curl up into the fetal position to protect herself. The asphalt felt cold and gravelly against her cheek, and with each kick her face was scraped against the rough surface.

'Fucking freak. Jesus Christ.'

Lola glanced to the side, upwards. The men were shouting even louder. One of them had a dark look in his eyes that she recognized. She'd seen that look so many times. Sometimes from the people she loved – the ones she had thought loved her.

'You fucking disgusting gay poofter!'

The kicks struck her hard in the diaphragm. The next kick – from the one with the kind face – hit her in the back so hard that it winded her. She tried to scream, but no sound came out.

Their voices got louder and louder. People hurried by, no one stopping to help her. She could no longer hear the men's words. The blows rained down on her so densely and so hard that she couldn't tell them apart.

Lola pictured P'tite's face as she lay at home in her bed, asleep, in her nightie covered in horses. She resigned herself to the fact that she would never see her daughter again. She could no longer put up a fight – she'd fought for so long and thought she was safe. She'd deceived herself into believing that she could be happy.

Lola pressed herself against the asphalt. She felt the chill of it as her body convulsed with each kick.

Then there was a voice. A familiar, wonderful voice. A voice that shouted so loudly that it rose all the way to heaven – angels must have heard it. Because the kicking stopped. When he sat down next to her and took her in his arms, Lola cried tears of happiness.

'I stopped for a cigarette, otherwise I wouldn't have . . .'

Rolf's voice broke as he cradled her in his arms.

Lola laboriously lifted up her arms and put them around Rolf's neck. She was safe after all.

17

It had been a mistake to come with them. With his advancing years and thanks to Rita's situation, Bertil Mellberg had become increasingly aware of his shortcomings. He wasn't sure how much he would be able to change. He was the man he was, and change wasn't something that had ever come to him easily.

He guessed that his colleagues assumed he'd escaped to avoid working. That might once have been true, but not now. He couldn't cope with death today – not when it was breathing down his neck and threatening to take the thing most dear to him.

That was why he was sitting in a crevice behind the houses, shivering. He'd heard the sounds at a distance – the voices, doors being opened and closed. Some of their colleagues from Uddevalla had found him while searching the area and looked at him very oddly. But he'd ignored them, merely shifting a few metres to allow them to search the crevice.

When they left, he heard them muttering among themselves. He didn't care. Nothing mattered anymore – all he knew was that if he went inside those houses and looked death in the eye, and was confronted with other people's grief, then he would crack.

He really ought to take the boat back and get away from the island. But his limbs wouldn't obey him. Once he had sat down, he couldn't get up again. He saw the boats carrying the media circling the island, and heard them snapping away with their huge cameras. A helicopter had been circling above them for hours. A sole lobster pot was just off the island, given away by the red buoy attached to it.

Under his icy palms, he felt the coarse granite. It would still be here when generations had come and gone. It was the only thing that endured. Bertil wouldn't be able to cope with being alone. He wouldn't survive without Rita. He shivered and stared out across the grey sea – his view broken only by small islands until the horizon dissolved into endlessness. There and then, he decided that, if he lost her, the sea could have him.

The decision was a relief. He wouldn't have to live on without her. He stood up and brushed himself down. Hopefully, he'd be able to head back to the mainland with the lifeboat right away. He didn't want to stay on this godforsaken island for another second. Death hung far too heavily over Skjälerö.

'Gösta? Gösta Flygare?'

Gösta had popped outside for some air after his second interview with Elisabeth Bauer – they'd had to terminate the first when she'd suddenly taken a dizzy turn. He turned around and saw Farideh Mirza walking towards him from the guest cottage. There was a brisk air to her.

'We've found something,' she said.

When Farideh told him about their discovery, his pulse quickened – before long, Gösta could hear it beating in his ears.

He hurried over to the main building and looked around for Patrik. Not in the living room, not in the study, not in the bedroom. He opened the door to the kitchen and found him at the draining board with Nancy the housekeeper, who was washing up teacups and spoons by hand.

'Patrik!'

Patrik looked up quickly in response to the tone of Gösta's voice, and he came towards him.

'Yes?'

'We've got a shirt with blood on it.'

'Where?'

Gösta glanced at Nancy, who had stopped washing up.

'Come on,' he said, and they went into the hall.

The two of them bent down to put on their shoes and Gösta said in a low voice:

'Rickard's shirt was in the laundry basket in the bathroom – there are blood spatters on it.'

'Oh crap,' Patrik said, pausing.

'Are we going to arrest him?' said Gösta.

Patrik pondered for a few seconds.

'I'll call the prosecutor right away,' he said.

Once outside the house, Patrik stepped to one side and pulled out his mobile. Gösta could tell from Patrik's expression when he returned what the prosecutor had said.

'Where is he?' said Gösta. 'I haven't seen him for a while.'

'In the shitter. He's hungover,' said Patrik.

He glanced at the cottage to the left. 'I just want to check in with Farideh. Then we'll get him. The boat's ready to cast off when we are.'

'I'll come with you,' said Gösta.

Patrik strode briskly away and Gösta tried to keep up as best he could. His legs no longer obeyed him as they once had, in spite of the countless rounds of golf in the summer.

When Patrik reached the cottage, he knocked on the door and spoke in a low voice to one of the forensics team in their full get-up. After a few minutes, Farideh came to the door. Her face looked tired and strained – many hours of focus and concentration had left their mark.

'So, you heard,' she said as she took off her hood and rubber gloves.

'Yes, Gösta told me what you found. I've been given permission by the prosecutor to arrest Rickard, but I've got a few questions for you first.'

Farideh shook out her long dark hair. Beads of sweat glistened at her hairline, and she wiped them away with her sleeve.

'Are we certain that it's Rickard's shirt?'

'Judging by the brand and the size, I would say it's a man's shirt, and it matches descriptions of a shirt worn by Rickard Bauer.'

'And the blood spatter?'

Patrik shifted his weight back and forth on his feet, while Gösta listened to him tensely from behind. Hedström knew how to do his job. He was asking exactly the right questions.

'My assessment right now is that they match the blood spatters that might have arisen when the person wearing the shirt shot the victims at close range. NFC will have to confirm that. But my experience tells me it's very likely.'

'Okay.' Patrik fell silent. Then he said hesitantly: 'It's just that . . . Would anyone be that inept? Throwing a bloodstained shirt into the laundry basket?'

'Wasn't he – by his own account – utterly hammered yesterday?' Gösta interjected.

He'd seen far greater ineptness in his time, and he knew Patrik had too.

Patrik nodded. 'Well . . . That's true. Let's bring him in. And we need to go another round with Tilde. After all, they were sharing a room.'

*　*　*

Erica laid out the clothes she had brought with her on the hotel bed. Getting dressed was a challenge. Firstly, everything was a little too tight thanks to the kilos she'd put on lately, and secondly she wasn't entirely sure how she was expected to dress. That culture called for black was a given, but would a sheer blouse work, or would she have to wear a black polo-neck?

Erica finally settled on the blouse and a pair of trousers with a comfortable elasticated waist. She quickly made herself up in front of the mirror. Foundation, mascara and a little lip gloss. She didn't feel up to any more effort than that.

She quickly double-checked the time and address on her phone. The exhibition began at seven o'clock and she estimated it would take her around fifteen minutes to get to the location near Odenplan.

She'd had a stroke of luck. Lenora – who was having her opening at Blanche tonight – was someone she'd known in the past. Back when Erica had been studying literature at Stockholm University, Lenora had been studying art history and their paths had crossed in the college bar. For a couple of years they had been inseparable, then life and their differences had taken them in different directions, but Erica still harboured fond memories of the many hours she and Lenora had spent drinking cheap red wine, talking about life and elusive love.

Erica had felt dishonest not explaining her hidden agenda when she'd texted Lenora to ask whether she could come to her exhibition at Blanche. Her old friend's obvious joy weighed rather heavily on her conscience, but it *was* going to be fun to see where Lenora's art had taken her to since they'd last met.

When they'd hung out, Lenora had mostly worked in clay and had often challenged people with her provocative sculptures. Judging by the description on the Blanche website, she'd carried on down that track. She was described as a 'post-feminist Judy Chicago on speed' who 'points the finger at the Swedish art scene's neo-materialist obsession'. Erica couldn't make head nor tail of that description. She'd understood even less of the review in *Dagens Nyheter* that she'd found when googling Lenora. Her work was described as 'a well-choreographed post-apocalyptic fantasy that turns everything the Swedish art scene believes itself to know about neo-materialism on its head, while simultaneously poking the most festering sores of the Anthropocene'. Erica thought that was a positive review but she wasn't sure.

After one final glance in the mirror, Erica picked up her bag and left the room. Emerging from the hotel entrance, she turned left towards the taxi rank on Kungsgatan where there were often cars waiting.

Once she'd given the address, she settled into the seat and pulled her phone out to see whether Patrik had been in touch. Still nothing. She checked the headlines. Nothing new, just speculation. No one seemed to know who the victims were yet, but there were pictures of three body bags being carried away by officers in white overalls. What the hell had happened on that island?

Erica gazed out of the window at the buildings they were passing. She pictured Louise's ponytail swinging as she surged forth on their power walks. Surely nothing had happened to her?

She was roused from her anxious thoughts when the taxi pulled over. She handed the driver her credit card without really knowing what she was doing. It felt as if she was in a fog.

She noticed the driver's quizzical expression in the rear-view mirror and pulled herself together. All she could do right now was find out more about any secrets at Blanche.

She smoothed her trousers and got out of the taxi. The entrance was unassuming and led down to a basement with brick vaults. A beautiful young girl in her twenties checked her name on a guest list and then admitted her graciously.

Erica felt out of place. This was as high culture as it got, and it wasn't usually a setting she was invited into. People wearing mostly black were talking in low voices around her. Some couldn't conceal surprised glances behind their black-rimmed spectacles when they saw Erica.

Over the rim of her wine glass, Erica spotted several members of the Swedish Academy, an internationally acclaimed opera singer, several senior politicians and a cousin of the royal family.

'Hello!'

Lenora hooted cheerfully when she saw Erica and flung herself around her neck. They hugged each other for a long time. As she often did, Erica reminded herself that she needed to get better at staying in touch with the people who meant something to her. But it was hard staying in contact with friends from Stockholm when she lived in Fjällbacka, and work and young children on top of that made it no easier. She knew Lenora was married, but she and her wife didn't have any kids, at least not as far as Erica knew.

'Show me what you've been up to,' said Erica, pointing towards the exhibition at the back of the room with a curious finger.

Lenora's eyes sparkled as she pointed at each of the pieces, explaining and gesticulating. Among others, there was a reclining vulva in ceramic with a tree growing from between the labia, and a stately erect penis squirting a one-euro coin from the glans.

Erica politely accompanied Lenora and did her best to match her enthusiasm, but no matter how much she tried, she struggled to really get it. Art had never been her thing, and she lacked both knowledge and a frame of reference. There was, however, no doubt that Lenora was gifted.

'Could I borrow you for a few minutes later on?' she asked, once they'd seen everything.

Lenora raised an eyebrow.

'I knew it wasn't my ceramic cunts you were interested in.' She laughed at Erica's guilty expression. 'I've already been chatting and sucking up to the polo-necks for an hour. I deserve a glass of wine at the bar.'

'Oh. I hoped there would be a bar,' Erica said with relief.

Lenora cocked her head, tossing her mane of black, curly hair.

'This is Blanche. The stronghold of decadence. Of course there's a bar.'

She set a course through the throng of cultural figures until they reached a bar in the corner. Another beautiful young woman in her twenties – surprisingly similar to the one who had let Erica in – was behind the bar.

'Two glasses of red wine,' said Lenora without asking Erica. She had remembered her preference from back in the day.

Once they each had a glass of the house wine, they sat down at a tall table.

'They seem to have a certain type working here,' said Erica, pointing discreetly at the cool blonde beauty behind the bar.

'That's Ole's type,' said Lenora.

'The exact opposite of Susanne,' Erica said thoughtfully, and Lenora laughed.

'Yes, there's something to be analysed there. But what I don't understand is where he finds them. It's as if he's got a secret factory somewhere pumping out young, leggy blondes solely for Blanche.'

'So his affairs aren't much of a secret?' said Erica.

She took a sip of her red wine – it tasted cheap and thin, but beggars couldn't be choosers. The murmur around them was polite and low-key.

'What do the other co-owners have to say about it?'

'About Ole's exploits?' Lenora snorted. 'He's been left to it for years, so it doesn't seem as if anyone much cares. Blanche owns several flats, and there have been plenty of rumours about how they're put to use. Susanne must be a master at turning a deaf ear.'

'Maybe they have an open marriage?'

'Half-open, if that's true. No one's ever seen or heard anything about Susanne and another man. No, Ole seems to cover that side of their marriage. And for some unfathomable reason she accepts it.'

'Marriage of convenience? Rumour has it in Hollywood that some male actors are married to conceal their homosexuality.'

Lenora ran a hand through her hair, which had an almost unnatural sheen in the bewitching light of the venue.

'Hmm, I don't know who'd care if Susanne was gay. As an author, it would frankly be seen as a PR advantage if she were a dyke. These aren't the days of Selma Lagerlöf and Karin Boye. I've also seen them here a fair bit, and I'm convinced that she loves him. Maybe too much.'

'And the other co-owners? Henning and Elisabeth? Rolf? What's your impression of them?'

'I guess Rolf is the reason why you're asking. There's been a lot of gossip after Rolf's death and there was talk of postponing my exhibition. But based on what I heard, the other co-owners gave instructions that the business should keep running as normal.'

Erica realized that Lenora hadn't seen the news about the murders on Skjälerö, but she chose to say nothing as yet. First, she wanted to focus on Rolf.

'So what do they say about Rolf? Are there any theories about the murder?' she wondered.

'Rolf was very well liked, despite his edgy and sometimes rather brusque manner. He saw people. He didn't care about status or wealth.'

'But the others do?'

'Yes, I'd say that they regard themselves in many respects as being above "ordinary people". But Rolf never did.'

'So no enemies?'

Erica noted with dismay that the red wine in her glass had run out and she wondered how that had happened so quickly. Lenora took her glass, went over to the bar and returned with a refill.

'Someone feeling starved of adult company?'

'Don't joke,' Erica groaned. 'But I'll be out of toddler life soon. We just have to dig in a bit longer. Although it seems I've started to hit the menopause. I didn't think that came until you were fifty.'

'Peri-menopause,' Lenora said sympathetically. 'It's shit.'

Erica took another sip of the wine. The second glass tasted a little better than the first.

'You asked me about enemies,' said Lenora, returning to their conversation. 'No, as far as I know Rolf had no enemies. Ole, on the other hand . . . Well, there's been a fair bit of muttering. It's not like the old days anymore. Men can't just do as they please. I don't have any details about the problems, but it seems to be generating some friction between the co-owners. Louise has been kept busy.'

Erica did a double take.

'Louise?'

'Yes, she's carried on overseeing the administrative side of things here – even after she became Henning's assistant. Given the rumours that the media have been digging into Blanche's dealings, she'll probably be kept very busy. And I'm not surprised by their interest. You can see the clientele for yourself. And thanks to Susanne, Blanche has a close connection to the Swedish Academy. It doesn't get yummier than rumours of scandal tied to people in and around our proudest and most internationally renowned institutions.'

'Did Louise work at Blanche before she worked for Henning?' said Erica.

She couldn't remember Louise ever having mentioned Blanche. She only talked about her role as Henning's right-hand woman.

'Yes, that's how she met Peter. She was already working here when he was married to Cecily, and after the accident she became his rock. And then by extension Henning's.'

'Ah, I see. I'd never thought about how she and Peter met.'

'They're a lovely couple and Louise has been so good with the boys.'

'Are you friends?'

'Well, it's actually Peter and I who are friends. We started hanging out pretty soon after you moved. But yes, Louise and I have always rubbed along. I don't know what the Bauers would have done without her.'

'We meet up when they're in Fjällbacka,' said Erica.

She pictured the photo of the three body bags being carried away by the officers in white overalls. It was starting to feel dishonest not to say more.

'Something else has happened,' she said slowly. 'On Skjälerö. At least, according to the tabloids. But there are no details about who or what, as yet.'

Lenora drew breath.

'What are you saying?'

Erica quickly pulled out her mobile and pulled up a tabloid website on it.

'My God.'

Lenora stared at the picture of the three body bags, her hand to her mouth.

Erica sat in silence while Lenora read the article. She listened to the hubbub around them and heard disparate words like 'dreadful' and 'awful', and she realized that the news was now spreading like wildfire.

'My husband is probably there,' she said, 'but I haven't been able to get hold of him, so I don't have any details.'

Erica had tried to refrain from speculation on who might be inside the three body bags, but once again she pictured Louise. Tears filled her eyes.

'Can't you try getting hold of him again?' said Lenora.

Erica hesitated, but then she took out her phone. She knew how strictly Patrik oversaw the privacy of investigations, but the anxiety was like a dull ache and she couldn't stand the vulnerability in Lenora's gaze.

Sorry if I'm bothering you but I need to know . . . Who are the dead?

Erica quickly sent off the text message. She put the phone down in front of her and saw the dots underneath the message indicating that Patrik was writing a reply. After a few seconds, the phone beeped.

Erica could hardly breathe as she read Patrik's text. It was impossible to take in what it said. She couldn't summon any words – instead she mutely held up the phone to Lenora.

Patrik had left the houses and was staring out to sea without really being able to take in the view. Exhaustion was hitting him in waves. It was early evening and they had been on the island since just before lunch, but the hours of intense focus had burned through all his reserves.

213

Yet he knew he'd have to keep going for another couple of hours.

They had taken a break and his colleagues were waiting in the courtyard between the houses. He needed a few seconds to himself before he could go back to them and continue.

Patrik took a deep breath and filled his lungs with fresh air before he made for the main house for the umpteenth time that day. He left Paula and Gösta outside while he and Martin went inside. He didn't foresee any problems, so there was no need for all four of them to go inside.

'Rickard. Tilde. We'd like you to come with us to the station in Tanumshede.'

'What the hell? Why us?'

Rickard quickly got to his feet. He ran his hand through his hair, making it stand on end. He still looked hungover and worn out, his eyes bloodshot and beads of sweat on his brow even though the room was cool.

Everyone's eyes were directed at him. Louise slowly sat up on the sofa she'd been resting on.

'What's going on?' she said sleepily.

Then it all caught up with her, and she gasped loudly. Patrik swallowed. He couldn't bring himself to look at Henning or Elisabeth, but he could feel their gazes.

'We've got a warrant for your arrest, Rickard. And we need to ask you a number of supplementary questions, Tilde.'

The crackling of the fire and distant voices outside were all that was audible. Then Henning spoke with restrained anger:

'What's this all about? There must be a mistake.'

Patrik gritted his teeth. He rarely had to do this kind of thing in front of the whole family, and it was only going to make the tragedy worse for everyone. But his job was to find the truth, and right now Rickard was where the evidence was pointing them. Those were the facts. Cold, hard facts.

'We're following the instructions of the prosecutor. You have to come with us, Rickard. We can't make you come with us, Tilde, but since it's in everyone's interest for this to be resolved, it would be good if we could have your cooperation to the greatest extent possible.'

Elisabeth groped for Henning's hand. Her face was ashen.

'Go with them,' she said insistently. 'Go with them so this mistake can be sorted out.'

'I'll call our lawyer,' said Henning.

He let go of Elisabeth's hand and headed for his study.

'Mum, it's only some dumb provincial cops. It'll all be fine.'

Rickard shrugged, but Patrik noted a glimmer of terror in his eyes.

'And I'll come with you. I'm not going to let Rickard go on his own.'

Tilde picked up her handbag and made for the hallway.

'I'll be back in a couple of hours,' said Rickard.

He followed Tilde and put on his shoes and coat. Then he held out his arms.

'So are we going or what?'

Patrik and Martin exchanged a glance. Arrogance was usually to their benefit. The more superior Rickard considered himself, the better.

'You'll regret this,' said Rickard once they'd shut the door. 'Don't you think we know powerful people? You'll be writing parking tickets in Lapland when we're done with you.'

He blustered on as they walked down towards the waiting boat, and Tilde ran along anxiously behind him. She slipped in her heels, which were wholly inappropriate for the rocks, but Martin caught her arm at the last moment.

'Thanks,' she managed to say, while Rickard looked at them in annoyance.

'My brother's dead. And my nephews. Can't we be left to grieve in peace?'

'We're doing our jobs,' said Patrik.

'So this is how they spend our taxes . . .' Rickard muttered as he got on board the boat with Tilde on his tail.

'He's not doing himself any favours,' Martin remarked quietly from behind Patrik. Paula and Gösta were going to stay on the island while the forensics team were there. The search of the island by their colleagues from Uddevalla was still incomplete, so they needed to leave a few officers.

'At least that damn helicopter has gone,' said Martin.

Patrick growled. He still wondered how on earth the press had managed to find out that something had happened so quickly, but he had a strong suspicion.

18

STOCKHOLM 1980

P'tite liked staying in houses, and she liked staying with Rolf and Ester. The grey detached house in Enskede had a big back garden and beds full of strawberries, rhubarb, carrots and sugar peas. Every afternoon, she and Ester would wander through the vegetable patch collecting their dinner in a big basket. She hadn't known that carrots and tomatoes could be so tasty. Daddy wasn't keen on vegetables, so it wasn't something they had very often, and when Daddy did buy vegetables they were tasteless and sloppy. The ones growing in Ester and Rolf's garden were completely different.

'Would you like rhubarb pie for pudding tonight?' said Ester, stroking her hair.

P'tite nodded eagerly. She'd never tasted rhubarb pie before her first night there, and it was the most delicious thing she'd ever eaten. She also loved eating stripped-back stalks of rhubarb that she dipped into a bowl of sugar before each bite. The mere thought of the blend of bitterness and sweetness made her taste buds tingle.

'When's Daddy coming home?' she asked, reaching for a huge, juicy strawberry.

She pretended the question wasn't all that important,

even though it was actually the most important question in the whole world. Both Ester and Rolf looked at her with sad eyes each time she asked, so she tried not to ask as often as she wanted to. But this time, Ester looked happy.

'Rolf called and said the doctor says she can come home on Saturday!'

'How many days is it until Saturday?' said P'tite.

Her heart was beating much harder now. She longed to see Daddy so much that she didn't know how all the longing fitted inside her.

'That's in four days' time. That'll be all right, won't it? Staying with us for another four days?'

Ester looked at her with gentle eyes. P'tite liked her. She liked Rolf too. They were kind. Not as kind as Daddy, of course. No one was like Daddy. But she liked them and it was fun staying in a house with a garden.

'That's okay,' she said.

Ester brightened up.

'Then we'll have to make the most of your time here. We'll cook all your favourites. Let's start with rhubarb pie tonight. And I thought we could have vanilla ice cream with strawberries for dessert tomorrow. And maybe you'd like to try my gooseberry cream for your breakfast in the morning? My granny taught me to make it – you have it with milk.'

'That sounds tasty,' said P'tite, trying the name for size in her mouth.

Goooooooooseberrrry cream. It sounded so funny. And everything else Ester had made for her had been delicious. She was sure she'd like goooooooooseberrrry cream too.

She took Ester's free hand in hers. To her surprise, she saw that it didn't make Ester happy. Her eyes had filled with tears. P'tite took the big strawberry she was holding in her hand and passed it to her.

'Here. It's the biggest one. You can have it.'

Ester hesitated. Then she took the strawberry and smiled. P'tite squeezed her hand contentedly. No one could be sad when they got a strawberry like that. She herself was bursting with happiness. Daddy was coming home soon.

19

Erica stopped at a 7-Eleven. She'd been overcome by a craving for something sweet – her bloody hormones were running amok.

She'd decided to walk back to the hotel from Blanche. The evening was unexpectedly pleasant and mild, and she'd been sensible enough to wear comfortable shoes rather than heels.

The atmosphere at Blanche had become increasingly gloomy as the news from Skjälerö had spread. Speculation had criss-crossed the room about who the three dead people were and what had happened. The winning version seemed to be that it was Elisabeth and Henning who had been killed by their son Rickard, who had then committed suicide. Erica knew the truth. And now so did Lenora. But she'd sworn Lenora to silence until the names were released to the press. Patrik had been clear in his text that the information couldn't be shared.

Erica peered through the large shop window of the 7-Eleven. Was she really going to go inside? But she would need a distraction when she got back to the hotel – she needed to watch a film or something so that she wouldn't think about what had happened on the Bauer family island. And if she was going to watch a film she'd need sweets.

Her feet seemed to lead her to the sweets inside the shop, where she helped herself to a bag of Dumle, another of Ahlgren's Cars, and another of salt liquorice.

The beautiful black and white portrait of Greta Garbo smiled at Erica welcomingly when she reached her room. She quickly changed into her loungewear and tied her hair up. She wanted to be in bed by a sensible time so that she could get as much as possible done in the morning, but it was still too early to go to bed and she hoped that Patrik might find time to call her.

She laid out her sweet buffet on the bed and began channel-hopping. In the end, she settled for a light-hearted comedy starring Jennifer Aniston and positioned herself against the pillows. But she had difficulty focusing – her thoughts kept wandering to the three body bags and to her mission in Stockholm.

Erica had no clear plan how to move forward. The threads were too sparse and she had nothing more than her gut instinct to go on. What usually helped her to advance was being led by her curiosity. What did she want to know more about? She reached for the notebook and pen lying on her bedside table and began to work.

She wrote 'Rolf' in the centre of the page and then drew lines coming off it. By the lines, she wrote 'Lola', '1980', 'fire', 'Blanche', 'rumours', 'Swedish Academy', 'exhibition', 'photographs', 'Skjälerö', 'Peter', 'massacre'.

She chewed on the end of the pen for a while before popping a couple of sweets into her mouth instead. Just at that moment her phone rang. It was Patrik. She tried to finish chewing as quickly as she could, but her mouth was still stuffed with sweets when she picked up.

'Are you drunk?' Patrik said in surprise.

Erica laughed.

'No, no. I've just been let loose on some sweets.'

She quickly became serious.

'How are you getting on? Are you okay?'

At first there was silence on the line, then Patrik sighed.

'It's very, very tough. For all of us. I'm at the station now. We . . . we've arrested someone.'

Erica managed to swallow her final sweet and was finally able to talk properly.

'Who . . . ? What can you . . . ?'

'I'll tell you more tomorrow. I can't do it right now. I've got a couple of hours ahead of me and then I'll get my head down, here at the station. Mum knows – she'll stay over with the kids. I can't handle seeing them right now. It would hurt too much.'

'Sweetie . . .'

Erica let the word linger between them.

'How have you been getting on?' said Patrik after yet more silence.

'We can talk about it tomorrow – or when you feel up to it. Do what you must – I just wanted to hear your voice. It would have felt weird not saying goodnight.'

'I know,' he said, and she could hear him smiling down the line. 'Good night, sweetheart. I love you and the kids.'

'I know,' said Erica. 'And we love you. Good night.'

They hung up and she sat there for a while with the phone in her hand. She realized she hadn't kept up with the plot of the film, but that didn't matter. It was mostly there to keep her and her thoughts company.

She reached for the notepad to carry on her mind map and stuck her hand into the open bag of sweets. It was already empty. She had guzzled the lot in record time.

Erica grimaced to herself and scrunched the bag up in her hand, making it rustle. Then she froze mid-movement. She slowly opened her hand and looked at the bag as it regained its original shape.

The Dumle bag.

A suspicion slowly began to take hold, and as she went back in time and began to put two and two together, the suspicion began to blossom into certainty. She stared at the bag.

For fuck's sake.

'Do you want to wait for your lawyer?'

Patrik sat down opposite Rickard. Martin was in the adjacent room with Tilde. They wanted to question them individually so that they had no opportunity to confer.

'Jakobsson's coming from Stockholm, so it'll take a while, and I've got nothing to hide.'

Rickard nonchalantly crossed one leg over the other and ran his hand through his hair. Patrik had noticed this was something Rickard did a lot, but he hadn't spent long enough with him to know whether it was a nervous tic or merely habit.

'Tell me about yesterday evening and the night again.'

'We've been through this already,' Rickard groaned.

Patrik waited.

'Okay,' he sighed at last. 'Again: after dinner, Mum, Dad and the others had something to discuss. There must have been a lot to drink, because I only vaguely remember Tilde and I going to bed. We'd been driven out of our own cottage and had to sleep in the kids' room.'

'Did you wake up in the night? Did you hear anything?'

Rickard shook his head.

'No, I slept like a fucking log. Didn't wake up until Louise began screaming . . .'

He ran his hand through his hair again. It was by now standing almost completely on end.

'Did Tilde wake up then too, or was she already awake?'

'She woke up then too.'

'Okay . . .'

Patrik ruminated on how to proceed. He wanted to get as many details as possible out of Rickard so that he painted himself into a corner before Patrik showed him what forensics had found.

'You said you weren't sure when you got to your bedroom, but do you know whether you undressed before you went to sleep?'

'I woke up in my underpants and Tilde was naked, so yes, I assume we did.'

'And you put your clothes on the desk chair in the boys' room?'

'No idea. It's all a fucking blur. I don't usually get so pissed, but I suppose I must have been pulled along by Ole. The man can drink. And Tilde was pretty far gone too. But you know, Rolf's death and all that had an effect.'

'Yes, of course it did.'

Patrik made a few notes in his notebook. The tape recorder had been running throughout the interview, but writing brief notes by hand helped him to marshal his thoughts.

'You said when we last spoke that you had a good relationship with your brother, but that there was some conflict in the family about your financial situation. Could you tell me more about that?'

Rickard snorted.

'I don't understand why you think this is so important. It's no biggie. I'm a bit short of cash, but I've got loads of irons in the fire, so it'll just take a little patience and then everything will be fine. I'll have more dough than Peter!'

He grinned. Then his smile faded.

'Fuck it, I keep forgetting . . .'

He leaned forward, resting his face in his hands. He rubbed his eyes for a few seconds before looking up at Patrik. His eyes were watery, but Patrik couldn't tell whether that was the result of tears or his hangover.

'I don't get why you're wasting your time on me. Why aren't you out there looking for the people who did this? Peter was a player in the finance world – there's probably all sorts of dodgy stuff going on that he might have found out about. There are a lot of slippery customers in big business, and something like that must be behind the murder. People must have come to the island by boat while we were asleep.'

Hand through his hair again. Patrik tapped his pen against the notepad. Then he said quietly:

'In that case, why did we find your shirt in the laundry basket with blood on it?'

Rickard stared at him. His hand was heading for his hair again, but he stopped mid-movement.

'What did you say you found?'

'We found your shirt in the laundry basket with blood on it,' Patrik repeated slowly.

'In the laundry basket?' Rickard swallowed noisily.

'Yes.'

Patrik said nothing else. A skilled interrogator knew that silence was his best ally. There was an inherent urge in people to fill silence, even when it was to their detriment.

'That's impossible.' Rickard shook his head. 'Someone must have put it there. I haven't shot anyone. I've never even held a gun.'

He shook his head again fiercely. 'Someone's trying to frame me. I swear. Someone shot them wearing my shirt. This is . . . My God. This is insane.'

Small beads of sweat began to appear on Rickard's brow, and he tugged slightly at the neckline of his top.

'By the way, you said . . . you said the shirt was hanging on the chair.'

'I didn't say it was hanging on the chair. I asked you if you remembered whether you'd hung your clothes on the chair when you went to bed. That's where your trousers were. But the shirt was in the laundry basket in the bathroom. Covered in blood.'

'This can't be happening.'

Rickard fell silent. He stared down at the table, his body shuddering.

Finally, he looked up at Patrik.

'I'm not saying another word without my lawyer here.'

Patrik stood up in disappointment. Their conversation was over until further notice.

'Did Rickard kill Rolf?'

Vivian's words fell heavily into the shocked silence in the living room. Elisabeth slowly turned her gaze to her. What was the woman on about?

'No, Rickard hasn't killed anyone. Not Rolf. Not Peter and the boys. He couldn't. He wouldn't. How could you even . . .'

Elisabeth collapsed on the sofa. It was impossible to stop the tears. This was a nightmare.

Henning emerged from his study and looked around.

'What's going on? I'd like to ask for a little calm. Jakobsson is on his way from Stockholm, Elisabeth. He got straight into the car. This is just . . . it's all a misunderstanding.'

Elisabeth took his hand and he sat down next to her on the sofa – all the energy he usually radiated seemingly gone.

'But what if it's true . . . ?' began Louise.

Her voice broke and she cleared her throat, before bursting out:

'You've always protected him, Elisabeth! You don't know what he's like! Not even you know what he's like, Henning! You've coddled him. He's spoilt and snotty and he hated Peter!'

Elisabeth tensed. It was like being struck.

'What are you saying? Do you seriously think Rickard

could have killed his own brother and the boys? You're in shock, I get it. But my God, you know Rickard! He could never kill them! And why would he kill Rolf? What possible reason could he have for that?'

To her chagrin, her voice rose to a falsetto and Henning put a protective arm around her.

'We're all grieving,' he said to Louise. 'There's no point in us turning on each other. Rickard and Peter had their differences like all brothers. But he didn't hate him.'

'Henning's right, Louise,' Ole said suddenly.

Elisabeth's eyes widened. She'd forgotten he was even in the room.

'I've known Peter and Rickard since birth,' he said. 'They were different, but they were like planets in a solar system. They didn't interfere with each other.'

Susanne nodded. 'That's what it was like, Louise. They've been so incredibly different from the very beginning, but they've never hated each other. I don't understand how you can claim something like that. It's bad enough as it is for Henning and Elisabeth.'

She turned to Vivian.

'And Rickard had no reason to harm Rolf. It's just a terrible coincidence that these two things have happened at the same time. Rolf's death must have been a break-in gone wrong. And Peter and the boys . . . Well, I don't know. That's for the police to work out. But no one here had any reason or desire to hurt them. That goes for Rickard as well. You know that, Louise. You're just upset and shocked.'

Susanne looked at Louise with pleading eyes and got no response.

'I want to go home,' Vivian sobbed. 'I don't want to be here.'

Her voice floated faintly across the room.

'The police said we were free to go,' said Ole, pointing to the officers still moving around outside the window.

'Then I want to take the boat to the mainland,' said Vivian.

'Ole and I will come with you,' said Susanne. 'We can book a room at the hotel for a couple of nights in case the police have any more questions. Then we'll head back to Stockholm. As long as you don't need us here?'

Susanne didn't look Elisabeth in the eye as she asked. It was apparent she wanted nothing more than to leave the island. *Well why don't you go then!* was what Elisabeth wanted to shout at her.

'Don't you worry,' she said instead. 'We've got Nancy. And Louise. We have each other. There's nothing we can do. And tomorrow our lawyer will be here – he'll bring Rickard home. We've got to get him and Tilde home. We have a funeral to arrange . . .'

Elisabeth marvelled at how absent her voice sounded. So distanced.

'We'll sort it all out, darling. Together. Louise will help us with everything.'

Henning put a hand over hers. She tried to draw strength from it, but the hand only weighed her down.

'He did hate Peter.'

Elisabeth stared at Louise sitting on the sofa. Everyone's eyes were on her. Louise stared back. Then she bent down and pulled an iPad from her bag. She swiped on something and turned the screen towards them.

'Peter's text messages get shared onto our iPad. I just saw what Rickard sent to him. Last night.'

Elisabeth couldn't take in the words on the screen – she couldn't.

Louise stood up.

'I'm going to the mainland too. I've already told my parents I'm coming.'

'Surely you're not going to . . .' Henning's gaze was still glued to the iPad. 'You're not going to show that to the police, are you?'

228

'They've already got it,' Louise said curtly.

She began to head for the hallway, but she stopped in front of Henning and Elisabeth.

'I've protected you for too long. It's cost me everything. This is enough.'

She turned to Vivian, Susanne and Ole.

'Are you coming? I've told the boat we're leaving. It'll sail in fifteen minutes.'

She grabbed her bag and headed for the front door.

Grief and confusion welled up in Elisabeth, but she could do nothing but quietly cry.

20

TUESDAY

Patrik woke up screaming in horror. He sat up on the narrow camp bed in the rest room at the station and cast the covers off. They were choking him.

Once again the images came back to him. The ones that had woken him. Images of the dead in their beds in Skjälerö. The blood. The staring, unseeing eyes. But instead of Peter, Max and William Bauer, it was Maja, Noel and Anton lying in the beds. It was their blood. They were the ones who could no longer see anything.

Patrik stood up abruptly to try and shake off the nightmare. Muttering, he went into the small kitchen to make a pot of coffee.

It was a little spooky being in the place on his own. He poured a cup of coffee when he had finished making it and went to sit on the station front step for a breath of air. The ventilation in the police station hadn't been modernized since the sixties, and after a night there it was hard to breathe. Worse, the nightmare refused to release its grip.

The traffic had started up on the road in front of the station, but so far it was sparse. The morning was raw and cold, but Patrik was wearing a coat warm enough to cope with the chill, and he'd brought a blanket from the kitchen to sit on.

Apart from his time at the police academy, he'd always lived in Tanumshede and Fjällbacka. Sometimes he thought he ought to have seen more of the world. Admittedly, he'd been abroad on holiday, but he'd never really had any adventures. Whatever good that might have done him. Erica and the kids were his adventure. And he had a job where he got to experience far more in a month than most experienced in a lifetime.

For better or worse.

The day before, he had done all he could to repress the sight of the dead boys. He'd gone through the day with tunnel vision, trying to focus on what needed doing, who had to be spoken to, and which questions he had to ask. All so that he wouldn't think about Max and William Bauer. All the blood.

But there was no escape at night. On several occasions he had woken in a cold sweat, their faces before him. He'd been involved in cases with dead children before, and each time he'd asked himself: how could he survive? How could he move on?

An old classmate drove past, saw Patrik on the step and waved. This was what he liked about places like Tanumshede and Fjällbacka. Everybody knew everybody. There was a sense of reassurance in that. There was always a neighbour who had seen something. There was always someone who recognized someone. And all those calls they received along the lines of: 'It was Bengt's lad who stole the neighbour's bike.' People could relate to each other.

The stark reality was that the vast majority of crimes were committed by someone known to the victim. Patrik had heard that as many as nine in ten murders were committed by someone close to the victim. The only people on Skjälerö had been the Bauers and their friends. The island was not in itself an impregnable fortress – it was definitely possible to get there by boat and land under cover of darkness. It just felt so far beyond anything that Patrik was familiar with, and he had statistics on his side, which meant it was reasonable to assume that it had been Rickard who had shot his brother and nephews.

The screenshot that Louise had sent the night before, with the text messages that Peter had received on the night of the murder, had been another piece of the puzzle. They would continue interrogating Rickard as soon as his lawyer arrived, at which point his messages to Peter would be something to add to the rest of their evidence. He would have a hard time explaining it all away.

A cold gust of wind went straight through his coat and Patrik shivered. The nightmare images from the night before resurfaced and he took a few sips of hot coffee, cradling the cup in his hands. There was something about families – that fine line between love and hatred. Functionality and dysfunctionality. Feelings that were so close together could easily be turned on their heads.

The tragedy for Elisabeth and Henning was so immense that he couldn't even begin to imagine what it must feel like. Their family had been crushed in one fell swoop. On Saturday they had celebrated their golden wedding anniversary. They'd had their sons, grandchildren and friends around them to raise a toast to their long and successful life together – their life as a couple and as a family. Two days later, only rubble remained. Their eldest son dead, their two grandchildren dead, their youngest son arrested for murder.

Things like that didn't spring into life from one day to the next. It must have been germinating, the situation deteriorating over the years before finally exploding in catastrophe. But what? How?

Maybe they'd never know. What happened behind closed doors often stayed there. Almost thirty years on, people were still speculating about what lay behind the Menendez brothers shooting their parents in America. Was it pure greed and indifference towards two parents who loved their children? Or was it frustration and anger that boiled over after years of abuse and sexual exploitation? No one would ever know. Perhaps the truth lay somewhere in between.

Patrik had seen Rickard's loathing for Henning boil over on Saturday. And he'd seen his hatred in the texts to Peter that Louise had shared with the police. Was Elisabeth part of the tragedy too – in her failure to teach Rickard that he couldn't have everything he wanted?

The cold from the step began to penetrate through the blanket, and Patrik stood up. The others would be arriving in half an hour. He'd called a briefing in the conference room. Rickard's lawyer was due at eleven. Before then, they needed to have gone through everything. Facts were their only path to the truth. Or as close as they could get to it.

'I'm struggling to adjust.'

It was early in the morning. Mette was standing by the window, surveying the still dark garden. Martin couldn't get enough of her silhouette, so replete with the round belly. He went over to her by the window, stood behind her and put his hands on her stomach. A few strong kicks showed the baby inside was awake and active, and he couldn't stop a big smile from spreading across his face.

'What is it you're struggling to adjust to?' he asked, kissing her neck.

She smelled clean and delicious and of the perfume on the top shelf in the bathroom cabinet, the one whose name he could never remember.

'Living with someone who goes off to work where they might get hurt or never come home again.'

'Oh, Mette.' Martin sighed and pulled her closer to him. 'You know the statistics. It's extremely unusual for police officers to even be injured in the line of duty.'

He turned her round so she could see his face.

'I know. But facts aren't exactly helping right now. The mere thought of those poor boys . . . It must be a lunatic who's responsible, and it's your job to find the monster.'

Martin gritted his teeth so hard his molars crunched. The memories from Skjälerö washed over him. What he had seen on the islands had only left him in brief moments since then, and he hadn't had much sleep. He agreed with Mette. Only an utterly callous individual could be capable of shooting two small children and their father while they lay defenceless, sleeping.

'I can't talk about it,' he said, running his hand over Mette's taut belly again. 'The only thing I want to talk about is which names we should add to the list for this cheeky monkey, which rose bush we should plant next to the gravel path, and whether we should do the small bathroom now or be sensible and keep it for later when we don't have a newborn to look after.'

'You *know* we're going to do the bathroom now,' Mette smiled, and they exchanged a glance of understanding.

She was right. Neither of them had any patience whatsoever, or the ability to wait. Things had to be done now, or preferably yesterday.

They had plenty of projects to be getting their teeth into, because the old house that Martin had inherited from Dagmar – a witness in a previous murder inquiry – needed a lot of love. Luckily, neither he nor Mette had any objection to dedicating their time and money to the old and beautiful late nineteenth-century house. In fact, it had been Mette who had fallen in love with the house the very first time he'd invited her round for dinner, and she had stayed there with him as if it were the most natural thing in the world.

Martin exhaled and felt his body relaxing against Mette's warmth. Their charming-but-demanding house would provide a home for their respective children, and soon for their first baby together. Sometimes he had to pinch himself to believe his good fortune – life had given him another chance at happiness; he'd been saved from the darkness he'd been in after Pia's death.

'Go. Do your job. Don't listen to me and my pregnancy hormones. I'll be fine.'

Mette stood on tiptoe to softly kiss him on the mouth.

'For sure?' he said.

'For sure.'

Martin kissed her one last time and then went out to the car. Before getting inside, he stopped and looked at the house. The legacy had led to so much more than he had ever hoped for.

As he drove towards Tanumshede and the police station, he tried to cling on to that feeling of happiness and gratitude. He needed it if he was going to cope with what the team had ahead of them.

Erica clutched the strip in her hand. She hadn't slept a wink all night, and as soon as the pharmacy on Drottninggatan near the hotel was open, she'd headed off to buy a pregnancy test.

She'd been staring at the strip for almost twenty minutes, but no matter how she turned it in the light and squinted there was absolutely no doubt: there was a distinct line in the small panel. Good God. She'd thought it was the beginning of menopause . . . but it was actually a bun in the oven.

She remembered the many glasses of red wine the night before with panic. Not to mention the considerable

235

volumes of booze knocked back at Henning and Elisabeth's golden wedding party on Saturday. The only consolation was that the fetus was in some kind of cocoon – the yolk sac, or whatever they called it – in the early stages, and supposedly wasn't affected by the mother's alcohol intake. But that might just be wishful thinking.

Finally, Erica threw away the strip and washed her hands with soap and water. The lack of sleep was clearly visible on her face in the mirror. It wasn't only the thought of pregnancy that had kept her awake. The news about Peter and the boys had been spinning around and around her head, and she hadn't been able to stop thinking about Louise. Her heart ached for her friend, but she didn't know what assistance she could offer to Louise in the pitch-dark abyss she must be in.

Erica had texted her before she'd gone to bed. She'd rewritten the message several times before sending it. What on earth could she possibly say? In the end she'd settled for a brief *I'm here for you, no matter what* and a heart emoji. It had felt utterly inadequate.

She hadn't received a reply, but she hadn't expected one either.

She dressed a little clumsily and unsteadily. She didn't know whether she was imagining it, but she thought she was a little nauseous. She wondered how far along she was. She'd been irregular for so long she was unsure when she'd last had her period.

She sat down heavily on the bed. What if it was too late to do anything about it? That was, if they didn't want to keep it. Surely they couldn't have another child? Not now . . . The twins were still little, fighting their way through the early years, but she and Patrik had begun to see light at the end of the tunnel. The mere thought of starting over with wakeful nights and nappies made her panic. Not to mention the thought of a difficult pregnancy. It left her so anxious she could barely breathe.

More than anything, she wanted to call Patrik and talk to him, but she knew this wasn't the right time for that. And she wanted to tell him to his face, not over the phone, so it would have to keep for when she got home.

Erica grabbed her coat and bag and left the room There was no point brooding – there was nothing she could do about the situation. She might as well follow her plans for the day.

The address was easy to find. She took the opportunity to take a walk in the weak sunshine, and she quickly warmed up even though it was chilly out. Newspaper hoardings screamed at her en route. 'Massacre on Skjälerö' thundered *Expressen*. 'Family murdered on island,' cried *Aftonbladet*.

Erica wondered what Patrik was doing now, how he was feeling and how he and his colleagues were getting on. She empathized with everyone involved.

Once she reached the door, she realized she hadn't given any thought to how she'd get inside – not to mention that she wasn't sure which flat it was. She knew it was the fifth floor, but there were probably lots of flats on each floor.

She leaned in closer to the window in the big, heavy door and used her hand to shield her eyes from the sun. Just inside there was an information board with the names of the residents and the floors they lived on. She noted the names against the fifth floor and dialled the first of them on the intercom.

It continued to buzz for a long time before Erica gave up. Then she chose the name of the next resident on the fifth floor. Elofsson, Å. After three buzzes, a husky male voice answered.

Erica spoke into the microphone as clearly as she could.

'Hello, my name's Erica Falck and I'd like to talk to someone who knows which flat had a fire here in 1980.'

There was silence for a moment. Then the door buzzed, and the lock clicked.

Erica took the small decrepit lift up to the fifth floor and read the plaques on the doors. Elofsson. She rang the bell. Almost immediately, she heard shuffling steps from within.

A man in his eighties opened the door, then backed away to admit her. He was neatly turned out in shirt and trousers with braces, and he had beautiful white hair and a beard.

'Come in, come in. I've put some coffee on,' he said, shuffling ahead of her to a small but bright kitchen.

Erica looked around curiously. She wondered if this had been Lola's flat, but she could see no signs of a dramatic restoration; the late nineteenth-century feel was intact, albeit a little battered.

Erica sat down at the kitchen table and waited patiently while the man poured coffee into beautiful and dainty espresso cups and set them down on the table.

'I'm afraid I don't have anything to go with it. Diabetes,' he said with a shrug.

'That's fine. I'm not supposed to eat stuff like that,' Erica said, sipping her coffee.

'I'm Åke,' the man said, after sitting down with some effort on the chair opposite her.

He regarded her intensely. 'Why are you interested in Lola?'

'You knew her?' said Erica, her interest piqued. Something in the man's tone when he'd said Lola's name had sounded familiar.

'Yes, I knew her. But tell me, now. Why are you interested in Lola?'

Erica carefully put her cup down on its saucer.

'A good friend told me about Lola and her death, and it got me interested. I write books about murders.'

'Those sensational things?'

Åke's mouth tightened at the corners. Erica shook her head.

'No, I wouldn't say so. It all began with my interest in people and their fates. And how things can sometimes go so badly wrong that someone gets murdered. What I try to do is bring out the individuals behind the headlines.'

'There weren't any headlines for Lola,' said Åke, apparently satisfied with her answer.

'No, and I find that strange. That there was so little written about the murder, I mean. Especially given . . . who Lola was.'

'Lola was wonderful,' said Åke, his eyes twinkling. 'Just wonderful.'

Erica took her notebook out of her bag.

'Do you mind if I take notes?' she asked, receiving an affirmative response. 'Were you close?' Erica continued.

'No. We shared the occasional cup of coffee, that's all. My dear wife and I were fully occupied with our teenage children – one of them had gone a bit off the rails. But I always appreciated chats with Lola – it was refreshing to talk to someone who didn't see the world the same way I did.'

'And her daughter?'

'Little P'tite. A ridiculously cute kid. She was Lola's world. And Lola was P'tite's world. Yes, it really was a tragedy. But you know the fire wasn't only in Lola's flat?'

Erica leaned forward with interest.

'No? Do tell.'

'That old hag Alm's flat was fire-damaged too. She went so crazy she no longer dared to have her grandson Sigge to visit any longer.'

'How old was he?'

'Same age as P'tite. I think they must have been six years old when the fire happened. They'd just thrown a party for her. The whole gang.'

'Who were the gang?'

'I didn't know them. I usually said hello whenever I met any of them in the lift or on the stairs. But there was a group of them that often came round to Lola's. Mostly late at night. Well, I was often up waiting for teenagers who never came home, so I'd hear them carrying on until pretty late.'

'Did you ever hear any quarrels from Lola's flat? Were they rowdy?'

'No, mostly laughter and music. The only time I heard arguments and shouting was the same day as the fire. A real bloody to-do.'

Erica paused, pen poised. A row at Lola's the same day she died?

'Did you hear any details?'

Åke shook his head. He stood up to fetch the coffee pot and refilled Erica's cup. Then he laboriously sat down again.

'The walls are too thick. I couldn't make out any of the words. But I thought I could hear both a man's voice and a woman's voice. But it was a long time ago. I told the police, although I don't think they even took notes. No one seemed very interested in finding out what had happened. Different times, you know . . .'

Erica nodded. No articles and the police hadn't cared. She had sniffed prejudice when she'd started doing her research, but it was still a grim realization.

'How badly damaged was the flat? Which one did she live in?'

'The one to the left of mine. And it was completely gutted. It has the same floor plan as when Lola lived there, but it's been completely renovated.'

Åke peered at her.

'Would you like to see it? I've got the key.'

'How come you have it?'

'I water the flowers for the family who live there, when they're away. They're in Dubai this week. Half-term break.'

'I'd definitely like to take a look,' said Erica, standing up.

Åke grasped the back of the chair and heaved himself up.

'Don't get old. If it's not diabetes, then it's gout. I supposed I'm going to go ga-ga soon as well.'

'The alternative is worse,' Erica said cheerfully.

Åke smiled wryly. 'Yes. At least until it isn't any longer. Come on, no need for your shoes, we can pop straight over.'

He took a key from a small cabinet on the wall by the front door and turned left after exiting. The neighbouring flat had 'Sandén' on the door and it was immediately apparent that a family with young children lived there. The hallway was full of big and small shoes, overalls, hats, scooters and bike helmets. It looked almost exactly like her own hall.

'Will they mind us coming in?' Erica asked, her gaze wandering.

It felt intrusive to enter someone's home without their knowledge.

'I'm assuming you won't steal or break anything? In that case, I don't foresee any issues with me showing you around. Right now it's not their flat, it's Lola's.'

Åke pointed further into the flat.

'This is exactly how it was laid out back then. Kitchen on the left, bedroom and wardrobe on the right, living room straight ahead. P'tite had her bed in the living room, but Lola had rigged up an alcove for the girl in that corner over there.'

He gestured from where he stood into the big bright room.

'The big trunk was over there too,' he said, lowering his gaze.

For a moment there was silence. That was where they'd found P'tite's body. Erica suddenly felt nauseous but fought against it.

Åke cleared his throat and continued the guided tour. He tapped against one of the walls. 'There used to be a door into the kitchen here. And you'll have to ignore the girls' bedroom – that didn't exist back then. The family living here now bought the studio flat next door and demolished the wall to make it bigger.'

'I get what you mean about it being completely refurbished.'

Erica looked around. The flat looked far more modern than Åke's, lacking all the period features.

'It was completely gutted. The fire destroyed everything.'

Erica walked towards the kitchen. She recalled what it had said in the investigation. Lola had been lying on the kitchen floor in front of the hob.

Erica knelt where Lola must have been lying, but the kitchen felt so new that she struggled to picture it.

She got up and went into the bedroom. It was light and airy with big windows. The walk-in wardrobe was almost like a room of its own, rather than the piece of furniture she had been imagining.

'This room looked like one of those . . . boutiques.' Åke gestured towards the bedroom and the wardrobe. 'There was a lot of Lola in here. Loads of beautiful clothes and high heels and bottles of perfume, and her wigs.'

'It sounds wonderful.'

Erica wished she'd seen the room when it was Lola's. She wished she'd got to meet Lola.

'Do you know anything about Lola's life before . . . well, *Lola*? Did she ever say anything?'

Åke hesitated.

'For me, there was only Lola. That was the way she wanted it. But . . .'

Erica stood quietly and waited.

'You know, it's so strange. I know she's gone and that I ought to tell the whole story because she's dead and her little girl's dead, and the only thing I can do for them now is to help the truth come out. Because I assume that's what you're after? The truth about what happened to them, I mean. But at the same time, it goes against the grain . . .'

Åke cleared his throat and took the plunge.

'There was a woman here. She called Lola "Lars". I'd never seen her before, and I've never seen her since that day. But Lola didn't want her here. They were in the hallway talking just inside the front door when I came up in the lift. I didn't want to eavesdrop, so I went into my flat and shut the door. But without hearing any details, I couldn't help but realize that Lola wanted that woman to leave. And I heard the woman call her Lars. And that . . . well, I didn't like it. I knew she wanted to be Lola. She wasn't Lars. And it feels wrong to even mention Lars.'

Erica spontaneously placed her hand on Åke's arm. He patted it.

'Look at me, getting all sentimental. But it's lovely to talk about Lola again. And her little girl. I've never forgotten them. And I'd very much like to know who killed them before I shuffle off this mortal coil. Or lose my marbles.'

'I can't make any promises. But I'll do my best. I also want to find out what happened to Lola and her daughter.'

Erica looked around the room and for a moment she thought she could make out the scent of perfume.

* * *

Henning put down his teacup and stared at the screen. Elisabeth was finally asleep. Only once the initial shock had given way had she been able to cry. It had been hysterical and bestial – as if her heart were being torn asunder. Which was probably not far from the truth.

It had begun after Louise had departed with Vivian, Ole and Susanne, and it had continued all night. She had been inconsolable.

This morning he'd managed to get her to take a Stilnoct. It was as much for his sake as hers. He couldn't stand to hear her grief.

His own feelings were confined – as if a roar had been trapped within him.

The cursor flashed on the screen. Henning wasn't sitting at the computer because he thought he'd be able to write anything – he was sitting here because it felt familiar. A familiar torment. He'd spent thousands of hours in that same spot. Agonizing. Feeling the anxiety seeping from his every pore. In a way, it had become his hair shirt and with the years he'd grown accustomed to the pain.

Right now he was trying to make use of the familiar situation to cope with this new torment – the one that hurt so much it made him want to crawl out of his own skin. But the flashing cursor provided him with neither relief nor anxiety. None of what had once been so important was now worth a thing.

Henning heard Nancy moving about in the kitchen. He had left the door to his study open to try and vanquish the sense of claustrophobia. He couldn't understand his own reactions – it was as if the walls were closing in on him.

He got up and went over to the window. He, Elisabeth and Nancy were alone on the island. Tilde had wanted to return to the island; she'd called them after she'd been questioned at the station, but Elisabeth had refused and told their daughter-in-law she'd have to stay at the hotel at their expense.

Everything was falling apart. The life they had carefully crafted together. Maybe it was karma. So many of their choices had been right for them but had been made at the expense of others. Perhaps this was exactly what they deserved.

The phone rang. It had been ringing constantly all morning. The media were hounding him, friends wanted to know how they were doing, the family's lawyer had tried to get hold of him. He'd rejected all their calls.

He sat down again at the computer. He tried to find comfort in the familiar anxiety summoned by the flashing cursor on a blank page. All those blank pages. Was that to be his response? Empty pages?

He closed the computer and pulled out his phone to call the lawyer back. He still had one son. That was all that was left to him.

The remorse was heavy to bear. Paula had to fight herself every step of the way to the conference room. What was her punishment to be?

'Patrik?'

Her voice sounded so pitiful – completely unlike her usual one.

Patrik was writing something on one of the whiteboards while Annika laid out coffee and biscuits.

'Yes?' he said absently, without looking at her.

'Can I have a word? In my office?'

'Of course,' he said, putting the marker down on the ledge of the board.

When they reached her office, she looked down at her feet in shame. She couldn't look Patrik in the eye.

'Yesterday you wondered how the press were able to get to the island so quickly . . .'

'Yes?' said Patrik.

His voice was gruff, and Paula forced herself to look him in the eye. When she'd got home the night before, Johanna had noticed something was up right away and Paula had promised to bring it up with Patrik first thing in the morning. But it was so hard.

'It was my fault,' she said. 'I had a brain fart and did something stupid. I did some horse trading with a hack and I . . . I said too much. I'm so sorry – it'll never happen again. And I'll willingly accept whatever punishment you impose.'

Paula's voice broke and she blinked away tears. The last few days had taken their toll.

'Okay, take it easy. Slow down and tell me what happened,' said Patrik, putting a hand on her shoulder.

She had to fight the impulse to throw herself into his arms in relief – that wouldn't have been very professional.

'What did you get from the journalist in exchange?' he said, pulling forward her visitor's chair so he could sit down.

Paula sat down at her computer and tapped a few keys. She turned the display towards Patrik.

'*Aftonbladet* is working on a big exposé on Blanche. They sent it to me this morning. They have an inside source who's given them all sorts of dirt. Strange payouts, secret emails, dodgy contracts. The lot.'

'You think the source is Rolf?' said Patrik thoughtfully as he read it.

'As a motive to kill him, it would be huge.'

'How does it tie in to the murder of Peter and the boys?' said Patrik.

It sounded as if he was thinking aloud rather than asking Paula a question, but it was something she had already thought about.

'Louise seems to handle a lot of the administrative side of things at Blanche. According to the article, she's identified

246

as the person who paid hush money to people, sorted out non-disclosure agreements, etcetera. And Louise was meant to be sleeping in that room that night. Peter and the boys may simply have been collateral damage.'

Patrik looked from the screen to Paula.

'So someone with a connection to Blanche had a motive to silence both Rolf and Louise? Both the informed source and the person in possession of damaging facts? That's not completely improbable. But who? And how does it relate to Rickard? We've got evidence to suggest that he shot Peter and his nephews. Was he paid to do it? Does he have his own interests in Blanche?'

Paula's phone buzzed. This can't be, she thought to herself as she read it. Then the laughter erupted. It was slightly hysterical, and Patrik looked at her in concern. She managed to stop laughing by coughing a few times. Then she held up her phone to show him.

'They've published the article. I sold my soul for an hour's head start with an article that everyone can read now anyway.'

'I'm not going to tell you off,' Patrik said gently. 'I know you get it. We all make mistakes, and there's no point dwelling on it. What we need to do now is get all our facts, all our questions, all our theories onto the wall. Briefing in five minutes' time. And stop hunching those shoulders. It's all fine.'

Tears of relief burned behind her eyelids. Once Patrik had left her office, Paula sent a text to her mother. Thinking of you. Should I bring anything tonight?

21

STOCKHOLM 1980

Lola anxiously examined her reflection in the mirror, but everything appeared to have healed as it should. She had refused to look at herself in the hospital.

She reached for her foundation and began to apply it to her face, smoothing an extra layer over the bruises which were still shades of blue and green. She could no longer wait for them to disappear – she needed to go back to work if she was going to pay her rent.

'Are you working tonight?'

P'tite had crept up behind her and wrapped her arms around her waist. She sounded uneasy.

Lola turned around and hugged her daughter.

'Daddy has to work. Otherwise we won't be able to eat.'

'I'm not hungry and I don't need to eat.'

P'tite buried her face between Lola's breasts, and she felt them moving inside her bra. She took P'tite's head and held her away so that she could look her in the eye.

'It was an accident. I didn't look as I crossed the road, which was stupid. From now on, I'll do exactly what I've taught you. I'll look left, then right, and then left again.'

'Do you promise?'

P'tite sobbed. Lola held her tightly and spoke seriously:

'I promise. I swear on your mother in heaven. I promise I'll never let anything happen to me again. Or you.'

The doorbell rang and both of them jumped. Lola grimaced as she stood up. She didn't want to think about how long the pain would last. She limped slightly as she made for the door and realized reluctantly that it would probably be a while before she was back in heels.

When Lola saw who was outside, she wanted to shut the door, but she opened it reluctantly and took a step back.

'I heard what happened,' said her sister. 'Not that you ever say anything.'

She stared at Lola reproachfully.

'Why would I?' said Lola.

'Things can't carry on like this, Lars. Don't you understand? It's dangerous.'

Her voice was loud and accusatory, and Lola had to stifle an impulse to put her hands over her ears. She hated hearing the name Lars. That was the name of a dead person. Someone buried long ago.

She spotted her neighbour Åke closing the grille on the lift over her sister's shoulder. He looked at them curiously.

'Come in,' Lola said reluctantly.

No matter how much she didn't want to invite her sister inside, she was even less keen to share this part of her life with others.

'Looks clean enough,' her sister said, striding inside. Lola had always detested the way her sister felt she owned every space.

'Why wouldn't it be?'

Her sister pursed her neatly painted lips.

'Is this Julia?'

'She's called P'tite,' Lola said, putting her arms protectively around her daughter.

'Where was she while you were in hospital?' her sister said, scrutinizing P'tite from head to toe.

'With friends,' Lola said curtly.

Her whole soul was screaming at the fact that her sister was in her home. She wasn't invited. She had long ago forfeited the right to be part of Lola's life – just like the rest of her family. Their parents were dead now, but she still felt the bitterness in her mouth at their cold condemnation.

'Lars! How could you let your daughter stay with friends instead of calling me? How old is she now? Five?'

Her sister's voice had the same tone of censure as their parents', and Lola grimaced again at the use of that name.

'Daddy's not called Lars, Daddy's called Lola, and I'm actually nearly six,' said P'tite, pushing herself against Lola and wrapping her arms around her legs.

Lola ruffled her hair. What a lovely, lovely child.

'I honestly can't fathom why social services allow this . . . situation.'

Her sister looked around the flat. The red rya rug in the living room, the collection of Lisa Larson plump ABC girls on the windowsill, the wigs in the bedroom . . .

Lola felt the flutter of terror in her breast. Her sister's words touched her deepest fear – that her choice would result in P'tite being taken away from her.

'We're managing just fine,' she said stiffly, taking a step back with P'tite.

'It's only a matter of time before something happens,' her sister said coldly, examining the kitchen in detail. 'Oh well. You know where I am if you need me. But you also know that the condition is that this nonsense has to stop.'

Her lip curled as she looked at Lola's hot pink nails.

'I think you should go now,' said Lola.

'Of course. I know when I'm not wanted.'

She made for the door but then turned around and looked at P'tite.

'Your father is stubborn. And stupid. But if you ever need help you can call me. I'll leave my number here.'

She pulled out a card and tucked it into P'tite's ruck-sack.

'Leave now.'

When the front door had shut, Lola knelt and hugged her daughter hard as she whispered:

'Nothing is ever going to happen. We have each other. That's enough.'

Her daughter hugged her back, equally hard. It was the two of them against the world. Just the two of them.

22

Ritorno on Odengatan was packed, but Erica had found a spot in the corner where she could sit with her laptop. She had always loved the classic patisserie, which had been there for sixty years and always gave the impression that time had stood still, with its dark interior and classic bakes.

Erica twisted and stretched her back as discreetly as she could. Then she pulled out her notepad and began to check her bullet-pointed list of what she needed to get done during her stay in Stockholm. It had been a long time since Lola was murdered. People would have moved or died. Those that were left might struggle to remember. Time was devastating to an investigation – that much she already knew.

At the top of the list was finding out how Lola had come to be living alone with her daughter. It was unusual for P'tite's mother to be out of the picture, and it must have been even more unusual in the eighties.

Erica had P'tite's personal identity number and through searches with the Tax Agency and population register, she had ascertained who were listed as her parents. Lars Berggren was registered as the father – which tallied with what she knew already. But the mother's name was Monica Sohlberg, deceased 30 August 1974. The same day that P'tite was born.

Erica continued to tap away. There was a Birgitta Sohlberg registered as Monica's mother, and she was still alive. And she had an address in Stockholm, thank goodness. In Bagarmossen.

It wouldn't take her long to get there by taxi now that the rush hour was over. Erica pulled out her phone and looked at the phone number on her computer. Should she call ahead and give advance warning of her arrival and what it was about? She tucked her phone into her bag and gathered her things. It was usually better to have the element of surprise on her side.

Erica quickly found a taxi and then it took twenty minutes to drive to Bagarmossen. The cab pulled over on a street below the animal hospital and Erica sought out the right number among the low blocks of flats from the fifties. An elderly man exited from the main door as Erica approached and she hurried to nip inside.

She found the right name on a black sign with white lettering on the right-hand side of the foyer and noted that Birgitta Sohlberg lived on the second floor. She took the stairs and stopped for a few seconds, panting, before she rang the doorbell. There was a welcome plaque hanging on the door with a picture of Jesus on it. Erica crossed her fingers that Birgitta would be in and breathed a sigh of relief when she heard footsteps on the other side of the door.

An old woman peered cautiously at her through the crack that the security chain allowed.

'I don't care what you're selling, I'm not interested. And if you're from the Jehovahs then you should know that Christ is already in my heart.'

'I'm not selling anything,' Erica said, trying not to smile

at the fact that she could be mistaken for a Jehovah's Witness. 'My name is Erica Falck. I'd like to ask you some questions about your daughter.'

'About Ingela? Why do you want to ask about Ingela?' said the woman, closing the door another centimetre.

'No, not Ingela. Monica.'

Birgitta was silent for a while. Then she pulled the door shut. Erica had time to curse her own pushiness before the chain rattled and the door opened.

'Come in.'

Erica followed the old lady into the hall. Everywhere she looked, Jesus was looking back. From paintings, tapestries and small porcelain and ceramic figurines. There were also crosses and Bible quotations dotted all over the place.

'Let's sit down in the living room. Viktor's doing his homework in the kitchen.'

'Viktor?'

Yes, my grandson,' Birgitta said, her eyes shining. 'He's lived with me for many years.'

Birgitta pointed to a floral sofa with a glass-topped wicker table in front of it, and Erica sat down. She'd never been in such a clean home. It made her own look like a crack den by comparison.

'You have a lovely home,' she said, and was rewarded with a smile.

'Thanks. Very kind of you to say. Well, I suppose I like to keep things in order.' Birgitta sat down at the other end of the sofa. 'So, why are you asking about Monica? She's been gone for many years.'

Erica cleared her throat. It was always a little nerve-racking having to explain herself. She never knew what might touch a nerve and what wouldn't, and over the years she'd encountered scoldings and hysterical fits of crying.

'I write books. About murders. I heard about Lola and her daughter through an acquaintance.'

'Lola . . .' Birgitta said the name slowly. 'It's been a long time since I heard that name.'

Erica decided to get straight to the point.

'As I understand it, your daughter was the mother of Lola's child. But the records show she died the same day the girl was born?'

'Yes, poor soul. May God have mercy upon her.'

Birgitta fidgeted with the edge of a cloth on the coffee table that was embroidered with the words: *Except a man be born again, he cannot see the kingdom of God.*

'This quote is from the Gospel of John. Have you accepted God into your heart?'

Erica shifted awkwardly.

'Hmm, well, I'm not that . . . ecclesiastical.'

'Do you have any faith?'

'As a child, I suppose . . .'

Erica's relationship with the church was complicated. In Fjällbacka and its surroundings there were still remnants of the strict, unforgiving religion that had kept the area in its grip for so long, making people live under the yoke of guilt and shame and in constant fear of God's wrath.

'That's good. Childhood faith is good.' Birgitta fell silent and looked out of the window.

'We were talking about Monica . . .' said Erica, bringing them back to the topic.

She heard someone moving about in the kitchen and assumed it was the grandson doing homework. She was surprised that Birgitta had a grandchild that young, but then again it might be a great-grandchild – that would be more likely . . .

'Monica was wild, even as a little girl,' said Birgitta. 'Never did as she was told. Quite the opposite. Well, I suppose both the girls got that from their father. The destructive part came from me.'

Erica looked at her in surprise. Destructive wasn't quite the word she would have used to describe the woman before her in her neatly ironed skirt and immaculate, high-collared blouse.

Birgitta seemed to spot her look, because she smiled.

'My need for order comes from the chaos in my former life. Before I found Jesus, I was deep in the abyss. My girls had a terrible childhood. Their father died when they were little, I was left on my own with them, and I was too young, wild and stupid to handle that responsibility. I shouldn't have been allowed to keep them.'

She didn't let her gaze shy away from Erica's.

'My daughters were basically left to raise themselves and they saw a lot they shouldn't have. Monica was the eldest, and she took it the hardest. In addition to looking after herself, she had to look after Ingela too. Things went the way they went. First booze. Then drugs. Then doing whatever it took to raise the cash for her habit. Burglary. Prostitution. And I was too deep in my own hole to help her. I only got sober ten years after Monica died. Around that time. By then she and the girl were gone.'

Her hand trembled as she fidgeted with the fringes of the cloth.

'Did you ever meet Lola? Or your granddaughter?'

'Yes. Lola once brought the girl to meet me in a park. I think she must have been around a year old. But I was . . . I was so broken that Lola was wise enough not to repeat that encounter.'

'Did she explain what had happened? To Monica?'

'She died during childbirth. Something went wrong and she bled out.'

'Did Lola say anything about how long they'd been together?'

'No, I didn't find out much about their relationship. I was in no shape to ask either. But I remember that he . . . sorry, *she*, said they were soulmates. I've always remembered that. I thought it was so beautiful. And it's brought me a lot of comfort over the years to know that Monica met her soulmate before she returned home to God.'

Erica hesitated but was too curious not to ask.

'But what was your perspective on . . . Lola? Given that . . .'

She looked around at all the crosses and Jesus figurines and felt ashamed for asking. But Birgitta didn't seem to take offence.

'When I met Lola, I still hadn't found my God and saviour. And the people around me were a motley crew. Who was I to judge? But I assume you mean my perspective on the situation . . . her . . . later on. A perfectly reasonable question. But you have to understand that my God is a forgiving God. He's forgiven me for my sins. And there are many of them. And the God I know in my heart is the creator of everything on Earth. That means He created us all just as He wants us to be. We all have our place. We all have our purpose.'

Erica smiled. It was a beautiful way to look at God.

'Grandma?'

A man who was surely in his early thirties was standing in the doorway clutching a colourful puzzle book about letters.

'Grandma, I spelled "banana".'

He smiled broadly and pointed to the book. Birgitta clapped her hands together in delight.

'Oh well done, Viktor! You're so clever!'

'I'm very clever,' Viktor said with satisfaction, before returning to the kitchen.

Birgitta watched Viktor go and then spotted Erica's quizzical look.

'Viktor is Ingela's son. As you may have realized, he has Down's syndrome. He's been living with me since he was a little boy. Ingela . . . Ingela wasn't quite up to it. But he's my joy in life. Him and Jesus.'

'How old is he?' Erica said curiously.

'Thirty-three. Some people with Down's can go to school and work like the rest of us, but unfortunately that's not the case for Viktor. His challenges are too great. He probably ought to be in day care, but he's very keen to go to school so I teach him at home.'

She smiled, making the wrinkles around her eyes deepen. 'For me, he's the proof that God created us in His image. There's no one more loving than Viktor. He's been made with just as much intention as the rest of us, if not more.'

Erica swallowed. Birgitta's bottomless love for her grandson made her throat tighten.

'Oh yes, Lola,' Birgitta added. 'She was a lovely person – that was all I needed to know. On the other hand, I was a little envious that her legs looked better in a skirt than mine did.'

Erica laughed. 'Yes, I've seen a photo of her, and she was incredibly good looking.'

'Wait!'

Birgitta leapt up and left the room. She was gone for so long that Erica began to wonder where she'd got to. Just as she was about to stand up, Birgitta returned with a black box in her arms.

'If you promise to return them, you can borrow these,' she said. 'Lola sent them to me, not long before she and P'tite were brought home to God. I think it was a way for her to invite me back into their lives again. Sadly, that didn't work out.'

When Erica lifted the lid of the box, she gasped. It was full of photos. Slightly yellowed, some with tatty corners.

Photos of Lola and Monica and P'tite. Her hands trembled as she thumbed through them.

'Thank you. I promise to take good care of them,' she said, standing up on faltering legs.

As they headed for the front door, Erica stopped in the kitchen doorway. Viktor was sitting at the table in deep concentration, his tongue at the corner of his mouth and a crayon in his hand. He was laboriously writing the word 'monkey' underneath a picture of a monkey, and he held up the book to Erica and his grandmother with a smile.

'Look! I wrote "monkey"!'

Birgitta went over and kissed him on the top of his head and put her arms around him.

'Thanks for letting me talk about my Monica. And Lola. I hope you'll be open to accepting God into your heart in future.'

Erica smiled.

'The God you describe is always welcome.'

Patrik stood in front of the two whiteboards in the conference room, preparing to start the briefing.

'What's our status with Rickard?' Mellberg asked from his corner of the room.

'I was going to start there. He's in custody, but we haven't been able to question him since yesterday because we're still waiting for his lawyer. He's due to arrive soon.'

'No confession?' said Mellberg, reaching for a shortbread on the plate that Annika had provided.

Patrik shook his head.

'He denies everything.'

'Does it seem genuine?' Paula asked.

Patrik hesitated before replying, trying to recall what he'd felt the night before.

'I don't know. It's hard to tell with Rickard. It feels like nothing about him is for real. But there is the alternative that he was so hammered he can't remember.'

'Did we take a saliva sample from him?' Martin asked.

'No, unfortunately not,' said Patrik.

He nodded towards the boards that he had prepared ahead of the meeting. The one to the left was full of pictures from the investigation. He pointed to a photo he had stuck to the board with a magnet.

'Last night I received a screenshot from Louise – Peter's wife – showing a text message that Rickard sent to Peter on the night of the murders.'

He read aloud from the photo:

Go fuck yourself, bastard.'

'Short and sweet,' Gösta said dryly. 'Am I the only one who thinks this is an open-and-shut case? Even if we haven't found the gun, we've got the blood-covered shirt and now we have a text showing Rickard's emotional state on the night of the murder. Sure, it's not an outright death threat, but it shows that he wasn't exactly fond of his brother. What time was that sent?'

'Three fifteen,' said Patrik.

'Do we have any indication from the medical examiner on the time of death?' said Gösta.

Patrik shook his head.

'Not yet. We're still waiting for all the analyses – both forensic and medical. The same goes for the evidence we secured at the scene of Rolf's murder. But I know Farideh is chivvying NFC along as best as she can. Given the media coverage, I suspect we'll get quick results.'

'Gratifying in this case, but unfortunate that that's what it takes,' said Gösta.

Patrik didn't disagree, but right now he was happy to take it and put up with the propensity to prioritize cases that were garnering extensive press attention.

Martin sat up straighter on his side of the table.

'What do we make of Rickard as the killer in Rolf's murder?' he said. 'Pretty plausible, right? Likely, even.'

'We don't yet have anything tying Rickard to the murder of Rolf,' said Patrik. 'We don't have a motive, and there's no forensic evidence pointing to him so far. No witness statements from the night in question place him at the scene. On the other hand, there isn't anything to indicate that it *isn't* Rickard.'

He looked at the two whiteboards. The one on the left was filled with pictures, the one on the right was empty.

'I'd like to play devil's advocate and go through everything we've got without any preconceptions. Let's not consider Rickard's guilt to be a foregone conclusion. Let's begin with the murder of Rolf and move on to the murder of Peter and the boys. All idle speculation is welcome – no idea or theory is too stupid; nothing is too irrelevant to bring up. Annika, can you take notes?'

'Yep. I'll take notes and I've set my phone to record. Go for it. I write quickly.'

Patrik turned to the empty board and picked up a marker.

'We know that Rolf Stenklo was murdered late on Saturday or early on Sunday. We're waiting for a more precise time of death from the medical examiner, but the body was cold when he was found, so he must have been dead for several hours.'

He pointed to a picture of Rolf's corpse on the left-hand whiteboard.

'As we understand it, he was at the gallery preparing for his exhibition, which was due to open yesterday – on Monday. He'd hung up frames with notes on which he'd written the names of the photographs that would later take their places. The framed photos themselves were stacked at the back of the venue. There were fifteen of them in total – worth around two million kronor. Someone came into the gallery during the night and shot him in the back of the head with a nail gun – a nail gun we believe was already at the scene. There was no sign of any fingerprints on the nail gun – it was probably wiped – and there doesn't seem to be any DNA either, but there were material fibres on the gun that our forensics team secured. Unfortunately, we can't say right now whether they were there before-hand, whether they came from Rolf or whether they belong to our killer.'

Patrik wrote keywords on the board as he spoke, under-lining some of them.

'Write "unplanned",' said Martin, pointing to the board. 'The fact that the killer used a weapon that was already there suggests it wasn't planned.'

'Agreed,' said Patrik, writing 'unplanned' on the board and underlining it.

He turned back to the team.

'We're going to ask Vivian about the exhibition and ask her to take a closer look at the photos from the gallery and see if anything strikes her. You formed a good bond with her, didn't you, Martin? Could you go and see her after we're done here?'

Martin gave a thumbs up.

'Good. Take that video I made of the gallery with you,' said Patrik. 'We've also got a bit more substance on possible motives, thanks to today's issue of *Aftonbladet*. Has anyone seen it and had time to read it?'

Everyone nodded.

'Great. This is something we need to look at more closely. Someone inside Blanche seems to have leaked all sorts of information that the management won't have wanted to see the light of day. Maybe Rolf was the source – in that case it's a motive for murder. But we still don't know whether that's the case, so let's keep an open mind and not get too attached to any particular theories.'

'If it looks like a horse and neighs like a horse, it's probably a horse and not a zebra,' Mellberg said glumly, crossing his arms.

'I don't think that's quite how the saying goes . . .' Martin said, but stopped when Annika flashed him a warning look.

Arguing the toss with Mellberg was rarely time well spent.

'On the other hand . . .' Patrik tapped the marker against his palm to emphasize his words. 'On the other hand, maybe that motive also ties in with events on Skjälerö. One person clearly singled out in the article as deeply entrenched and involved in Blanche's affairs is Louise. And she was meant to be sleeping in her bedroom.'

'Okay, but what would Rickard's motive be – in relation to Blanche – for killing Rolf and then Louise?' said Gösta. 'If we're toying with the idea that she was the real target.'

He reached for a biscuit.

'We should look into Rickard's connection to Blanche,' said Patrik. 'Has he been involved in any way? From what I've been able to deduce from the first article in the series, there's a whole bunch of dirt coming to light. Sexual assault. Young girls' silence being bought. Bribes to members of the Swedish Academy related to betting ahead of the Nobel Prize in Literature being announced. Holes in Blanche's accounts. There's a long list.'

'Bloody hell,' said Gösta. 'Posh nobs. But they all shit like the rest of us.'

Mellberg chuckled, his stomach wobbling.

'Nice one, Gösta. Well put,' he said, holding up a greasy thumb still covered in biscuit crumbs.

'Look, I don't get it,' said Martin. 'Exactly who has been singled out by the papers?'

He had a deep wrinkle of concern between his eyes, which always formed when he didn't have the full picture.

'I'm not going to claim that I've got a hold on the whole mess,' said Patrik. 'That's something we'll have to work to map out. But as I understand it, it's largely Ole being accused of using his status at the club to sexually exploit young women.'

'And what about the others? Henning, Elisabeth and Louise?'

'They've covered up for him. They've allegedly used power, cash, favours – well, any currency you can name – to keep the women in question quiet.'

'Holy shit, that's awful,' Martin said with disgust.

No one contradicted him.

'We also need to look at whether Rickard might have been paid to carry out the murders,' Patrik said, turning back to the board. 'He's desperate for cash – several people around him have said as much when we spoke to them. In other words, we need to request details of his accounts and check whether there have been any big deposits lately.'

Patrik underlined 'Rickard's bank statements'.

'Sorry to go on about this, but I still don't want us to become fixated on Rickard. It almost feels too simple – we need to consider other possibilities. For example, whether a person or persons unknown came to the island by night. I also think we should look more closely at the possibility that Louise was the actual target.'

He looked at the whiteboard before turning back to his colleagues.

'When I spoke to Rickard out on the island, he said something that I haven't been able to let go of. He said Peter had begun looking into the death of his first wife. She died a couple of years ago in a hit-and-run. Rickard said Peter had even hired someone to do some digging. There's something there that I think we should be looking at ourselves.'

He wrote 'Peter's wife, hit-and-run' on the board.

'Does anyone have anything to add? Oh yes, Martin. We haven't had time to ask about how the interview with Tilde went last night. Did it give us anything in relation to Rickard's alibi?'

'No, she says the same as he does. That they went to bed together. That they'd both had a lot to drink. And that they slept all night and only woke up when Louise screamed in the room next door.'

'No discrepancies in their stories?' Patrik asked.

Martin shook his head. 'No, but we know how unreliable alibis from loved ones can be. So the value of her testimony is questionable at best.'

'I agree. That's enough for now. We've got plenty to be getting on with. I'll remain in touch with Farideh and as soon as we get the reports from the autopsies and the results of our other analyses, I'll let you know. The search for the gun is still ongoing. I also thought I'd have a chat with Louise about Blanche. Apparently, she's staying with her parents. Paula, would you come with me?'

Paula nodded briskly.

'Gösta, can you investigate the hit-and-run angle? Martin, you take Vivian and try to find out more about the exhibition. Annika, can you review Rickard's bank statements as soon as the prosecutor secures them? And Mellberg . . .'

Patrik looked at Bertil, who held up his hands in a parry.

'I'm already up to my eyeballs. There's . . . a lot of admin on a case this size.'

Patrik raised his eyebrows but gave an internal sigh of relief. Mellberg always did the least damage from the sanctuary of his office while he was having one of his naps.

'Then let's get to work,' he said, glancing one last time at the whiteboards.

For a moment, he felt overwhelmed by the chaos and gigantic scale of four murders in forty-eight hours. And he couldn't help but think that time was getting away from them.

It felt good to be alone for a while in the car. Without his colleagues. Without, Martin thought to himself with a dash of shame, Tuva and Mette. He loved family life, but he also appreciated a little alone time occasionally.

He took the coast road through Grebbestad to reach Fjällbacka. It took a little longer than the road inland, but there was something about seeing the coast during the autumn. In the summer, getting through the small villages by car was hopeless. They were teeming with tourists, people were ambling along in the middle of the road, and it was generally enraging.

The calm of autumn and spring was completely different. It was as if the coastal communities relaxed, unfolded themselves and showed their very best side. The logical part of him knew that these small villages would never survive without tourism. Two months provided a livelihood for twelve. All the same . . . When you were a permanent resident, it sometimes felt like being invaded by a horde of locusts laying waste to all in their path.

Martin slowed down as he approached Sälvik. He'd called ahead to Vivian to warn her he was coming. She had no car with her, so he was able to park right by her house.

Vivian opened the door the moment Martin got out of the car.

'Come in,' she said in a subdued voice.

She looked tired and worn out. Her plait lay tangled and unkempt on her left shoulder.

'Look at the state of me! Sorry. I . . . I don't seem to be able to get a grip on things.' As if she were reading his thoughts, she gently touched a stain on her shirt.

'Sorry we keep intruding like this,' Martin said – and he meant it.

It was always uncomfortable questioning a person who had just lost someone, but at the same time he knew it was the loved ones more than anyone else who wanted the police to do their job and give them the answers they needed.

'Come on, let's sit on the terrace,' she said quickly.

They walked through the house and onto the terrace, each sitting down in a wicker armchair.

'We've got a few things we'd like to follow up on,' Martin said, clasping his hands in his lap. 'Firstly, I'd like to start by asking whether you've thought of anything since our last conversation? Related to Rolf or that night on Skjälerö?'

Vivian shook her head.

'No. I would have got in touch right away if I had. It's beyond comprehension – it's like a nightmare. Peter and the little boys . . .'

'We're doing everything we can,' Martin said. 'But what's your gut feeling? That there's some kind of connection with Rolf's death or that it's a macabre coincidence?'

Vivian heaved a trembling sigh. 'I have a hard time believing they're not related. But I've no idea how. Or why. Everyone liked Rolf. Just as everyone liked Peter. It's a completely different matter when it comes to Rickard – but Peter was a gentle, stable, warm person.'

'Do you believe Rickard would have been capable of doing this?'

'Peter and the boys? Or Rolf?'

Martin didn't answer, merely carried on looking at her. Vivian wrung her hands in her lap.

'I don't know,' she said. 'I've never been very close to Rickard. I know that Elisabeth and Henning are completely against the idea. But there's something that . . .'

Rickard's never been told no his whole life. Well, I haven't known him as long as that, but long enough. And Rolf told me he'd always been like that. I should add that Rolf was his godfather.'

'I heard.'

'Of course, he was never that involved,' said Vivian with a slight sigh. 'Not as far as I know. Maybe things were different when Rickard was younger – when Rolf and Ester were married. You would have to ask Elisabeth if you thought that might be relevant. But during our marriage, they were only sporadically in touch, and always in connection with Henning and Elisabeth. They didn't have a relationship of their own.'

Martin contemplated her, noting her tired gaze. He thought about Rolf's career and how much support Vivian must have given him behind the scenes.

Silence descended between them. Down at the shore, the reeds were bending in the wind. Big chunks of seaweed were floating in the water. They must have blown in during the storm, Martin thought to himself. He shook himself, seeking to return to the conversation, and turned back to Vivian.

'You said you weren't all that involved in Rolf's exhibition in Fjällbacka. Can you tell me more?'

'In the past, I've always been very involved, and we worked together as a team. Rolf was responsible for the creative side – the artistic bits – and I handled the practical and administrative details. "The boring bits" is how many would describe it, but I loved it. Organization and structure have always been my thing. Don't let the bohemian front fool you.'

She smiled wryly and Martin was once again struck by her natural beauty. She had made no effort to stop time – there were no peculiar interventions to smooth out wrinkles or fill out her skin. The crow's feet around her eyes testified to life lived, and he personally thought it was much more beautiful than the artificial form of youth that appeared to be in fashion.

'But not this time?'

Vivian shook her head.

'Something about Rolf was different over the last year. He was more absent. I had a hard time getting him to make decisions about things, he was forgetful, he was late, sometimes he was abrupt and snappy in a way he hadn't been before. Offhand, I'd say something was bothering him. I even asked him on a few occasions. He always got angry and told me I was wrong and that I should leave him alone. So I let it be. Perhaps I should have been more assertive. Then he might not have . . .'

Her voice died away.

'We've got a video of the gallery,' Martin said. 'Would you mind watching it?'

Vivian's mouth trembled slightly as she agreed.

Martin pulled out his mobile. He held it so that they could both see the display, and they both peered at it. Vivian's hair grazed Martin's arm as he started the video.

Patrik's recording panned across the bright space with its high ceiling. Vivian started when she saw Rolf's body on the floor. Martin placed a hand on her arm. In the video, the forensics team were visible, working away in their white overalls, and then Patrik had filmed the walls covered in cheap frames with blank sheets of paper in them.

'Rolf's placeholders,' said Vivian. 'So that he could move the photos around until he felt they were in the right places.'

The video continued along the back wall where the photographs were lined up neatly alongside each other.

Vivian grabbed Martin's arm.

'I never got to see them,' she said. 'I never got to see which photographs he was going to exhibit.'

She gasped as the camera panned past the photos for the exhibition.

'Lola!' she exclaimed.

Martin paused the video.

'You recognize the woman in the photograph?'

'Very well. I knew the exhibition was about Rolf's past, but not that . . . The funny thing is that Rolf's talk about the past got me chatting to your boss's delightful wife Erica about Lola in particular.'

Martin smiled. Vivian wasn't the first to think that Patrik was in charge of things at the station.

Vivian pointed to the mobile where the paused video was still visible.

'We've got a copy of this particular photograph at home in the flat. I really do like it a lot. It's called *Innocence*.'

'Do you know anything else about Lola?' Martin asked.

Vivian put her hand on Martin's mobile, almost touching the picture of Lola.

'She was a trans woman murdered in the early eighties. Long before I met Rolf. She and her daughter died horribly.'

'Were both murdered?' said Martin.

His pulse quickened. Might there be something in this?

'Yes – it was unsolved, so I was talking to Erica about it, and saying she ought to write a book about Lola's death. I actually think she went to Stockholm to find out more.'

Martin nodded. Patrik had told him that Erica was in Stockholm doing research for a book.

'Can you tell me anything else about the pictures?'

Martin started the video again and Vivian began to sob.

'It seems to have been an exhibition about Lola and the people around her. And about Alexa's – the club where she worked. Rolf first became friends with Lola when she was working there. Alexa's was the "in" place in Stockholm at the time. He always said that she was the wisest person he'd ever met, and that their souls had clicked after three Hot Shots. I think that was probably the only time I ever heard Rolf say anything about souls.' Vivian smiled.

'So it wasn't through Rolf's profession as a photographer?'

'No, no. I know he took quite a lot of pictures of both the staff and patrons at Alexa's. Including Lola. But their friendship wasn't based on the fact that she was in front of his lens. Rolf once said that he loved her wisdom, and she loved his kindness. Apparently, she hadn't had much of that commodity in her life.'

'There appear to be fifteen photographs,' Martin said, returning their focus to the video.

'Yes, and I think that matches the number of placeholders on the walls. Could you . . . ?'

Martin scrolled back through the film and started to play it again. He counted the frames on the walls. Fifteen.

'Wait,' Vivian said, so abruptly that Martin jumped. 'Could you go back a bit?'

Martin paused and moved backwards frame by frame.

'There! Do you see?'

Martin looked at the screen. On one of the scraps of paper, there were two titles.

'Rolf sometimes did that when he was going to hang two sister pieces next to each other,' Vivian said slowly.

Martin squinted to get a better view.

'It looks like one of the titles is *Innocence*. And that's the portrait of Lola. But I can't quite see what . . .'

'*Guilt*,' said Vivian. 'The other photo was going to be called *Guilt*.'

'Are you familiar with that photo?'

Vivian shook her head.

'No; I'm pretty sure it's not any of the photos in the video. But if there were sixteen names on the walls . . .'

'Then there's a photograph missing,' said Martin. 'Is it at all possible to work out what the picture might be? From the negatives, maybe?'

'Negatives? That's not really how things work anymore. The pictures are on a hard drive, but I've never had access to it. It's probably in Rolf's studio in Stockholm. I'm going home in a day or so – I can check then.'

Martin slipped his mobile back into his pocket.

'Thanks,' he said, standing up. 'I'd be grateful if you could.'

Beyond the window, the wind continued to whip the reeds. The question of guilt hung heavy in the air.

'Come in, come in.'

Louise Bauer's mother Lussan opened the door to Patrik and Paula, glancing nervously outside. Patrik guessed she was worried the neighbours would see the police calling.

The house that Lussan and Pierre were staying in was just above the old Badis hotel and the houses were undeniably close together with clear lines of sight. On the other hand, most of them were empty and shuttered at this time of year. The sea views were sought after by moneyed property owners who didn't even bother to keep a single light on.

'They're turning that into flats, apparently,' said Lussan, pointing towards the former hotel.

A hotel and spa venture a number of years before hadn't ended well, and the building was now empty and desolate.

'I dare say it'll be a good investment,' said Pierre, Louise's father.

He approached and shook their hands formally. He looked straight out of an advertisement for some antiquated English confectionary brand with his well-pressed trousers, white shirt and grey waistcoat. Lussan was not informally dressed either – she wore a dark blue tailored suit and gleaming pearls around her neck. Patrik hid a smile. This wasn't exactly how he and Erica dressed at home.

Lussan waved her hand dismissively.

'We can't think about things like that at the moment, Pierre. Not in the midst of this awfulness.'

'Yes, I'm sorry . . .' Paula began, but she was interrupted by Lussan's heavy sigh.

'The newspapers really are beastly. I can't understand how they are permitted to make such outrageous claims. We know Henning and Elisabeth well – ever since Louise and Peter were married – and they are the most upright, solid people I have ever met. As for Susanne, she is a literary legend – she would never condescend to such a thing. Although Ole has always seemed a little nasty. He's a bit of a mess and he always struggles to keep his hands to himself, so as far as he goes, I can very well imagine what they're saying is true. But naturally all of this has taken place without Louise's knowledge. How can they have the nerve to claim that she's involved in shady deals?! Pierre and I are both shocked to the core. I haven't slept a wink all night.'

Lussan gestured that they could sit down on the sofas positioned in front of the window facing down towards the bay. Valön was right outside, and Patrik caught a glimpse of the white buildings at the old children's holiday camp through the trees.

Patrik glanced at Paula as they each sat down in an armchair. He knew they were thinking the same thing: how could the media scandal currently raging around Blanche be what was bothering Louise's parents most?

'Louise is resting, but I'll go and fetch her,' said Pierre, making his way down the hall.

Lussan sighed loudly again as she draped herself against the corner of a sofa. Patrik looked around. So this was how the other half lived. Everything was white, white, white. In his mind's eye, he pictured what this living room would look like after half an hour with the twins, and he shuddered. Toddlers and a white home were incompatible.

'This is the home of some good friends of ours – they lent it to us while they're at their place in Spain,' said Lussan, as if she'd read his thoughts. 'Giggs and Joy are wonderful people. We got to know them when we were in Marbella for a charity gala, and when it transpired they had a place in Fjällbacka, well, it was meant to be . . . Of course, they knew Skjälerö and the Bauers and had even bumped into Louise at Zetterlind's bakery on occasion. Small world.'

Lussan shook her head, making her diamond earrings sparkle. Well, Patrik assumed they were diamonds. They had an altogether different lustre to the ones that Erica bought on the high street.

'So when they heard we were coming for Henning and Elisabeth's golden wedding celebrations they insisted we borrow their house instead of staying at the hotel, and of course we couldn't possibly decline. This house is a real gem and Joy has done a tremendous job restoring and decorating it.'

'Would you like some coffee?'

Louise's voice brought Lussan's torrent of words to a temporary halt. A knot formed in Patrik's stomach when he saw her haggard face. He knew he needed to be professional, but it was hard to detach himself from the fact that she had lost her entire family at a stroke.

'Yes, please,' he said.

Lussan waved impatiently to Pierre that he should sit down while Louise went to the kitchen, which opened off the living room, and began to make coffee in a big, shiny machine that looked like it would be better suited to a busy coffee shop than a domestic setting.

Patrik's phone beeped and he apologized and switched it to silent, but before putting the phone with its display face down on the grey marble coffee table, he read the text he'd received from Gösta. Gösta had asked him to ask Louise for the name of the private detective that Peter had engaged to investigate Cecily's death.

'There's milk in the jug if you want it,' said Louise, putting a tray down in front of them. Then she sat down on the sofa at a distance from her mother.

'I was just telling the officers how dreadful it is that the papers are treating you this way, especially given the circumstances. Frankly, it's a legal scandal. We've asked our family lawyer to see what can be done about it, haven't we, Pierre?'

Pierre nodded as he took a sip of his coffee. Patrik could see that Louise was gritting her teeth. Then she said:

'Mum, none of it matters. Peter and the boys are dead – that's the only thing I care about. Let the papers write whatever they want.'

'I still think it's dreadful,' Lussan muttered, reaching for her cup.

'What can I help you with?' Louise said to Patrik and Paula.

She pushed her dark hair backwards. She had bags under her eyes and didn't seem to have slept a wink since Patrik had last seen her.

'Has Rickard confessed?' she went on, her blue eyes flashing.

'We can't comment on the investigation,' said Paula.

'No, of course not.' Louise pursed her lips so hard they turned white. 'It's just . . . It's hard waiting.'

Lussan leaned towards her and patted her on the hand. Louise withdrew it.

Patrick watched them. He hadn't previously reflected on how similar they were to each other since they had

275

such vastly different personalities, but the eyes were the same, as were the hairlines. He guessed that a younger version of Lussan must have been the spitting image of Louise.

'How did you and Peter meet?' said Paula.

Louise smiled faintly.

'At Blanche. I started working there around a year before Cecily – Peter's first wife – died. At first, we just said hello and exchanged pleasantries when he came in to see Henning or came to our events.'

'And then?' said Patrik.

He took a sip of the coffee. Good grief, it tasted good. He glanced towards the giant contraption in the kitchen. How much did one of those things go for? Two months' pay?

'Then Cecily died. Peter was in mourning. And he was also a single parent. One night, he stopped by looking for Henning, but Henning wasn't there, and Peter and I got talking. It was so simple, somehow. I was a pillar amidst his grief. A friend when he needed a friend. Eventually, friendship turned into something else . . .'

Louise couldn't continue. She blinked away the tears and buried her face in her hands.

'They were such a fine couple,' said Lussan, patting Louise gently on the shoulder. 'We were thrilled when we heard Louise and Peter Bauer were a couple. As a parent, you grow anxious with the passing of the years when your only child doesn't meet anyone. She wasn't exactly in the prime of her youth, and since Louise can't have children there are many people who might not want to commit to a relationship . . .'

'Lussan!' Pierre said sharply, fixing his gaze on his wife.

She snorted but fell silent.

Louise straightened her back, wiped her eyes and looked at Pierre.

'It's okay, Dad. Mum's right. I was well on my way to being left on the shelf, and the fact that I can't have kids was definitely part of that. The men who wanted to start a family filtered me out. But Peter and I . . . We were perfect for each other. And it was as if the boys became mine. I couldn't have loved a biological child any more than I loved them.'

She wiped her eyes with her sleeve as the tears continued to flow. Unlike Lussan and Pierre, she was wearing a sweatshirt and loose-fitting loungewear trousers.

'It was incredible how well-matched Peter and Louise were – it was as if you were the same person,' said Lussan.

'Yes, it was almost weird,' Louise agreed. 'He spoke Russian after spending two years in Moscow as an exchange student. I studied Russian at university. He played tennis, I played tennis. We both loved opera and realized we'd even been to the same performances on two occasions, sitting a few rows apart.'

'You were made for each other,' said Pierre, shaking his head gloomily. 'Terrible. So terrible.'

Patrik tapped his knuckle on his mobile.

'Rickard mentioned that Peter had hired someone to investigate Cecily's death. How did that come about?'

Louise sighed; her gaze drifted to the view beyond the window.

'It was an idea Peter got into his head in the last year. I don't know why.'

'But it was a hit-and-run?'

'Yes, which makes the whole thing so tragic. But Peter began to see conspiracy theories behind it. He claimed someone had deliberately run Cecily down. The police looked into it and concluded it had probably been sheer bad luck. She was in the wrong place at the wrong time. Most likely a drunk driver.'

'Was there anything in particular that made him believe there was more to it?' said Paula.

Louise shook her head slowly.

'Not that I know of. Both boys went through a phase of asking a lot of questions about their mum. It might have been related to that. Amplified by Peter's feelings of guilt.'

'Guilt? Why guilt?' said Patrik, furrowing his brow.

His coffee cup was empty. He glanced longingly at the coffee machine.

'Survivor's guilt, isn't that what they call it?' said Louise. 'I think he wanted to do something – anything – to avoid feeling powerless in the face of the boys' loss of their mother.'

'Do you know who he engaged?' said Patrik.

Gösta must have hit the buffers on tracking down a name, he thought to himself, and was instead hoping Louise might know. But she shook her head.

'No, he never said. He knew I thought it was unnecessary and couldn't lead anywhere. So he didn't talk to me about it. Didn't Rickard know?'

'No, he didn't know who it was either.'

Damn it. Patrik shuffled irritably in his armchair. It might be possible to find the details via Peter's call logs on his mobile or via his bank statements, but it made it infinitely more cumbersome.

Lussan perked up. She pointed to Pierre.

'You guys were talking about it not long ago! When Louise and Peter came down to see us in Skåne. I know I heard you discussing it. Didn't he say a name then?'

Pierre cocked his head to one side.

'Yes, he did say a name. But blast it, I can't remember.'

He grimaced and Lussan glowered at him in annoyance.

'Think!'

'If Dad can't remember then he can't remember,' Louise said, sounding just as annoyed as Lussan.

But Pierre snapped his fingers and sat up straighter.

'Reidar! I don't remember the last name, but I'm certain his first name was Reidar because I made a joke asking Peter whether he'd hired Reidar from *Rederiet*.'

'Reidar,' Patrik said with satisfaction.

It was an unusual name. He couldn't imagine there was a plethora of private detectives in Stockholm, either. One by the name of Reidar ought to be easy to track down. He had another idea but pushed it to one side for the time being. He wasn't sure whether it was a good idea or a bad idea.

'Could we talk about Blanche?' he said, deliberately choosing not to look at Lussan.

Her thoughts on the matter were already obvious. And she did indeed snort.

'Of course,' Louise said quietly.

'There are a lot of allegations in the press right now,' Patrik said cautiously.

'Nonsense,' Lussan snorted, clutching her pearl necklace.

'I haven't read what they say,' Louise said quietly. 'But I can imagine.'

'Do you think it has anything to do with the murders?' said Paula.

There was a silence for a long time.

'I don't know. Maybe.'

'How do you think it might be connected?' said Patrik.

'Things got complicated. It started small. Then it got out of hand for all of us.'

Lussan stared at her daughter. She opened her mouth to say something, but after a sharp look from Pierre, she closed it again.

Louise continued in a low voice.

'It's all connected. It's hard to explain. One thing led to another. Like a drop of water eroding a stone.'

She got up abruptly and went to the kitchen.

'We need more coffee,' she said, beginning to rattle around the machine.

Patrik guessed she needed a pretext to give her time to think about what she should say. He decided to give her that break.

Soon, they had fresh coffee in their cups and Lussan's lips were tightly pursed as if she were physically trying to prevent herself from talking. Once again, it struck Patrik how similar she and her daughter were.

'I think they had good intentions when they started Blanche,' said Louise. 'It was supposed to be a cultural forum – a place where new talent could meet the establishment and where contacts could be formed. And I suppose in many ways it still is. But over time, personal motives and needs came into the picture. When I started there, it was already ingrained but it took me a while to notice. And by the time I did, it was too late. I loved my job. Peter and I had found each other. I'd become part of the family. So I became part of the solution.'

'The solution?' Paula asked.

'Yes, I'm good at cleaning things up. It's always been a talent of mine,' Louise said dryly. 'And it's a trait that's come in handy at Blanche.'

'What do you mean by "cleaning up"?' said Patrik.

'One of my jobs was to pay off the women that Ole crossed the line with, so that they kept their mouths shut.'

'Louise!' Lussan said shrilly. Her face had turned fiery red. 'I don't think you should say anything else until you've spoken to our lawyer. Don't you agree, Pierre? She can't just . . . What's the word? The one they say on TV? Incriminate herself.'

'Mum!' Louise yelled, making Lussan jump.

She pursed her lips again. Louise continued, her voice now subdued and resigned.

'I handled the payments, I drafted the agreements, I wheedled, I coaxed, I did everything I could to keep a lid on things.'

'And the others knew about this? Ole, Susanne, Henning, Elisabeth – and Rolf?'

'Yes. And eventually even Peter knew,' said Louise. 'He realized pretty recently what was going on. He borrowed my computer, and the folder containing the non-disclosure agreements and the amounts paid was open.'

'And Rickard? What was Rickard's role in this?'

Louise hesitated. Then she took a deep breath.

'Rickard was blackmailing Blanche too. He wanted to be paid off not to tell Henning what he'd found out.'

'Which was?' said Patrik.

He held his breath.

'That Rolf was his father. Not Henning.'

Next to her, Lussan dropped her coffee cup onto the marble table.

Birgitta's photos were scattered across the hotel bed. Erica handled them with care because they were well-thumbed and fragile, and she knew how much they meant to Birgitta. It felt as if she'd been given a gift – a unique and beautiful one.

She had already seen Lola in Rolf's photograph, which had also been wonderful and intimate, but this was something else. The pictures were like a story. Snapshots from reality in faded colour. A bygone era that was now casting its shadow into the future.

Erica carefully sorted through them. Lola with Monica. Lola with P'tite as a baby. Lola behind the bar at what had to be her place of work. A shot outdoors, two smiling drag queens linking arms with Lola outside a bar. They looked so happy. Erica caressed their faces with her finger. It was surely the same bar Lola had worked at. The name of the place was visible behind them: Alexa's. Erica made a note in the notebook and underlined it.

Erica had set aside the photo she was most fascinated by, but now she picked it up again. There was something special about that photo. It radiated love in a different way to the photos of Lola and Monica. The couple in the photo were blurry, as if they'd been caught mid-movement. Lola was being embraced by a man in whose arms she seemed to feel safe. Her face was turned towards the camera, and she was clearly in love and happy. But it was impossible to tell who the man was – the only thing visible was a grainy back.

Erica sighed and put the photo down on the bed again. She sent a text to Lenora. Fifteen minutes later she had a reply. Through her huge network, Lenora had managed to find the name and address for one of Lola's colleagues from Alexa's.

The damp was lingering in the air and people were hurrying along Kungsgatan. The address Erica had been given was five minutes' walk away. As she arrived, it began to drizzle, and she hurried in through the main door.

The flat was above a Thai restaurant and Erica could hear the hubbub of the patrons through the walls. The building was neglected and in real need of renovation. Even the cleaning seemed to have been neglected, and she wrinkled her nose at the stench of urine that hit her in the stairwell. The smell turned her stomach, and she stifled a wave of queasiness. At least now she knew why she so easily felt nausea, but it was cold comfort. She resolutely pushed away all thoughts of pregnancy. Not now.

The plaque embossed with 'Johan Hansson' was on the right-hand door on the first landing. Above this there was a Post-it note on which it said in pink lettering 'Maggie Vinter design'. There was no bell, so Erica knocked gently.

There was no sound on the other side of the door, so she knocked a little harder. Eventually, she heard shuffling footsteps. A lock clicked and the door opened. Erica slowly raised her gaze. The person in front of her was tall. Almost two metres.

'Erica? Lenora called and said you were on your way. Of course, she forgot to mention how good looking you are! Even better than in your photo! That photoshoot in *Amelia* really didn't do you justice – whoever did your make-up should have been fired.'

'Aw shucks.' Erica felt herself blush.

'Johan, by the way.' A hand with pink fingernails was proffered. 'When I heard a famous author was coming to visit, I just had to change into my Maggie Vinter look.'

Johan let his hand glide along his silky emerald green trouser suit with sash waist and wide, flowing legs. It deftly covered a voluptuous bust formed by a generously padded bra, and the neckline was discreet. Erica was immediately overcome by a sense of covetousness.

'Come in, come in, my sweet.'

Erica followed Johan curiously into his flat. After the dank stairwell, the flat was like an irresistible box of chocolates and Erica couldn't help purring with happiness. It was personal and inviting, and there were incredible fabrics, edging ribbons and boxes of buttons all over the place. The flat was otherwise bright and boldly Scandinavian, with plenty of designer furniture she could pick out, thanks to her occasionally obsessive browsing of antiques auctions.

'What do you make?' Erica said with fascination, fingering a pink sequinned fabric.

'Stage costumes. Melodifestivalen. Shows. Cabaret. Music videos. I'll do stuff for basically anything where they're not asking for less is more. At first, it was for my own drag shows, but word of my creations got around.

If you want something that's glittery, over the top and makes you stand out in a crowd . . . well, you come to Maggie Vinter design.'

'Heavenly,' Erica said, stroking a purple boa.

Her own wardrobe was dominated by black, white and beige, but that didn't stop her from being fond of glitter and bright pink.

'Sit down, my sweet. Sit.'

Johan patted a white Arne Jacobsen Model 3107 and moved a neon yellow piece of tulle. He sat down opposite her and pushed over a box of chocolate pralines.

'Dark chocolate. One a day keeps the sugar cravings away and it doesn't sit on your hips unnecessarily. When you're over seventy, there aren't many vices left that you can enjoy if you want to keep your figure.'

He eyed Erica from head to toe.

'Do you always dress this tragically? Girl, you've got the figure – it's a real pity to hide it in this unflattering way.'

Erica looked down at her outfit and realized there was no point protesting. She'd packed and dressed for comfort and wholly ignored aesthetic considerations. Today's suitcase ensemble was a pair of slightly pilled black trousers which had – for full disclosure – previously served her as maternity trousers. Nothing was as comfortable as a wide-ribbed waistline, especially now she'd put on a few pounds. She hadn't even realized when packing them just how fitting they were. Her top wasn't in any better nick; it was an old favourite from H&M made of some sort of knitted synthetic that had been through the wash a few too many times. There were loose threads hanging from it here and there, and the sleeves had begun to fray.

Johan was right: she really ought to update her wardrobe. She was still wearing clothes she'd bought in the nineties. Patrik was even worse. He had a T-shirt from the Scorpions' Wind of Change tour that he'd refused to throw out even though it looked moth-eaten.

'How did you know Lola?' Erica said, concealing her frayed sleeves under the table.

Johan perked up. He took a moment to respond. Erica gave him the time he needed – she got the feeling that Johan was being conveyed back in time in his memories, which was exactly what she wanted.

'We often tended the bar together at Alexa's,' Johan said eventually. 'We liked working together and usually tried to synchronize shifts. Lola was a dream colleague. Always showed up on time, always did her job, didn't give drinks away to her mates and was never drunk on duty. Alexa's had a few hopeless cases over the years. But Lola was a rock. She was also always happy. That's probably what I most remember about Lola – her *joie de vivre*. And her blue notebooks.'

'Blue notebooks?'

'Yes, she always had a blue notebook with her in which she wrote during her free moments. She got through a couple in the years we worked together.'

'What did she write?' said Erica.

This was the first time she'd heard anything about notebooks.

'Lola dreamed of becoming an author, but I never got to read anything she wrote. No one did.'

'Do you know whether she ever submitted anything? To publishers?'

Johan removed an invisible speck from his trouser suit. He reached for a chocolate praline and took a bite.

'I don't think so. The only thing she said about her writing was that it was a whole story. *Everything* had to be finished.'

'And you've no idea what she was writing about?'

Johan held out his well-manicured hands.

'It's not like we didn't ask. We even teased her about the constant writing. But she just smiled . . . like a sphinx.'

'Did you spend time together when you were off duty?'

Laughter from restaurant patrons below penetrated through the floor. Johan stamped his foot angrily and the laughter died down.

'Things were calmer when there was a haberdashery shop downstairs,' he said irritably before looking back to Erica. 'Yes, we hung out a bit, but Lola had her posse. They were pretty inseparable.'

'Rolf and the rest of them?'

Johan nodded.

'It was a pretty odd collection of people. But as far as I understood it from Lola, it was their passion for literature that brought them together.'

'How were things back then otherwise? Were there a lot of places for . . .'

Erica hesitated, unsure of which word to use to avoid treading on tender toes. She was ignorant in this respect and didn't want to come across as clumsy or prejudiced.

But Johan smiled.

'For LGBTQ people? Or do you just mean trans people like Lola? Well, fortunately things have moved on a bit since the eighties. After everything that happened to Lola, I became an activist in the RFSL and while I'm a homosexual man who likes to dress in women's clothing, I've familiarized myself with trans issues for Lola's sake. I have to go back a bit further than the eighties to give you the context.'

'Please do,' said Erica.

She held up her notebook with a quizzical look.

'Take all the notes you want, dear girl,' said Johan. His gaze took on a dreamy look. 'Until the sixties, there weren't really any ways for trans people to meet. Nothing official anyway. But then cautious contact began to take place through pornographic magazines – of all places. One of them was called *Raff.*'

Johan laughed, lost in memories.

'Lola and I talked about that a lot when things were quiet at the bar. One of the pioneers in the Swedish trans community – Eva-Lisa Bengtson – made contact with Erika Sjöman via the magazine. Erika had been a mariner and had come across a copy of the American magazine *Transvestia* and I suppose that inspired them. Anyway, they placed an ad in *Raff's* sister publication *Piff* about creating a meeting place. They got answers from trans people the length and breadth of Sweden and that led to the opening of Sweden's first club for trans people. They called it Transvestia. It became a safe place for many people who had previously cross-dressed in solitude. And it wasn't only trans people who were drawn to it – there were lesbians, gays, people with all sorts of orientations and fetishes, a number of them drag queens like me . . . Well, everyone who was hiding in the shadows at the time.'

'How long was Transvestia around for?'

'Only until 1969.'

'And when did Alexa's come into the picture?'

'That's what I was getting to. It was a blessing when Alexa's opened in the mid-seventies because it became one of our most important gathering places. Homosexuals and bisexuals, trans people, drag queens. Everyone came there, just like they had previously done at Transvestia. The difference was that it wasn't only for us. Everyone was welcome. Everyone went there.'

Erica looked up from her notebook.

'Excuse the stupid question, but what's the difference between a drag queen and a trans woman?'

Johan flashed another smile at her. Erica got the feeling that he liked having such an attentive listener at his disposal.

'A drag queen is a cis man – so that's someone born a man who sees himself as a man – but likes to dress in women's clothes.' Johan had quickly added the last part when he'd seen Erica's thoughtful expression. 'Drag is a way of playing with the expression of gender. Often – but not always – it's used to explore the boundaries of femininity or masculinity.'

Once again, a dreamy look subsumed Johan.

'I've always been a big, tall guy, but there's something about the feminine that attracts me. I tried to resist, but in the mid-seventies when I was around twenty, I finally dared to venture into these clubs, and it was like coming home. As a drag queen, I could live as my full self. It was a big step for me.'

Erica was moved by Johan's honesty and his fearlessness as he told his story. She could sense the brokenness between the lines and realized that Johan had many scars from his childhood.

'Can we go back to Alexa's?' she asked.

'Absolutely. I started there around 1977 and Lola started not long after I did. But we already knew each other before that. I knew Monica, and that was how I met Lola.'

'What did you make of her life with Monica? And – forgive my complete ignorance – but was Lola considered hetero or lesbian?'

'Monica and Lola were never together,' Johan said with a snort. 'Lola wasn't interested in women. She wasn't a lesbian.'

'But what about the daughter?' Erica said in confusion.

'Monica and Lola were close. They lived together like a family, but they were sisters. Not lovers. I can guarantee that it's physically impossible that the girl was Lola's. She would never have slept with a woman. She was a heterosexual woman in every way except her innate physical condition.'

'But she took the girl as her own?'

'Yes, she did. She promised Monica she would take care of the girl. Monica was in deep with her addiction and selling her body to fund it. It was impossible to know who the girl's biological father was. Even for Monica. But I know Lola loved P'tite as her own. She was her everything. And they put Lola down as the father on the birth certificate, so Lola never had any problems with securing legal custody. She was hers in every way except biologically. Lola once said that P'tite called her Daddy because she wanted P'tite to remember Monica as her mother.'

'Do you know if there was anyone else in Lola's life?' Erica said curiously.

Johan nodded. The sound from downstairs intensified again and he stamped his foot hard on the floor.

'Yes, there was a man. But she was very reticent about him.'

Erica looked up from her notes.

'Do you know anything about him?'

'No. She was good at keeping her secrets. But she was in love. She was always a little more radiant when she'd seen him.'

Erica pondered. No men had been questioned in connection with Lola's and P'tite's deaths. That had the potential to be a very interesting avenue of enquiry: a love story gone wrong . . .

Erica took the plunge and asked another question she suspected might be sensitive.

'What about hormones and surgery in the eighties? Was that something Lola considered?'

'Yes, she did. In 1980 you could get surgery in Stockholm as part of the transition to being a woman. Before that, you had to go to Copenhagen or Casablanca. But the operations were still at a very experimental stage. The same was true for hormone treatment. The side effects were terrible. I know Lola began taking hormones before Monica died, but when she became responsible for P'tite she stopped. She didn't want the side effects to make her feel so unwell she couldn't care for the child. So she bore the burden of living in a man's body for the girl's sake. But she always intended to continue her transition to being a woman as soon as P'tite was a little older. It was her big dream. And she said that writing helped her to manage her big decisions in life.'

'In the blue notebooks?'

'Yes. The blue notebooks were her lifeline.'

Erica helped herself to a praline and felt it melt in her mouth. She had to finish chewing it before she could ask the next question. Below them, laughter rose from the restaurant.

'Was mixing with people from outside your circles the way Lola did common?'

'Yes and no. Many were living double lives. They had a life with us, their true life. And then they had a life that was acceptable socially and to society alongside that. Many had wives and children. Or husbands and children. From the outside, they were living a conservative life. It was probably pretty unusual to be accepted in the straight cis world as a trans woman in the way Lola was. But her posse were cultural folks, so I dare say that explains it.'

Johan laughed.

'How did Lola get to know the group?' said Erica.

She hesitated, then took another praline. If she couldn't drink wine any longer then she might as well eat chocolate.

'Via Rolf. They got to know each other at Alexa's. Then it was Rolf who introduced her to his friends because of her interest in writing. And after that they were inseparable.'

'You've heard Rolf's dead?'

'Yes, I have, sadly. What happened?'

'No one knows. I . . . I thought I would find out more about Lola and P'tite and what happened to them, but my thoughts are also drawn to Rolf and his murder. He was going to do an exhibition on his past, according to his wife Vivian. She showed me a photo of Lola. It was called *Innocence*. Do you know anything about it?'

Johan shook his head slowly.

'No, not a clue. It's been years since I heard from Rolf. He dropped off the radar after Lola's death. I don't even think I've met him since then. Actually, no. I tell a lie. It depends on how you look at it. I haven't had any contact with Rolf, that's true. But he tried to get in touch a couple of weeks ago. I had my hands full with costumes for Alcazar's new show, so I didn't have time to take his call. Then I forgot all about it. So I never called back.'

'You don't know what he wanted? He didn't leave a message?'

'No.'

Johan shook his head apologetically, making the curls of his long dark wig tumble around his face and shimmer.

'And you don't have any leads on who the man in Lola's life was?'

'No, nothing concrete. I suspected he was married, but Lola never said as much. That was just my reading between the lines.'

Erica asked the question buzzing away at the back of her mind.

'Could it have been Rolf?'

Johan hesitated.

'I'd be lying if I said I hadn't thought the same,' he admitted.

As Erica left the glitzy flat, she felt the pieces of the

jigsaw beginning to fall into place. The picture of Lola in Rolf's bedroom had been bothering her in some way. Now, all of a sudden, it felt much more logical.

'How did you get on with Louise?' Gösta asked when he met Patrik and Paula in the corridor.

'Let's sit down.'

Patrik led the way to the kitchen and Gösta and Paula followed. Martin was already there. He had his back to the wall and his feet up on the chair next to him, but he took them down when they came in so everyone could have a seat.

'Coffee?' Gösta asked as he picked up the pot and poured himself a cup.

Patrik and Paula quickly shook their heads.

'I don't think I can hack station coffee after what we were just served,' Patrik said, sitting down next to Martin.

He patted him on the leg.

'How's Mette feeling? Is she longing for you to get back to working regular hours?'

'Yes, it's a bit much for her right now and she's doing most of the heavy lifting with Tuva and Jon. But she knows the score, and so far, she seems to think life as a police officer's wife is totally okay.'

'Wife?' Paula said meaningfully.

Martin blushed all the way up to his hairline.

'Police officer's cohabitee, I suppose.'

'So when . . . ?'

'Let's change the subject,' Martin said, folding his arms. 'For instance, it turned out that there is most likely a photograph missing from the exhibition. It's called *Guilt*. The tricky bit is that Rolf didn't say much about the exhibition, so Vivian doesn't know what it was of. But it may have been of a trans woman called Lola. I think your wife is looking into that.'

He looked at Patrik, who swore under his breath. Bloody Erica and her nose for mysteries. He would have to text her after this meeting.

'We need to unravel that,' Patrik said, scratching his head.

The long hours were beginning to take their toll and his back reminded him that the camp bed at the station was best used for brief naps rather than full nights.

'We've also turned up something of interest,' said Paula. She exchanged glances with Patrik before she dropped the bomb:

'According to Louise, Rickard was blackmailing the management at Blanche. For big money.'

Martin let out a low whistle.

'Why were they letting him blackmail them?'

'To protect Henning,' said Patrik.

'Protect him? From what?'

'The knowledge that he's not Rickard's father.'

Gösta froze, his coffee cup halfway to his mouth.

'What the hell are you saying? Henning isn't Rickard's dad? Then who is?'

Paula and Patrik looked at each other again. Patrik indicated that she could take the lead. Paula raised her eyebrows and said:

'Rolf.'

'And Rickard knew that?' said Gösta. 'And was being paid out of Blanche's coffers not to tell Henning?'

'Yes, that was how Louise explained it,' said Paula.

Martin cleared his throat.

'What should we do about Rickard? His lawyer got here a couple of hours ago. Should we continue the interrogation?'

'No, let's leave him to sweat for a while longer.' Patrik drummed his fingers against the tabletop. 'I'm hoping for at least a preliminary report from Farideh in the morning, and we can hold him for up to seventy-two hours. I want as much material as possible before we speak to him again.'

'Did you find out anything about the private detective?' Gösta asked.

'We did, as it happens. Louise's parents had talked to Peter about it on some occasion and remembered that he was called Reidar. I reckon that should be enough for us to locate him pretty easily.'

'I'll get on that right away. Then I'll call the guy.'

Gösta stood up and pushed his chair towards the table. Patrik held up a hand to stop him.

'No, hold off on contacting him. Erica is in Stockholm. If you can get hold of a number and address, why don't we ask her to talk to the detective?'

Gösta's brow furrowed, but then he nodded.

'Right you are. I'll find out the details.'

'I'm going to chase Farideh up,' said Patrik. 'Paula, can you keep digging through Blanche's dirty laundry? Martin, try to find out more about the missing picture. Ask galleries, photography connoisseurs, etcetera. See if you can find anything online – there must be places to sell stuff like that. And check whether there's anyone around Rolf who might have been familiar with the picture and knows what it's of. For example, did he have an assistant?'

They left the table. On his way past the coffee pot, Patrik hesitated. Coffee was just coffee. He poured himself a cup and headed for his office. It was going to be another long night.

23

STOCKHOLM 1980

'Six! I can't believe you're turning six on Saturday!'

Elisabeth pinched P'tite's cheek as she passed by. P'tite's cheeks flushed with joy.

'Yes. Only three days to go! I'm having a party! With Sigge!'

Elisabeth stopped.

'Who's Sigge?'

Lola exhaled a perfect smoke ring and winked.

'P'tite's boyfriend.'

'No he's not!' P'tite said, stamping her foot.

Rolf laughed.

'Don't tease P'tite. She's never going to have a boyfriend. Uncle Rolf has made up his mind!'

'No, I'm never going to have a boyfriend,' P'tite said, stamping angrily off towards the bedroom.

'My goodness, to think that she's almost six years old. A grown-up lady,' said Susanne, wrapping her arms around Ole's neck.

'She'll be starting school soon,' Lola said, unable to conceal her pride. 'She's so excited about learning to read, count . . .'

'And making new friends!' Ester said warmly. Her gaze

had lingered in the direction of P'tite's retreat for a long time.

'Yes . . .'

Lola didn't know how to articulate her feelings about P'tite starting school. The others lived such . . . normal lives. They would never understand.

Rolf looked at her from under his blond fringe and said gently:

'You're worried about how they'll treat her when they find out about her dad . . .'

Lola felt the love washing over her. He understood her like no other. He'd got to know her in depth through his lens, but that wasn't what defined their relationship. He *saw* her. Always her.

'Yes. I'm terrified.'

The words tumbled towards the shabby tabletop. The cigarette in her hand had almost burned down and she tapped it against the porcelain ashtray in the shape of a polar bear – one of the few things she'd taken from her childhood home.

'She'll do beautifully,' said Ester. 'She's tough. She's loved.'

Henning and Elisabeth were silent, but they exchanged a glance. Lola saw it.

'You don't agree?'

Elisabeth hesitated. Then she said:

'It's not easy for kids. And you're on your own. Are you sure you don't want to . . . rekindle contact with your family?'

Lola shook her head fiercely. She lit a new cigarette and took a deep drag before slowly exhaling the smoke.

'My sister was here,' she said.

'Oh?' Rolf said in surprise.

Lola took another puff.

'She was here. She judged me. She left.'

'But did you give her a chance?' said Elisabeth. 'Maybe things have changed? Maybe your parents . . .'

'They died a couple of years ago,' Lola said, swirling the red wine around in her glass.

The flames from the candles made the wine glow and she contemplated the ruby-red liquid in her glass intently.

'But why didn't you say anything?'

Ester put a hand over Lola's and almost burned herself on the tip of the cigarette.

'To me, they've been dead since the very moment I walked out of their front door. I wasn't welcome. I wasn't their . . . their child.'

'But your sister?' Elisabeth persisted. 'Isn't there any way you can reconnect? Doesn't she understand? Blood is blood, after all.'

Rolf gave Elisabeth a sharp look and she fell silent. Ole watched them both with an amused smile. For a moment, he looked as if he was about to say something, but Susanne gently placed a hand on his arm and the room fell silent.

Lola gestured to P'tite, who had emerged from the bedroom and was now doing pirouettes on the kitchen floor in front of the hob. P'tite crawled into her lap and Lola kissed her on the head. She looked around the kitchen. Then she raised her wine glass.

'P'tite is my family and in three days' time we're going to throw a roaring party. That's all I want to think about right now.'

'I'll drink to that,' Rolf said, raising his glass.

The others hurried to do the same.

Lola closed her eyes and leaned her cheek against the crown of P'tite's head. The only family she needed was here.

24

Erica ended the call. She'd been on her way into the lobby of the Haymarket when Patrik had called, but now she turned on her heel and headed for the taxi rank round the corner.

There were two cars waiting there. Erica got into the one at the front and gave the driver the address Patrik had supplied her with. Apparently, Peter had engaged a private detective to investigate Cecily's death, and the man was based in Årsta. She leaned back and closed her eyes for a moment but almost immediately regretted it when she felt the nausea welling up.

She looked around for something to throw up into if push came to shove but found nothing. Instead, she opened the window and put her face to the crack. The taxi driver watched her anxiously in his rear-view mirror, probably concerned at the possibility of having to remove vomit from his back seat. She tried to smile at him, but he didn't look particularly reassured.

What a turn-up: Rolf's exhibition had been going to be about Lola. The nausea eased a little as Erica thought about it. She would have liked to see that exhibition.

'We're here,' the driver said, pulling over.

He was doubtless relieved that Erica hadn't thrown up.

She paid and got out, standing still for a moment and breathing until the final remnants of the nausea were gone. She put a hand on her belly, but quickly took it away again. No – she couldn't think about the reason for her nausea; if she did that, she'd end up stuck in thoughts that took her nowhere. First, she had to tell Patrik. Then they could work out what to do together.

Reidar Tivéus had an office at Årsta torg. It was years since Erica had last been in this neck of the woods, but the square still looked like she remembered it. It was as if time had found a crack in the space–time continuum at Årsta torg, where everything stood still decade after decade. Flaking, faded signs. Businesses that seemed to be asleep, or at least very, very dozy.

The office was next door to a hairdresser. It was on the ground floor, with large windows with the blinds drawn down to hide the interior from both the sun and people's curious eyes. There was no bell, so Erica tapped on the glass door, which had rather grubby, drawn-down grey blinds. A sign that read 'Reidar Tivéus, private detective' showed that she had at least knocked on the right door. No one answered and she knocked again. After waiting for a while, she tried the door handle and the door opened.

'Hello?'

Erica stepped in and looked around. The office looked like it could feature on a TV show about hoarders. Folders, stacks of papers and newspapers covered every available surface.

A door towards the back rattled and opened. The man who emerged buttoned his trousers over a huge belly and carefully smoothed his shirt.

'Sorry, I didn't hear anyone come in,' he said with a big, beaming smile.

He proffered his hand and Erica took it after some

hesitation, given where he had come from. But the handshake was warm and firm.

'Please, take a seat. I'll clear this chair,' he said, laboriously making his way between the stacks to a chair in front of his groaning desk.

Reidar unceremoniously removed the huge heap of papers weighing down the chair and dumped it on the floor. A gentle cloud of dust rose from the stack, and Erica discreetly wiped the seat before sitting down.

He nudged the desk slightly so that he could fit behind it, and then sat down with a loud sigh.

'You wouldn't think I was an elite athlete in my youth,' he said, with a smile that extended to his eyes.

Erica didn't really know what the polite response to this statement should be, so she said nothing and merely smiled. The private detective reached for a framed photo on his desk.

'The 1980 Olympics in Moscow. I nearly took the bronze, but Lars-Erik Skiöld beat me to it.'

He shook his head regretfully. The photo depicted a young and decidedly slimmer Reidar wearing a skin-tight wrestling suit.

'Impressive!'

Erica meant it, although she could hear she mostly sounded polite. Since she had a hard time even motivating herself to take a walk if there wasn't a coffee shop at the end of it, elite athletes won her undying admiration.

'I don't suppose you came here to talk about my ancient sporting career. Do you suspect your husband is sleeping with his secretary? Maybe you need help finding a sibling you've just found out about? Do you want to dig up some dirt on your business partner? For all this and much more, Reidar is at your service.'

He held out his arms and flashed another big smile at her.

It was impossible not to be charmed by Reidar Tivéus, private detective.

'I'm helping the police with an investigation. Peter Bauer and his sons were shot dead on their island near Fjällbacka. One of the things the police want to look into more closely is the rumour that he hired you to look into his wife's death.'

Reidar stared at her. He'd gone pale and his smile had disappeared.

'Peter's dead? And the little boys?'

Erica nodded. She assumed he didn't keep abreast of the headlines.

'Yes, on Sunday night.'

'Jesus Christ,' Reidar said, looking a little sick. 'But yes, it's true that Peter engaged me to take a closer look at the hit-and-run.'

'Do you know why?'

Erica's nose was intensely ticklish from the dust and she was trying to hold back a sneeze.

'He told me he wanted to find out who the driver was. Which I can understand. The police didn't succeed on that front, but it's not like they tried all that hard. "Probably some drunk driver" to quote the investigating officer when I asked what the police knew.'

'There's nothing in the file that hints at the identity of the driver? It's been years since Cecily died . . . Do you know why Peter waited this long to start looking for her killer?'

She could no longer contain the sneeze.

'Bless you.'

'Thanks.'

Erica wiggled her nose to try and get rid of the ticklish feeling.

'I've no idea why he hired me now,' said Reidar. 'But from what I know about the grieving process – I encounter it a great deal in this line of work – it takes time to heal from grief. It can be paralysing. Maybe it was only now that he was in a place where he could bring himself to grapple with it?'

'That sounds plausible,' Erica said thoughtfully. 'He was in a new relationship too – a good relationship – so that might have given him the security to confront it.'

'You see!' Reidar said, once again holding out his arms. 'But to answer the first part of your question: no, there's nothing in the formal investigation that gives even the slightest lead on the driver, but please bear in mind that I use the term "investigation" very loosely. They didn't do much to find out who it might have been. It wasn't a priority.'

'And how far have you got in your own enquiries?'

'Peter only took me on a few weeks ago. I warned him up front that I wouldn't have much time in the first few weeks, since I had another big case to wrap up. I've only really been focusing on Cecily's death for the last few days. So far, the results have been pretty slim.'

'Could you tell me a bit about the circumstances of her death? I've heard so little you can assume I don't know anything at all.'

Her nose was tickling again, and she tried to wiggle it to avoid sneezing before realizing how absurd she must look.

'They were at their place in the country. Brevik in Tyresö. We're talking July four years ago. Cecily went running every day. The same route. The same time. She went out at eight and ran for about an hour; she was usually home by nine. By the time it was going on ten o'clock, he was worried. So yes, then he called the police . . . Cecily was found not far from their house – about twenty minutes away, given her usual pace. No witnesses.'

'No one saw anything?'

'No, not according to the police report. But I don't think the cops went to the trouble of asking around much. According to Peter, there wasn't much traffic at that time of day in July.'

'So no one saw her get run over and the driver fled the scene,' Erica said thoughtfully. 'Could you show me on a map exactly where she was found?'

Reidar looked dismayed.

'Sorry, I don't have a map.'

'I've got one on my phone,' Erica said, pulling up her mapping app. She searched for 'Brevik, Tyresö' and pushed the device over to Reidar.

'I've still got an old Nokia. You'll have to show me how to use one of these things.'

'Okay, so where was their house? Was it a year-round place, or just a summer house?'

'Summer house,' Reidar said, squinting at the display she'd pushed over the desk to him.

He took a minute or so to get his bearings and then pointed at a spot at the tip of a promontory.

'The house was there. Now, let's see where she usually went running . . .' He pointed to one edge of the display. 'Can you keep going that way?'

'Yes.'

Erica dragged her fingers on the display to make the map move to the right. Reidar pointed at a road winding its way through what looked like countryside.

'That's where she went running. And here's . . .' He leaned forward and slowly followed the bends in the road. 'Here's where she was found. On this corner. You've got woods on one side, and it banks away steeply down to the water on the other. There are houses at the bottom of the hill, but they're hidden by the trees.'

'That looks like a deadly spot to go running – I know

303

what drivers are like on country roads,' Erica said, following the twists and turns of the road with her gaze.

'Yes – Peter said he was always worried when she went out, but she insisted it was safe. I actually checked on the accident rate in the area, and there had been a number of incidents prior to them putting up the speed camera the year before Cecily died.'

'Speed camera?' Erica said, sitting up straighter. 'Where is it located?'

Reidar leaned over the screen again, squinting. He pointed at a spot a couple of kilometres away from the location where Cecily had been found.

'Here. Sneakily it's at the bottom of a hill where the limit suddenly changes from fifty to thirty. I dare say plenty of drivers who don't know the area get done there.'

Erica memorized the location Reidar had pointed at. An idea had slowly begun to take shape.

'Would you mind if I took photos of the pages from the investigation?'

Reidar pulled a bound file from the middle of a stack on his desk with uncanny precision.

'It's not my case any longer, given that it was Peter who hired me – take whatever you need.'

Erica gave him a look of gratitude and carefully took photos of the two pages of the police report.

When she emerged into the fresh air after carefully navigating her way through the stacks of paper, she took a deep breath. Finally her nose had stopped bothering her. She checked her watch: it was high time she was on her way to the hotel to pack up and catch her train. She would call her police contact Frank from the taxi. What she was going to ask him for was difficult – but not impossible.

* * *

Vivian had spent the whole journey to Stockholm imagining what it would feel like stepping through the door to the flat in Södermalm. Her and Rolf's flat. Now it was just hers. He would never take another step in there; his voice would never again be audible from the bathroom as he sang some old favourite in the shower.

Vivian dropped her bag onto the hall floor. Rolf's things were still in the cottage they'd rented – she hadn't felt up to packing them up. All she had wanted was to get home. It would all work itself out later, somehow.

She went into the living room and sat down on the sofa, not knowing what to do next. What did you do when the man you loved was gone?

She had lived for many years before Rolf. She ought to know how to live without him. Yet it still felt impossible.

They hadn't had a perfect relationship. Sometimes she'd been overcome with jealousy at the life Rolf and Ester had shared. He'd always spoken about her with such love in his voice. And sometimes when Henning, Elisabeth, Ole and Susanne were wandering down memory lane – memories that had included Rolf and Ester – those dark emotions had almost consumed her. But she and Rolf had also had something unique.

On the train, Vivian had read all the articles about Blanche over and over. And reading between the lines, she'd recognized Rolf's voice. He must have been the one who had given all the information to *Aftonbladet*, but she couldn't understand why. There was a lot about the last year she hadn't understood, and that still didn't make sense.

Where had he gone all those times she hadn't been able to get hold of him? Before, they had always agreed the plan for the day and they had always known where the other one was – not in a controlling way, but just because they liked to be part of each other's days. But then that had disappeared from one day to the next. She had noted that Rolf had begun to keep secrets from her. Any attempt she had made to get him to explain had only made him retreat even further into his shell.

Then there were the letters. The big, white envelopes that had been arriving in recent months with no return address. She regretted not opening any of them. But they weren't in the habit of opening each other's post.

Vivian had never seen where Rolf had put the letters. Had he thrown them away? Maybe he hadn't . . . What was more, the young and sympathetic policeman had asked her to see whether she could find out any more about the missing photograph, *Guilt*. She had already called Rolf's most recent assistant, Rafael, from the train but he hadn't known anything about the exhibition either. However, Rolf's studio was only a stone's throw from the flat and if there was anywhere he would keep something important to him, it would be there.

Vivian stood up. She finally knew what to do.

Darkness had fallen on Fjällbacka by the time Patrik drove home. The car's headlights were reflected in the garage door as he sat there, taking deep breaths in order to change focus from his job to being a dad and son before he went inside. Erica was due back in an hour or so, and he wanted to relieve his mother and get dinner ready. Fatigue was dragging him down, but he refused to give in. The fact that Erica would soon be home dissipated some of the fog of exhaustion. He always missed her when they were apart, and he loved that he still did. There were so many other couples in their circle who barely wanted to be in the same room as each other and were only maintaining Project Family for the kids' sake.

He and Erica had sworn never to end up there, and it didn't feel like it was a looming risk.

'Hello?'

Patrik shouted from the hallway as he took off his shoes and was rewarded with what sounded like a herd of elephants. All three children came running and hurled themselves at him.

'Goodness me! What a welcome!'

Patrik hugged and kissed each of them but gave Maja an extra-long hug. He knew she took a lot of responsibility for her brothers when he and Erica weren't at home, and it didn't matter how much they tried to tell her she didn't have to. It was simply in her nature.

'Granny and Gunnar have done loads!' said Anton, tugging him along. 'Come and see!'

'Done? Loads?'

A tight knot formed in Patrik's stomach. He knew deep down that it might not have been a great idea to sleep at the station, leaving his mother and Bob the Builder alone in the house for a couple of days. His sons' eager faces told him his concerns were justified.

His mother clapped her hands together in delight when she spotted him, which did nothing to reassure him. What had she been up to?

'Boys, boys . . . don't spoil the surprise. Let your father see for himself. Close your eyes, darling.'

'Mum . . .'

Patrik groaned, but Noel and Anton were dragging him along holding a hand each and he realized he was backed into a corner.

'Close your eyes, Dad! Close them!' they yelled, and he reluctantly did as he was told.

This did not bode well. He knew his mother and her husband all too well.

'Come on!' the twins continued to shout, and with his eyes shut he allowed them to guide him forward.

'You can look now!' his mother said happily.

Patrik steeled himself and then opened his eyes.

Good God. Erica was going to go apeshit.

The cursor flashed on the screen. He was once again sitting at the computer looking at a blank page. That was his only source of comfort at the moment.

If Henning looked out to the right through the window, he could see the cottage surrounded by police tape fluttering in the wind. Were they allowed to go in there now? Were they allowed to clean up? Who would do the cleaning? Nancy? She'd known Peter since he was little. She'd seen the boys here on the island since they were born. How could they ask her to clean it up? To wash away the boys' blood? Peter's blood?

Henning blinked away the tears and turned back to the screen and the flashing cursor.

He knew everyone was waiting. Or rather, they had been waiting. Surely no one could expect any writing from him now? Everyone would understand that he couldn't finish the tenth book – the final instalment in his decalogy. Things had fundamentally changed, and he didn't have to deliver. Not anymore. The Nobel Prize was his without the series being complete – so amazing were his achievements. No one could take that away from him. Or could they?

Henning stopped mid-movement. Could they take it away from him now? They hadn't made the announcement yet. Before that, nothing was certain. Before that, they could be influenced by all the lies being spread around the world. Well, lies and lies. Some of it was true. But things weren't as black and white as they looked in newspaper print. The articles left no room for life's shades of grey.

Had they paid off the girls Ole had slept with? Yes, of course they had. None of them could deny that. But it wasn't how it sounded. The girls and women had all had their own agendas. They had sought out Blanche like moths to a flame, hoping to gain success, fame and attention. They had wanted to be close to the epicentre of culture with people who were someones – people who mattered. They had used their femininity. And Ole was weak.

Henning hadn't fallen for the siren calls. It was a blessing that he was impervious to them. But Ole was weak in the flesh and those women had exploited that. And for that, Blanche was having to pay – twice over. The verdict in the court of public opinion was unjust.

Henning moaned. He couldn't lose any more. He'd lost Peter and the boys. Perhaps even Rickard. But the man he was – and even more importantly the man he was about to become – couldn't be lost.

Hands trembling, he rang the Permanent Secretary of the Swedish Academy.

'Hello, this is Henning. Thanks. Yes, it's terrible. Elisabeth and I are devastated. Yes, yes. I've read that too. It's dreadful how they twist and turn . . . Yes, quite. That's exactly how we feel about it. I just wanted to make sure that there hadn't been any change in what we discussed a couple of days ago? No. Yes, exactly. The Academy is above such worldly things. And it's all based on misconceptions, prejudices and sometimes nothing more than downright lies. Opportunism. Yes, well you know yourself how hungry the culture groupies . . . Yes, by any means. But that's a relief to hear. Of course, nothing has the same meaning any longer in light of our loss. But it does provide a glimmer of joy in this dense darkness. Thanks. I'm grateful for the Academy's continued support. Yes, I'll let Elisabeth know. We appreciate your solicitude. Thank you.'

Henning hung up. Thank God the Academy was made up of sensible people. People who could tell the sheep from the goats. The prize was still his. His name was going to be chiselled into the halls of immortality. And he no longer had to stare at a flashing cursor.

He hesitated. Then he sent a text to Louise. She of all people would understand the significance of the news that the prize was guaranteed to be his regardless of the tragic circumstances. And she needed to be there, with them.

What was more, he could do with Louise's help to clean up the mess at Blanche and unburden Elisabeth of the preparations for the funeral. His wife was far too fragile to handle it. But Louise was a rock – and the family needed her right now. She could book a cleaner to handle the cottage.

'I'll come with you tomorrow!'

Bertil slapped his hand on the kitchen counter to emphasize his words. Ernst vacated the kitchen in terror, seeking out a quieter part of the flat. At the same moment, the streetlight outside dimmed and the room became even darker. Bertil shivered. It felt like an omen. He hurried to switch on the light by the window and then looked at Rita.

She smiled quietly at him, but it was such a faint and forced smile that it pained Bertil.

'There's no need for that,' she said. 'I'll manage just fine by myself. You've got an investigation to look after. Those poor kids on Skjälerö . . .'

'Patrik can deal with that. You and I both know that Patrik is really the man in charge of things at the station, and he has been for years.'

'Well, I know that. I didn't realize you did too.'

He looked at her and saw the sly smile she was unable to conceal.

'I'm lazy, not stupid,' he replied, sitting down heavily on one of the kitchen chairs.

'Yet another thing I love about you,' said Rita.

She came closer and he grabbed her by the waist and pulled her down onto his lap.

'Are you sure this chair will take the weight of us both?' she said, wrapping her arms around him.

'If not, there are always new ones at Ikea.'

Bertil leaned his head against hers and closed his eyes. They synchronized their breathing as they had done so many times before.

'Aren't you afraid?' he said, his eyes still closed.

Rita hugged him more tightly.

'I'm terrified. I'm not just scared of dying – I'm scared of the nausea, the weakness, the uncertainty. And I know it's vain, but I'm scared of losing my hair. I know the doctor said some people prefer to shave it off before it happens, but . . .'

'You'll be just as beautiful without it,' Bertil said, opening his eyes to look at her. 'And it'll grow back.'

'Yes, I know. And it *is* vain to worry about that kind of thing. But it's the most palpable thing to worry about, so that's what I'm trying to do. I'm pushing the unknown away.'

'You're not going to die.' Bertil's voice broke and he shook his head firmly. 'You're not going to die.'

'None of us know that,' she said calmly. 'Now might be my time. Or later. It's not something we can control.'

'I can't live without you.'

He buried his face in her neck and breathed in her scent.

'If things go that badly then you'll cope,' she said, but she also pressed herself closer, and Bertil felt the pulse at her collarbone quicken.

'I won't,' he managed to say even though his chest ached so much.

'Yes you will, I promise, my love.'

311

'You're not the one meant to be comforting me.'

'You'll get to comfort me in time.'

'What if I'm not strong enough?'

It was his innermost fear and his voice faltered. She took his face between her hands and held it some distance away. With her gaze fixed on his, she said gently:

'You're stronger than you think. And I'm grateful to have you by my side.'

'I won't be able to do it,' he said dejectedly. Tears were flowing without him being able to stop them.

'Yes you will,' she said, gently cradling him in her arms.

'Hi sweetie!'

Erica kissed Patrik's cheek and took her shoes off with a sigh of relief. The train had been both hot and delayed, and her feet had swollen up considerably.

'It's good to have you home again,' said Patrik, but something in his voice made Erica look at him suspiciously.

'Okay. What have you broken? What have you bought that was much too expensive or unnecessary? Who did you sleep with?'

Patrik smiled stiffly.

'You may come to wish that it was one of those options.'

'Oh no.' Erica hung up her coat and looked at him, her hands limp at her sides. 'Explain.'

Then her hand flew to her mouth.

'Kristina and Bob the Builder have been here,' she exclaimed. 'What the hell have they done?'

'I think it's probably easier if I show you.'

Patrik led Erica towards the kitchen, and she followed hesitantly. She came to a halt in the doorway, her jaw dropping.

'What on earth?'

'Honestly, I find you get used to it after a while. I don't think it's too . . .'

Erica glared at her husband, and he fell silent. She couldn't believe her eyes.

'Roman arches? Salmon pink? Who's the designer? Barbie? Oh no, that's right. Your mother.'

Erica didn't know whether to laugh or cry.

'But they've done a nice job in the garden,' Patrik said, his voice slightly desperate as he waved his hand in the direction of the outside.

'They've had a go at that too?! How did they have the time? And the energy? Shouldn't they be old and tired? Instead of two lethargic, compliant pensioners, we've got two interior designers on speed.'

Her voice rose to a falsetto and left her breathless. Erica sank down onto one of the kitchen chairs. Only then did she spot the new seat cushions.

'Lemons? *Lemons?*'

Patrik held up his hands to placate her.

'They can be changed,' he said resignedly. 'And cupboard doors can be repainted.'

'And the Roman arch?'

'We did say we were going to knock that wall down when we redo the kitchen.'

Erica stared at the wall and realized that Patrik was right.

She shook her head.

'Good God – can't a person even go away for a couple of days without seeing their home transformed into an eighties pizzeria?'

'Sorry. I should have kept an eye on things.' Patrik looked guilty as he laid the table. 'Did you eat on the train? I've warmed up some of Mum's lasagne.'

'I'm famished,' Erica said, inhaling the aroma of toasted cheese.

You could say what you wanted about Kristina, she was a good cook.

'Anyway, there's no need for an apology,' Erica said, wiggling her toes to get her circulation going. 'You've got far more important things to be dealing with, and you're right, we can repaint, and we were actually planning to take down that wall. It's only stuff. Now that's dealt with . . . How are you getting on?'

Patrik served each of them a big helping of lasagne and sat down opposite her.

'Wine?'

Erica waved her hand dismissively.

'No, not tonight.'

Patrik raised an eyebrow but didn't say anything. Instead, he began to tell her about everything that had happened since she'd left for Stockholm.

'So Rolf is Rickard's dad?' Erica said, wide-eyed, as she took a big mouthful of lasagne before reaching immediately for her glass of water in a panic. 'Wow, I didn't realize it was this hot.'

She took a couple of sips of water.

'Would you like me to blow on your food?' Patrik said in amusement, and Erica stuck her tongue out at him.

She'd missed him so much she ached. She'd spent so many years single and had been totally fine with that, but now she couldn't imagine life without Patrik at her side.

Her thoughts grazed past the issue she knew she had to raise with him, but she wanted to postpone it for a while longer.

'I wonder if Henning knows that,' she said instead, blowing on a new mouthful of food.

She wasn't going to make the same mistake twice.

'No idea,' said Patrik.

He stiffened when he heard a sound from the children's bedrooms upstairs, but relaxed when there was no follow-up noise.

'What was the vibe like at Blanche?' he said. 'It must have been at boiling point.'

Erica rocked a hand to and fro.

'News about Peter and the boys spread while I was there, but the articles about Blanche hadn't been published yet. I dare say the place is in chaos by now.'

'My God, Henning and Elisabeth must be going through hell. Peter and the boys dead. Rolf dead. Rickard as the prime suspect. And now their life's work is mired in an unparalleled scandal.'

'Their lives have been ruined in the space of a few days,' Erica said slowly.

She hadn't thought about it like that before, but it was the truth. From all the happiness and rejoicing of last Saturday when they had been at the pinnacle of their lives – personally and professionally – to the nightmare they now found themselves in. Everything now like shattered glass around their feet.

'I wonder what's going to happen to the prize,' Erica said as she chewed her way through a big chunk of lasagne.

'What prize?'

'There was a rumour on Saturday that Henning is going to be awarded the Nobel Prize for Literature. I wonder what'll happen to that following *Aftonbladet*'s articles. It can't be a given that it's his for the taking any longer.'

'But surely the scandal has nothing to do with his books? Surely that question has to be judged separately?'

Erica put down her water glass.

'That's how it would be in a perfect world, but I have a hard time believing that the Swedish Academy is completely neutral on the issue. And it must be a tough situation for Susanne.'

'I can't imagine either Henning or Elisabeth being all that bothered about a literary award right now,' Patrik said.

'Probably true. But it's not just any old prize – it makes you an eternal star in the literary skies.'

'Still . . .' said Patrik. 'Their son and grandchildren have been shot dead. Worldly things surely don't mean much in that context. Speaking of dead children: how's your investigation into Lola and her daughter going?'

'Slow progress. But isn't it a bit of a coincidence that Rolf's final exhibition was going to be focused on her?'

Erica told him about her conversations with Lola's neighbour, Birgitta and Johan.

'I've also got a copy of the full police file. Could you ask Pedersen to look over the autopsy report?'

Patrik grimaced and glanced at her apologetically.

'He's pretty busy processing what we sent him – alongside his usual workload.'

'Okay, I get it. But if you get the chance, could you ask him?'

'Yes, but I can't promise any more than that. I'm going to speak to him tomorrow and find out how far he's got, and if I get the chance I'll ask then. But I don't think he has time. Just so you know.'

He held up his hands deprecatingly.

'That's all I ask,' said Erica.

'How did you get on with the job I gave you? The private detective?'

'Oh, he was a character all right. But it went well. I've got copies of the full police report. All two pages of it. But I don't have anything concrete to offer. Peter Bauer simply seems to have wanted to find out who ran his wife down and then did a bunk. Perfectly reasonable, if you ask me.'

Erica avoided Patrik's gaze. There was a small possibility that she might be able to find out something crucial that would help him, but that would have to wait. Right now, she had something to tell him that couldn't wait

316

any longer. The plaster had to come off. She took a deep breath and said:

'I'm pregnant.'

There was a loud clatter as Patrik dropped his fork on his plate.

25

WEDNESDAY

Patrik aimlessly shuffled some papers on his desk. He didn't really know how to take the news that Erica was expecting. On the previous occasions, he had been happier than he had thought was possible. But now they had three children and life was – to put it mildly – intense, but they could see the light at the end of the tunnel as they got past the early years.

Neither he nor Erica had ever been particularly fond of the baby years and mostly regarded it as heavy toil with zero sleep and extreme stress to boot. Could they manage it one more time?

He shuffled the papers around the desk again. There was a ton of work to be done, but after a night spent pondering, he was so tired he could barely formulate a sensible thought. But he had to. Rickard was still in custody but there wasn't long left until the prosecutor had to make a decision on whether to have him remanded. The prosecutor would probably be that way inclined, but Patrik still wanted a confession. There was something that felt wrong, and they still had nothing to tie Rickard to the murder of Rolf – the man they now knew to be Rickard's father.

Patrik sighed and decided to apply the advice he gave others when a task felt insurmountable. It had been his grandfather who had always said: *How do you eat an elephant? One bite at a time.*

Right now, Patrik felt like he had an enormous elephant in front of him. It had been a long time since he'd felt this overwhelmed. The case – the cases – were merging into each other, subsuming one another. It was all too sprawling, too dreadful, too improbable that this had all happened at the same time by chance. And then there was the media constantly calling Annika in reception and trying to get hold of every officer on duty in the station as they filled page after page with dark headlines about people mixed up in the case. The press was like a constant, disruptive noise – like a buzzing fly always within earshot but out of reach.

He reached for his notepad to start figuratively dicing up the elephant. He quickly wrote down the things he considered top priorities and decided to start with the elephant's trunk, which in this case was Pedersen, the head of forensic medicine in Gothenburg.

Pedersen picked up on the first ring.

'I was about to call you.'

The voice was familiar after their many years working together. They had long ago done away with all the pleasantries and always got straight to the point.

'I don't have everything as yet – we're not done,' Pedersen added. 'But I do have some findings to report, so you've got something to be getting on with.'

'Why, thank you,' Patrik said, and found himself almost bowing slightly.

He knew how bogged down they were in forensic medicine, but he suspected that the two children lying on the shiny autopsy tables meant everyone was prioritizing this case and very probably working around the clock.

'How's the investigation going otherwise?' Pedersen asked.

'Oh, it's fine. We've had a few preliminary findings from NFC through Farideh. She's had to pull some strings. She's been a rock.'

'See – you'll get used to her,' Pedersen said with a chuckle.

'I suppose I will. And like I said, she seems sharp.'

'She is. We've already established a great partnership. Anyway, why don't we go through what we've got so far?'

Patrik turned to a fresh page in his notebook. He knew he would also receive a written report from Pedersen, but taking notes while he listened helped him to focus and structure his thoughts.

'Let's start with Rolf. Well, we know the cause of death, so no surprises there. A shot to the back of the head with a nail gun. He probably had no idea what was about to happen.'

That was some consolation at least, Patrik thought to himself.

'Okay. What else? Anything else of interest in Rolf's autopsy?'

Pedersen paused for a moment. 'He almost certainly had only months left to live.'

'What are you saying?' Patrik straightened up in his chair.

'Advanced cancer.'

'Fuck me. Is it at all possible that he wasn't aware of it?'

'No, not given the spread and where I found tumours. He must have been having quite a bit of trouble. He'll have seen a doctor. There should be details in his medical records.'

Patrik mulled this over thoughtfully. How did this relate to everything else?

'And Peter and the boys?'

'We're talking about pure execution. The kids likely died in their sleep. Each had a shot to the forehead. Close range.' Pedersen's voice was gruff. 'I suspect Peter woke up when the boys were shot because he took two shots – one of them went through his left hand before it hit his head. The eldest of the boys still had a bullet in the back of his skull. It was a through and through on the youngest – the bullet ended up in the headboard. In Peter's case, one bullet was still there while the other was in the wall.'

'Jesus Christ.'

Nausea rose up within him. The thought of the baby in Erica's belly threatened to overcome Patrik, but he quickly pushed it aside. Distancing himself was the only possible way to keep a cool head and carry on working.

'What state were the bullets in?'

'There were fine traces of rifling from the barrel. If you find a gun, we'll be able to match it. Do you know any more about that, by the way?'

Patrik checked his emails. The ballistics expert's report had finally arrived.

'A classic. What springs to mind if I say Bond?'

'Walther PPK. Not just Bond. It was the standard police sidearm until the eighties: 7.65 calibre, full metal jacket ammunition.'

'That's right. And if the bullets are in as good nick as you say, then it may even be possible to find something in the database,' Patrik said, thinking aloud.

Pedersen didn't answer – he realized it was a rhetorical statement. NFC had probably already started a database search.

'By the way . . .' Patrik said quickly before Pedersen had time to hang up. 'I have a favour to ask. Well, it's Erica asking the favour.'

Pedersen laughed dryly.

'Normally I'd say no on the spot without even asking how big a favour, since we're drowning in work. But since it's Erica, at least tell me what she wants.'

'You want to be in the acknowledgements for her next book, don't you?' Patrik grinned.

It felt good to lighten the mood after the gloomy subject matter they'd been discussing.

'Of course. It's my only shot at immortality,' said Pedersen. 'So . . . What does your distinguished wife want help with?'

Patrik briefly summarized the Lola case.

'So that's Erica's next book?'

'Looks that way. She's been in Stockholm for a couple of days doing research, and she dug up some of the old investigative file. To describe it as thin is probably the kindest thing I can say. My guess is there was a degree of transphobia at play – but if that's true then it's awful, given that Lola had a kid who also died in the fire.'

'People's bigotry never ceases to amaze,' Pedersen said gloomily. 'But let me guess. Your dear wife would like me to glance over the autopsy report?'

Patrik managed to force out a yes, feeling slightly ashamed. Then again, Pedersen was a grown adult who was perfectly capable of saying no if he didn't want to do it.

'Of course I'll help. Email it over and I'll have a gander.'

'It'll be in your inbox in ten minutes,' Patrik said gratefully.

'Give Farideh a ring.'

'Right away,' said Patrik.

When he'd hung up, he looked at his spider diagram. Then he underlined *Rolf dying* with several thick lines. It wasn't necessarily of significance, but something told him that it mattered – that it was a piece of the puzzle that fitted into the whole somehow or other. He just needed to figure out how.

26

STOCKHOLM 1980

'When do I get to read it?'

Lola glared at Rolf while keeping a watchful eye on P'tite, who was on the swings in the playground at Vasaparken.

'I got to read the poems you wrote. Why is this so different?'

Rolf waved merrily at P'tite, who waved back.

'By the way, Ester and I loved having her to stay with us. Despite the sad circumstances. You know that you only have to ask if you need help – she's always welcome at ours.'

'I promise to get better at that.'

Lola waved to P'tite too and tried to master the impulse to rush over and stop her from going so high. She had to let P'tite fly. She had promised Monica that.

'Don't you trust me enough to let me read it?' Rolf continued, his expression hurt.

Lola put her hand on his arm. The sun was beating down on them, making beads of sweat run down their lower backs. She raised her face to the sun, luxuriating in its beams. She loved the sun – she loved the colour it gave her. During the summer, she always sat on the balcony for a spell every day clutching a foil-covered tray under her chin to help her tan along. Sun was good for the health. The more the better.

'There's no one I trust more than you, Rolf,' she said, her face still turned towards the sun. 'You know that. And there is no one whose opinion matters more. That's precisely why I don't want you to see my work in progress piece by piece. I want you to see the big picture.'

She turned her head towards him and tapped her long red nail on the thick blue notebook.

'This will be done soon. The story is coming to an end. And if it turns out the way I think it will, it's going to be beautiful, strange, special and something that no one has ever read before.'

'That sounds incredible,' Rolf said, a warm smile spreading across his face – the smile she liked so much. 'Have you thought about showing it to Elisabeth? I know she's looked at some of your shorter works. She's so keen to publish something by you. I'd even say she's itching to publish something by you, with her as your editor.'

'Of course I'm going to take it to Elisabeth. Who else? So once you've seen it, Elisabeth will be the first to read it. But until then the words are mine alone.'

Lola tapped on the blue cover again.

'I understand how you feel about your family,' said Rolf. 'Mine weren't much to write home about either. The last time I saw my old man, I knocked out his front teeth. I was sick and tired of being beaten.'

'My wounds are only on the inside,' said Lola, and it was as if the sun no longer warmed her. 'Frostbite. No one ever beat me with their fists. Only their words. I grew up in a cold place you can't even imagine. Everything had to be correct. Everything had to be just right – polished. I was a strange bird from the very beginning, and I've always known I wasn't the person my family thought I was.'

The image of a bird brought an old memory to life.

'When I was little, I often read a story about two birds who found an egg in their nest and decided to brood it as their own,' she said, looking at Rolf. 'But when the egg hatched, it wasn't a chick – it was an alligator. And it grew and grew and grew until it was so big it no longer fitted into the nest. So the bird parents decided to teach it to fly, because that was the only thing they could imagine their child would do. They pushed the baby alligator out of the nest and he flapped his legs for all he was worth. But instead of flying, he tumbled straight down into the water below the tree, where he found the world he hadn't ever realized he was missing, but that he knew from that very moment was his. In the story, the alligator's bird parents were happy for him. They were happy because the child they had raised in their nest had found his home. There wasn't a happy ending like that in my story.'

Rolf caressed her tanned cheek.

'I'm sorry. But you have us now. And P'tite has us too.'

He brightened up when P'tite came running towards them.

'Daddy daddy daddy! Can I buy an ice cream?'

'Here. You can have five kronor from me.'

Rolf pulled his wallet out and produced a five-kronor note, and she skipped off happily towards the ice cream kiosk. Lola knew that P'tite would spend ages there deliberating before she finally settled on a Pear Ice – both because she liked the flavour and because she loved the surprise of the small picture that came inside the packaging.

'You're spoiling her.'

'It's a true pleasure,' Rolf said, grinning from ear to ear.

'Sometimes she's so incredibly like my grandmother,' said Lola. 'The only person who saw me for who I was. P'tite's named after her.'

'But I thought . . .'

Rolf couldn't hide his astonishment.

'That she wasn't mine?' Lola smiled. 'A perfectly reasonable assumption.'

She bowed her head.

'Yes. I prefer men. But Monica . . . I loved her more than I've ever loved anyone else. And she loved me and wanted me to love her the same way. I so dearly wanted to. And I figured if I just gave it a chance, but . . .'

Lola shook her head.

'I am who I am, and I could only love Monica in a different way to the way she wanted. But P'tite still somehow came into the world. There aren't any other possible candidates, because Monica wasn't . . . she wasn't working then. And we were so unspeakably happy that it happened. Monica would be so proud if she could see P'tite now.'

P'tite approached them holding a Pear Ice – already dripping down her hand – and Lola put her notebook into her handbag to avoid getting ice cream on it.

'My sister says she wants her,' she continued thoughtfully. 'Apparently she and her husband can't conceive, and in my sister's eyes that's an imperfection. But in her perfect world, P'tite would just be part of the backdrop rather than a unique person.'

Lola fell silent as P'tite got close enough to hear. The ice cream was gone – only the stick remained. And the picture.

'Look. There was a hedgehog in this one!'

P'tite eagerly held out the small picture, which was now sticky from ice cream. Lola took a handkerchief from her bag, spat on it and began to wipe her daughter's mouth.

'Ew!' P'tite exclaimed, but Lola didn't stop until her daughter was clean.

She took the messy stick between her thumb and forefinger and passed it to Rolf.

'Bin this for me, will you?'

She wiped P'tite's hands carefully with the handkerchief, and then cleaned the picture of the hedgehog.

'Can I play now?' said P'tite, looking longingly towards the kids running around the park.

'Of course!' Lola said, waving her away.

'Is everyone coming on Saturday?' Rolf asked.

'Yes, all of you lot. And Sigge.'

'Oh yes. The boyfriend.'

'Um, I think it'll be a while . . .' Lola angled her face towards the sun again. 'Poor kid. Sigge's mother is God knows where, and his grandmother can't cope with him. She just wants to be shot of him.'

'P'tite's lucky to have you for a father.'

Lola leaned forward and kissed him on the cheek.

'And I'm lucky to have you.'

In the distance, they heard P'tite's laughter rising wild and free into the clear blue sky.

27

'Hello!' Anna bellowed. 'Welcome home! Can I get a Hawaiian?'

Erica dashed into the hall with a grumpy expression.

'You knew?' she said accusingly to her sister. 'You saw what they were doing and did nothing?'

'Did nothing? I helped Kristina find the right shade of salmon pink for your cupboard doors. She was drifting towards something at the terracotta end of the scale, but I thought something a little more like apricot was the right fit . . .'

'If you weren't holding the world's cutest niece, I'd box your ears! Hand over the kid and go and savour your handiwork, you Quisling.'

Anna passed Fliss over. When she entered the kitchen she laughed so hard tears ran down her face.

'I didn't see it finished! My God, I'm dying.'

She wiped away the tears as she continued to giggle.

'Yup, I died too. It was a nice surprise to come back to last night. A trip back in time to the eighties. I'm only grateful they didn't conjure up a tapestry too.'

'Well, there were samples . . .'

'Shut up!' said Erica, slapping her laughing sister.

'You've been talking about doing the kitchen for years. I thought this might be a good kick up the backside,' said Anna, grinning.

Erica snorted, put Fliss in a high chair and made them each a cup of coffee.

'Well, you do have a point. The process has been shortened by around two years – that's about how long it would have taken us to pull our fingers out. Now there's no choice. That wall has to go.'

She regarded the Roman arch with a shudder.

'You should have known better than to let that pair in here unsupervised,' said Anna.

Her sister opened one of the cupboards and took out a wafer for Fliss.

'I learned the hard way. Which means that next time I go away you have the honour of looking after three young kids. Nice, huh?'

Anna shuddered before sitting down at the kitchen table.

'Speaking of which, how was Stockholm? Did you turn anything useful up? Is the new book going to be about Lola?'

Erica nodded. She told Anna briefly what she'd found out and how desultory the police investigation had been.

'No one has bothered to find out what happened to Lola and her daughter. Not for all these years. Her closest friends – they were like family to her – just moved on. All of them: Rolf and his wife, Henning and Elisabeth, Susanne and Ole. Right up until Rolf decided to exhibit his photos of Lola and her friends.'

'Have you talked to Lola's biological family?'

'I've only had time to scratch the surface. What I do know is that Lola broke off contact with them long before the little girl was born. But a sister apparently turned up shortly before Lola's death. I'd obviously like to talk to her if she's still alive. A lot can happen in forty years. But first, I'd like to get a second opinion on the autopsy report.'

'Did both of them die in the fire?'

Anna gave Fliss another wafer. The first one had been partially eaten and then spat out and was now lying in a damp heap on the table.

'Yes and no. Lola had two gunshot wounds to the head, which was the cause of death. But P'tite had smoke in her lungs and the cause of death was listed as carbon monoxide poisoning. They found the little girl inside a trunk. Lola was in the kitchen in front of the hob.'

Anna shook her head.

'It's not like you can ask her old circle what they know . . . Even though it was Vivian who first mentioned Lola to you.'

'No, I can't really give Henning and Elisabeth a bell and say: "Hey, I'd like to chat to you about Lola." That'll have to keep for later, once they've had time to grieve.'

'How is Louise, by the way?' Anna asked. 'Have you talked to her?'

'No.' Erica shook her head. 'I don't really know what to do. I don't want to intrude. But I also don't want to be that friend who doesn't get in touch.'

'Text her and say you're there for her if she needs to talk. Then it's up to her.'

'Yes, I guess that's smart,' said Erica. She didn't need to tell Anna that she had already done just that. And it wouldn't hurt to send another text.

Then she took a deep breath.

'I'm pregnant.'

'What?'

Anna shouted her reply and Fliss was so startled she began to cry.

'No, no – sorry, sweetheart, sorry. Here, have another wafer.'

Anna stared at Erica in shock while the little girl calmed down.

'I thought it was the menopause, but apparently I'm up the duff,' Erica said with a sheepish smile.

'Well, uh, congratulations eh? What does Patrik have to say?'

'I think he's in shock too. I told him yesterday evening and I could hear him tossing and turning all night.'

Anna got up and began to pace around the room. Erica knew how she felt. She had been wandering around the house like a lost soul that morning.

'So what are you going to do?'

'I'm not actually sure.' Erica looked down at the tabletop. 'I felt very, very done with this. The same is true for Patrik. At the same time, it's a big decision, not . . .'

'Only you can decide whether you're up to it and want to do it all again.'

Anna put a hand over her sister's.

'Then there's the whole age thing. The risk . . .'

'You can find out about that in advance.'

'Ugh, I don't know if I'm brave enough to have amniocentesis. That needle . . . And the test itself comes with a risk of miscarriage.'

'No, no. There are more modern ways now. I don't remember what it's called, but they start with a simple blood test. And you can do it sooner than the old test.'

Erica looked up at her little sister.

'I'll have to call the maternity clinic and ask. But still, I don't know if I want . . .'

'Start by finding out how the land lies. Then you can make up your minds.'

'Sounds sensible,' said Erica. 'You're almost forgiven for that arch.'

'I think it's very you.'

'Oh shut up.'

Erica began to relax. Everything would work out somehow. She had Anna. And she had Patrik.

It hadn't been possible to reach Farideh by phone – she was out on a job, according to her voicemail. Patrik drummed his fingers impatiently on the desk. He wanted her pieces of the puzzle before he moved on. At the same time, Pedersen's words about Rolf were gnawing away at him. Somehow, it felt like Rolf was the key to both cases and therefore to Rickard.

Patrik went into the corridor and over to Gösta's door. He knocked on the frame of the open door.

'Fancy joining me for a chat with our suspect?'

'Of course. But his lawyer isn't here right now. Do you think he'll agree to talk?'

'We'll see.'

Patrik headed towards the custody unit and felt himself adopting his grim face. He hoped Rickard had been humbled a little by his detention.

'Rickard? I'd like to ask you a few things. Do you want your lawyer present?'

Rickard looked up at Patrik. He seemed tired and dejected – there was no trace of the man who had refused to talk without his lawyer.

'I just want to get out of here. Anything. Ask me anything.' Gone was the snotty tone and the superior gaze. 'When will you decide whether to release me or not?'

'We can hold you for seventy-two hours. We're onto day three. After that, we can request that you be remanded. That means we can hold you for a fortnight, then we have to hold a new remand hearing. Didn't Jakobsson inform you of this?'

'Probably,' Rickard said tiredly. 'I'm struggling to focus and the days all merge into one. Are you going to remand me?'

'There's a lot pointing to your guilt – enough that you're highly likely to be remanded. But if you help us with our investigation, that may change. We have a few question marks and were wondering whether you'd discuss them with us?'

'Go for it,' Rickard said, getting up from his bunk in the small room where he was being held.

They headed for the interview room and Patrik and Gösta sat down opposite him at the table.

'Tell us about Rolf,' said Patrik, watching Rickard closely.

'Rolf?' Rickard said indifferently. 'What do you want me to say about him?'

'Rolf was your father.'

Rickard started. He stared at Patrik and Gösta.

'How the hell . . . ?'

'We know you were blackmailing Blanche.'

Rickard remained silent, looking down at the table. Then he looked up defiantly.

'What do you want me to say? I saw an opportunity and I took it.'

'Why Blanche in particular? What made you think they would pay to keep quiet about it?'

'For Dad's sake. Henning, I mean. He doesn't know a thing. They've always protected him and Mum.'

'So it was Susanne and Ole who approved the payments?'

'And Louise. Nothing happened at the club without Louise's say-so. But yes, I figured they were already used to paying hush money, so why not cut me in on the deal?'

There was the cynical smile that so bothered Patrik.

'How did you find out that Rolf was your father?' said Gösta.

'He told me himself. Made a big deal out of it. He asked me to come to his studio in Stockholm and he showed me a load of pictures of trannies he was going to exhibit. He was waffling on about coming to terms with the past. Then he asked whether I knew that I was his son.'

'Had you suspected anything?' Patrik asked curiously. Rickard shook his head.

'No. I had no idea. And I'm absolutely certain Dad doesn't know either. He'd never have been able to handle it.'

'So that's why Susanne and Ole were paying – via Blanche?'

'Yes. For them, Blanche is everything. Well, mostly for Ole. Susanne has the Academy. But if it's important to Ole then it's important to Susanne.'

'Was Rolf going to tell anyone other than you?'

'I didn't get that impression. I don't think he wanted to cause any trouble for Mum. It felt as if he wanted . . . I don't know . . . to stop having to keep the secret? Perhaps he was having some kind of mid-life crisis? I don't know. I had to swear not to tell Mum that I knew.'

Rickard looked down at his nails and poked at a cuticle. He was becoming more and more like his nonchalant self now that he was out of the cell.

'He was dying,' said Patrik. Gösta looked at him in surprise. 'From what I've understood, he only had months left to live. Cancer.'

'Jesus.' Rickard frowned. 'I suppose that explains it.'

'If your father had found out that Rolf was your father, how do you think he would have taken it?'

'He would have gone completely nuts. Henning has a temper . . . There are not many people who know that. Mum's been tiptoeing around him their whole marriage. If Dad doesn't get his own way, then . . .'

Rickard shook his head, so that his fringe fell across his face. He brushed it out of the way with his usual practised movement.

'So if Rolf had told him . . . ?'

Rickard punched his hand into his palm in reply.

Patrik said nothing, but exchanged glances with Gösta.

'I didn't do it,' Rickard said wearily. 'Not Rolf. Or Peter and the boys. I could never do that. And where would I have got a gun from? I've never owned a gun and I don't have a clue where you'd get hold of one either. And I . . . Damn it, I loved Peter. And the boys. And Rolf had never done anything to me. I had no reason to kill him. He was worth more to me alive – given the money I was getting from Blanche.'

He had been gesticulating but now his hands came to rest on the table.

'You could continue blackmailing them even with Rolf dead,' said Patrik. 'The information remains true.'

'Yes, but without Rolf alive it loses a whole lot of its edge. It would be a lot harder for Dad to be pissed off at a dead man.'

'Or maybe Rolf found out about the blackmail and confronted you?' said Patrik.

'I may be a shit, but I haven't killed anyone. Ask Tilde. She knows I was in bed all night.'

'A partner's testimony in this situation has less weight than the forensic evidence.'

Patrik cracked his knuckles. It was a habit he'd picked up lately.

'The forensic evidence is wrong. I didn't do it.'

'That remains to be seen,' Patrik said, standing up. Gösta followed his example. As they led Rickard back to the cell, he looked just as dejected as he had when they'd brought him out. The last thing they saw before they shut the door and locked up was Rickard on his bunk, staring into space.

Patrik and Gösta walked all the way back to their offices in silence. The only thing that could be heard was the tread of their feet.

'So what do you think?' Gösta said at last.

Patrik hesitated. The facts didn't correlate with his gut.

But his intuition had the benefit of many years' experience. He sighed deeply.

'I don't have a fucking clue. But I'm going to call Farideh, so let me get back to you on that . . .'

He went into his office and picked up the phone. He needed some more answers and hopefully Farideh could give them to him.

Vivian stretched and rubbed her eyes. She had been searching for hours. She had turned the studio upside down and had completely lost track of time. She'd nodded off for a while on the daybed on several occasions, but she had spent the lion's share of the night searching.

The studio looked like it had been broken into. Everything was ripped out, strewn across the floor. But nowhere had she found any sign of the envelopes that Rolf had received or the missing photograph – *Guilt*.

Admittedly, she didn't know what she was looking for. She didn't even know what *Guilt* looked like. She had found a lot of other things linked to the exhibition – thoughts on what he was going to say with the photos of Lola – but *Guilt* was only named in the odd place.

Why had Rolf kept this from her? And what other secrets had he kept? Secrets that might have led to his death . . .

Vivian looked around in resignation. Had Rolf actually kept the envelopes and photo somewhere else? There were countless storage companies around the city, and he could have rented space from any of them. Then again, she knew what Rolf was like. He liked to keep his things close. He would never trust an unknown company. If he had hidden anything then it would be here.

Vivian sank to her knees in the middle of the floor. The studio was on the ground floor, a stone's throw from their flat, with high windows letting in plenty of light. It had been she who had found the place, and she had immediately realized that he would love the floor in particular. It comprised wide wooden floorboards that had been worn to a pale grey patina by footsteps over the decades. It creaked when you walked around – something that had become a soundtrack to Rolf's shoots in the studio. While he preferred to shoot on location – in the setting, in the situation – he had still done countless shoots here over the years to pay the bills: celebrities, politicians, royalty and the plain old rich who were prepared to pay to have their portrait taken through Rolf's lens.

Vivian ran her hand over one of the grey boards. Her eye was caught by something in the far corner. She squinted. Then she hurried closer and closer until she got to the corner and saw what her eye was reacting to.

One of the planks was a slightly different shade to the others. It looked newer. She pressed it lightly. The plank bowed a little, but it seemed to be nailed down.

Vivian looked around for something to prise it loose with and found a table knife in the jumble on the floor. She carefully inserted the knife into one of the cracks around the board. It gave way with surprising ease. The nails were only for show – none of them were actually embedded into the wood beneath.

There was a cavity under the plank, running under the floor. Vivian squinted, but it was too dark to make anything out. She turned on the torch on her mobile and shone it down there. There was a clutch of folders in a crate. The crate was too big to lift up through the hole, so on some occasion the other boards must have been loosened and replaced with the box in situ. But it was no trouble at all to remove the folders – there were so few she could pick them up with one hand.

Vivian fanned the folders out in front of her. There was nothing written on them, so she would have to open each one to see what was inside.

The top one contained the envelope she'd told Martin about. She recognized the handwriting on the front. It seemed the contents were still inside, and it was just as she had thought: information about Blanche. Every time they had covered up Ole's indiscretions. His abuse of young women. Of course it was.

Vivian trembled when she realized that the next folder contained love letters. The handwriting was florid and hard to read, but she quickly realized that they were letters from Elisabeth to Rolf, from the time when Rolf had been married to Ester. The words jumped off the page at her: longing, passion, love, despair, sorrow, hope. They had been considering a life together – that much was apparent from several of the letters – but their correspondence increasingly reached the conclusion that it was impossible. They couldn't leave what they had – they couldn't hurt their spouses and break up their families.

There was also confirmation of what Vivian had always suspected: that Rickard was Rolf's son. She had never said anything about it to Rolf, but it was obvious whenever they were in the same room. At least to her – no one else seemed to have noticed.

The final letter was Elisabeth's farewell, dated 1978. They had decided to end their affair but do all they could to remain friends. Based on what Vivian had seen over the years, they had succeeded in those intentions – something few people ever did.

The final folders contained negatives. They poured out of the first one she opened. She picked them up and held them to the light one by one. All of them were from the same period as the photos for the exhibition. Lola at work. Lola with P'tite. And Lola in her kitchen with her friends: Susanne, Ole, Henning, Elisabeth and Ester.

Rolf behind the camera – a constant presence but out of sight. Now that she knew, she could see the love between

Rolf and Elisabeth. The way he photographed her, the way he aimed his lens at her face as it caught the light in Lola's kitchen. Part of Vivian felt compassion for him. It couldn't have been easy to sacrifice himself – to give up his love for what was right and proper. At the same time, she felt jealousy tearing at her breast. She had never felt as if she were Rolf's great love – not compared with Ester. And now definitely not in comparison with Elisabeth.

The final folder was thin and light. Vivian removed the elastic band holding it together and opened it. It contained only one negative in addition to a quickly developed, small-format photograph. She turned the picture over. On the back it said 'Guilt'.

Vivian had found a copy of the missing photograph. The question was what to do with it – and whether she *wanted* to do anything with it.

Patrik lunged for the phone when he saw who was calling.

'I was on a job,' said Farideh. Patrik's most recent attempt to track her down had been fruitless.

'Yes, I heard. Look, I spoke to Pedersen, and he thought you had something for me.'

Farideh sighed softly. 'Yes and no. I've received various preliminary notifications, but there's still a lot outstanding. You can have what I've got so far.'

'Okay, shoot.'

Patrik regretted his choice of words immediately. Given the circumstances, it was tasteless to say the least, but Farideh didn't seem to notice.

'Let's start with the fibres from the nail gun. Silk. Black. I can't provide any more detail than that, but if you find where they came from then NFC should hopefully be able to match the fibres to a fabric.'

'Okay,' said Patrik, scribbling rapidly.

It was no different than with Pedersen – he would

receive a written report from Farideh too, but he had made it a habit to take his own notes.

He closed his eyes and pictured what Rickard had been wearing on the night of the golden wedding party. A black dinner jacket. Admittedly almost all the men had been wearing dinner jackets or dark suits.

'I'll get Rickard's jacket from the night of Rolf's murder brought in.'

'Great,' Farideh said dryly. 'Then there's Rickard's shirt. The blood is from the victims. There's blood from all three of them on the shirt, and the spatter is consistent with the shots being fired at close range. Nothing remarkable in that respect. And we've tested for DNA on the inside of the shirt and only found Rickard's.'

'So everything indicates that he was wearing it when the murders were committed?'

'Yes.'

'Any trace of gunshot residue on Rickard's hands?'

'On the shirt but not the hands. But he may have been wearing gloves. Not entirely logical, given that he didn't protect his shirt, but from what I've understood he was extremely intoxicated. I've seen drunk killers do weirder things. Alcohol has its own logic.'

Patrik knew that Farideh was right in that respect, but it was yet another piece in the puzzle that didn't really fit.

'The bullets? Pedersen said they were in good condition.'

'Yes, none of them had been badly damaged. There was clear rifling, and NFC should be able to match them to the murder weapon if we find it. The bullets have been added to the system and a search against other crimes has been initiated, but it'll probably be a week or so before we have a result.'

'I've double-checked with our gun expert and it's a Walther PPK; 7.65 calibre, as you said.'

'Which isn't all that helpful,' said Farideh, though Patrik

thought he detected the sound of satisfaction. 'One of the most common guns out there. But, again, if you find the gun then we'll be able to match the bullets to it.'

'I'm not at all hopeful on that front,' said Patrik. 'If I were the killer, I would have chucked it in the sea. We've had divers looking, but you know what the waters are like in those parts.'

'Deep, dark and murky,' said Farideh. 'I'm inclined to agree. But hope is always the last light to go out, right?'

'True,' said Patrik, examining his notes.

He had written 'gun' in large letters and underlined it. 'Anything else?'

'No, I'm afraid that's all I've got at the moment. I don't know if it's given you any leads, but it may help to tie the murderer to the crime somewhere down the line. And Rickard Bauer seems to be an excellent candidate. Right?'

'Oh yes, I'm with you on that. Everything points to Rickard. He had both motive and opportunity, and the forensic evidence seems to point to him. But . . .'

'But you're not completely satisfied,' said Farideh.

Patrik was silent for a moment. Then he said:

'No, and that's probably the best way of putting it. I don't feel completely satisfied . . .'

'Well then, we'll have to keep going. And if I get a match on the bullets then I'll call you right away.'

'I'm counting on it.'

Patrik hung up. The most tangible task he'd got from talking to Farideh was that he needed to secure Rickard's dinner jacket. He would have to go out to the island again. He grabbed his coat from his desk chair and went down the corridor to get Gösta. The man was always angling for a boating excursion.

* * *

Erica edged forward in the car, searching for the right number. She pulled onto the driveway of the house in question and parked her Volvo next to a gleaming navy-blue Bentley. She opened the car door carefully to avoid knocking against the other car – scratching it would probably cost her a year's salary.

Louise opened the door. Erica had been surprised when her friend had replied to her text almost immediately, and had asked whether she could come round. Erica wasn't sure what to expect. She'd never been very good around the grieving, and if she was honest she felt uncomfortable in settings that included members of the so-called upper classes, which most definitely included Louise's parents.

Erica had only met them in passing at the party, but she saw them frequently in the pages of the women's weekly magazine that Kristina gave her uninvited each week. If they weren't at the races, it was a gallery opening or some royal wedding. Judging by the pictures, Louise's mother owned a vast selection of small, chic hats. Erica wondered whether she herself owned any hats and concluded that there was a rather tatty sunhat on the top shelf of her wardrobe.

'Come in,' Louise said, stepping aside for Erica.

Erica looked around. The interior was bright and tasteful – a long way from her own salmon pink.

'God, this is lovely,' she said impulsively – immediately regretting it. It sounded far too materialistic, given the circumstances.

'It's beautiful,' Louise said tonelessly, leading the way to the living room.

'Oh hello there!' chirped Louise's mother Lussan, who leapt forward to greet her.

Her father Pierre also came over and pumped Erica's hand. Being famous came with its advantages. There was a frisson of excitement for people from all walks of life in meeting her.

'Do you want coffee?' said Lussan, guiding Erica towards the sofa while Pierre began to tinker with a big, shiny coffee machine.

'How are you feeling?' said Erica, studying Louise.

Louise didn't reply at first. It broke Erica's heart when she saw the state she was in. It was as if she had become . . . transparent. That was the best description Erica could think of. She didn't look like she'd washed her hair in days, and her clothes were hanging loosely off her body as if she had lost several kilos from her already slim figure.

'It's hard,' Louise said finally, her gaze wavering. 'I don't really know where to go. Peter and the boys were . . . my home.'

'We've said we'll stay with her as long as she needs us,' Lussan said, touching the pearls at her throat.

Erica was always fascinated by people who dressed up at home for no particular reason. Her own domestic attire looked like it had been stolen from a homeless person.

'Henning wants me to join him and Elisabeth on the island,' Louise said in her lifeless voice.

Pierre deposited several coffee cups on the table and then sat down.

'I'll probably go in a couple of days,' Louise added.

'How are they doing?' Erica said gently.

She took a sip of her coffee and had to stop herself sighing with pleasure. This was completely unlike her usual cup of coffee at home.

'I've spoken to Henning, but not Elisabeth. I don't think she's up to it. But Henning . . . Well, I guess he's like a lot of men of that generation. Strong, silent, teeth gritted, focused on the job.'

Lussan sighed.

'At first Pierre and I thought that Henning and Elisabeth must be innocent,' she said from her corner of the sofa. 'That dreadful man Ole must have deceived them. But there's been so much in the papers now that I don't think you should be mixing with people like that. It brings shame on your father and me.'

'They're my family too,' Louise said in a low but clear voice.

Lussan snorted but after a sharp glance from Pierre she turned back towards Erica.

'Has your husband said anything else about Rickard? I know the police aren't meant to talk about their cases at home – Pierre's uncle was a chief of police in Stockholm in the eighties – but maybe the rules aren't as strict out here in the sticks? Has Rickard confessed? Your husband paid us a visit with a charming female colleague, although it feels a little strange to see a woman in a police uniform. It somehow doesn't seem quite . . . natural. You know, we're not as strong as men – that's how nature created us – so if I were a man I wouldn't feel nearly as safe with a female officer at my side.'

Pierre cleared his throat and Lussan lost her train of thought.

'Oh sorry, what I was asking was whether Patrik had said anything about Rickard? The most compassionate thing he could do for us would be to confess.'

'Us,' Louise said, pursing her lips.

'Yes, we're actually part of this family too,' said Lussan.

She pointed to her cup, which she had drained, and then looked at Pierre, who went over to the machine.

'He must be the one who murdered Rolf too. How dreadful . . . But then again, you always hear about these serial killers in America. Thank goodness we're spared such things here in Sweden. All we have are the gang shootings. It feels like they're brandishing guns on every street corner. Good God, it makes you wonder why we live here, doesn't it? It's like Rwanda.'

'Well, they had a civil war in Rwanda – not gang shootings,' Louise said wearily.

Lussan glared at her.

'You know very well what I mean. The socialists have ruined Sweden. Not to mention Reinfeldt with his "open your hearts" thing. We're seeing the results of that now. I've told Pierre umpteen times that we ought to leave the country for Spain.'

'Spain's crime rates are much worse than Sweden's.' Louise turned to Erica. 'In case it's not obvious, my mother has been a Friends of Sweden voter for a number of years . . .'

Louise raised a sarcastic eyebrow.

Erica felt the sudden desire to get up, get into the car and drive home to her cosy kitchen with its Roman arch and salmon pink cupboards. This wasn't a home. It was an icebox.

'I'm afraid we have the same rules out here as in the big city,' she said. 'Patrik can't share anything about his work at home, so I don't know any more than you do.'

That wasn't quite true, but she had no desire whatsoever to reveal anything to Lussan.

'Then I must ask . . .'

Lussan's voice suddenly became vivacious and she took both of Erica's hands in hers. Erica had to fight the impulse to quickly withdraw them, instead managing to carefully prise them loose on the pretext of reaching for her coffee.

'What case are you working on for your next book? I'm a big fan, and it's such a luxury to be able to ask a famous author like you direct questions.'

Louise rolled her eyes at Erica, who winked back. This was her bread and butter at every social gathering she attended.

'It was actually Vivian who tipped me off about the current case. And I can't guarantee it'll turn into a book – I'm still in the research phase, so anything can happen. But it has a connection to the exhibition Rolf was meant to be having here in Fjällbacka. He took a series of photographs of trans women in Stockholm in the eighties. One of them became one of his closest friends – Lola.'

'Lola?' Louise said, looking at Erica.

Lussan snorted loudly.

'Deary me, I don't think we need to give their kind too much attention – say no more.'

She got up and made for the kitchen. Pierre followed her and Erica could hear them muttering to each other irritably. She guessed he was lecturing his wife on how to behave. She hadn't thought this kind of narrow-mindedness existed in the present day. Even if Lussan voted for Friends of Sweden.

'But I want to hear more,' said Louise, leaning in towards Erica. 'Tell me about Lola.'

So Erica told her what she knew about the fire, about P'tite, and about her meetings in Stockholm with people who had known Lola.

'And Rolf's exhibition was going to be about Lola?'

'Lola and her friends in the trans community. But Lola also had other friends – you know them. Through Rolf, she got to know Henning, Elisabeth, Susanne and Ole. And Ester, Rolf's first wife. I think their club is probably a play on the title of Christer Strömholm's photobook *Friends of Place Blanche*, which was about transgender people in the Pigalle district of Paris. It's not too much of a stretch to suggest that the name is probably a tribute to Lola. From what I understand, they were very close.'

'They've never said anything about it,' Louise said in a low voice.

She turned to her parents, who were still muttering in the kitchen.

'Hey, pull yourselves together. You're embarrassing yourself in front of Erica. We're well into the twenty-first century now.'

She turned back to Erica again.

'I think it sounds like a great idea, and I'd love to read more about Lola. Based on what you say, she sounds like someone the world deserves to get to know.'

Warmth had come back into Louise's voice, and Erica smiled at her.

'Yes, that's the way I feel too.'

Erica had come to admire and like Lola based on what she had heard, and that feeling only intensified the more research she did.

She glanced at the time. 'You'll have to excuse me – I have an appointment in Tanumshede. But I can pop back later if you like.'

She reached across the table and took Louise's hand.

'No need – it was nice of you to come by for a bit. But I was going to ask you a favour . . .'

'Anything,' said Erica. She meant it.

Louise hesitated.

'I'm going to stay here for a few more days but then I'll head out to the island, as I said. But . . . could you give me a lift? You have a boat, right?'

'Of course,' Erica said in surprise.

Louise had never asked for a lift before.

'I'd appreciate the company. It will be . . . hard to see it all again. You won't have to stay on the island long, but it would feel easier if you were there.'

Erica patted Louise's hand.

'Of course I will. Just give me a shout and I'll take you out there whenever you like. Weather permitting. I'm not a good enough captain to pilot my boat through a storm. So calm conditions, please, if I'm taking you out.'

'I promise I'll arrange that.'

Louise smiled and stood up at the same time as Erica. She escorted her to the door and leaned against the doorway. Her face was pale and drained.

'I'd love to hear some more about Lola some time. And I'd like to see the photos from the exhibition. I could do with something else to think about.'

'Talk to Vivian – I'm sure she can make the arrangements. And if there's anything, call me. I'll be straight round.'

'I promise.'

Louise blew her a kiss and closed the door.

'I don't understand why Louise doesn't just come here. In a week or so, she says . . .'

Henning snorted and furrowed his brow as he bit into a warm scone from the plate Nancy had set down on the table.

It was almost two o'clock, but his body still felt drained. He and Elisabeth had each taken a sleeping pill the night before and he could still feel it.

'We have to give her the time she needs,' Elisabeth said in a low voice.

Henning looked at her with concern. She was getting leaner by the day. She barely ate, and now she was merely nudging her food around the plate.

'Of course, but she's also got a job to do. She made a commitment. And we need help with the burial. What's more, we need to plan for the first onslaught from the press when the Nobel Prize is announced, and then for the award ceremony itself.'

Elisabeth didn't answer. She spread more jam onto her scones without making any attempt to eat them.

'Why don't we go to the mainland and try to see Rickard?' she said at last.

Henning finished chewing before he answered.

'I've spoken to the lawyer. Jakobsson advises that we should keep our distance – given that the media circus has finally begun to die down, it wouldn't be the best idea to give them anything new to write about. Visiting Rickard would almost certainly be turned into a negative.'

'He's our son.'

'He's in safe hands. Jakobsson is handling the situation.'

Elisabeth didn't answer. Nancy came in with a pot of fresh coffee and put it on the table.

'Can I get you anything else?'

'No thank you, Nancy,' said Elisabeth.

Nancy gave her a concerned look. She'd made all her favourites, but nothing seemed to be whetting Elisabeth's appetite.

'I need to order some tails,' Henning said, reaching for another scone.

He spread it thickly with butter and enjoyed the sensation of his teeth sinking into the melting butter and then the freshly baked dough.

'How can you think about that now?'

Elisabeth stared at him. He wondered what had got into her. She'd always been his champion. Every success with his books, every literary prize, every positive review from *Dagens Nyheter* to the *New York Times* . . . Elisabeth had always been right behind him, applauding. He shared her grief over Peter and the boys. And Rolf too, for that matter. But surely it was possible to hold two thoughts in your head at once? Wasn't that the mark of a civilized human being?

'I think Peter would have been the first to say that we shouldn't let a crazed madman deprive us of the joy at what I – we – have achieved over a long career. The Nobel

350

Prize in Literature is the crowning glory on the work of decades. Thousands of hours of blood, sweat and tears. Peter would never have wanted to deny me that. Nor would Rolf . . .'

Henning pointedly got out his iPad. He had no desire to carry on talking to Elisabeth if this was the mood she was going to be in. He pulled up the *Expressen* website. It had been a tremendous relief to see the headlines about Blanche falling further and further down the page as the days went by. People's memories were short. The scandal would soon be forgotten.

When the home page loaded on his screen, he stared at it in horror, unable to process what he was seeing.

'What now?' said Elisabeth.

Henning turned the screen towards her. It was the lead story. *Reliable sources say Henning Bauer will be announced as the winner of the Nobel Prize in Literature tomorrow. Is he a worthy recipient?*

He swallowed.

'Someone's leaked to the media.'

'This isn't good,' Elisabeth said in a low voice.

Henning grimaced.

'No, it's not.'

28

WEDNESDAY, A WEEK LATER

Erica and Patrik were sitting at the kitchen table, staring at the computer. There was an unread email.

The blood test results had come back more quickly than they had expected, so now they were sitting here a week after Erica's visit to the maternity clinic in Tanumshede.

The email was right there in their inbox.

'I don't want to open it yet – let's eat first,' said Erica.

'Okay, you're the boss.'

Patrik pushed the laptop aside and Erica opened the oven.

'The potato gratin's ready. You lay the table and I'll plate up.'

'You just want to take the credit for cooking it. Typical. I've been slaving away over a hot stove, putting my soul into it, only for you to steal the glory at the last minute.'

'I thought we were both acutely aware that I'm incapable of making a dish like this.'

Erica smiled as she gestured to the tenderloin stew with its honey and balsamic sauce simmering away on the hob and the potato gratin she had taken out of the oven.

'True. Are the kids settled?'

Erica glanced towards the living room. The twins were

indeed sitting slightly too close to the TV watching a programme, while Maja was on the sofa with her iPad bingeing YouTube videos. She was currently obsessed with The Swedish Family, which followed family life with the kids Alma, Harry and Laura. Right now, that meant Erica and Patrik were hearing so much about that family that it was like living under the same roof.

'So when are we going to get started on the kitchen renovation?'

Patrik pointed to the arch as he put out plates and cutlery for himself and Erica. The children had already eaten; Erica and Patrik had been craving a grown-up dinner in peace and quiet for a change.

'I've almost got used to it.' Erica laughed and turned off the hob. 'But joking aside, this spring? I can check with Dan and Anna.'

Patrik gave a thumbs up and held out his plate. At first, they ate in silence – this was a favourite meal. Herb garden beef tenderloin was the name of the recipe, and it had become a classic in their household.

'How's the investigation going?' Erica said between bites.

Patrik shrugged despondently.

'We're plodding along. But the prosecutor believes Rickard is the killer, so we're pushing towards charges. Everyone is satisfied that we have an answer.'

'Except you.'

Erica reached for the salad bowl and added some to her plate.

'Yes, except me. And I don't have anything concrete to go on, except that we didn't find anything to tie Rickard to Rolf's murder. He hasn't managed to give us an alibi for the murder, and he certainly may have had a motive. But I must emphasize it's only *may have*. He also denies that Rolf knew about the blackmail.'

'You haven't got anything else due in from forensics that you're pinning your hopes on?'

'Yes and no. The bullets haven't yet been matched to anything in the database, but it can take ages to get an update from NFC. And the fibres on the nail gun didn't match Rickard's jacket, and we can't round up all the guests' jackets like this after the fact.'

'Why only jackets?' Erica said, serving herself more potato gratin.

She was constantly hungry now – there was no stopping once she had started eating.

'What do you mean?' Patrik said, putting down his cutlery.

'Well, you've found black fibres. High-quality silk. Why does it have to be a jacket? Not many jackets are made of silk, are they? Isn't it likelier the silk came from a dress? Which guests were wearing black dresses?'

'You're right about that,' said Patrik. 'Bloody hell. I'm drawing a blank on what people were wearing. I would have remembered if they were naked, but their clothes . . . nope. Nothing.'

'You've already collected pictures from the party – you checked them to confirm alibis – so you could take a look to see which women were wearing black dresses. I remember a few dresses that weren't black. Louise was wearing blue, Susanne's was green, and Elisabeth's was red. So you can start by ruling them out. Then all you have to do is peruse the photos . . .'

Patrik cleared his throat, picked up the ladle and added more sauce to his plate. He loved drowning his food in sauce, while Erica was much more sparing.

'Have you heard any more from Vivian? About the missing photograph?'

'No, it almost feels as if she's avoiding my calls. I'm not quite sure what's going on with her. What about you? How's work on the book going?'

'I'm going up to Stockholm in two weeks' time to see the publisher. They like what I've sent so far. Of course, they're pretty keen for the book to end with the killer finally being caught.'

'Isn't that almost impossible after this much time? The case is colder than a freezer.'

'I've got an idea. It's pretty far-fetched and crazy, but I don't think it's completely impossible. But it's the same as it is for you. I'm waiting. Everything always takes way too long. Now I'm hoping Frank will get in touch with some exciting news.'

'By the way, did you see the actual news? The Swedish Academy issued a strong denial that Henning Bauer is in the running for the Nobel Prize?'

'Yes, I saw. You have to feel sorry for Henning. I know it's only a prize and he's lost so much more. But it must still smart. To have been so close. To effectively have something taken away from him before he'd even got it. And from what I understood of Henning, the Nobel Prize would have been of infinite significance to him – for many reasons. Vanity for one thing.'

'I can understand the Academy's position,' Patrik said, taking even more sauce despite Erica raising her eyebrows in amusement. 'After the debate that's been raging, it would have been impossible. People see the literature prize as theirs – as Sweden's prize. They want the recipient to be worthy.'

'Well, I think it was pretty dubious from the start – it stank of nepotism. They're so entangled with each other. Susanne has a clear conflict of interest. It wouldn't have gone down well. But the books are supposed to be great.'

'You haven't read them?'

'No, they've been on my list of books I ought to have read for ages. But I always plump for a good thriller or a feelgood novel instead.'

'What are they about?'

'They're a tribute to womankind. Nine parts. The series is considered to be the biggest and most beautiful tribute to woman in the modern age. There's a rumour that there's going to be a tenth, but I don't know. It's been seven years since the last one, and Henning has always been reticent about whether there will be a tenth or not.'

Erica's phone buzzed and she picked it up to read the message.

'Louise just asked if I'd take her out to the island first thing in the morning. We discussed it earlier.'

'Why you?' Patrik said in surprise.

'I was wondering the same thing. But I think she wants the company of someone she feels safe with. It's the first time she'll have been back to the island since . . . after what happened.'

'Well, I guess that's reasonable. Why don't we pull the plaster off now?'

Patrik took Erica's hand and stroked it with his thumb. She hesitated at first, then she said:

'Okay. Let's look.'

Patrik reached for his computer and opened it.

The sunset over the inlet to Fjällbacka was incredibly beautiful. Dashes of orange, pink, red and purple blended into broad brushstrokes across the sky as the sun slowly descended behind the bare archipelago islands. In spite of that, the sunset wasn't as beautiful as it was when witnessed from Skjälerö – nothing beat that.

It was almost time to return there. Louise was almost done with what she needed to do. It was a process – it always had been. So many people couldn't see the big picture – they lived their lives with their sights set solely on individual pieces of the jigsaw. She had always been good at doing whole jigsaws.

Patience. It had been a watchword throughout her life. She had never taken hasty decisions on impulse, weakness or what she wanted in the moment. Instead, she kept her eye on the prize and approached it step by step.

She thought back to her childhood. She had often felt like a prisoner with Lussan and Pierre. All the rules, all the requirements, all the expectations she had to live up to. Yet she had given them what they had wanted. She had been the daughter they wanted even though they had so little in common. Well, that was over now.

A flock of seagulls passed by outside the window. Noisy, loud and constantly hungry. William had loved the gulls on Skjälerö and to Henning's chagrin he had fed them the moment he got the chance. He'd even named them. Quite how he could know which was which no one had ever managed to determine. But William had merely shrugged and said: 'They look different.'

Louise thought the gulls looked identical. Sometimes, she felt the same way about people. There was so little that separated them. Their pettiness. Their selfishness. Their greed. Their pursuit of whatever it was that formed their currency. Money. Honour. Power. Sex. People were small. Narrow-minded. With a few exceptions.

She felt no compassion for people. Everyone chose their path – even if they didn't realize it – and every decision had consequences. Even hers. But she was strong. She had been forced to be. Nothing worth having was easy to get. That was what the people around her had so much trouble understanding.

The flock of seagulls swept past again. It sounded as if the birds were laughing at her. Maybe they were right to. Perhaps she was someone who ought to be laughed at. Lussan always had done. In her eyes, Louise had never been good enough, no matter how much she had followed the rules.

Louise smiled wryly as the gulls sailed on towards the harbour. No matter what happened, she was still the one who'd had the last laugh.

29

STOCKHOLM 1980

'Wow! A Freestyle! Thanks!'

P'tite flung her arms around the neck of first Henning and then Elisabeth. After bouncing up and down with joy, she sat down on the floor to open the packaging containing a yellow Walkman and headphones.

'It's too much,' Lola said, but she couldn't help smiling when she saw her daughter's happiness.

Henning winked and ruffled P'tite's hair.

'We're rich. Well, my wife is. I'm just a struggling author.'

He nudged Elisabeth in the side and she snorted. P'tite threw herself onto the next present from Ole and Susanne and hooted with joy at that too.

'A Rubik's Cube! They're soooo cool! Sigge, look!'

P'tite held up the multicoloured cube to show Sigge, who was sitting shyly at the kitchen table.

'I'm going to learn how to do it in record time,' said P'tite, reaching for the final present on the table – the one from Rolf and Ester.

It was more of a card than a wrapped-up parcel. P'tite held it up to her eyes and slowly tried to read it. It took her a while to get through the letters.

'Daddy, daddy, daddy, I'm getting riding lessons!'

She stood up and hugged Ester and Rolf ferociously.

Lola sighed.

'How am I supposed to find the time to take her there?'

'That's the beauty of it,' Ester said with a tired smile. She'd seemed run down lately. 'Rolf and I will sort it all out. We'll pick her up here, take her to the stables, which are near us in Enskede, then we can eat at ours and give her a lift home.'

'It's all part of our cunning plan to snaffle more time with P'tite,' Rolf said.

'Transparent. But nicely done.'

Rolf pulled out the camera and took a couple of photos of P'tite, who was now sitting on the floor, turning her Rubik's Cube in intense concentration. Then he turned the camera towards Lola, who immediately straightened up.

'You have to warn me before you take a photo. A girl's gotta have her posture and pout just right.'

'The best photos are always when the subject doesn't know they're being photographed.'

'Maybe. You've actually taken a couple of great pictures of me and the girls,' Lola said, blowing a kiss to Rolf.

She clapped her hands together.

'Right, cake! P'tite asked for Princess Cake and that's what we're having. Sigge, could you fetch spoons? Henning, would you mind getting the plates off the top shelf?'

Soon everyone was gathered and P'tite blushed when Ole gave her a piece that wasn't on its side and told her it meant she was going to marry.

She immediately toppled the slice over.

'Sigge and I are never going to get married. But we'll still live together and have children.'

Sigge's face went bright red.

'That's the right attitude, P'tite,' said Ole, high-fiving the birthday girl.

'What are you doing that for? You're married too,' Elisabeth said, helping herself to a slice of cake.

'I mostly thought how great it was to see the new generation being so much wiser.'

Susanne slapped his arm.

'Budge up so that I can get you all in shot!'

Rolf held up the camera and directed the others to move in closer and closer.

'Say cheese!'

'CHEESE!'

P'tite laughed and even Sigge smiled. Lola swallowed a lump that was forming in her throat. She'd lost a family but gained a new one.

She'd finally come home.

30

THURSDAY

Erica hadn't slept all night, and she didn't think Patrik
had either. They'd been up until two o'clock talking it
over from every angle without reaching any conclusion.
In the end, they'd gone to bed and lain back to back,
each staring at a wall.

*Increased likelihood of defects. We recommend you contact a
doctor for further examination.*

The mere thought of that email gave Erica the chills.
She was so tired she barely knew her own name, and
she and Patrik had embraced almost in desperation before
he had gone to work. His face had been completely ashen.

The boat, an old wooden jig that had been Erica's father's
most prized possession, was moored in the harbour by
Badholmen. Most people had already taken their boats out
for the winter, but Erica and Patrik always managed to
leave it until the last second. Louise was already waiting
for her when she arrived. She looked freshly showered, her
damp hair in a ponytail at the back of her neck, her face
bare with no make-up. There was a small bag next to her.

'You're travelling light,' Erica said, hugging her friend.

Even through the autumn coat, she could feel how
thin Louise had got.

362

'I don't need much.'

She held onto the mooring rope as Erica climbed aboard.

'Thanks for taking me,' Louise said, throwing her bag into the bottom of the boat before smoothly jumping in.

She held onto the rope until Erica had got the motor going and then pushed gently against the quayside so that Erica could reverse out of the mooring.

'No wind,' Louise said, pointing towards the horizon as they left the harbour with Fjällbacka at their backs.

'As per your request.' Erica managed a laugh in her spot at the stern of the boat with the tiller in her right hand. 'I'm not a bad captain, but I still don't like high seas.'

'They're not nice,' Louise said, closing her eyes as she looked up into the sky.

There were small drops of seawater spattering her face.

'How do your mum and dad feel about you going back to the island?'

'They weren't happy,' Louise said, without looking at Erica. 'Especially not now after the latest stories. They wanted me to go home with them to Skåne.'

'But you didn't want to?'

'You know what they're like.'

Louise smiled wryly and Erica didn't reply. She undeniably had a point – Erica would have gone mad after spending a day in the same house as Lussan.

'How's Henning?'

Erica had to shout to be heard over the sound of the water.

'Shit, or that's my impression. There's nothing he's wanted more than to win the Nobel Prize.'

'It must be awful to come so close and have it wrenched away when it's within reach.'

'Yes. Terrible.'

Louise still had her eyes closed.

'And Elisabeth?'

'I don't think Elisabeth gives a fuck about the prize. The boys were her world. With them gone . . .'

Louise's voice changed and became muffled. She shuddered and crossed her arms.

'Elisabeth has always supported Henning – in everything. Why, I've never understood. He hasn't been anything like as loyal in return. And he was a nobody when he met Elisabeth. A poor, unknown author of pretty mediocre short stories, while she was the daughter and heir to one of Sweden's most important and richest publishing families. I can see what he saw in her, but I can't understand why she fell for him – except that I've seen a couple of old photos so I know he was very handsome. I'm . . . I'm glad that she at least found some love elsewhere.'

'You mean Rolf?' Erica couldn't conceal her curiosity.

'Yes, Rolf. I've read her love letters to him. Vivian found them this week. Along with a whole bunch of Rolf's photos from back in Lola's day. She called me and asked what I thought she should do with them. She didn't want to contact Elisabeth – she thought it was too sensitive. I was so intrigued that she photographed some of them on her phone and sent them to me.'

'Did she find the missing photograph too?' Erica said excitedly. 'Why didn't you say anything?'

'It's none of my business. I told Vivian she should contact the police. I don't know what happened after that.'

'She hasn't been in touch. Do you mind if I tell Patrik? And do you have the photos and letters? Could I see them?'

'Sure,' Louise said. 'Tell Patrik that Vivian has what he's looking for. She also found some anonymous letters sent to Rolf airing Blanche's dirty laundry.'

'Wait! I'll call him.'

Her call didn't connect. The reception was terrible. Erica swore and quickly sent him a text instead. She crossed her fingers that it would be able to send. It did, and she stuffed her phone back into her pocket.

'So what did Vivian say? Did she work out who sent them? And what was the photograph of?'

'We'll get onto that in due course,' Louise said, pointing to Skjälerö, which was rapidly approaching. 'We're here.'

Erica was almost gnashing her teeth. She wanted to know now. But she knew from experience that it rarely paid to push people who weren't ready. And she guessed that Louise was occupied processing her emotions ahead of her return to the island.

'Shit! Stop!' Louise said, standing up. She pointed. 'That's William's lobster pot. I don't want it to be left out here. He was so proud of it. It might go missing.'

Erica steered back towards the lobster pot. Once she was close enough, Louise hauled it in and tipped it into the boat.

'Any takers?' Erica asked.

Louise shook her head.

'Nope, it's empty.'

She pushed it underneath the seat and sat down again, gazing towards the island.

Erica glanced at her friend. She couldn't imagine what it felt like for Louise to return. But there was no going back now.

'Sleep badly?'

Paula looked at Patrik with concern as she sat down in the chair in front of his desk.

'Yeah, rough night.' He rubbed his eyes.

'Everything okay?'

Paula continued to look at him, but Patrik waved her question away. He didn't want to think about the results, about Erica's tears, about their worries.

'Oh, just one of those nights. It's probably a full moon. Right, what do we have here?'

'Gösta and Martin have gone to a house where there's a cleaner complaining about a bad smell. One of those ones by Badis. She says it smells as if something died in there. It's probably some rat in a corner, festering away. But best they go and check it out. And Pedersen and Farideh have both been trying to get hold of you. They couldn't get you on your mobile.'

'One of my little bandits pulled the charger out last night and used it for her iPad instead.'

Patrik pulled his phone from his pocket and plugged it into the charger by his door.

'Can I borrow your phone for the time being?'

Paula handed over her mobile.

'Do you want to be alone?'

Patrik shook his head as he pulled up Farideh in the contacts list.

'Nope. Stay where you are.'

Paula directed her gaze out of the window to try and give him a little space. Patrik smiled and tapped on the display.

'All right? It's Patrik. You wanted to talk to me?'

'Yes. I've got an interesting development in the case. You know the bullets I sent off for analysis?'

'Yes – from the murder of Peter and the boys?'

'Exactly. From a Walther PPK. We've got a match.'

'You're kidding!'

Patrik sat up straight so quickly that his chair scraped against the floor and made Paula jump. He tapped on the speakerphone button.

'My colleague Paula is here. She's listening in. You said you had a match for our bullets. From another murder?'

'Yes. The rifling is identical to two bullets from a murder in 1980. Victim was one Lars Berggren. A trans woman found in her burnt-out flat together with—'

'Her daughter,' Patrik said, staring at Paula who frowned at him uncomprehendingly.

'Yes. How do you know that?' Farideh said in confusion.

'She was called Lola and the daughter was called P'tite. There are . . . there are connections between Lola and the people involved in my investigation.'

'The odds of that being a coincidence are incredibly long,' Farideh said.

Patrik bit his lip.

'You haven't found anything else out about the gun?'

'No, there aren't any other hits – only the murder of Lars Berggren. But I hope that's of use?'

'Probably. I don't know how right now, but it will be. Pedersen has been trying to reach me too – seems I'm Mr Popular today. I'll call him right away and see what he wants. The ketchup effect . . .'

'Yes, that's often what happens. Call Pedersen and I'll keep you posted if anything else turns up. I'm still working on getting a better identification of the fibres we found, but the material isn't sufficiently unique. It wasn't a match to Rickard's jacket.'

'My sensible wife pointed out that since they were silk fibres, it was more probable they came from a dress. I think it was probably me who got waylaid by the idea that they came from a jacket.'

'Of course. Your sensible wife is obviously right. And that gives me an idea. Let me check and get back to you.'

'Do that. Be in touch. And thanks.'

Patrik ended the call and stroked his chin thoughtfully. Thoughts were bouncing around his head, but ever so slowly he was beginning to see the contours of something in his consciousness. He couldn't really put his finger on it yet, but he knew that this piece of the puzzle was of crucial significance.

Rickard had been a small child when Lola had been killed, and couldn't have shot her. Admittedly, he could have found the gun used then and used it now, but that seemed far-fetched. And there were other, more likely possibilities.

'Call Pedersen before you get too wrapped up in your thoughts,' said Paula.

Patrik shook his head to collect his thoughts and then looked up Pedersen's number. Pedersen picked up on the first ring. He got straight to the point.

'Good thing you called. I've been taking a look at the autopsy reports you sent over on behalf of Erica, and I think something must have gone wrong.'

'Wrong?' said Patrik.

He was on speakerphone again, and the phone was between him and Paula.

'Yes. You said it was a trans woman – who would be shown in the report as a man – and her daughter that died.'

'Yes?' said Patrik, feeling impatience beginning to creep in. If only Pedersen would hurry up . . .

'You must have got the wrong end of the stick. The bodies belonged to a man and a boy.'

Patrik's jaw dropped in surprise and he stared at the mobile where it lay. Something was wrong. Something was very, very wrong.

'Be careful – it can be slippery,' Louise said as she got out of the boat. She pointed to the rocks where the jetty ended.

'Hey, this ain't no Stockholm-dwelling city girl you're talking to,' Erica said, snorting as she moored the boat with a bowline.

Louise clutched her bag in one hand and the lobster pot in the other and waited for Erica.

'Are you okay?' Erica said gently once she had caught up.

'I'll survive,' Louise said, but Erica could see that she was gritting her teeth.

They made for the main house. Louise walked around the end of the building, put down the lobster pot and then seemed to hesitate with her hand on the door handle. After taking a deep breath, she entered with Erica on her heels.

Henning came towards them in the hallway. His usually well-kempt hair was standing on end and his knitted waistcoat was buttoned up unevenly. Erica realized that he was hammered even though it was still early in the morning.

'Louise! Louise!'

Henning flung himself around her neck and she stood there stiffly, her arms by her body, before she responded to his embrace.

'Where's Elisabeth?' she said gently, looking around.

'She's resting. She's always resting these days,' Henning complained.

He went back to the living room and straight to the bar.

'Whisky?'

He proffered a bottle, but both Louise and Erica shook their heads.

'Well, I'll have a snifter,' he said, filling his glass to the brim with whisky.

The liquid was only contained by surface tension.

'Nancy, Louise is back!'

Nancy was standing in the doorway wringing her hands. She looked at Louise with pleading eyes, and Erica saw Louise deliberately turn away.

Henning pointed to Louise and Erica.

'Didn't I say we'd eat lunch early once they arrived? Is it ready?'

He turned to face them again.

'I've asked Nancy to make grilled mackerel with boiled potatoes and spinach sauce. You love that, don't you Louise?'

He swayed slightly on the spot.

'It was Peter who loved it,' said Louise.

'Well then, we'll have mackerel with spinach sauce because Peter loved it,' Henning said, waving his arms about so that some of the whisky splashed over the rim of the glass.

'Sit down, everyone – I'll fetch Elisabeth. We're going to eat together. All of us. I can't get my head around that modern nonsense of sitting in front of the television to eat, or eating in shifts. Families should sit down to eat together. Families and guests. And today we have a distinguished visitor. A visiting author. Who knows . . . maybe one day you'll win the Nobel Prize . . .'

He almost lost his balance as he bowed to Erica and even more whisky splashed onto the floor.

Erica writhed with discomfort, wishing she was far away.

'Hmm, well hardly.'

'Never say never. If anyone had told me as a young writer when I managed to get my first work published that one day I would have been in the running for the Nobel Prize in Literature, I would have said it was impossible.' He took a few unsteady steps. 'Why, there you are, my dove.'

Henning pointed to Elisabeth, who had entered the living room without them hearing her.

'It was thanks to her that I won . . . well, I mean, *almost* won the prize. They ended up giving it to that Asian no one's ever fucking heard of, but still. I was close! It was when I met my dove that I got my inspiration. My muse . . .'

'How much have you had to drink, Henning?' Elisabeth grimaced.

'I've drunk as much as I want. Just as much as I want. For the first time, I'm doing exactly as I please. Not what you want, or what your family wanted.'

370

He wagged a finger at Elisabeth. Her reaction was immediate.

'What *I* want? What my family wanted? Have we been living on the same planet? Throughout our marriage, we've only done as *you* wanted. Both I and the children have adapted to you. In everything! The great writer. The grand man of letters – above all the trivial concerns of daily life that the rest of us have faced. You couldn't be troubled with such things . . . You needed to write. You shut yourself away, hour after hour, day after day, week after week, year after year. You sat in your study while the boys and I sat outside longing for your time, for your love . . .'

Henning took a few gulps of whisky.

'The boys were fine,' he said, waving the glass about. 'And you had exactly what you wanted. You could show me off at your salons without being ashamed. On the contrary, I elevated your status even more in literary circles. The star publisher and her star author of a husband. The power couple.'

'Let's eat. Maybe you'll sober up.'

Erica glanced at Louise. It was a little too early for lunch, she thought, but nothing seemed as it should be in this house any longer. It felt as if she'd stepped straight into a war zone.

They sat down at the large dining table. Henning put down his whisky glass with a clatter by his place at the end of the table. Elisabeth had taken her seat at the other end and Louise and Erica sat opposite each other on the long sides. Erica felt as if she were at a dinner with her dysfunctional parents who were on the brink of divorce.

'How's Rickard?' she asked Elisabeth in order to break the uncomfortable silence.

'He's really not doing well, if I'm honest,' Elisabeth said, her face softening. 'He's innocent. You know that too, don't you, Louise? That he's innocent . . .'

Elisabeth's voice was pleading. Louise sat in silence before turning to Henning.

'Do you know that he's not yours?'

Erica started. What was Louise up to? Not even Patrik had wanted to bring this up with Henning – certainly not until they knew whether it was relevant to the murder inquiry.

Henning would probably have found out sooner or later, but here and now? Erica looked at Louise in confusion but she didn't meet her gaze, staring fixedly at Henning instead.

'Of course I know he's not my biological son,' said Henning, looking down into his whisky glass. 'I've always known that. I'm not as stupid as they think. I saw the looks. It was actually quite touching – Elisabeth probably thought it was love.'

He laughed and Elisabeth gasped. Her eyes filled with tears.

'You knew? But why . . . ?'

'Why didn't I say anything? Do you want to know? It was rather amusing, if I'm honest. Your game. Your little lies. Your little subterfuges. Like little children. And Rickard. Well, it fitted nicely with the picture – the picture we wanted to project to the outside world. Elisabeth and I and our two boys. Raising someone else's bastard was a small price to pay. But it was very obvious that he wasn't mine. He was weak.'

'Your . . .'

Elisabeth's words failed her. Her hands were gripping the table tightly.

'After everything I've done for you,' she gritted out.

'You've been holding that over me for all these years,' Henning said, raising his voice. 'You've had my balls in a vice. And yet you have the gumption to claim that *I* was in charge.'

Erica shifted her gaze between Henning and Elisabeth. She understood nothing of what they were saying but Louise was completely calm sitting opposite her. She was even smiling slightly.

Erica didn't know how to compose herself. She picked up her phone to see whether Patrik had replied to her text message and to distance herself from the hellish lunch she'd been forced into. Reception was temperamental in the islands to say the least. She mostly had zero bars – occasionally two. No reply from Patrik. On the other hand, she had received a text from Frank.

Don't know if this is what you asked for, but have managed to pull up three hits from the period you specified. Photos in your inbox.

Erica felt her heart beat a little faster. She pushed her chair back, mobile in hand, and excused herself.

'Sorry, I have to check an important email. I'll be right back.'

No one seemed to take any notice of her. She headed for a room that looked like a study so that she could check her emails in peace and quiet. The reception was lousy here too, and she realized she ought to have requested the Wi-Fi password. Yet slowly but surely, the email with its attachments began to load. Three images. Just as Frank had said. The first two were completely unfamiliar. But the third face made her gasp. Time slowed down. Everything came to a standstill. Everything she had known, everything she had believed, was turned on its head. She tried to call Patrik but it wouldn't connect. Frustrated, she sent him a brief text message and forwarded the email she had been sent. Then she put her phone back in her pocket and tried to compose her features before reluctantly returning to the dining table.

* * *

'Patrik!' Paula came running into his office. 'You know the call-out Martin and Gösta responded to? We have to go there!'

'The bad smell in the house by Badis?'

'I'll explain in the car. Come on!'

Patrik grabbed his coat and ran after her. When they had almost reached the car, he ran back inside, pulled out the charger and picked up his phone before hurrying to the car park. Paula explained briefly what she knew, and Patrik's face was grim as he pulled onto the driveway of the familiar house by Badis.

'Shit,' he said as he turned off the engine.

'We didn't make the connection to this address. It was you two who came here to talk to them,' Martin said apologetically when he came to meet them by the car.

'How bad is it?'

Patrik got out of the car and looked up towards the white house.

'As bad as you can imagine and then some.'

Patrik swore again and followed Martin towards the door. He stopped there without entering.

'Farideh?'

'They're five minutes away. We've secured the crime scene – only Gösta and I have been inside. The cleaner called us in the second she smelled it. She didn't dare go in any further.'

'Good. Let's wait for the team,' Patrik said, trying to maintain his composure.

Part of him wanted to see what they were dealing with right away, but his rational side knew how important it was for their work to keep the crime scene as pristine as possible.

While they waited, Patrik pulled out his phone and entered his PIN – at least it was now charged to half full. The messages began to roll in. Two were from Erica. He read them quickly and felt panic rising. He followed the instructions in the second text and checked his emails. When he saw the photo she had sent, his pulse quickened.

At that moment, Farideh and her forensics team arrived and he ran over to her.

'Can I come in with you?'

She hesitated before agreeing.

'Put on an overall and use your common sense.'

She pointed towards the car containing the equipment. He quickly donned the same protective gear as the forensics team and followed them into the house. The stench hit him in the hall.

'The bedroom!' Martin shouted from outside, pointing to the left.

They came to a halt in the doorway to the bedroom. Then Farideh began to issue orders in a low voice. Patrik was paralysed.

'If you're going to get in the way then you'll have to go,' Farideh said, shoving him gently to one side.

He took a few steps back until his back was against a wall. He stood there, his brain trying to process what he was looking at. It was a bloodbath. Lussan and Pierre were in their bed. Both appeared to have had their throats cut, and someone had also stabbed them countless times in the chest and head. The rest of their bodies weren't visible as they were under the covers.

The blood had gone everywhere. On the bed, the walls, the ceiling. The violence was so excessive that only someone with tremendous, vengeful fury towards the couple could have done it.

Patrik's mouth went completely dry as he forced away the nausea that was threatening to take over. He tried to gather his thoughts and get his facts in order, but the blood kept blanking everything else out. It looked like a Jackson Pollock – one of the few artists he was familiar with.

And the stench. Good God.

Lussan and Pierre seemed to have been in the bed for a good while, perhaps as long as a week judging by the putrefaction. The nausea welled up again – not only because of what he was seeing and because of the smell . . . No, it was because of the theories that were running amok in his head, leading him to one single conclusion: Erica was in danger.

Unable to stop himself, Patrik rushed away. Outside the house, he tore off his overall and ran towards the car, shouting to his officers on the scene.

'We have to go! Now!'

Martin and Gösta exchanged a glance but immediately obeyed. They ran towards the police car they had arrived in, and Paula was already behind the wheel of hers and Patrik's.

'I want to drive,' Patrik said, sweat pouring down his brow.

Paula shook her head, shifted into reverse and floored it down the drive.

'Not on my life – you're way too agitated. I'll drive. Where are we going?'

'Skjälerö,' said Patrik. 'We're going to Skjälerö.'

Erica couldn't tear her gaze away from Louise. She sensed the fury simmering under the surface.

'Tell me more about how you wrote the books, Henning,' Louise said, her voice louder. 'About all the hours you spent in your study, crafting them, laboriously assembling sentence after sentence. All while Elisabeth took care of the chores you didn't want to sully yourself with.'

She laughed in a way that Erica had never heard before.

'Where did the ideas come from? The inspiration? You always say that Elisabeth is your muse. Is that true? Then why no tenth book, Henning? You can't claim there wasn't meant to be one. After all, it's a decalogy. Right?'

'There are nine books,' Henning slurred. 'And there were always meant to be nine books.'

'So why have you been sitting at the computer staring at a flashing cursor for years? Can you explain that?'

Elisabeth looked at her in shock.

'Louise? I don't understand . . .'

'No, you don't, because you're naive. Henning is something far worse. Your sin is defending him all these years. Cleaning up after him. Lifting him up when he didn't deserve to be. He's a small, small man, Elisabeth. You of all people ought to know that – having lived with him all these years.'

'I don't understand where this is coming from.'

Elisabeth looked at Erica as if seeking an explanation but Erica could only shake her head slowly.

Louise reached for the bag at her feet. Without a flicker of expression, she pulled out a pistol and laid it on the table in front of her. Elisabeth gasped but Henning didn't seem to understand what was going on. He muttered and refilled his whisky glass before sitting down heavily on his chair again.

Erica looked at all three of them. Enough was enough.

'Cecily. That was you, right?' said Erica.

She met Louise's gaze without wavering.

'What are you talking about? What about Cecily?' Elisabeth looked from Louise to Erica. In the silence, all that could be heard was the wind against the window and Henning's muttering into his whisky glass.

Louise smiled as she fingered the gun.

'Yes, that was me.'

'You really must explain what you're talking about!' Elisabeth's voice rose to a falsetto. 'And why do you have a gun?'

'How did you know?' said Louise.

'My police contact in Stockholm just sent me a photo.

It took a week to dig it up. You were caught in a speed trap in your getaway.'

Louise nodded. 'I remember the flash. I thought that was curtains. But as luck would have it, the police exhibited not even the slightest investigative skill. They were more than willing to write it off as an accident.'

Erica stared at the woman before her – so unlike the smiling Louise who paced ahead of her on their power-walks. She'd never seen the real Louise – not until now.

'Why did you kill Cecily?'

Louise fingered the butt of the gun gently as she contemplated her answer. Finally, she looked at Erica.

'It was my way in. I'd been studying Peter for years before I managed to bag the job at Blanche. When I started there, I had the chance to get even closer to him. After a year, I knew everything. What he liked, what he didn't like, what he laughed at, his favourite foods, how he liked his martini, whether he was a cat or dog person, his TV preferences, his favourite Bond. I had everything I needed to be the perfect wife. There was only one small detail in the way.'

'Cecily.'

'Yes – he was already married. But that was relatively easy to overcome, and the grief made him extra vulnerable. When he needed someone, I was there.'

'What are you . . . What's she saying? Henning? Are you listening to this?'

Elisabeth was twisting and turning on her chair. Erica couldn't look at her – if she saw her grief and despair she wouldn't be able to continue her conversation with Louise.

But Louise continued without Erica having to say a word. It was as if she wanted to get it all out into the open – her burden of many years.

'She was so predictable. She went running on the same route every day she was in the country. All I had to do

378

was wait until she was alone with no witnesses nearby. I waited at the beach at Telegrafbacken three days straight. The first two, there were cars coming at the wrong time. But on the third, there wasn't a car. So I floored it and ran her down.'

Her voice was devoid of emotion. Louise might just as well have been talking about the price of a pint of milk.

'And when Peter began digging into it, you killed him?' Elisabeth gasped for breath.

'No, no, you don't understand,' said Louise. 'It had nothing to do with Peter's enquiries. My plan was always to kill Peter and the boys.'

Now Henning came to. He looked at her over the rim of his glass, struggling to focus.

'Elisabeth? Did she say she killed Peter? And Max and William?'

'Yes.'

Tears were pouring uncontrollably down Elisabeth's face. She made to get up, but Louise picked up the gun and waved it in her direction, ordering her to sit down.

Elisabeth slumped back onto her chair. Erica tried to surreptitiously check her phone.

Louise looked at her almost in amusement.

'It's okay, you can check your mobile.'

'Then I will,' Erica said, pulling it out.

She had several missed calls and messages from Patrik. Her pulse was pounding in her ears as she read what he'd said. How had she ended up in this nightmare? In her mind's eye, she saw Maja rolling her eyes as Noel and Anton were at their rowdiest, and Patrik's intense gaze as he leaned in to kiss her. She stifled a sob.

From the corner of her eye, Erica saw Louise watching her.

'They've found your parents,' she said. Her voice faltered slightly.

Louise nodded.

'Yes, I guessed they would. The cleaner was due. But I'll get to that. It has to be told in the right order.'

There was another flash on Erica's display. After glancing at Louise, who gave her permission, she tried to pull up the message. Her palms were so sweaty it took several attempts. Finally, she was able to read it.

She frowned. That couldn't be right.

'What?' said Louise.

Elisabeth made another attempt to stand up, but Louise merely waved the pistol at her without a word and Elisabeth sank down again.

'I asked Patrik to get an expert to review the autopsy report for Lola and P'tite.'

'And?' Louise cocked her head to one side.

'There seems to have been a big mistake. If indeed it was a mistake . . .'

'Yes? Why don't you tell your rapt audience?'

She pointed the gun at Elisabeth and Henning. Elisabeth was visibly trembling.

'P'tite's body wasn't a girl. It was a boy.'

The room fell silent. The truth was slowly beginning to dawn on Erica.

'Looks like we've got company,' Louise said languidly, pointing through the window. Erica stifled a sob as she spotted the lifeboat mooring and Patrik, Gösta, Martin and Paula coming ashore. Soon this would be over, one way or another.

'You know who killed Lola?' said Erica.

'Yes, and that's why you're here – so you can write your book with the whole truth about Lola. Henning? I think you should tell us who killed Lola.'

Henning looked tired and dejected. He looked at them with watery eyes.

'It was me,' he said. 'I'm the one who killed Lola.'

31

STOCKHOLM 1980

'It's not a party if you don't have a breakage,' Lola said cheerfully as she swept up the remains of the wine glass Ole had knocked off the kitchen table in his eagerness to assert that Stieg Larsson's *The Autists* was a new advance in literature. The debate had been so heated that the shards had lain there until everyone had calmed down.

'Thanks for a wonderful afternoon! I ought to stay and help clean up, but I was due back at the office ages ago,' Elisabeth said, moving a kitchen chair that had ended up in the doorway to the hall.

'And I need to drop in on my writing group,' said Henning. 'Who knows – maybe I'll turn out something big one of these days.'

'You will,' said Lola. 'I'm sure of it.'

'We'll join you,' said Ester, nudging Rolf. 'You've got a studio session in half an hour.'

'I'm selling my soul for money,' Rolf said dramatically, but he still stood up.

Before they left, they all hugged the happy birthday girl, who had left the grown-ups when they had started talking about books and authors. She had gone to play with Sigge in the living room. Then the flat became quiet and empty. Lola returned to the kitchen happy and satisfied. What a party!

The doorbell rang as she tipped the pieces of glass into the bin. She hurried to open it. Rolf smiled at her.

'Sorry, beautiful,' he said, proffering an envelope. 'Ester told me off for forgetting to give this to you and P'tite.'

Lola took the envelope. What could it be?

'Open it,' Rolf said, still smiling.

Lola couldn't hold back her tears when she saw what was inside.

'Rolf!'

There were a number of photographs of her and P'tite that Rolf had taken that day in the playground. P'tite swinging ever higher towards the sky. Lola's eyes closed, her face towards the sun. And Lola with P'tite in her arms. Photographs where they were smiling at the camera, photographs where they were smiling at each other and where Lola could see the love between a parent and her daughter. Between P'tite and Lola, her father.

'I don't know what to say.' Tears were flowing now. 'Rolf, what you capture with your camera, it's so . . . Thank you so much.'

She hugged him.

'It's nothing,' Rolf said offhandedly. 'Must rush or Ester will lose it.'

'Give her my thanks. And thank you again. For everything!'

Lola closed the door and wiped away the tears with the back of her hand.

'I'm such a drama queen,' she muttered. 'So maudlin.'

She'd barely made it back to the kitchen before the doorbell rang again.

'Did you forget something?' Lola said when she opened it.

And there he was. The man who was the light of her life. Her everything.

'Hello,' said Henning. 'I don't think anyone saw me.'

She didn't know why he was back – they hadn't agreed anything – but she was grateful for every moment in his presence.

Lola took his hand. Touching him was like grazing a force field – he made her thrill with joy.

'Now that you're here, you can help me tidy up the kitchen.'

Lola washed up the final bits and pieces, constantly aware of Henning's presence. After returning the last cup to the cupboard, he wiped his hands on a tea towel and hung it on the oven handle.

He went over to Lola.

'I've been longing to kiss you all day.'

His hands made their way under Lola's hair to her neck. He pulled her close and she felt as soft as putty in his arms.

'Can't we send the kids off somewhere?' he muttered, his lips against hers.

She shook her head while the tip of his tongue sought its way into her mouth.

'No, I can't. I've promised them popcorn and a story. We . . . another time . . .'

'I have such a hard time resisting you,' Henning said, caressing the outside of her panties.

Lola groaned.

'Soon . . . soon,' she said, tearing herself loose. 'I'm going to heat some oil on the stove for the popcorn. You have to help me keep an eye on it. It'd be a pity if the whole flat burned down.'

'Mmm, hot,' Henning said.

He stood behind her at the hob, put his arms around her and began to kiss her neck.

'Down, boy!' Lola said, laughing as she wriggled free from his grip again. 'Why don't you go to my wardrobe and fetch my present for P'tite. It's next to the grey army box. A purple parcel. I decided to give it to her after everyone had left.'

'Okay then,' Henning murmured, giving her a final kiss on the neck.

Lola stiffened.

'What was that? It sounded like something from the hall.'

'I didn't hear anything.'

'I thought that . . . I suppose it was just P'tite and Sigge.'

'Probably. I'll get that present.'

Henning wandered off and she heard him rummaging through the wardrobe. The oil in the pan was beginning to get hot.

'Did you find it?'

No response. She went after him.

'What are you doing? You have no right to look at that!'

Henning was sitting on the bed with the grey metal box in his lap, reading the first of her blue notebooks.

'This is incredible!' he said. 'Why haven't you shown us these?'

It was as if she were wading through a mire as she moved towards him.

'I haven't given you permission to read that!'

Lola tried to wrench the book from his hand, but he pressed it to his chest and laughed as he held her at arm's length.

'You're so touchy!' he said. 'And why do you have a gun?' Henning pointed to the pistol – a Walther PPK – which had been slipped in among the notebooks in the box.

'It was my father's. I took it when I left. He and the rest of the family taught me that there are people who hate people like me and I wanted to protect myself. Now put everything back in the box!'

Henning continued to laugh. He grabbed the whole bundle of blue notebooks teasingly, stood up and waved them around.

'These are the ones I'm not allowed to read?'

'I said give them to me!'

Suddenly the tears were flowing just as they had done when she'd seen Rolf's photographs. But now it was out of anger and sadness. Maybe even out of horror. The books were her life's work and she didn't want anyone to read them before she was finished. Not even the man she loved.

There was a hissing sound from the kitchen and Lola realized to her horror that she had forgotten the pan of oil on the hob. She catapulted herself towards the kitchen with Henning on her heels, making it to the hob just in time to prevent the oil from catching fire. She moved the pan off the ring but left the gas burning.

She turned to Henning, who was holding the notebooks over his head while smiling at her provocatively. She jumped and tried to take them from him, but he was a good bit taller than she was and she had no chance of reaching them.

'This isn't funny!' Lola said, stamping her foot.

She grabbed hold of him in order to reach higher but that didn't help. The blue notebooks were out of reach.

'Suck me off and then you can have them.'

'Don't be stupid! The kids are at home.'

'They're probably in P'tite's corner behind the drapes. They won't see. Come on, Lola.'

'Stop it! Henning! Stop it!'

Lola tried to reach the books again but he only held them higher. In her frustration, she began pummelling his shoulders and ribs with her fists.

'What the fuck are you doing?'

Henning's smile had died away and something dark had appeared in his eyes. He held the books in his left hand and pushed her with his right. Lola momentarily lost her balance but then righted herself and struck his stomach even harder. She landed her punch and Henning groaned.

Anger made her eyes flash. She hit him again, hard. Then he twisted his right hand and curled it up. The fist hit her jaw with full force and she fell backwards, her head bouncing off the hard metal edge of the hob. Everything went black.

32

'It was an accident,' Henning said, his voice trembling.

Erica could only stare at him. She had been thinking of nothing but Lola's fate for weeks and wondered what secrets she was hiding . . . Good God.

A stifled exclamation from the doorway made everyone turn that way. Nancy. The housekeeper was holding her hands up in an appeal to Louise, who brandished the gun indifferently as she said:

'This has nothing to do with you. You're free to go. But tell the cops that only Patrik is to come inside. The others have to stay outside or I'll shoot Erica.'

Erica's whole body stiffened. When she saw the darkness in Louise's eyes, she couldn't help thinking back to when she and Louise had first met – at the playground on the mainland. The sun had been shining, and Maja and William had laughed in the way that only kids could laugh as they competed to see who could go highest on the swings.

Nancy hesitated for a second. Then she did as Louise told her and headed for the front door.

'I didn't mean to hurt her,' said Henning. 'I was just fooling about, there was no malice intended. But she got so . . . bloody angry.'

'Those books were her everything,' said Louise. 'She wrote in every spare moment she had. And she was almost done. She only had to finish that last book and then the series would be complete. She didn't want to show it to anyone until she was done. Could you really not respect that?'

Louise's voice cracked and Erica was suddenly certain that her suspicion was true.

'You're Lola's daughter,' she said softly.

Henning and Elisabeth stared first at Erica, then at Louise. Louise's uncannily blank face contorted.

'Yes, I'm P'tite.'

'That . . . that can't be right!' Elisabeth gasped.

The front door slammed, there were footsteps and then Patrik appeared in the doorway.

'Nancy said I was allowed to come in.'

Tears pricked Erica's eyes as she met his desperate gaze. Calm, she wanted to say. Calm.

'Yes, come in,' said Louise. 'And there's no need to worry. I'm not going to harm Erica. I need her to tell the world about what happened. I want her to write the book about Lola. But she has to know everything.'

'She killed them,' said Henning, sounding almost sober. 'She killed Peter, Max and William.'

'Is that true?' said Patrik, and Louise nodded almost imperceptibly.

Patrik pointed quizzically at the chair next to Erica's and Louise allowed him to sit down.

Patrik took Erica's hand as he sat down. They squeezed each other's hands very tightly.

'I'm assuming that you weren't foolish enough to bring your gun with you,' said Louise.

'That's correct. But I do have to ask . . .' he said, staring at the pistol in Louise's hand. 'Where did you hide the gun? We searched the whole island.'

'Erica? Have you figured it out?' said Louise.

Erica frowned. Her pulse had slowed down at the mere sight of Patrik, but her thoughts were still racing. How was she supposed to know where Louise had hidden the gun? She had no idea. Then she recalled their journey there.

'The lobster pot. The gun was in William's lobster pot.'

'That's right. I rowed out and put the gun inside it – then when we returned today all I had to do was fish it out. Pretty slick, even if I do say so myself.'

'And Rickard?' Patrik asked. 'The blood on the shirt?'

Louise snorted. 'That's not hard to work out. I made sure Rickard and Tilde took plenty of sleeping pills so that they slept heavily. Then I sneaked in, put Rickard's shirt on over a long-sleeved top so that I didn't leave any DNA and then wore it when I fired the gun. Then I dropped it in the laundry basket.'

'But why?' cried Elisabeth.

Louise looked at her, almost pityingly.

'I never meant to hurt *you*, Elisabeth. You're as innocent in all this as Lola was. Peter and the boys were innocent victims too. And Cecily. Even Rickard, despite being an utter shit. The only person who isn't a victim is Henning. And I wanted . . . I *needed* to do to him what he did to me. I wanted to deprive him of everything. But first I had to get close.'

'And that's why you married Peter?' said Erica.

'It was my ticket into the family,' Louise confirmed. 'And it was even easier than I'd thought it would be. Men love their own reflections, so I became Peter's mirror image. And with Cecily gone, that was easy. Then I made sure that I became indispensable to Henning. I became his right-hand woman – the daughter he'd never had. And you never suspected a thing, did you, Henning? You loved having someone who was at your beck and call,

389

who made sure your life was frictionless and who flattered your ego.'

Louise nonchalantly waved the gun around. Elisabeth let out a sob and Erica squeezed Patrik's hand even harder.

'You're so talented, Hen! You're a literary giant, Henning! You're a divine writer, Henning!'

Louise mimicked herself in a shrill voice. Henning's head was lowered, his gaze on the table.

Louise continued in the low voice she'd been using since she'd pulled out the gun.

'Only I knew you for the impostor and liar that you are. Not just a killer, but a thief. You not only stole a life but a life's work. And Elisabeth . . . you never suspected a thing did you? My God, you of all people ought to have known that he has zero talent!'

'Henning, what's she talking about?' Elisabeth said in confusion.

'Yes, what am I talking about? Are you going to tell her, Henning, or shall I?'

'Go to hell,' Henning said in a low voice, refusing to meet her gaze.

Louise smiled her warped smile at everyone around the table.

'I'll take that as a request to go on with the story,' she said. 'Let me tell you what happened that day. My sixth birthday. After my birthday party, the whole group left our flat. But you came back, didn't you, Henning? You wanted to be with Daddy. You thought I didn't know. But children see everything. I didn't want Sigge to hear what you were doing, so I told him to hide in the trunk. He thought it was a game and he got in and closed the lid. I put a stick through the loop so that he couldn't open it until I wanted him to come out. Then I pulled the drapes around my bed and curled up there. My new Freestyle was in my rucksack, so I got it out and turned on the music at top volume so that I didn't have to hear. But after a while, there was a bang and I could smell burning from the kitchen. I got scared and ran in there with my rucksack in my arms. It was horrible. The stove was on fire – there were big flames licking the ceiling. Daddy was lying on the floor completely still. There was blood everywhere, and her eyes were open. I screamed and screamed but she didn't wake up. I tried to drag her into the hall but she was too heavy and I hurt my knee on Daddy's pistol that was lying on the floor. The smoke from the fire was making my eyes sting, so it was even harder to breathe. I realized I had to get out of there. I put the gun in my bag and ran down the stairs as quickly as I could to get help, but no one saw me – or wanted to see me – even though I was crying and shouting at the top of my lungs in the street. But someone must have called the fire brigade because fire engines came blaring up and pulled over by our building and I thought they'd help Daddy. But that didn't happen. Flames and smoke were bursting out of the windows of our flat. I stood there trembling in a doorway across the street with my rucksack in my arms and I saw the firemen come out and shake their heads. I was only a kid, but I understood.'

'Where did you go?' said Patrik.

'I'd been given a card by Daddy's sister Lussan when she came to visit and she and Daddy had a fight. She gave me the card and told me to call her if I had any problems. It was in my rucksack where I kept all my most important stuff, and I called her from a phone box. She told me to go round the block and she picked me up in her big car. Then they arranged everything. Did you know that you can arrange anything if you've got money and contacts? Especially back in 1980. I wasn't P'tite anymore. Or even Julia. I was Louise. Lussan and Pierre's adopted daughter. Pierre's uncle was a chief of police in Stockholm and he used his contacts to ensure I got everything I needed for a new identity. I don't know the details – or at least, I didn't know the details until I got Lussan to explain before . . . before she died.'

'I've seen what you did to her. That was a lot of anger,' Patrik said in a low voice.

'What do you mean? What's happened to Lussan?' Elisabeth's voice broke.

Louise looked at her calmly.

'Lussan and Pierre are dead. I killed them.'

'My God,' said Henning.

After being unmasked, he'd slumped over and looked completely absent. Erica wondered whether he'd taken in what Louise had said. Now he downed a big gulp of his whisky.

'Lussan and Pierre bribed Sigge's grandmother to keep her mouth shut about Sigge dying in the fire. He was only reported missing a few weeks later, and no one connected it to the fire. They kept the autopsy results quiet. Money. Contacts. Power. No one ever questioned who I was. And we never talked about Lola. It was strictly forbidden. The whole family was ashamed of Daddy – even after she died. That's why Lola left them and never looked back. But I couldn't leave. Where was I supposed to go? I didn't have anyone else.'

'You had your grandmother,' said Erica.

She wanted to feel sympathy for what had happened to P'tite, but when she saw Louise's cold gaze she just couldn't.

'I was six years old,' Louise said in that peculiar, emotionless tone that had subsumed her voice. 'I didn't know what my grandmother was called or where she lived. I had no way of finding her. I was stuck with Lussan. And it was terrible. She was terrible. Their life was terrible. But I learned everything I needed to become the right wife for Peter when I grew up. And I had the right background and family tree to be admitted to the Bauer family. Lussan was overjoyed at my "good match". She didn't understand a thing – stupid old Lussan. And she got what she deserved in the end.'

Louise's gaze shifted to Henning and her eyes narrowed.

'Just like you, Henning Bauer. You're an evil, bitter, narcissistic man who built his life on a lie. You were a gold digger when you met Elisabeth – a talentless dilettante of an author whose ambition exceeded his ability and who changed his last name to that of his famous wife. You knew right away what you had in your hand when you read Daddy's books. You knew what a gold mine they were. And you wanted to make it yours.'

She raised the gun and pointed it at Henning.

'And now you've got what you deserve too. I've taken everything away from you. Your sons, your reputation, your prize. You have nothing left.'

Henning lifted his head and stood up unsteadily.

'You little whore . . .' he hissed.

Louise began to laugh.

'Now the mask comes down and everyone can see you for who you are. I shot your son and your grandsons with the same gun you used to kill Daddy. Symbolically worse. Like a Greek tragedy, as you'd say at Blanche.'

'What do you mean?' Henning swayed on the spot as he stood at the end of the dining table. 'I pushed her and she hit her head.'

'But that's not what killed Lola,' said Patrik, and Erica started. She pictured the preliminary investigation file lying in front of her – why hadn't she thought of that? 'Lola died from two gunshot wounds. Fired from the same weapon that killed Peter and the boys.'

'Lola was shot? No. No!' Henning sank back down onto the chair. 'I didn't shoot Lola,' he whispered.

For the first time, Louise's terrifying indifference cracked.

'If Henning didn't kill Daddy, then who did?'

Louise looked around wildly. Her eyes were so wide that the whites were glistening.

No one replied.

Eventually, Elisabeth cleared her throat. Hectic red spots had begun to form on her cheeks and she looked oddly defiant. Then she began to talk.

33

STOCKHOLM 1980

Elisabeth had crept back into Lola's flat. Now she stood hesitantly in the hallway, pressing herself into the coats hanging there. She wasn't sure what she was doing, but the uncertainty had been gnawing at her for so long that she could no longer take it. Henning's excuse about his writing group had made her desperate. She knew the group didn't meet today. She had discreetly followed him to find out, and her heart aching, she'd seen him return to Lola's flat.

Elisabeth could hear his and Lola's voices from the kitchen as she crept along the hall. She saw what she had been dreading. Her husband kissing another . . . another *man*.

Because that was the truth of it. They might all say Lola was a woman, but Elisabeth knew you couldn't paper over biology with words.

The nausea rose and she blinked away the tears that were stinging her eyelids. Another woman would have been bad enough, but another man was more than she could bear to think about. She'd loved Lola as much as the others, but that was before she'd . . . before *he* had got into bed with her husband.

The mere thought of their bodies, naked, close, Henning caressing Lola . . . it gave her the shivers. She could barely take in the betrayal and the humiliation. The disgust made her body shake. The disappointment in them both. She had thought Lola was her friend. And Henning – her husband – her beloved.

She moved silently further into the flat and looked around carefully before going into the living room, where rays of sunshine were forming patterns on the large red carpet and the trunk by the wall. P'tite was nowhere to be seen, but the drapes around her bed were drawn and there was a faint thump coming from within. Good. The girl was occupied.

For a long time, she stood there quite still. Her rage made it difficult to think clearly and rationally. Why was she still in Lola's home? She had wanted to know, and now she knew. She was done here. But she padded across the room to the other doorway into the kitchen, where she peered around the frame. Henning was holding Lola – they were flirting and kissing each other. His hands were caressing Lola, and she was moaning like a cat in heat. Elisabeth was on the brink of bawling at them, throwing herself at them and hurting them as much as they were hurting her, but a clicking sound startled her and she backed away. Nothing happened. Lola said something to Henning and then there was silence. After waiting for a while, Elisabeth ventured another peep into the kitchen. It was empty.

Then she heard agitated voices. Henning's. And Lola's. Henning rushed back in. He was holding something above his head – something that Lola was trying to get at. Elisabeth heard Henning ask Lola to suck him off, and fury dimmed her vision.

Suddenly, Lola hit Henning – pummelling his chest with her fists. Henning raised a clenched fist and struck Lola clean on the jaw. Her arms flew out, she staggered backwards and the back of her head hit the hob with a loud crack.

The silence afterwards was horrible.

Lola was lying on the floor, lifeless – and Elisabeth saw her future passing before her. Prison for Henning. Their two sons would grow up without their father. Shame brought on her good family name. She couldn't let that happen. Henning was weak. But she was strong.

She crept back into the hall, past the kitchen and to the front door which she opened and closed with a slam before rushing into the kitchen where Henning was.

'My meeting was cancelled, so I came to help Lola clean up . . . My God, what's happened?'

Henning was standing next to Lola's body like a statue, his face ashen.

'She . . . she fell,' he said, a sob catching in his throat. There were several blue notebooks strewn across the floor. 'I . . . I changed my mind too and came back. We . . . we were arguing about her diaries. I read one and saw she'd written about . . . her fantasies about me. Fantasies that might be misinterpreted in the wrong hands.'

Elisabeth wondered whether Henning could see her disgust.

'Take them, leave, destroy them. I'll take care of this.'

'But . . .'

'Do as I say,' Elisabeth said sharply. 'Get out. Destroy the diaries.'

Henning nodded. He picked up the books from the floor and almost ran out of the flat. Elisabeth looked around. All the evidence had to be destroyed. Nothing could lead back to Henning.

There was a pan filled with oil on the gas hob. One of the rings was still on and Elisabeth leaned over to pick up the saucepan, but she screamed when a hand grabbed her ankle.

'Henning . . .' Lola rattled, sitting up. She put a hand to her head. 'Where is he? He hit me.'

'He's gone,' Elisabeth said, half-choking. What was she going to do now?

Lola stood up laboriously. She limped into the bedroom and over to a box on the bed. It was grey and fairly large. Elisabeth followed her. When Lola opened the lid, she peered over her shoulder curiously. Inside the box there was a gun.

'He's stolen them.'

'Stolen what?' said Elisabeth.

The rage was coming in waves. She didn't know how to handle everything she was experiencing. Her old love of Lola was mixed with her new hatred of her.

'My books,' Lola said through gritted teeth. 'I'm sorry, Elisabeth, but I'm going to call the police and report him.'

Lola limped back to the kitchen.

Elisabeth looked down into the box again at the pistol. She couldn't think straight. Everything was simultaneously crystal clear and murky. Her right hand reached out for the gun of its own accord – she grabbed it and made for the kitchen. Lola had the receiver in her hand and she had begun to dial. Without trembling in the slightest, Elisabeth raised the gun and fired. Two shots.

Lola looked at her in surprise. Then she slumped to the floor.

Elisabeth wiped off the gun with her skirt, laid it beside Lola and then poured the oil from the saucepan over the kitchen counter, the hob and the still-ignited flame.

As she left the flat, she heard the flames crackling. She hurried away. Then she stopped mid-step. P'tite! But she kept going. It couldn't be helped. What was done was done.

34

'You've let me think for all these years that I killed Lola.'

Henning's face was red and blotchy. Beads of sweat glistened on his brow.

Elisabeth looked as if she was shrinking.

'I . . . I couldn't do anything else. You had left. And I couldn't go to prison. It was better for you to believe that . . . And we were lucky. Nothing happened. No one wanted to investigate the murder of someone like that.'

'Someone like *that*,' Louise said through gritted teeth. 'Daddy was *someone like that*. And I've always believed Henning was the murderer.'

She slumped over on her chair. Then she raised the gun and took aim at Elisabeth.

'I should have hated you for all these years. Both of you. I'm glad I killed your son and your grandchildren, Elisabeth. You hear me?'

Elisabeth pressed her hands to her face but said nothing. Patrik squeezed Erica's hand and quickly asked Louise:

'But what about Rolf? Why did you kill him?'

She lowered the gun and looked at him blankly.

'I didn't kill Rolf.'

'But who . . . ?' Patrik said in confusion.

'I killed Peter and the boys because Henning loved them. And Cecily to get into the family. But Rolf? I had no reason to kill him.'

Louise rose from her seat and stood behind Elisabeth, who was sobbing with anguish.

'Daddy loved Henning. And Henning betrayed her. But he didn't kill her. *You* did.'

Louise put the gun to Elisabeth's temple and wrapped her left arm around her throat. She leaned forward and spoke very closely in Elisabeth's ear.

'Why did you have to kill Daddy? To protect Henning? You didn't even love him. You loved Rolf. I've read your love letters. And Henning didn't love you. Was it for the sake of your reputation, Elisabeth? For the family name? Because word couldn't get out that your husband had slept with *someone like that*? A freak. That's what Lussan called Daddy. Before I killed her. Imagine calling your own sibling a *freak*.'

Louise pressed the pistol harder against Elisabeth's temple and Elisabeth whimpered.

'It wasn't luck that no one investigated the murder. It was Lussan and Pierre using their contacts. If Pierre's uncle – the chief of police – didn't want something to be investigated then it wasn't. No one cared about Daddy. No one.'

She moved the gun in a circular motion against Elisabeth's temple. Tears were pouring down Elisabeth's cheeks.

'You realize that Henning deceived you too? The notebooks he took weren't diaries. They were the books he later published under his own name. Henning shouldn't have received the Nobel Prize – Lola should.'

'Why did you wait so long?' Erica asked. She was now sitting so close to Patrik that she could feel the warmth of his body. She needed that comfort.

'I've been waiting my whole life. Time means nothing. The only person who ever meant anything to me was Daddy. And I'm the only person who ever cared about Lola. I thought it was Henning who killed her. But for my revenge to mean anything, he needed to have as much as possible to lose. When I found out he was going to win the prize he'd been longing for his whole life, I knew I was ready. I knew all my years of preparation were at an end. I wanted to take everything that mattered to him. His family. Blanche. His honour.'

'Was it you who sent the papers to Rolf? About Blanche?'

'Yes,' Louise replied. 'He had started asking questions about Blanche, and I realized he'd become suspicious. So I gave him what he needed. It was the perfect opportunity.'

'Did you know why he was asking questions?' said Patrik.

'No. Maybe he was just sick of all the bullshit.'

'He was dying.'

Elisabeth gasped and Louise tapped the pistol against her head.

Patrik continued:

'Rolf only had months left to live. I think he wanted to come to terms with the past and I think the exhibition was part of that. So there *was* someone who cared about your father. Don't forget the names of the pictures. *Innocence* and *Guilt*. I received the missing picture from Vivian on my way over here. And you've already seen it, haven't you?'

Louise nodded.

'Can I pull it up on my phone? And show it to Henning and Elisabeth?'

'Why do we have to see that awful picture?' Elisabeth had suddenly straightened up and was trying to free herself from Louise's grasp.

'Shut your mouth!'

Louise pressed the gun into her again. Then she ordered Patrik:

'Show it!'

Patrik pulled up the photo on his mobile and showed it first to Erica and then held it up to Henning.

Henning's gaze, however, was frozen and the corner of his mouth was twitching. Then his body began to shake. His eyes rolled upwards, showing the whites. Before anyone could do anything, he fell to the floor.

The convulsions intensified as he lay there. It looked as if he was frothing at the mouth.

'Henning!'

Elisabeth cried out like a wounded animal.

Patrik lunged towards Henning and then shouted at Louise.

'He needs help!'

Louise stared at Henning, loosened her grip on Elisabeth's neck and lowered the gun.

Elisabeth reacted in a flash. She wrenched the pistol from Louise's hand and shot her in the chest.

Louise's eyes widened. She stood there for a few seconds swaying before she collapsed.

'Erica! Get help!' Patrik shouted, rousing her from her shocked reverie.

Erica dashed out of the dining room, away from the blood and screams. Paula, Martin and Gösta were standing in the space between the houses, and she told them to call for help and then go inside to help Patrik. Not until she was alone did she notice that she was crying. It took a while for her to calm down enough to return to the dining room.

She stopped in the doorway. The scene before her made her gasp for breath. Henning lay where he'd fallen. His body was still spasming. Martin was clutching his head and trying to clear his airways. On the other side of the table, Patrik was kneeling beside Louise and pressing his hands hard against her chest. Even so, the puddle of blood under her body was growing.

'The chopper's en route,' said Gösta. 'It's five minutes out.'

'Let's hope they make it in time,' Patrik said grimly.

Paula had disarmed Elisabeth, who was standing still, her arms limp at her sides, staring at her husband's body.

'I took care of everything for all those years,' she whispered. 'The kids, the house, his career. While he sat in his study writing. He was the artist. The genius. He took the applause and the credit while the kids and I lived in his shadow. And it was all a lie.'

'You lied too,' Erica couldn't help herself saying. 'You let him believe he'd killed Lola.'

Elisabeth seemed oddly calm.

'True. But doesn't that make his lie even worse? He stole the work and the credit from someone whose life he thought he had on his conscience. He's a weak man. I see that now. I should have seen it sooner. Although I suppose I've always known. Henning has always been dazzled by shiny things. My name must have been an irresistible temptation to him.'

A damp patch spread across the front of Henning's trousers as he lost control of his bladder. Elisabeth's face contorted with disgust. She walked over to the sideboard and poured herself a large whisky.

Outside there was the sound of a helicopter on approach to Skjälerö.

Patrik stared out to sea through the terrace windows at home. The view was infinitely beautiful, but he couldn't take any of it in. He was still filled with the fear of what could have happened. Recent events had once again shown how fragile life was. He could have lost Erica on the Bauers' island.

Erica was his life. His everything. Well, so were the kids. But he and Erica were the foundations – it was out of their love that the family grew. He would be lost without her. And Louise could have taken her from him.

'Food in half an hour.'

Erica's voice made him jump, and then her hands settled calmingly on his shoulders. He automatically put his hand over hers to feel more of her warmth. She squeezed it but then sat down in the wicker chair next to him.

'I was so scared,' he said.

'Me too.'

Erica took a blanket and draped it over her legs.

'I can't seem to shake the fear from my body,' he said.

Erica shivered despite the blanket and looked at him tenderly.

'We've been here before,' she said, smiling gently. 'It'll pass. Eventually. One day you'll have nothing to worry about except how we remove that bloody Roman arch.'

Patrik squeezed her hand.

'I hope you're right. But it just feels like it gets worse over the years.'

'Have you heard anything from the hospital?' she said.

'Louise is out of surgery. No one knows how it's going to pan out. Henning is going to survive, but they don't know how bad the brain damage is.'

'Jesus Christ.' Erica sighed and tucked her legs under herself on the chair. 'Imagine living a lie for that long.'

'Are you talking about Louise or Henning?'

'Both really. Louise spent her whole life shape-shifting into the person she needed to be to get into the Bauer family. And Henning took the credit for an oeuvre and talent that wasn't his.'

'The newspapers are already devouring it,' Patrik said glumly. 'They'll love it when they find out all the details.'

'Don't read all the crap.'

'What are you going to do about the book? About Lola?'

Erica took a deep breath and looked out to sea.

'I think what's happened makes it even more important to tell Lola's story. I spoke to Vivian earlier. She's going to let me use Rolf's pictures from the exhibition in the book. And she's going to hold his exhibition, but she said she'll wait until I release the book.'

'The photographs are amazing.'

'Lola was amazing.'

They sat in silence for a while as the sky blazed outside. Soon the sun would dip down into the sea. Darkness arrived ever earlier at this time of year.

Erica squeezed Patrik's hand. 'Are we going to talk about the elephant in the room?'

'You mean the bun in the oven?'

It was a weak attempt at humour and Erica didn't smile. She merely nodded. He leaned forward and stroked her cheek. She was right. This wasn't a conversation they could postpone any longer.

35

STOCKHOLM 1980

'Damn it!'

'What?' Ester replied in response to Rolf's sudden outburst.

'I left my scarf at Lola's.'

'Pick it up next time. You've already gone back once.'

'No, no, it's blue, and you know what Lola's like. If she likes it then it'll vanish into the black hole that's her wardrobe.'

'Okay, but hurry so that you're not late. The client doesn't like waiting.'

'The client . . .' Rolf muttered.

He hated the commissions he had to take to keep a roof over his head and put food on the table. Prostitution: that's what it was. This time it was the board of a major company being photographed. Serious men in double-breasted suits who wanted to radiate money and power as much as they could. Utterly disgusting.

He climbed the stairs two at a time and had to stop outside the door to calm his breathing. He wasn't as fit as he had once been. He tried the door handle carefully. He didn't want Lola to notice he was there. If Lola got talking, he'd never leave . . .

The scarf was on a hook in the hall. For a brief moment he pressed it against his cheek. He couldn't tell Ester the real reason why it was so important for him to get it back, but he wondered if she knew anyway. There had been something up with her behaviour lately.

Elisabeth had given the scarf to Rolf. Sometimes he thought he could still smell her scent on it. It smelled of love and sorrow, a mixture that made his heart ache. He missed her so much, but it had been necessary for them to break it off. Love couldn't be built on lies and betrayal. He loved Ester and Elisabeth loved Henning. Not in the same way they loved each other, but the wounds that would be torn open if they sought divorce would never heal and maybe they would never be happy together. You couldn't build your happiness on someone else's unhappiness.

Sometimes – when none of the others were looking – Elisabeth would give him a look filled with so much emotion that he felt dizzy. And Rickard was a constant reminder of their love. The fact that he was Rolf's had been obvious the first time he'd seen the boy. But Henning would never survive that truth. So Rolf had buried it deep within himself, just as he had hidden her letters.

Rolf involuntarily took a few steps further down the hall with the scarf in his hand. That was when he heard a sound from the kitchen. He looked in through the doorway and started. Then he carefully raised his camera and fired off a series of shots. His heart was pounding in his ribcage. Henning. And Lola.

It would crush Elisabeth if she knew that she and Rolf had sacrificed their love for something that was a lie. He paused to see whether he was angry. No. He couldn't be angry, because what his lens had captured was pure unadulterated love. Like his and Elisabeth's. Lola's face shone when it was cupped between Henning's hands.

Her lips opened longingly under his when he kissed her, as if they were the only two people in the world. It was impossible to feel anger. Love was love – in whatever shape it took.

Rolf slowly lowered the camera and crept out of the front door. Lola and Henning's secret was safe with him.

36

TWO WEEKS LATER

The appointment had been made. The results from the amniocentesis test had meant that after much anguish and discussion, Erica and Patrik had agreed it was the only sensible option. They had neither the time nor the energy for another baby – let alone a child they knew might face difficulties in life.

Yet she was shocked at how hard the decision hit her. When the train pulled into the station in Stockholm, Erica realized she had spent the entire journey watching the landscape outside whizz past the window without seeing it.

Her first meeting was with her publisher. The taxi stopped outside the stately doors on Sveavägen and she stood there for a while clutching her small suitcase. Lola's story had taken an unexpected turn, and the story she had thought she was going to tell had turned into something else entirely. She hadn't yet decided what to do about it. The case had succumbed to the statute of limitations, since Lola and Sigge had been killed before 1985. No one could be convicted for those murders.

The press still hadn't caught wind of that part of the story, but Louise's face had been plastered across the front pages. She had survived the gunshot wound to the chest and confessed to the murders of Cecily, Peter, Max and William – as well as Rolf's murder, even though she had initially denied that.

Lola hadn't been mentioned at all. That would all change when Erica's book came out and she wasn't sure how she felt about that. There was one person she needed to talk to before she could make a final decision.

After her meeting with her publisher, she strolled to her next appointment. Her publisher had been concerned and somewhat unsympathetic about her hesitation, but she had provided no explanation. This was between her and Elisabeth.

Erica hesitated for a moment before ringing the bell. The flat was on Strandvägen and was in the same building as Svenskt Tenn. The whole stairwell exuded money.

When Elisabeth opened the door, Erica was immediately uncertain. She didn't exactly have a plan for what she was going to say, or what she was going to ask, and Elisabeth looked as cool and unmoved as she had done at the golden wedding celebrations. Her outfit was expensive and elegant. Each strand of hair was perfectly positioned. It was as if the scene in the dining room on Skjälerö had never taken place.

'Come in,' she said, showing Erica towards a huge living room with one meticulously manicured hand.

Erica had to force herself not to gape open-mouthed. This wasn't a flat . . . it was an *apartment*. It was enormous and perfect in every respect. There were no Roman arches to be seen.

'Coffee? Tea? Something stronger?'

'Coffee is fine, thanks.'

Elisabeth motioned discreetly to a woman Erica hadn't even seen until now. Nancy.

Erica greeted her in surprise.

'Henning! We have a visitor!'

Elisabeth spoke loudly and clearly as she headed for an assortment of soft white sofas. Erica drew breath sharply. It was a shock to see Henning. She hadn't seen him since he'd been on the floor of the dining room back on the island, having suffered what had turned out to be a stroke.

'He can hear and understand everything we say, but his movement has been severely restricted as much of his body is paralysed,' Elisabeth said in a soft voice. 'He can't talk anymore. But like I said, his brain is all there.'

Elisabeth leaned over the wheelchair and wiped some drool from the corner of Henning's mouth with a handkerchief before she sat down on the sofa, carefully smoothing her skirt.

'Thank you – *both* of you – for seeing me,' Erica said, as Nancy handed her a cup of coffee. The housekeeper had set down an overburdened tray on the coffee table.

'Biscotti?'

Elisabeth gestured towards the plate of Italian almond biscuits.

'No thanks,' Erica said, clearing her throat. 'Uh, I've just had a meeting with my publisher . . .'

She glanced at Henning, unsure how to express herself in his presence. She had honestly been expecting to speak to Elisabeth alone, and now she wasn't quite sure what she dared or wanted to say.

'You can speak quite freely in front of Henning,' Elisabeth said, as if reading her thoughts. 'We have no secrets from one another any longer, do we, darling?'

Once again, she wiped drool away from the corner of his mouth.

'Well, there are a few things to discuss in relation to my new book,' Erica said, her gaze wandering between Henning and Elisabeth. It was like being in a bizarre nightmare. 'The publisher is completely on board with me finishing it based on what I now know. But I'm not sure . . .'

'What does Louise say?'

Elisabeth sounded business-like.

'Louise wants Lola's story to be told. As it is. As it happened.'

'There you have it,' Elisabeth said, holding out her hands.

'But . . .' Erica stammered. 'It'll be very hard . . . on you. Won't you contest the publication?'

'No,' Elisabeth said, taking a sip of her coffee.

Erica looked at her in bewilderment. Then the pieces of the puzzle began to fall into place, one by one.

'Something has been bothering me ever since we were in the dining room with Louise,' she said. 'I haven't been able to put my finger on it. But there was something you said. Something along the lines of: "Do we have to look at that awful picture?" How did you know what it was of, if you didn't see it that night at Rolf's gallery?'

Elisabeth smiled and reached for a biscotti. Then she turned and pointed to the wall behind Erica.

'Beautiful, isn't it? I'd go so far as to venture that it's one of Rolf's best. What do you think, Henning?'

Erica turned around and looked in the direction that Elisabeth was pointing.

A huge print of *Guilt* was hanging on the wall.

'I bought it from Vivian. The negative too. Thanks to the sale, she can afford to keep the flat. She was very grateful.'

Erica turned her gaze to Henning. His left eye was twitching and he seemed to be trying to say something, but all that was audible was a low groaning.

'I didn't know Rolf was dying so I couldn't understand why he wanted to ruin everything. For all of us.'

'You went to the gallery during the party?'

'Yes. I was drunk and a little angry that he hadn't come to the party. He'd become an increasingly morose old man and I . . . I suppose I wanted to tell him off. Or like always, it was just an excuse to see him.'

'You still loved him?'

'I've always loved Rolf.' Elisabeth said this with her gaze fixed on Henning. 'But I thought I was sacrificing our love for something that was bigger than us. I thought I was sacrificing love for a great man – that Henning had something permanent to leave as his legacy. In my own conceit, I wanted to be part of that. And what Henning went on to write – what I believed he had written – it was so . . . beautiful. So perfect. So full of love. No author had ever captured the female being so perfectly.'

Then she snorted and shook herself, as if trying to rid herself of something sticky.

'Henning always said I was his muse. How could I take that away from him?'

She stroked his hand. Then she turned her gaze to the photo again.

'When I saw the photo in the gallery that night, I pleaded with Rolf not to exhibit it.'

'You didn't want Henning's affair with Lola to become public?'

Elisabeth shook her head. 'It would have brought disgrace on us. And scandal. But that's not why. Look at the photo. What do you see? You have to look beyond Henning and Lola.'

Erica looked at the picture again. She didn't understand what Elisabeth meant. Then she shifted her eyes from the kiss – from Henning and Lola – to the background. And suddenly she understood. It was only when the photo was blown up to a large format that you could see it.

'You're in the picture.'

'Yes. Rolf must only have seen that when he enlarged it. Not even Louise saw it when Vivian sent her a small copy. But if Henning saw the enlarged photograph at the exhibition then he would realize I had been lying. That I'd been in the flat far earlier than I had let on – that I had seen them together. He would put two and two together. I couldn't let that happen.'

'So you shot Rolf with the nail gun to keep the photo a secret. But your dress was red. They found black fibres on the gun.'

Elisabeth smiled again.

'You missed the fact that I changed later that night into a wonderful Oscar de la Renta. In black.'

'So why is Louise claiming to have killed Rolf?'

Elisabeth stood behind the wheelchair. She put her arms around Henning and caressed his chest.

'Louise and I have cut a deal. Lola's murder and the child's have timed out. It doesn't matter what you say in print about my role in that. I'll simply deny everything. Your word against mine. Rolf's death would see me go to prison. I would never survive. But I can live with shame. So she's taking the rap for Rolf's murder in return for me not preventing the truth about Lola being told. And I'll personally ensure the nine books are reissued under the correct author's name. Won't that be nice, Henning? Lola will finally have her name on the cover.'

She was speaking quietly into his ear. He made a few guttural sounds, but nothing comprehensible.

Erica stared at the couple. There was something grotesque about the whole situation. She felt as if she were appearing in some grisly horror movie.

'Just to be absolutely clear. You're saying I can tell the *whole truth* about Lola in my book and by extension about all those of you who were around her?'

Elisabeth slowly stroked her husband's head.

'Yes. I'm not going to prevent you from telling the truth. Why would I? It's all gone. Peter. The boys. Rickard is . . . Rickard. Blanche is closing its doors. The board at Bauer's have made it known that they'd like me to retire. Or as they put it, I should "enjoy my autumn years". Although I'll tell you this much: there's a sense of freedom in no longer having anything to lose. And we have each other, don't we Henning? Isn't that right, my sweet? We have each other. I'm your muse. Until death do us part.'

Henning gargled something inaudible. Erica thought she could see panic in his eyes, but it was hard to tell since his facial movements were irregular and jerky. A small part of her felt sorry for him. He was going to stand naked and exposed to the world. Then she thought about Lola and her sympathy was diminished. Lola had considered her friends as family, and they had betrayed her. The only thing Erica could do now was tell the world about Lola.

When Erica emerged back onto the street, she glanced up at the windows of the apartment one last time. It was no longer a home. It was a prison.

A note pinned to the black door read *Closed*. Rickard Bauer carefully tried the door handle before taking out a key and unlocking it. He looked around before entering. Not that it mattered if anyone saw him, but he wanted to retain the feeling that he was slipping under the radar. He didn't want a soul to know where he was.

It was strange being at Blanche when it was closed. He had only ever visited the club when it was full of life and movement. Now it was deserted, and in the pitiless daylight the joint looked seedy. All the imperfections and dirt were visible. No place suited him better right now. The public spotlight had been shone on every part of his life and that of his family over the last few weeks, revealing their sins. Now there was nothing left to expose. Nothing more to lose.

Tilde was at home in the flat. She didn't even know he was back in Stockholm. She had called him countless times but he hadn't been able to bring himself to answer. That part of his life was over. She was part of who he had been, not what he was now.

Rickard entered the austere office that Ole and Henning had shared with Louise, and looked around. Everything was untouched. It looked like the owners had simply walked away leaving everything behind, which was admittedly more or less the case. And none of them would ever return. Blanche would never reopen. No one would ever sit in this office again, because the veil of secrecy had been lifted and exposed them all.

He retrieved some cushions from the sofa in the anteroom to the office and laid them out as a bed in a corner. The armrest cushion and a blanket served as his pillow and covers. Slowly and stiffly, he lay down on his side. He was completely exhausted, but every time he closed his eyes he saw Peter and the boys. He saw them alive. He saw them dead. He didn't know which was worse.

A wasted life was a heavy burden to bear, he reflected. His time in custody had forced him to examine his own self for the first time in his life. What he had found filled him with shame. Without expensive watches, fast cars and lavish holidays, he was nothing. He had no skills, owned nothing that was his or that he had created, because everything had been served up to him. And he hadn't even been able to see the value in that.

In the cells, he'd realized that he didn't miss the evenings with the boys in Ibiza, his handmade Italian shoes, the slap-up dinners in smart restaurants or the shopping sprees with Tilde. He hadn't given them a single thought. What he missed were the moments with Max and William, seeing Peter's face light up when he was looking at his sons, the trips on the boat to Skjälerö with sunshine and saltwater on his face, or falling asleep to the sound of screeching seagulls. Thousands and thousands of things that had nothing to do with money and extravagance.

Sooner or later, he had to get a grip on his life. The terrible thing, and what scared him, was that he knew what he *didn't* want, rather than what he wanted. He was a middle-aged man who didn't know who he was, and there was no one left around him who could help him to figure it out. Everything was in tatters.

The only thing he knew with any certainty was that he would have given anything for another moment with Peter and his nephews. A spell on his belly on the rocks with bait on a crabbing line, with William's and Max's laughs and excited chatter in his ears as they slowly reeled the line in, now covered in tiny crabs. He would have given a kingdom for a single moment like that.

The Bauer men didn't cry, but tonight Rickard cried himself to sleep.

'Bertil!'

Rita shouted from the bathroom. Bertil dropped the wooden spoon he had been stirring the stew on the hob with and ran to her, closely followed by Ernst.

'What is it? What's happened? Are you unwell? Are you in pain?' He stared at her in panic.

She held out a hand to him. It was full of hair.

'It's started,' she said, and he could tell she was fighting to hold back the tears.

Bertil pulled her close and she shook against his breast, shedding the first tears she'd cried since getting the news.

'Let it out. Cry all you want,' he said, stroking her back.

Bertil's top was damp all the way down his front by the time Rita pulled away from him and wiped her eyes dry with her sleeve.

'Sorry,' she said, with a sob.

He looked at the woman he loved and was filled with so much love that it pushed aside his fears.

'Don't apologize. It's crazy to play the hero. I know you want to be strong, but you don't have to be for me.'

'You're right, I know that. It's just so hard. My hair . . .'

Tears welled up again and he wiped her cheeks. Then he opened the bathroom cabinet, took out his shaver, and stood behind her in front of the mirror.

'You know, I've always thought Demi Moore as G.I. Jane is one of the sexiest things on legs.'

'I don't think you've ever mentioned that before,' Rita laughed through her tears.

'I'm sure I have. Many times. See, you don't listen to me.'

Rita shook her head and wiped her face again.

'So why don't you do old Bertil a good turn and give him some G.I. Jane,' he added. 'In a relationship, it's the give and take that matters. And sometimes you have to stand up and be counted. I must warn you that I'll probably have the horn, but I think you'll just have to live with that . . .'

'Bertil!'

Rita slapped him on the shoulder, but she was laughing instead of crying. She looked in the mirror. There was a bald spot at her left temple where the clump of hair had come out.

'It's coming off one way or another,' she said. 'We might as well get it over with.'

Bertil carefully ran the shaver in one long sweep from the crown to the back of her head. Large hanks of hair fell to the floor. Rita's lower lip trembled, but there were no more tears.

Afterwards, he kissed Rita's bare head and hugged her for a long time. Then he turned the shaver on and applied it to his own head.

'Bertil! What on earth are you doing?'

'You think you're the only one who's allowed to be sexy in this family?'

'You're crazy,' she said, but she grinned as he shaved his head.

Eventually, his head too was completely bare. He put his cheek to hers and said:

'Two sexy devils.'

Rita gave him a long look before turning towards him and taking his bare head between her hands. She kissed him hard on the mouth.

'I love you, Bertil Mellberg. Never forget that.'

He kissed her back. There was nothing about Rita that he could ever forget.

Erica had saved her visit to Birgitta for last. After saying goodbye to Elisabeth and Henning, she had visited Lola's old neighbour Åke and had then seen Johan Hansson at his colourful studio where they had both cried over Lola's fate. But the visit to Birgitta was particularly special.

Erica didn't know how much the old lady followed the news, and she'd considered calling first to prepare her for what she was going to hear. But in the end she'd decided she wanted to tell her face to face.

Christ was staring at Erica from every direction as Birgitta invited her into her home again. Erica was clutching the box of photographs she had been lent. All the images had now been scanned and carefully filed on her computer.

'I don't know if you've heard? Do you follow the news?' Erica said cautiously.

Birgitta shook her head. 'No, no. All I need to read is

the Bible. There's so much misery on the news and hearing about war and famine and people behaving badly leaves me so depressed.'

'Then you don't know?' Erica said, nervously smoothing her trousers.

The feeling that she might say something that Birgitta classified as a miracle made her shiver.

'I've found out what happened to Lola,' she said. 'And P'tite.'

'Oh my goodness gracious,' Birgitta said, putting her hands to her throat. 'I think I'm going to have to sit down before you tell me. I'm just going to check on Viktor. He's learning his numbers at the moment. He's so clever.'

Birgitta disappeared into the kitchen but returned almost immediately.

'He's fine. Tell me.'

'It's a long story and I'm going to tell you the whole thing. But I want to tell you the most important bit first. Monica's child – your granddaughter – is alive.'

Birgitta gasped. 'No, no, I don't believe you. It can't be . . .'

Erica put her hand on Birgitta's and told her everything from the beginning. As she spoke, tears flowed down Birgitta's cheeks.

'The poor thing. The poor, poor thing. How hard it must have been for her. Of course, that doesn't excuse what she did, and she'll have to answer to the Lord. But still . . .'

'I've got a lot of sympathy for Louise too. She was only a child when everything was taken from her. I think she would be pleased to hear from you, if you thought you could bring yourself to get in touch. Maybe even visit her? I know what she did goes against everything you believe . . .'

'The thing I believe in most of all is forgiveness,' Birgitta said gently. 'If Jesus could forgive Judas for his betrayal of Him for thirty pieces of silver, I think I can find it in my heart to forgive the sins of Monica's little girl.'

Erica patted her hand lightly and they sat there together quietly. The silence felt healing. She had no idea how long they sat there, each woman absorbed by her own thoughts, but in the end she turned to Birgitta and asked a question.

'Do you mind if I help Viktor for a bit? With his Maths?'

'Please do,' the older woman said, wiping tears from her cheeks. 'He talked about you for days after your last visit. He'll be so happy.'

'Thank you,' Erica said, going to the kitchen.

Viktor beamed when he saw her.

'Hello! I don't remember your name!'

'My name is Erica. Can I take a seat? Maybe you can teach me some Maths? It's never been my strong suit.'

'I'm great at Maths,' Viktor said exuberantly, pulling out the chair next to him for Erica. 'This is an eight. You can make it using two circles next to each other, or you can do it without even lifting your pencil. Look.'

He proudly demonstrated an eight and Erica praised him.

'If you take two fours and add them up it makes eight!' he added.

'You're great at counting!'

'I know!' Viktor said, colouring in a number four with a purple pencil. 'I'm great at lots of things. I know numbers, I know letters, and I've learned to swim!'

'Wonderful!' said Erica.

'I like you,' Viktor said, putting his arms around her.

Erica felt the warmth of his hug spreading through her body, dissolving all that had been difficult and all that she had been grappling with. Suddenly what had been complicated became very, very simple. Four plus four made eight. And one plus one made three.

Author's afterword and acknowledgements

As ever, there are many people to thank. Above all, I'd like to thank my husband Simon for his constant support. I'm also eternally grateful to the rest of my family, who are always there for me. My publisher John Häggblom is my rock and a joy to work with, and the same goes for the rest of the gang at Forum, headed up by Pia-Maria Falk and Clara Lundström. Thanks to Lena Sanfridsson and Rebecka Cronsten who read the manuscript with eagle eyes. A big thank you to my agents at Nordin Agency.

Fact-checking is a very important part of my work, and I've had a lot of help making sure things are right. Thanks to Anders and Annika Torevi for keeping me on the straight and narrow when it comes to Fjällbacka's intricacies. Kelda Stagg MSc, a crime scene investigator with the Stockholm Region Police Authority, has helped me to get to grips with all matters forensic, ensuring as much accuracy as can be achieved in a crime novel. It has also been of the utmost importance to me to understand and accurately describe trans history and the trans community insofar as this is possible, and I must acknowledge the first-rate assistance of Sam Hultin in this respect.

Eleonora von Essen and Lena Läckberg Ivarson read the manuscript and offered valuable feedback.

There are many people in my midst who are sources of joy, inspiration and motivation when it comes to my writing – it would be impossible to name them all, but I would like to particularly mention Henrik Fexeus.

Dialectal words and expressions are always tricky to render correctly. With regard to Skjälerö, I chose to base it on the Norwegian origins of the Bohuslän expression: *skjeller*.

Sometimes as an author, in spite of rigorous research and fact-checking, you have to be a little elastic with the truth for the sake of the story. All errors are therefore my own.

Camilla Läckberg

If you enjoyed *The Cuckoo*, don't miss *The Ice Princess*, the thrilling first novel in the Patrik Hedström and Eric Falck series.

Discover how it all began…

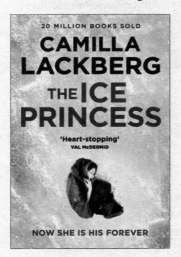

A small town can hide many secrets

Returning to her hometown after the funeral of her parents, writer Erica Falck finds a community on the brink of tragedy. The death of her childhood friend, Alex, is just the beginning. Her wrists slashed, her body frozen in an ice-cold bath, it seems like she's taken her own life.

Meanwhile, local detective Patrik Hedström is following his own suspicions about the case. It's only when they start working together that the truth begins to emerge about a small town with a deeply disturbing past…